What on earth could have happened in that room? To all intents and purposes it seemed that the five people involved had simply stood up, walked out onto the balcony and hurled themselves into the night. Absolutely nothing was manifest to indicate their reasons for doing so. It was senseless. Insane. As one wry officer was later heard to remark:

'It was a bit like the *Marie Celeste* really – only without the water.'

PHILIP FIRST

# The Great Pervader:

A Participatory Report on the State of
Things in General

PANTHER
Granada Publishing

Panther Books
Granada Publishing Ltd
8 Grafton Street, London W1X 3LA

Published by Panther Books 1985

ISBN 0-586-06416-8

Printed and bound in Great Britain by
Collins, Glasgow

Set in Times

Excerpt from 'World Without Love' by John Lennon and Paul
McCartney reproduced with the kind permission of Northern
Songs Ltd, ATV Music Ltd, 19 Upper Brook Street, London W1V
1PD. (Thanks to the anonymous wandering Sufi for the Blame,
and special thanks to Abat's Essential Services for just about
everything else.)

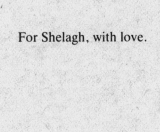

For Shelagh, with love.

# PART ONE
# Peripheral Consequences

'I don't care what they say
I won't stay in a world without love.'
                    Lennon & McCartney.

'God is food.
Eat well.'
Iddio E. Scompiglio.

# 1

This is how it went . . .

'What on earth can they be up to?' the old man said, wiping the condensation from the window-pane with his sleeve. He screwed up his eyes and peered back out into the night. 'Daphne, come and have a look, your eyes are better than mine.'

'I don't want to look,' his wife replied irritably. She sat in her armchair in front of the electric fire. 'Come away, Henry. What does it matter? What business is it of ours?'

'But it's the middle of winter,' he insisted. 'And it's almost ten o'clock, and it's raining, too! There's something odd about this. Dammit, I wish I could see better.'

'There's nothing odd about it at all. Henry, I do wish you wouldn't be so inquisitive. Honestly, you'll give us such a bad name. I don't know what the neighbours must think, seeing you standing there all the time staring out of the window like that . . .'

'I always thought that was what windows were for,' Henry mumbled. He wiped the pane again where his breath had misted his vision. 'There's something funny going on,' he said.

'Henry, come away. Come and watch television. The news will be on in a minute.'

'But they're just standing there, Daphne. Five of them standing there on the balcony, eight, nine floors up. It must be freezing up there!' The window was misting over again and he rubbed at it in annoyance. 'And their clothes . . . Daphne, there is definitely something odd going on up there. Look at them, they're dressed in light clothes! No coats or anything. Daphne, look!'

Reluctantly the old woman left the comfort of her armchair and made her way over to join her husband by the window.

'I don't know what's wrong with you lately,' she muttered, then squinnied her eyes up and stared into the darkness. 'Where? I can't see a thing. Where are you looking, Henry? Show me.'

'Up there,' he said, pointing. 'See? Two men and three women. The women haven't even got their shoulders covered.'

'Well, they're probably all drunk or something,' his wife replied, unimpressed. She pushed her face closer to the window. 'They do look excited about something, though. But what does it matter? I expect they're just watching the fireworks.'

'What fireworks?'

'It's Bonfire Night, Henry. November the fifth.'

'Yes, I know. But I haven't seen any fireworks around here.'

'They've got a better view from up there,' Daphne observed. 'They can probably see fireworks all over London. Now, close the curtains and come and watch the news.'

'Just a minute,' Henry said. 'I want to know what's going on up there. I don't think they're watching fireworks at all. Not dressed like that. They could see just as easily through the window without coming out onto the balcony. Keep your eye on them, Daphne. I'm going to get my binoculars.'

He left his wife at the window and went into the kitchen to retrieve his binoculars from the windowsill where he always left them in order, he said, that he might observe at close hand the various wild birds that alighted in their tiny backyard. As he shuffled back into the living-room, the binoculars slung around his neck, he was startled by a sudden sharp cry from his wife.

'Henry! Henry! Quickly! Oh my God!'

Henry rushed back to the window. Daphne's face was pressed against the glass and she was shaking violently. One hand groped in the air behind her until it came into contact with his arm, which it then gripped like a vice.

'Daphne, what's wrong?' he cried. He winced with pain. He tried to unfasten her hand whilst at the same time staring out of the window to locate the cause of her agitation. Only one man was now visible on the balcony.

'Daphne, let go! Whatever's got into you?' Her strength astonished him. Suddenly she released her grip on his arm and turned to face him. Her face was grey and he could hear her teeth clacking together as her jaw trembled.

'Pull yourself together, Daphne,' he said. 'What's happened?'

'Henry, they jumped,' she said very quickly.

'What!'

'They jumped. They just climbed over the railing and jumped. Henry, the police . . . Phone the police.'

But Henry was back at the window.

'Henry!' his wife cried tearfully. 'Please!'

He rushed across the room and grabbed the telephone from the top of the teak sideboard then took it back to the window as his wife collapsed into a chair.

Even as he was dialling Henry glanced outside and saw the last man on the balcony leap out into the empty night. At the very last second he seemed to change his mind. He grabbed wildly into space, managed to grasp the lower rail, and was left hanging by his fingertips nine floors above the street.

0

When the first police-patrol vehicle pulled up outside Kimberley Mansions, London W.2., a motley cluster of urban noctophiles had already formed around the four smashed bodies on the pavement. The gathering continued to grow by the second and an atmosphere of barely contained hysteria could be sensed radiating from its core.

Already a handful of the ladies present had passed out at the ghastly sight that met their eyes, or, to their embarrassment, thrown up reflexively like drunks at a party; and more than a few of their male counterparts were turning green around the gills.

Be that as it may, nobody had actually seen fit to leave.

Well turned-out young men in snappy suits stared in morbid fascination, their arms held protectively around weeping wives and girlfriends who could only bear to look through parted fingers. Drink-plied businessmen had paused between rendezvous and, finding themselves suddenly sober, not moved on. Strollers, out sampling the cold evening air with their dogs, interrupted their constitutionals to peer curiously over the shoulders of those who had arrived before them. Their pets, aroused by the scent of blood and fresh meat, whined and growled excitedly, sniffed at each other's genitals and wound their leads around the legs of those persons nearest to them.

Bruisers, cruisers and late-night liggers were drawn like flies. Oafs, hags and lounge-lizards, all apparently oblivious to the constant drizzle and near freezing temperature, came and rubbed shoulders with magistrates and winos, and strained together on tip-toes, silently cursing the fact that they couldn't see a damned thing.

The first police officer had threaded his way through the conflux and up to the main entrance of the building when the second patrol-car arrived. By this time the road and pavement were jammed almost solid.

13

Far above all this a man still hung screaming from the ninth floor balcony.

This was evidently the cause of some confusion amongst the still dilating crowd. Many people seemed to be having difficulty in deciding which way to look. For those near the back the problem was less severe: realizing that they had no hope of viewing the corpses, they simply fixed their attentions on the dangling man overhead. But those near the front were faced with a dilemma.

The man above them had failed repeatedly to haul himself back onto the balcony. Instead of attempting to conserve his energy he was kicking out frantically into space and bawling at the top of his voice. The consensus of opinion down below was that if he kept this up he would drop quite soon.

Now, those at the front of the crowd who had already taken in the bloody remains on the pavement were somewhat reluctant to shift their eyes from the dangling man in case they missed something. However, due to the proximity of the front wall of the building, they were obliged to tip their heads well back in order to view this. Consequently many of them were beginning to suffer from stiff necks.

In addition, they were being jostled by those behind who wished to make their way to the front. To avoid stepping in the mess at their feet entailed glancing down at frequent intervals – which in some cases caused an uncomfortable sensation of giddiness – and it was also necessary to lean backwards from time to time to inhibit the persistent forward surges of those in the rear.

This combination of discomfort and anxiety was creating a good deal of stress. Tempers were becoming frayed. Elbows were being surreptitiously dug into ribs and toes were deliberately stepped on. There was a lot of bad feeling in the air.

More policemen arrived. They fought their way roughly into the crowd and stoically endeavoured to disperse persons who were not at all inclined towards being dispersed.

The fire brigade rounded the corner at the end of the street in a truck mounted with a turntable ladder. There they halted, siren blaring, their passage blocked by the queues of cars and accumulating herds of onlookers that were flooding the narrow road. Immediately behind them an ambulance added its siren to the din.

The screams of the man hanging from the balcony were lost beneath the clamour of sirens and the irate honking of car horns.

His audience continued to grow. Lights blinked on along the street and the windows and balconies of surrounding buildings began to fill with avid neighbours.

Husbands and wives could be seen clutching one another and uttering such things as: 'Oh my God, poor man!' and 'Why doesn't somebody do something!' Those who were neither clutching nor uttering were kept busy pushing back indoors startled, sleepy-faced children who had been woken by the uproar.

A frail old lady on the balcony adjacent to that from which the man hung closed her eyes tight and covered her ears with her hands. In a high-pitched, quavering voice she recited the Lord's Prayer, tears streaming down her face as her snowy-haired husband leaned out over the steel safety-rail and thrust his walking stick towards the unfortunate man, saying dodderingly,

'Grab hold of this, son. We'll help you.'

What would have been achieved had the dangling man been capable of grasping the stick will never be known, for Fate had decreed that the old fellow's gesture be in vain: the end of his stick fell well over a yard short of the man's outstretched fingers.

At that moment a helicopter, complete with camera crew who had been filming major firework displays from the air, appeared chuckering noisily out of the sky. It descended as far as its pilot dared take it, then remained hovering high above the street. A BBC television news cameraman hung death-defyingly out of the side hatch and focused his zoom lens on the drama beneath him.

The following day millions of viewers all over the country were to switch on their television sets to witness this scene: On a ninth floor balcony way above a London street an old lady stood in an attitude of despair. Her eyes were screwed shut and she had her hands over her ears and was mouthing something as if in protest at the pandemonium around her. At her side a hoary-headed old man, presumably her husband, stood with his head turned towards the camera and, apparently in order to aid the cameraman, indicated with a walking stick the presence of a man who, in obvious panic, swung helplessly from the neighbouring balcony.

It was too much for any civilized person to take. From that day and for weeks to come the old couple's lives were made hell. An outraged public, having misconstrued the entire scene, rose in righteous indignation and took justice into their own hands. The old couple were deluged with poison-pen letters and obscene

15

telephone calls. Their friends and neighbours shunned them. The local stores refused to serve them and their pet corgi was attacked and cruelly mutilated by a gang of local children.

In desperation the couple were eventually forced to go to the BBC and plead for air time in which to put forward their case and straighten out the terrible misunderstanding. Their request was granted and they were given a spot on the early evening news which was later repeated for the benefit of those who had not caught it first time around.

The day after their broadcast they were once more overwhelmed with letters and telephone calls, only this time from horrified and abject citizens nationwide. Cheques totalling thousands of pounds poured through their letterbox. Interflora delivered enough bouquets to beautify an abattoir, and members of the local community banded together and purchased a brand new video recorder which they presented at a special celebratory dinner party thrown in honour of their new champions. Even the local kids went out and bought a 56lb bag of Winalot for the crippled corgi.

Back at street level the fire brigade were making no further progress. A squad of beat-bobbies, aided by several firemen, were striving to force a path through the crowd wide enough to enable the turntable ladder to be driven up to the building's forecourt.

By this time the dangling man's screams had turned to sobs and pleas. His strength was failing him rapidly and he seemed barely able to retain his grip.

Inside Kimberley Mansions the first policeman had reached the door to apartment seventeen, from the balcony of which the man hung. Discovering it to be locked he tried ramming it but, far from access, gained nothing more than a badly bruised shoulder.

Below him and ascending rapidly via lift and stairs were several of his colleagues, including two CID men. It was at that point, with salvation only a matter of seconds away, that the dangling man's strength finally gave out.

There was a communal gasp from the onlookers as his hands were seen to part company with the iron baluster he had been clinging to. With a last drawn-out shriek of horror he dropped flailing through space to add himself sickeningly to the cannibals' stew that had been his companions.

● ● ● ● ●

# 2

It is difficult to imagine what the police could have been expecting to find as they smashed their way into number seventeen, Kimberley Mansions. Undoubtedly, though, they must have sensed it would not be pleasant.

What strange and potent force could have been at work to cause a group of presumably normal and respectable persons to take their lives in such a gruesome manner? It was unprecedented.

Was there a fanatic loose inside with a gun? Or a crazed fiend with a bomb strapped to his chest?

Perhaps it was more sinister than that. Certainly, considering the few facts that were so far in evidence, just about anything was to be expected. Was it possible that the deceased were all members of some weird religious sect, and that death, for them, was viewed as the perfect climax to an evening of frenzied orgiastic ritual – Perfect Consummation, The Ultimate Gift, etcetera? . . .

Equally conceivable was the notion put forward later by one Sunday newspaper that they were all the victims of a perverse obligation laid upon them at birth – or even before – by their parents, who were themselves acting out of fear of the consequences should they refrain from doing that which was demanded of them. If that were the case, and some macabre pact with the Devil had been signed, then perhaps suicide was the only possible means of escaping a fate that was too horrible to even contemplate.

The possibilities were endless.

Suffice to say that minds boggled and imaginations ran riot; and it was amidst growing, though tacit, speculation that the door was finally forced open.

The scene that lay waiting was something nobody had been expecting.

The first policeman through the door rushed immediately, though with caution, through the lobby and into the lounge. Discovering nothing there to threaten him he crossed the room to the balcony, unaware that the man he had come to rescue was no longer requiring his assistance. He then turned back into the lounge and stood gawking along with his fellow officers.

The room was immaculate.

Soft music crooned through the speakers of an expensive hi-fi system and attractively prepared but largely untouched food lay waiting on salvers and dishes.

The chic, ultra-modern furniture was spotless and the soft, beige, deep-pile carpet looked as though it had hardly been stepped on. Nothing more than a few errant crumbs had tumbled to the floor.

Glasses containing wine, whisky and various other alcoholic beverages stood unemptied on shelves and tables and the last vestiges of a long cigarette still smouldered in a marble ashtray. The lights had been turned down low.

Strategically placed around the walls and adorning most available furniture tops were a dozen or so birthday cards, implying that the purpose of the gathering earlier in the evening had been to celebrate the passing of another year for somebody resident in the apartment. In fact, the room was set as though in the middle of just such an informal, low-key get-together. The only things missing were the people.

Baffled policemen regarded each other with empty expressions. Why were the walls and carpet not spattered with blood? Why was there no mad axeman squatted chuckling on the bookshelf? Where were the items of discarded clothing that might suggest an impassioned orgy, or the chaos that would indicate the passing of a gang of roving boot-boys out for a lark? At the very least there should have been something overturned or smashed: the inevitable consequence of a drunken brawl. But there was nothing. Nothing at all.

A systematic search of the entire flat was instigated. As silent policemen moved to comply the two detectives put their heads together and conferred. Both were nonplussed.

What on earth could have happened in that room? To all intents and purposes it seemed that the five people involved had simply stood up, walked out onto the balcony and hurled themselves into the night. Absolutely nothing was manifest to indicate their reasons for doing so. It was senseless. Insane. As one wry officer was later heard to remark:

'It was a bit like the *Marie Celeste* really – only without the water.'

As the search progressed the mystery deepened.

In the main bedroom a man and a woman were discovered lost together in ecstatic abandon on black satin sheets. With loud music blasting through stereo speakers, and oblivious to the fact that only minutes ago their families and closest friends had flung themselves to their deaths, the couple were fast approaching mutual glory when the first uniformed officer entered the room.

Too close to fruition to be aware of anything else they squirmed and heaved in pre-orgasmic rapture as the room quickly filled with bug-eyed policemen eager for something to put in their reports.

A young police photographer, quick to spot red hot action in the making, was at the bedside in a flash. He snapped away diligently, capturing forever on film the last climactic throes of the pair, who, though suddenly drastically aware of their situation, were so far over the brink as to be incapable of any form of voluntary physical coordination. In horrified ecstasy they shimmied and jerked together as a phalanx of appreciative policemen looked on.

0

The entwined twosome in the main bedroom were gently disengaged and provided with blankets with which to cover themselves (their clothes being temporarily expropriated for investigative reasons). They were then escorted to separate rooms and grilled intensively by the two detectives. Not surprisingly both were in a state of considerable distress and the few answers they were able to give to the questions put to them were of negligible value to the police.

The girl, a nineteen-year-old model named Jill Richmond, was already hysterical when led from the bedroom. Upon being informed of the horrible deaths of those persons with whom she had been sharing her evening such a short time ago, she broke down completely.

A doctor was summoned. Following a perfunctory examination he administered sedatives to the girl and had her admitted to hospital, admonishing the police in no uncertain terms for their lack of artifice.

Jill was considered well enough to be discharged from hospital the following morning. However, whilst making her way home she discovered to her horror that overnight the press had gone to town on her. Her picture was splayed across the front pages of the tabloids, alongside such headlines as: 'Naked Model In Mass Suicide Mystery', 'Girl Enjoys Sex As Best Friends Die', and 'Dead People In Model Sex Shock'. With her career in ruins, her family outraged and her mind shattered, Jill returned to her small, comfortable, bachelor-girl apartment and slashed her wrists with a razor-blade.

She was saved by a freelance journalist who, during her absence and in the hope of providing himself with a scoop, had rigged up a couple of concealed microphones in her flat and then installed himself in the loft with a portable cassette-recorder. Persuaded by her silence that she had gone out again, the journalist had lowered himself back into the flat in order to avail himself of the lavatory. He discovered Jill sitting unconscious on the bathroom floor, sopping wet in a lake of her own blood.

Less than twelve hours after being released from hospital she was re-admitted, this time barely breathing. There was, of course, an immediate outcry: How was it that the girl, surely a prime suspect, was not in police custody? How was it that she had been allowed to leave hospital when she was obviously not fit to do so? Why was there nobody to escort her home?

Rumblings of discontent prevailed, but satisfactory answers did not.

Jill's companion in the bedroom, and also the owner of the apartment, was one Samson Tallis, a dynamic and successful young record executive, employed in the Artistes and Repertoire division of *EMI* The party that evening had been to celebrate his thirtieth birthday. His wife, Corinne, was one of the five deceased.

He, too, was taken completely unawares by the news that, whilst he had been busy in the next room adulterating his marriage, his wife and friends had hurled themselves over the balcony. Though less inclined to hysterics than his co-partner in crime, Tallis was nevertheless severely affected and entered into a condition which the interrogating officer later described as 'frozen disbelief'.

For approximately two and a half minutes he sat in stunned silence. His mouth hung rigidly open and his fingers clutched tightly at the blanket he had wrapped around himself. He appeared unconscious of anything said to him.

Eventually his head was seen to move very slowly from left to right and then back again. His mouth closed and his breathing grew slightly deeper. Then his head began to tip slowly forward. As it did so his left hand rose to cradle his descending forehead. In this attitude he leaned forward and placed his left elbow on the table in front of him. He was a very worried man.

The extent of Tallis's shock is perhaps most graphically illustrated with the first words he was to utter upon emerging from his brief catatonia. They were (in a slurred voice):

'I don't understand it. I just do not understand it. It's inconceivable that they would do such a thing. Not without telling anyone. And on my birthday, too . . .'

Samson Tallis was later removed to his sister's home in North London where he was sedated and put to bed. A police guard was stationed outside the house.

● ● ● ● ●

# 3

Soon after the eye-opening discovery of Samson Tallis and Jill Richmond in the main bedroom there occurred another curious incident which was to contribute even further to the already complex and enigmatic situation the police were confronted with. It was the unearthing of a man secreted inside a cabinet adjacent to the kitchen sink.

Initially this discovery was regarded by all concerned as being the decisive factor that they had all been hoping to find. Here, apparently, was the missing piece in the jig-saw; the *primum mobile* behind the bizarre occurrences of that evening.

But this, in fact, was not the case.

The man was sitting literally crammed into the cabinet, there being a minimum of space available inside. His knees were drawn up tight to his chest, his arms were wrapped around his shins and his head lay at a remarkably uncomfortable angle, sandwiched sideways between his knee-caps and the ceiling of the cabinet. He had his eyes shut tight and was gabbling incomprehensibly to himself in a voice that was little more than a strained whisper.

The kitchen, incidentally, was the only room in the entire apartment in which anything remotely indicative of a disturbance had been evident. It wasn't much, to be sure, but it did add a welcome hint of discord to an otherwise uncanny semblance of normality: A large kaolin bowl containing what appeared to be a kind of fruit trifle had fallen from the sideboard and shattered on the floor. Bone-like shards of broken pottery now lay amid the trifle which, a curious mixture of strawberries and lychees, sponge cake and flaked chocolate, oozed pink juices, custard and cream, and spread itself in a visceral heap over the linoleum tiles. The sight had been enough to send one policeman reeling for the lavatory-bowl, believing himself to have stumbled upon the remains of yet another victim of the evening's atrocities.

On the sideboard itself, beneath the serving-hatch which opened into the lounge, sundry small items lay in disarray, as though knocked over by someone in a hurry.

The man in the cabinet was hauled out and seated at the kitchen table to await interrogation. He was very small, less than five feet in height and weighing well under one hundred pounds. His clothing consisted of a pair of ill-fitting denims held up by an old, striped tie, a dirty green tee-shirt and a pair of pink ballet shoes. He had neglected to shave for more than a week and his jet-black, curly hair sprawled in an unruly mass about his head. All this, together with his strange, piercing blue eyes, persistent jabbering and the fact that he was quite liberally smeared with the very same trifle that now adorned the kitchen floor, made him odds-on favourite amongst those officers still supporting the mad-axeman hypothesis.

The little man sat fearfully at the table, squeezing his hands and gazing about him in a strangely disorientated manner, his eyes shifting from one burly policeman to another as though uncertain of who they were. As he was obviously not English, and had not responded to anything put to him in that language, the interrogating officer, Detective Inspector Cyril Bellows, had questions thrown at him in a variety of languages.

This, too, proved ineffectual; the man possessed all the characteristics of an out-and-out screwball.

Bellows was contemplating having him removed to the local police station when something happened to throw new light on the matter.

Samson Tallis was at that moment being ushered back along the hall to the main bedroom to collect some clothes in order that he might be taken to his sister's home. As he passed the kitchen door he happened to glance somewhat dazedly in and catch sight of the Inspector and his suspect. His vacuous expression changed immediately. He halted at the door and stared at the tiny scruffy man. Pointing a finger at him he turned to his escort and demanded in a belligerent tone of voice:

'What's he doing still alive?'

The Inspector looked round in surprise.

'Do you know this man, sir?' he asked Tallis.

'Know him? Of course I bloody know him,' Tallis replied. 'The man's a lunatic. Look, what's going on here?'

This was precisely the same question the Inspector had been asking himself. Leaving two constables with the man, who was still babbling quietly and apparently oblivious of Tallis's presence, he joined Tallis at the door, deftly sidestepping the mound of trifle on his way.

'If I could just have a word with you in the next room, sir.' He ushered him back into the hall.

'Yes, but what's going on?' Tallis repeated indignantly. 'Why isn't he dead?'

Three minutes later Inspector Bellows returned to the kitchen with the information, gleaned from Tallis, that the small man sitting at the table was an artist named Rogelio Ramon Reyero who spoke something approaching perfect English, as well as several other languages, and who had been a guest at Tallis's birthday party. How that had come about was not altogether clear as Tallis evidently detested the man.

However, what *was* clear was that Reyero had been the only person present in the lounge, other than the five now deceased, when Tallis had made his exit along with the delectable Miss Richmond. Reyero, then, should indeed hold the requisite information which would unravel this bizarre mystery.

Bellows seated himself at the table beside Reyero and said softly, 'Rogelio.'

For the first time since being dragged from the cabinet the man fell silent. His eyes swivelled slowly to peer uncomprehendingly at Bellows.

'Rogelio,' Bellows repeated, 'I want you to tell me what went on in there.' He indicated the lounge with a backward jerk of his thumb. 'What happened, lad? Eh? You can tell me.'

The strange little man fixed his interrogator with a crazed stare. He looked over towards the serving-hatch, then back to the Inspector. Very quietly he said,

'Space.'

'Eh? What was that, lad? I didn't quite get that.'

'Space,' Reyero repeated, his eyes vacant now and staring inwards with a haunted look.

'What about it?' the Inspector asked.

'I observed it,' the little man stated. 'I didn't intend it. It was an accumulation.'

He looked at the Inspector as though pleading with him for something. Bellows rubbed his jaw thoughtfully.

'I don't quite understand you,' he said presently. 'Can you explain in a little more detail?'

Reyero was silent. He looked like a man undergoing indescribable mental torture. As he stared at the table, his hands rubbing together fretfully in his lap, his eyes began to mist with tears.

'Too much malcontent,' he sobbed, burying his face in his hands. 'Oh, too much malcontent!'

Bellows turned to one of his constables.

'Any of this make any sense to you?' he asked.

''Fraid not, sir,' the man replied.

'No, thought not.' He turned resignedly back to Reyero, saying, 'Rogelio, come on, lad. You can trust me. I'm your friend.'

The artist's sobs began to subside. As he looked up again his face became stricken with alarm. He gripped the table edge so that his knuckles turned white, and asked in a strangled voice:

'Still here?'

'Who?' the Inspector said, thinking he was probably referring to Samson Tallis. Reyero's eyes shone imploringly.

'The Great Pervader!' he cried. He had begun to tremble.

'What? The great what?' Bellows said.

Reyero was gasping now in obvious terror.

'I didn't intend it,' he cried. 'Oh God no, it wasn't my fault! Please!'

'What didn't you intend? Who are you talking about?'

Reyero rose suddenly out of his chair, screaming, 'The Immanent One! The Essence Of All Things! I summoned Him! I summoned Him! Oh please, no!'

He collapsed over the table in a jumble of sobs and moans. Bellows looked on, bemused.

Just then a uniformed constable entered the kitchen and approached the Inspector.

'Information from HQ, sir, concerning the suspect,' he said.

'Yes, go on,' Bellows told him.

'Rogelio Ramon Reyero: a moderately successful artist based in London these past four years. Age uncertain and origin obscure, but believed to be of Latin-American descent, though raised in California.'

The Inspector groaned.

'There's more, sir,' the constable continued. 'Reyero has spent the last eight months in a psychiatric hospital following a severe mental breakdown. He was only released two weeks ago.'

Bellows rubbed his eyes.

'Well, who would have thought it?' he said tiredly. He walked around the table and lowered himself onto one knee beside the broken artist.

'Rogelio, can you tell us more?' he coaxed, gently, like a loving, caring pal. 'We have to know what went on. We must know how those people came to die. Did you do it, lad?'

He was answered by a long, drawn-out moan. The artist did not look up.

Bellows climbed laboriously to his feet. 'Okay, take 'im down the station for questioning,' he snapped. 'And don't let anyone near 'im till I get there!'

'Just a second, sir,' one of the constables guarding Reyero stepped forward. 'You might like to have a look at this.'

He held out a small book in a protective polythene wrapper, which the Inspector accepted with a raised eyebrow.

'Found it on the suspect, sir,' the constable explained.

Bellows examined it. It was a green, leatherette bound, pocket-sized volume entitled: 'The Book Of Imaginary Hauntings,' by Iddio E. Scompiglio. Inside was a selection of what appeared, at first glance, to be short pieces of verse. One page was marked. On it, and underlined in red ink, the Inspector read:

> There is One in Existence
> Who cannot be reduced to less,
> In Whom decay is not inherent,
> And Whose Connection
> Is entirely dissolved.
>
> The One Transcends Awareness,
> Yet still Awareness
> Recalls the Specious Form.
> Knowing this we must accept,
> And know the Great Pervader.

The Inspector scanned this a couple of times, flicked through a few more pages, then handed the book back to his constable, saying, 'What exactly does this say to you?'

The constable shrugged. 'Nothing, sir. Just some obscure, arcane gobbledygook as far as I'm concerned.'

'And yet you seemed to think it would benefit me to read it?'

'Well . . . yes, sir. This "Great Pervader" referred to in the, er, poem, obviously has some kind of significance for the suspect. I thought it might be pertinent.'

'You thought it might be pertinent . . .' Bellows echoed. 'Tell me, constable, do you think it might help me to solve this case?'

The officer swallowed uncomfortably. 'Well, sir, things being as they are, it's, er, rather hard to say at the moment.'

Bellows stared at him for a few seconds.

'But would you say, constable,' he continued, 'that, working from the premise that this little green book does have some especial significance for the suspect, it is likely to have a particular bearing on this case?'

The constable stiffened. Staring beyond his superior he said, very formally, 'I would hesitate to make such a claim at this point in the investigation, sir.'

Bellows pushed his face up close to that of the constable. 'I'm bloody glad to 'ear it!' he growled. 'Now, stop playing Sherlock bloody 'Olmes and get this 'ead case and 'is bleeding gobbledygook down the bloody station and keep them there till I arrive! Got it?'

'No you don't.' Before anyone could make a move a man strode briskly into the kitchen and over to Reyero. It was the doctor who had earlier been summoned to attend to Jill Richmond.

'What's this, Inspector?' he demanded angrily, eyeing the detective over a pair of thick, tortoiseshell spectacles. 'Another victim of your interrogation techniques?'

He put an arm around Reyero's shoulders and tried to ease him back into a sitting position. The little man wouldn't budge.

'This man is a hospital case,' the doctor declared. 'There is absolutely no question of his being taken to anywhere other than the hospital . . . And if you wish to argue that point, Inspector,' he added, seeing the hostility on Bellows' face, 'I suggest you follow me downstairs. There is a whole army of journalists waiting outside who would no doubt love to sink their mandibles into a nice succulent case of police brutality.'

Bellows glared at him but said nothing. Instead he crossed the kitchen to the sideboard and plugged in the electric kettle. Blowing air tunelessly between his teeth, he wandered through the lounge and out onto the balcony.

The drizzle had ceased and below him most of the crowd had dispersed – only a few stragglers were still hanging on in the hope of further entertainment. A flurry of press-men and women had gathered around the entrance to the building, their access barred by two sturdy policemen stationed there. Directly opposite a hot-dog vendor had set up his stand on the side of the road. He stood alone at its side, stamping his feet and blowing his hands in a halo of lamplight.

The fire brigade was no longer in evidence. Neither were the bodies on the pavement, all five having been removed by ambulance once a way was cleared. Confused chalk outlines and one or two dark stains on the concrete surface were all that remained to show where they had been.

Inspector Bellows shook his head. He thought about his dinner. He should have been on his way home now, would have been if all this had not occurred. No doubt when he did get home his dinner would be all shrivelled and crusty in the oven. He gazed distractedly down at the heads of those beneath him. Out loud he said to himself, 'No doubt some came and fell in love.'

'Beg pardon, sir?' It was the young detective sergeant who was his assistant on the case.

'Oh, nothing,' Bellows murmured, turning back into the lounge. 'Just musing on the fact that I wasn't born a dustman.'

● ● ● ● ●

# 4

The file on the strange affair at Kimberley Mansions remains open. Although the police did attempt to bring a charge against the demented artist, Rogelio Ramon Reyero, he never actually appeared before the court. Judged unfit to plead due to extreme psychological imbalance, he was committed for an indefinite period to an institution for the insane. As far as anybody is aware he remains there still.

An open verdict was recorded on the five deceased as the police were unable to offer anything even resembling concrete evidence. Many a sage head was subsequently shaken in consternation.

But what did happen that night? What was it that induced five sane persons to commit such a terrible act? There is only one way to tell.

On the following pages is a minute-by-minute account of the entire evening. Commencing some time prior to the arrival of the first guests, it records every word that was spoken and every deed that was done that night, right up to the party's ineluctable climax.

Thus: Samson and Corinne Tallis are at home, preparing for what promises to be an interesting time for all. It is Guy Fawkes night, 5th November, 1980. The time is six forty-five. Outside it is cold and dark and miserable . . .

# PART TWO
## Those Who Are About To Die . . .

'From the crucible of hope the truth shall emerge.
Let us hope that it is not burnt.'
Iddio E. Scompiglio,
from
*The Book Of Imaginary Hauntings*.

# 1

'That was Dinah,' Corinne Tallis called out, replacing the telephone receiver and making her way back into the kitchen. 'She and Pete won't be coming.'

Her husband, Samson, was in the lounge. He was fixing himself a large scotch.

'Good,' he said, without looking up.

Corinne ignored him. She turned her attention back to the plate of *sashimi* she had been putting the final touches to when the telephone rang. She was having difficulty arranging the delicate slices of raw sea-bream into shapes resembling breaking waves. She did not seem to be able to get it the way the book said. No matter how she rolled or curled the pale flesh it didn't look right. It lay untidily in small, flaccid, shapeless heaps on a jumbled back-drop of lettuce leaves, chopped radish and chrysanthemum sprigs.

Looking around her at the colourful array of dishes she had set out, Corinne worried that she had done too much. She also worried that she had done too little. She wished she had hired a professional caterer instead of attempting it all herself. She asked herself whether perhaps it would have been wiser to be a little less experimental, a little more conventional.

Samson poked his head through the serving-hatch.

'Why?' he said.

'I beg your pardon?'

'I said, why?'

'Why what?'

'Why aren't they coming?'

'Oh, they can't find a babysitter.' She turned distractedly to face her husband. 'Why ask? You're not interested. You didn't even want them to come.'

Samson gave an insouciant shrug.

'No, it's true, I didn't want them to come,' he said with a vaguely pompous air. 'I can't stand them. But that doesn't necessarily mean I'm not interested in their reasons for declining such a rare and thrilling opportunity to spend an evening in our company.'

He grinned and took a mouthful of scotch, swilling it around his mouth before swallowing it.

'So they couldn't find a sitter for their brat . . .' he mused out loud. 'Did they contact the zoo? I'm sure they could have deposited it overnight in the reptile house. I think it would feel quite at home there.'

Corinne, having abandoned for the time being her *sashimi*, crossed the kitchen to the hot-plate where the contents of several pans were warming. She was feeling somewhat absent. Her mind was in a dozen places at once. Her environment confused her. Even now, after almost six months living here, she still sometimes had difficulty getting her bearings in this big, new, open kitchen. From time to time she even caught herself wishing she were back in their old, cramped, basement flat in Streatham.

'Do you think that's in any way significant?' Samson asked. He was leaning on his elbows and making circular motions with his whisky glass in the air in front of him, studying it impartially.

'Do I think what is in any way significant?'

'That out of, how many was it? twenty? invitees, less than half are actually coming?'

Corinne looked at him questioningly. She opened her mouth as if about to say something, then changed her mind. Then she noticed what he was doing with his glass.

'Samson, be careful with that drink! You'll spill it on my trifle!' She crossed the kitchen and moved the kaolin bowl along the sideboard to where it was in less danger of being splashed with alcohol.

'Oh, that's what it is,' Samson said, staring ruefully at the trifle. 'I did wonder.'

He withdrew his head and sauntered out of the lounge and into the kitchen. He was a good-looking man of about average height and a body that was just beginning to teeter on the verge of a slump. Throughout his teens and early twenties he had kept himself in reasonable trim with squash and football, but in the last couple of years his interest in these activities had begun to dwindle. As a consequence, and due to his increasing interest in alcohol, he had lately acquired a paunch.

He stood in the centre of the kitchen, tugging abstractedly at his dark, droopy moustache and gazing at Corinne, who had her back to him and was now fiddling with some *tempura*. He was dressed this evening in a brick-red, Fiorucci two-piece suit, burgundy shirt with gold cuff-links, and a tie that matched the suit. His deep-burgundy, moccasin style shoes were In Town. His hair, which was thick and dark brown, without the slightest hint of encroaching grey, was cut in a fringe and layered so that it fell neatly over his collar and ears.

He looked like a young, dynamic, successful A & R man.

He paid no heed to his steadily developing gut.

When he gazed at himself in the mirror, which he did quite frequently, he failed to notice the sag of his cheeks and the lines around his eyes. What he did see, and which never failed to make him wink and grin and adjust his tie if he was wearing one, was that he was still an awfully attractive hunk of man. And lately he had been growing restless.

'What is all this, anyway?' he enquired, nodding expansively to include the many plates, dishes and pans of food.

Corinne looked round to see what it was he was talking about.

'It's all a bit experimental,' she said in a voice that belied just how important the success of this experiment was to her. 'I've based it mainly on Japanese cuisine. A kind of oriental smorgasbord, I suppose you could call it. I thought it would be more convenient than a full sit-down meal.'

'An oriental what?'

'Smorgasbord. You know, a sort of buffet.'

'No, I didn't know.' He drained his glass and began tinkling the misshapen ice-cubes that lay in the bottom. 'It certainly doesn't sound like something one would be particularly anxious to sink one's teeth into.'

He was thoughtful for a moment, then, 'I don't know, though. On second thoughts, perhaps it does . . .'

Walking over to his wife he peered over her shoulder.

'This is *sashimi*,' she said, gesturing with one hand.

'It doesn't look very well cooked.'

'It isn't. It's raw.'

'Raw!' Samson exclaimed with distaste. 'Raw fish? You're joking!'

'No.' She passed on quickly to another plate. 'Those are omelette rolls with Japanese salad, this is skewered chicken, these are a selection of oriental sauces I'm mixing, and that is *tempura*. I've done that with an assortment of vegetables and seaweed.'

'My God!' He stared one by one at the plates in front of him.

'It's delicious,' Corinne assured him. 'I've been doing a lot of reading up on it. It's a very healthy diet. Do you want to try some?'

Samson shook his head.

'Why did you have to do all this?' he demanded. 'You know I don't like foreign food. Why couldn't you stick to English food?'

'It *is* English food,' she told him. 'Most of it, anyway. I've simply done it in a slightly different way. It's time you stopped being so finicky. Just try some.'

'No.'

Corinne shrugged indifferently.

'I'm going to fix myself a Harvey,' Samson muttered. He strode back into the lounge and over to the drinks' cabinet. There he began blending the ingredients for an extra-potent, somewhat arbitrarily concocted Harvey Wallbanger.

Corinne watched him a little apprehensively through the serving-hatch. She wanted to ask him not to drink any more before the guests arrived, but she was reticent. She could never be sure what his reaction would be these days.

'Samson,' she said tentatively, 'go a bit steady on the booze, will you.'

'I'm all right,' Samson replied curtly, dropping four ice-cubes into the shaker. 'Just having a little drink to calm me down after a hard day.'

'Yes, I know. That's fine. But I don't want you to get drunk, especially not this early in the evening.'

He turned on her irritably. 'Why not?'

'Oh Samson! You drink too much lately. You're always drinking.'

'I am not always drinking. Don't exaggerate. I'm quite capable of knowing when I've had enough.' He was pouring the drink into his glass now. 'And anyway, why shouldn't I get drunk if I want to? It is my birthday, after all. I thought you were supposed to have a good time on your birthday. I thought that was what birthdays were for. That's what I intend doing, anyway. Having a bloody good time.

'After all,' he added pointedly, 'it isn't as if I need to worry about my performance later on, now, is it?'

Corinne was silent at this.

'Well, is it?' he asked again.

'Samson, let's not go into that again.'

'Why not? I think we *should* go into it again. I think we should go into it in depth.'

'Samson, *please*!'

'What?'

'You're deliberately trying to provoke me.'

'I'm not.'

'You are. You know you are.'

'Listen, who started this? I was quite happily minding my own business, mellowing out for the evening ahead until you started griping at me.'

'I wasn't griping at you. I just –'

'You were griping at me, Corinne. Don't try and tell me otherwise.'

'Samson, why do we always have to be at loggerheads? Why can't we discuss things in a reasonable manner?'

'Why discuss anything at all? Why not just keep quiet and let me get on with my drink?'

Corinne sighed. 'Please don't get into one of those moods again. I can't cope with them.'

'*You* can't cope with them?' Samson exploded suddenly – and it was impossible to tell whether he was serious or not. '*You* can't cope with them? Jesus Christ, what about me? I've got no choice! I *have* to cope with them! I've had to cope with them for thirty years!'

With reluctance Corinne admitted defeat. She was all too familiar with the strange, maddening twists her husband's arguments could take. She had little hope of countering them. An argument with Samson was, by its very nature, a capricious, tangential, involuted affair which generally left her floundering and speechless. It was best to leave him be. That was usually what he wanted.

She turned back into the kitchen.

A minute later, as she was pondering spices for her Genghis Khan *nabé*, she heard Samson call out, 'Where's the dope? I fancy a joint.'

She tensed. She put down the fork she was holding and pressed her fingertips against the cool, melamine worktop.

'There isn't any,' she called back.

There was a short pause, then, 'But I ordered some black and half a dozen Thai sticks from Arlo last week. He promised to deliver them yesterday.'

'Arlo telephoned this afternoon,' Corinne answered, with a sense of something unpleasant impending. 'He's stopped dealing – for the time being, anyway. He says he's getting paranoid about a Bedford van that's been parked across the street from his house for the last two weeks. He thinks it's the police. He thinks they're watching him and keeping a record of the comings and goings at his house. He said to apologize to you. He said – and I quote – he's really blown out by it all. It's a beeg sheet hassle, but the peegs are out to get him thees time and it just eesn't cool.

'He put the phone down then,' she went on, smiling faintly to herself. 'He was calling from a public call-box and he mumbled something about the lines being tapped. Personally I think he's just burned out another couple of billion brain cells . . . and it sounds as though this batch may have been crucial.'

She waited now. She sensed her husband's silence as it left him. It spread through the lounge and crept menacingly into the kitchen. She felt it hovering, poised like an invisible stiletto at the nape of her neck. His feet padded softly in its wake and the light tinkle of ice and glass informed her of his presence immediately behind her.

Presently, in a voice weighted with contained emotion, he said, 'Did you try anyone else?'

She spotted his tack – he was aiming it at her. She picked up the Genghis Khan *nabé* and turned, holding it defensively between them. 'No, I did not try anyone else. I don't know anyone else. You're the one who smokes the stuff, not me. You see to all that.'

'When did Arlo call?'

'This afternoon. I told you. About three.'

'Why didn't you telephone me at work?'

'Oh Christ, Samson! I've been rushed off my feet from the moment I got up this morning, trying my best to organize this party for you. I didn't think to call you. I haven't had time. The matter went straight out of my head as soon as I put down the phone.'

Samson's arrogant features were set. His eyes were filled with reproach. His head and shoulders were inclined slightly towards her. Everything about him told Corinne that it was all her fault.

40

'So there's no dope,' he said.

Corinne dropped her eyes to the *nabé*.

'No,' she said, 'there's no dope.'

'Well, I can see this is going to be one hell of a great birthday party for me,' he accused her. 'No dope, I'm told I'm not allowed to drink, my wife gives me raw fish and seaweed to eat – no doubt the fish is filled with mercury and the seaweed is radioactive! Christ, all we need now is for thermo-nuclear war to be declared! That would round it all off rather neatly, wouldn't it!'

Corinne moved away.

'Fuck!' Samson cried acrimoniously. He stood, stiff with rage in the middle of the kitchen. 'Fuck! Fuck!'

He glared at the mock parquet floor.

'Corinne! Fuck!'

'Maybe someone will bring some,' Corinne said patiently.

'Well, it's no good relying on that,' he snapped. 'Fuck! There must be someone!' He strode from the kitchen. 'I'm going to make some phone calls.'

'Can you keep an eye on things in here as well, please?' his wife called after him. 'I have to get ready. They'll be arriving soon.'

His answer was what she expected.

Nothing.

0

Corinne sat down on the edge of the double bed with her back to the wall-to-wall, fitted wardrobe mirrors. She closed her eyes and placed her hands on her knees, tried to breathe calmly and evenly in an attempt to instil tranquillity into her agitated mind.

It was no good. She had too much to think about. It had become so important to her that this evening be a success. She didn't really know why, it was hardly a front-page event, but she had been planning it for weeks and had devoted a lot of time and effort to its organization. She desperately wanted it all to go well.

And yet she had a horrible and irrepressible feeling that it was going to end up an unqualified disaster.

Corinne felt like crying – she always seemed to feel that way these days. And she wanted to sleep, to lie back on the bed and sleep deeply with no worries to harry her and no crazy dreams to ransack her oblivion.

Heavy on her mind, amongst other things, were the friends and relations she had invited this evening. So many had declined, Samson was right. Jane and Werner, for instance, had already booked seats for the theatre; Alice and Mick were on holiday skiing in Zermatt; Terry was in bed with a heavy cold; Clive and Louise, like Dinah and Pete, were unable to arrange a babysitter; Oscar and Geoff were going to a bonfire party, and Claire was more than frantically busy with her language classes . . . all perfectly reasonable excuses, but Corinne could not help wondering – and it hurt her to think this – whether they might not be absolutely genuine.

In addition to all this, something – she didn't know what it was but she put it down to the fish – had evoked strong, tender memories of Tamasin.

Tamasin was a kitten that Corinne had purchased to keep her company soon after she and Samson had moved into Kimberley Mansions. She had never owned a pet before, neither had she thought of owning one. She was always much too busy.

But a year ago Samson's father had died, bequeathing him a patrimony that was not to be sniffed at, and Samson had decided then that it would no longer be necessary for his wife to go out to work.

'There's really no need any more,' he had said. 'We're laughing now. We're relatively affluent, and I'm expecting promotion at any time, so as soon as we move into this new apartment you can stop.'

Corinne had protested. She liked her job – she worked as an assistant displays director for ClimbDown Enterprises, a small but thriving company, specializing in video promotions for the music industry and for various large chain stores around the country. She did not want to give it up.

Samson, however, was adamant. He thought it was absurd that she continue to go out to work when they did not need the money. He could not fathom her reasoning. And he considered it demeaning, too. It did not fit in with the image of himself that he wished to project.

So eventually, reluctantly, Corinne had concurred. Four years of marriage had taught her that dispute was pointless when Samson's mind was made up. She could have held out, might possibly even have won, but it would not have been worth it. He would have found ways of making her pay.

One afternoon soon after this, as she was making her way home from a visit to the hairdresser, she had happened to glance in at the window of a nearby pet-shop. Her attention was caught by a small, fluffy, tabby kitten. It was sitting alone, dozing in the corner of a large hutch. As she gazed the kitten's eyes opened and it yawned and focused its gaze on her. Its eyes were beautiful: big and wide and yellow, and it seemed to be imploring her with its tiny expression to liberate it from the awful, wood-and-perspex prison where it was being forced to live. With silent longing it seemed to Corinne to be telling her that it didn't understand how it came to be there, that it didn't have a mother, nor any brothers or sisters, not even any companions to play with, and that it had never asked to be born into such a lonely, cheerless world of sodden sand, rough, groping hands and inadequate meals.

And there was promise, too, in the way it looked up at her. It promised her that if she would just come in now and pick it up for a moment, hold it gently against her bosom, stroke its soft fur and play with it, maybe take it home with her and give it something nourishing and toothsome to eat, then in return it would reward her a million times over by filling her long, empty hours with amusement, companionship and joy.

It wouldn't shit on the carpet, it said, as if reading her mind. No way. And it wouldn't scratch the furniture too much, either. Nor would it bring home other, less desirable felines that it might encounter on its night-time prowls. All it wanted, it said, was to be loved.

Just get me out of here, it begged her. *Please!*

So Corinne bought it.

For a while Tamasin was given the run of the apartment. She was cute and playful, as kittens always are, and Corinne grew very attached to her. Tamasin, in turn, grew very attached to Samson – an affinity which was not reciprocated. Samson was far from keen on having an animal about the house. He resented being clambered over when he was trying to watch television or listen to music. He found it difficult to come to terms with having his clothes clawed, his skin lacerated and his magazines and newspapers regularly torn to shreds. And when one night he had awoken in a panic to find himself unable to breathe due to Tamasin, who was curled up fast asleep on his face and preventing oxygen from gaining access to his respiratory tract, he had blown up.

'Bloody cat's out to get me,' he had complained bitterly to Corinne. 'It's trying to suffocate me in my sleep!'

'She's just displaying affection,' Corinne tried to placate him. 'She likes to sleep in the warmest place.'

'Fine, we'll put it in the oven tonight,' he retorted.

When it happened a second time he had banned the kitten from the bedroom.

'I don't know what it was doing there in the first place,' he accused his wife. 'The bedroom's no place for a cat. And especially this one. It's bloody psychopathic!'

It was six weeks ago now that Tamasin had disappeared. Corinne missed her terribly. She supposed that she must have somehow wandered off and lost herself. It was quite likely that she had been run over or something. It upset her to think about it. She tried not to dwell on it too much.

0

Corinne opened her eyes and the room assaulted her. Samson was responsible for this room. She had had a more or less free hand in furnishing the rest of their home but Samson had insisted that the main bedroom be left to him. Hence the black satin sheets and crimson coverlet, the coral wallpaper and carpet and the lilac curtains. Hence the expensive hi-fi system, the television and video recorder, the sound-proofed walls and ceiling, the fitted wardrobes with externally mirrored doors, and the soft-focus David Hamilton prints on the walls. It was hardly an environment conducive to relaxation.

Now Corinne lit herself a Dunhill mentholated and turned to look at the full length kaftan robe that lay draped across the bed beside her. She had bought it a few days earlier after spotting it in the window of a boutique in Kensington. Samson had not yet seen it.

The robe was loose-fitting and comfortable and bore a gorgeous, kaleidoscopic Indian design on a white background. It was a truly beautiful robe. Corinne had fallen in love with it the instant she had set eyes on it.

But as she looked upon it now, a scintilla of doubt slipped cagily into her mind. Was it perhaps just a teeny bit 'ageing hippy'?

Putting down her cigarette she stood up slowly, and with a feeling of reluctance turned to face herself in the full length mirror.

She was big.

She was obese.

She was grotesque.

With a pained expression she turned away again.

Corinne had started putting on weight several months earlier, shortly after her thirtieth birthday, in fact. Up until then she had been a pretty, slender young woman. Now she was an overweight hag. Quite suddenly flesh had begun to accumulate on her and, despite diets, exercises and pills, she had been unable to arrest the process. The upshot was more than a stone of flab spread about her body in places where before there had been none.

She had begun to dislike herself. She could no longer imagine herself as being in any way desirable. Whereas previously she and Samson had enjoyed an enthusiastic and mutually satisfying sex-life, she now found herself turning cold at the very thought of intimacy, and, with one excuse or another, rejecting all but his most ardent advances.

It was three weeks now since she had permitted him to make love to her. It had been in the dark. She herself had ensured that the light went out, she did not want to see Samson's face when his eyes took in the folds of surplus flesh that hung on her belly and flabbily bolstered her arms and thighs. However, she was quite certain now that had she not switched it off, Samson would have.

She did not have an orgasm that night.

Samson disliked fat women. He had told her that many times and she could quite understand it. But she was hurt by his unsympathetic attitude towards her now. He acted as though it was her fault she was fat, as though he thought she was gaining weight deliberately in order to spite him.

She picked up the robe from the bed and held it against her, turned again to confront her reflection. It *was* a lovely robe, she thought. It really did suit her. It wasn't ageing hippy at all. Quickly she slipped out of the jeans and blouse she was wearing and put the robe on. She let her arms float out from her sides so that the magnificent butterfly sleeves were displayed to their fullest effect. The loose cut and the white colour both helped disguise the shape of her body, she thought, and the contrast of colours set off her shoulder length, brunette hair rather nicely.

Now she looked at her face. She stepped forward and studied it more closely. Her eyes were puffy; heavy pouches had formed beneath them. Her cheeks were pasty and slack and she looked old. She turned her back on herself, picked up her cigarette and sat down again.

Drawing in a deep lungful of cool smoke she turned her face to the candy-pink ceiling and slowly exhaled. Samson had wanted to have a mirror there, too. Full length on the ceiling, directly over the bed. But she had put her foot down at that, objecting in principle to Samson and his voyeuristic and narcissistic inclinations, which she did not sympathize with, and also, perhaps a little carpingly, to the cost. Samson had extravagant tastes. Unlike her he had never had to scrimp and save. He had no notion of what it was like to have to do without.

Surprisingly, he had let her have her way about the mirror. This came as a relief, for she had balked when it came to revealing the real reason for her demurral. The true bone of her contention was that she could not bear the thought of having to look at her bloated form last thing every single night and first thing every single morning. She often wondered now whether that was Samson's reason, too.

0

Samson was in the lounge, hunched forward on the sofa with a hydrochloric scowl on his face. He was sucking the life out of a Lambert & Butler International-size filter tipped cigarette, and mouthing indelicacies at the round, travertine, occasional table in front of him. He was huffy. Inflamed. Seething. He was *really* pissed off.

Five telephone calls had turned up nothing. There was no dope to be had from anywhere at such short notice.

'My bloody birthday,' Samson muttered dismally between his teeth. 'My bloody, bloody birthday.'

It all seemed so grossly unfair to him. That this could happen on today of all days was an unspeakable transgression against everything he held sacred. It was inadmissible. It was *profane*.

'That twat Arlo,' he growled, 'that bloody, freaked-out twat Arlo.'

How was he supposed to get through this so-called party now? What was he supposed to do? It really wasn't funny.

Maybe someone will bring some, he thought. Like Corinne said. He hoped so.

Samson half got up from the sofa, half made to move to the telephone and give it one more try, then changed his mind and sank back again.

This is all wrong, he told himself. It shouldn't be like this at all. It's my birthday. I'm entitled to have fun.

As the moments passed his bitterness began to give way to puzzlement.

So I don't have any dope, he thought. Is that really such a tragedy? Can't I have myself a good time without it?

He pondered on this question for a little while and came up with the answer that it was, in theory, possible to enjoy oneself without resorting to cannabis resin. And he was determined that, one way or the other, this was exactly what he would do. It was, after all, *his* day, and he could, therefore, do just as he liked. Go ahead and have a good time, regardless.

Looked at from this angle the problem seemed marginally less grim. He felt his mood ascend a little.

Yes, he thought. Yes, I'll do just that. I'll have myself a bloody good night to remember.

He chewed over this for a minute, grinning to himself. Positive thinking, that was the key. Reaching for his drink, he stood, toasted the second sofa opposite him, and downed it in one gulp.

It came to him now that he did not have the vaguest idea who was coming that evening. He decided to remedy this forthwith. As he was leaving the lounge he recalled Corinne's request that he keep an eye on the kitchen whilst she was changing. He poked his head around the door; everything appeared to be all right. It was really rather a handsome spread she had prepared, he thought, despite being largely foreign. A most impressive little smorgasbord.

He smiled at this. He *had* encountered the term before, of course, but to him it was a misapplication. To him it conjured up images of mixed groups of scantily clad and utterly naked Scandinavians besporting themselves intimately, and with unaffected gusto, in the privacy of their own homes. He could somehow not equate it comfortably with raw fish, seaweed and rice-balls.

He sauntered back into the lounge, fixed himself another Harvey and a Dubonnet-and-lemonade for Corinne, and carried them both through into the bedroom.

● ● ● ● ●

47

# 2

Corinne was sitting at her dressing-table when her husband entered the bedroom. She looked around, an expression of mild shock on her face as he handed her the drink he had fixed. It was unusual for him to do anything like that without being asked.

She watched him seat himself on the bed, and when he returned her gaze, looked away. She felt strangely oppressed by his presence, and nervous, as if it were a stranger sitting there. In some ways, of course, it was. She could hardly claim to be in close harmony with him these days.

She felt she ought to say something, the silence bothered her, but she did not know what. She wondered if this was something that happened in all marriages – was the entire world putting on a brave face?

Presently she said, staring at her glass, 'I was just thinking about Tamasin.'

She wished immediately that she had not said it. There was no point. Samson was not going to respond in any way. She had really just put it in to give a small voice to her melancholia, and to fill in an empty space.

Samson was silent, tugging thoughtfully at his moustache. He knew what had happened to Tamasin, but he wasn't saying anything. He felt it was best this way. He knew he would never be able to make Corinne understand.

The truth concerning Tamasin was this:

One night, a short while after barring the kitten access to the bedroom, Samson had had a dream. In the dream he was a hunter, rugged and daring. He was scouring the North-American Rockies for a marauding grizzly bear that had been terrorizing the area for months and which no one else had had the guts to go after. Samson wasn't scared. He had tackled bears before. He had tackled packs of starving wolves, too. And bull mooses. In fact he had tackled just about everything there was to tackle and he had emerged triumphant and unscathed.

There was a reward out on the bear's hide but Samson wasn't interested in that. He just wanted to kill it.

He was advancing across a small clearing, his shotgun held firmly and lovingly before him in both hands, making his way towards the den where he knew the bear to be sleeping. Earlier he had doped some water and left it outside the bear's hideaway. He had seen the bear drink it so he knew now that it would be sleeping. All he had to do was walk up and shoot it as it snored.

He had reached the entrance to the den and was peering into the gloom when he was startled by a loud noise behind him. He spun round. There, less than six yards away, where he knew it could not possibly be, was the bear. With a mighty roar it reared up on its hind legs. It was gigantic. It was thirty feet tall.

Before Samson could collect his wits the bear had swatted the shotgun from his hands. Samson cried out in horror. The bear slobbered. It advanced, towering, and picked him up. Its fangs glinted in the sunlight as it clutched him in a vast, irresistible embrace.

Samson kicked and struggled. He tried to scream but no sound emerged. The bear held him tight. It wasn't hugging him to death, it was smothering him. It had his face crammed into its great, soft, ursine belly. His mouth was full of hair and flesh. He couldn't breathe.

He felt something pop, felt blood trickling down the side of his face and into his mouth. He was sick inside. He was dying.

Samson awoke at this point with a sharp cry. He was perspiring heavily and his body was convulsed in its struggle to draw air into its lungs. Curled up and still purring blissfully on his face was Tamasin. Somehow or other she had slipped into the bedroom without either he or Corinne seeing her – she must have followed them in when they retired for the night and hidden herself until they were asleep.

He pulled the kitten off his face and breathed deeply. There was a sour, brackish taste in his mouth which he was unable to identify, and he could still feel the warm, sticky blood of his dream on his cheek and ear. It was several seconds before it dawned on him that the kitten had urinated over him in its sleep.

Retching now, and blind with rage, he grabbed Tamasin by the scruff of the neck and leaped from the bed, opened the window and tossed her out into the night, calling after her, 'And you don't get back in till morning!'

Then, swearing, he charged into the bathroom to sponge himself down and rinse his mouth with Listermint.

It was as he was returning to the bedroom that it struck him. He stopped dead in his tracks.

'Oh Christ!'

Too late, he had remembered that they no longer occupied a small, two-bedroomed basement flat in Streatham but were now nine floors up in a fashionable apartment block in W.2.

Samson quickly donned a dressing-gown, located a torch and left the apartment. As he descended in the lift to the street he tried to persuade himself that there was still a chance. After all, he recalled, cats did have nine lives. And they always landed right side up . . .

After a brief search he had found the tiny, shattered body in the road outside the concierge's back door. He crouched over it for some time, gazing at it blankly and trying to decide what to do. Eventually, resignedly, he had scooped it up and placed it in a discarded Kentucky Fried Chicken carton he found lying in the gutter. Then he buried it deep in the bottom of a nearby litter-bin.

Corinne, who had slept through the entire episode, never got to hear a word of it.

0

Samson leaned forward on the bed, with his elbow on his knee, and tightened his lips across his teeth. He said, 'Who exactly is coming tonight?'

Corinne busied herself with her earrings in the mirror. They were single pearl droplet earrings, a birthday present from Samson four years ago.

'Oh, there aren't many coming,' she answered evasively. 'Only about half a dozen, I think.'

'Yes, I gathered that. But what I am endeavouring to ascertain is, who exactly are these nameless, faceless persons that I have been condemned to play genial host to?'

His tone was light, and as she looked at him she recognized with relief an amused sparkle in his brown eyes. His mood had changed in less than fifteen minutes. She assumed he must have come up with some dope from somewhere.

'Or is it a big secret?' he continued, with exaggerated concern. 'I do hope not. You know how I hate surprises.'

'No, it's no secret. Of course not,' Corinne said. She hesitated, then, 'The Baileys are coming,' she ventured, 'Gerald and Margaret.'

She wondered whether this was the right place to start. The problem was, that of the guests who were coming there was no one whom Samson was likely to prove particularly hospitable towards. One or two of them she knew he actually disliked, and the remainder she wasn't really sure about. Samson was pretty disparaging about almost everybody he came into contact with. He had no close friends of his own, so it was often impossible to gauge his true feelings about a person. Corinne hoped to introduce them to him now in some sort of order of ascending or descending preference. She couldn't quite decide which was best.

'The Baileys,' Samson echoed tonelessly. He bowed his head and brought his left hand up to his brow. 'Oh Christ.'

Corinne's heart dropped. 'But I thought you liked the Baileys,' she protested, though she had never thought anything of the kind.

Samson looked up and fixed her with a meaningful visage.

'They are a pair of turkeys,' he said. 'Numpties, the both of them. You know that.' He smiled grimly to himself. Despite this piece of news he still clung tenaciously to his resolve to enjoy himself at any price. 'Farts,' he added. 'I mean, Margaret . . . well, she's not *so* bad, I suppose. You know, I can tolerate her for a little while, providing she doesn't say anything. But Gerald . . .' He let out a brief sigh. 'Well, Corinne, you know as well as I do, the man's completely full of faeces!'

'Don't be awful,' Corinne scolded him. She was smiling secretly. Her husband had a certain way with words.

'Well, it's true,' Samson insisted. 'God, what on earth made you invite them?'

'I like them! Margaret's an old friend. You know that. And I haven't seen her for months.'

'That's something to be thankful for, I suppose. What are they "into" these days?'

'Much the same things, I think. The Clog Shop seems to be doing quite well, from what Margaret was telling me on the phone the other day. You know, they've got the exclusive rights to those Scandinavian clogs they started importing last year? They've taken off fantastically. And Margaret's still making her beauty products in her spare time.'

'Is she having any success?'

'Not very much, I don't think.'

'No, she wouldn't, would she.'

'Oh yes,' Corinne sniggered and put her hand to her mouth. 'Gerald's taken up Kung Fu.'

Samson's eyes opened wide with delight.

'What?'

'Kung Fu.'

He laughed out loud and slapped his leg.

'Gerald Bailey? Kung Fu?' he shrieked. He put down his drink and leapt to his feet, began bounding about the room, chopping and kicking vociferously at everything in sight. Corinne watched him, laughing to herself. He sparred stiffly with the open door, then jumped in front of the mirror and menaced himself with an extended fist, an open hand and a curled upper lip. Now he wheeled awkwardly, almost toppling, and advanced upon Corinne.

'Yaa!'

He aimed a clumsy kick, followed it with a limp chop, then turned, vaulted into the hallway and disappeared with a yell.

Presently he returned, panting heavily, and sat down again on the bed.

'Oh wonderful!' he gasped. 'Oh perfect!'

After a minute spent regaining his breath he asked, 'How long has he been doing that?'

'About a month, I think.'

Corinne's spirits had lifted. She felt better now. She looked better, too. She was beginning to think that perhaps this evening might be a success after all. Looking at Samson she saw the man she had married, the man with whom she had first fallen in love. He hadn't really changed and neither had she. They had just allowed their marriage to grow stale, vapid. The outside world had slipped between them and they had failed to see it and had turned away from each other. Surely the situation was not irremediable? Not if they both worked at it?

She picked up her Dubonnet-and-lemonade and moved to sit down beside him on the bed. Then she recalled what she had to tell him next. Perhaps this is a suitable time, she thought, while he's in such a good humour.

'They're bringing Rogelio,' she said hastily.

'Who?'

'Rogelio.' The name caught slightly at the back of her throat as she repeated it. She sipped at her drink.

'Rogelio who?' Samson enquired, puzzled.

Corinne inhaled deeply and enunciated the appellation, 'Rogelio Ramon Reyero,' as if the very sound might bring a hail of fire and brimstone into her home. She watched her husband's face solicitously, saw his expression change from enquiry into cognition, range through incredulity and astonishment, and emerge finally as righteous indignation – all in the space of a couple of seconds.

'You mean that little wart-hog of an artist friend of theirs?' he demanded.

She nodded.

'They're bringing him here?'

She nodded again.

Samson stared at her uncomprehendingly. 'I don't believe it. I don't believe it. I mean, why? What for?'

'They don't have any choice. They're looking after him. He's been staying with them since he was released from hospital a couple of weeks ago. They *have* to bring him with them, they wouldn't be able to come otherwise. He's too unstable to be left alone.'

'Oh great. Fine. Wonderful. He's too unstable to be left alone so they bring him around to my house so that he can babble and scratch and spout his gibberish that nobody else can understand and generally make life exceedingly difficult for all concerned. Jesus Christ, Corinne, this is my home, you know, not fucking Broadmoor! It's my birthday, too, remember? I'm supposed to have fun on my birthday!'

'Samson, shush!' Corinne admonished him now with annoyance. 'He isn't as bad as you make out. He's a talented man and he's been through a very trying time. You have to make some allowances. I don't – '

'Talented, my arse!' Samson scoffed. 'The man's a total no-no! He lives in cloud-cuckoo land! I think they've got a bloody nerve bringing him here.'

Corinne's voice hardened. 'Samson, I don't want you picking on him all night. He's still convalescing and it will do him good to get out and mix with a few people. But don't you *dare* piledrive him. He won't be able to stand up to it.

'And as for them bringing him here, *I* told them to. This is my home as well as yours and I want to see Gerald and Margaret, and if they don't bring Rogelio they won't be able to come.'

'Well, that's not such a terrible thing, is it?'

'You're so predictable, sometimes,' Corinne parried. She watched him wince almost imperceptibly, knowing how it stung his ego to be thought of as predictable.

She wanted to move off the subject now, draw Samson's attention away from Rogelio, but she felt she had to say something in the little artist's defence.

'He *is* talented,' she said. 'He had those two exhibitions over here last year, and both of them were quite successful. Some of his paintings have sold for as much as £800. He is a bit odd, I know, but I like him. He has an interesting mind.'

Samson wasn't really listening. He was smouldering at his drink and reflecting on his resolve of a few minutes ago. It was growing more difficult to hold on to by the second. The obstacles just seemed to keep on mounting. He heaved a sigh. Nevertheless . . .

'I always want to mother him,' Corinne was saying. 'He's so vulnerable. He has such a "little boy lost" look about him. I find him very appealing.'

'About as appealing as a vulture's crutch, if you ask me,' came the riposte. 'Comparably malodorous, too.'

Samson drained his glass and lay back on the bed with his hands behind his back.

'They worship that little nitwit,' he said. 'I can't understand it. They act as if he's some kind of guru or something. Is he still on his big religious kick?' Receiving no reply he went on, 'You know what he said to me the last time I saw him? It was after that last exhibition he had in Piccadilly. God, what a lot of crap that was! Splodges and straight lines, that was all I saw. Chimp scrawls. And do you know what he said? I was standing at the entrance, waiting for you to finish yapping to whoever it was you were yapping to, and he came over, all scruffy and falling apart, and he looked up at me and he said in that half-strangled voice of his: "You are trapped in your radiations. It makes me unhappy to see you this way."

'I couldn't quite believe he'd said it! I mean, it's not exactly the kind of opener you expect from someone you've only ever nodded your head to twice in your life, is it?'

Corinne smiled. 'And what did you say?'

'I told him to go fly a DC 10. Shrunken twerp.'

Having said this Samson was silent for a little while, tossing notions around in his young executive's brain. After a minute or so had passed an indulgent grin began to spread across his face. He was gradually bringing himself around to accepting the inescapability of the artist's presence in his home. He was even, in a slightly perverse way, beginning to look forward to it. He chuckled abdominally and his body bounced a little on the bed.

'What are you laughing at?' Corinne asked, smoothing her new robe on her heavy thighs.

'Your out-to-lunch artist friend,' Samson replied. His face was merry, his eyes laughing inwards.

'What about him?'

'I was just thinking . . . He's such a – ' he broke off and began to chortle loudly, rolling onto his side on the crimson coverlet.

'What?' Corinne urged, laughing too. Samson's laughter was contagious. 'Samson, tell me.'

Samson paused and looked up at her, his eyes bright and wet with mirth. 'Have you ever noticed how small he is?'

'Yes. Of course I have. He's tiny.'

Samson raised himself onto his elbows. 'He's like a scraggy little doll, isn't he.'

'Yes.'

'Well, you know how, when he sits on a chair, his feet don't touch the floor?'

Corinne nodded. 'Yes?'

'Have you ever noticed that, when he stands up again, they *still* don't touch the floor!'

He fell back on the coverlet, laughing heartily. Despite herself, Corinne laughed too. She felt a tinge of guilt for doing so but she could not help herself. She laughed less demonstratively, though, into her hand.

Wiping the tears from his eyes, Samson asked brightly, 'Who else is coming?'

Corinne reached for her Dunhills.

'Julia,' she said.

'Julia? From downstairs?'

She nodded, lighting her cigarette.

This was more bad news. For the first time Samson found

himself thinking in terms of a conspiracy. He said, 'What made you invite that ugly dyke?'

'Don't call her that! That's a horrible term! And you don't know anything about her. You do that all the time. You make arbitrary judgements about people – judgements which have no foundation whatsoever – and then you pass them on as fact. That's slanderous, Samson. It's malicious.'

'I stand corrected,' Samson said, mildly surprised at her outburst. He pulled a white handkerchief from his trousers pocket and waved it in the air. 'Julia, as far as either of us is at present able to ascertain from the currently known facts, is not a dyke.'

'She is ugly, though. And a man-hater. You must concede that much.'

Corinne did not reply.

'Back to my original question, then,' Samson said. 'What made you invite Julia to my birthday party?'

'I don't know, really,' she said vaguely. 'I ran into her in the post office the other day and we walked home together. I just happened to mention that it was your birthday and we were having a bit of a party, and I asked her if she would like to come along.'

'You asked her if she would like to come along . . . Well, I'm sure she'll turn out to be the life and soul of the party. I'm sure she'll turn up with a bottomless well of amusing anecdotes and hilarious, off-the-wall jokes that will keep us all entertained from beginning to end. I mean, we both know how Julia's charm and wit are renowned throughout the Eastern Counties. I'm surprised she's been able to find the time to fit us into her busy schedule.'

'Samson, don't be unkind. I feel sorry for her. She lives all alone in that flat down there and she doesn't seem to have any friends. I don't think she's got any family, either. She never goes out, you know. She was telling me, she just can't afford to. All her money goes on the flat – imagine having to keep a place like this on social security – and she hardly has enough left over to even feed herself.'

'Why doesn't she go out and get herself a job, then?'

'She says she's tried several but there's no hope. They all want younger girls.'

'I wasn't talking about dancing. She's obviously not going to have any success there, it stands to reason. But if things are so bad she can always go out and work in a factory or something. Or she could probably get work stripping again in the pubs. They're not fussy who gets up on stage as long as they've got a hole between their legs. And she did it before. She must have contacts?'

Corinne shook her head slowly from side to side. 'I don't know,' she said. 'Poor Julia, she doesn't seem to enjoy life very much.'

'Neither would you if you had it crawling all over you.'

'That's not funny!' she snapped. 'And neither is it true!'

Samson shrugged indifferently. He had been planning to follow up with an enquiry into Julia's current life-expectancy, knowing that the woman had already made three attempts on her own life, but he thought better of it. Instead he decided to change the subject.

'Is that the lot, then? Or do you have yet more wagonloads of scintillating guests queueing up to torment me?'

'That's all – except for Jill,' Corinne replied, her cheeks tingling a little.

Samson's face lit up.

'Aah, Jill,' he crooned. 'Of course. I had forgotten about her.'

This was untrue. He had not forgotten about her at all. Jill Richmond had been fairly prominent in his thoughts for a week now, ever since his initial encounter with her at Dingwall's, a trendy Chalk Farm nightspot.

Samson had been there in his official capacity as a talent-spotter. One of the bands playing support that evening had earlier submitted a demonstration tape to EMI which had aroused no interest whatsoever amongst Samson's colleagues. However, having little desire to return home before midnight at the earliest, he had decided to wander down there on the pretext of checking them out live.

He had spotted Jill immediately. She was blonde and exceed-ingly pretty, a cynosure in a jerking, weaving jungle of benighted human forms. He homed like an American Cruise on her rolling curves and hollows, her welcoming crevices and dips. To him, her wide, smiling eyes sparkled a personal promise and her crimson lips seemed to pout an invitation to intimacy. And her pert little teenage backside . . . aah, Samson saw, so badly in need of a good spanking.

He had sidled up to her on the dance-floor, eased her away from her female partner and introduced himself. He perceived within seconds that she was captivated by his suavity and waggish charm. And when he revealed to her that he was a highly-paid, fast-rising executive in the music industry he thought she looked mightily impressed.

He had flirted unashamedly with her throughout the next two numbers then taken her aside, bought her an orange juice (which was all she would touch), discovered she was a model and quite new to London, had her own flat and was unmarried, jived with her some more and was about to invite her to dinner when the band finished their set and she excused herself. She was with the band, she explained, and she had to leave with them now as they had another gig at the Rock Garden in an hour's time.

Not to be outdone, Samson had recklessly shoved his address into her hand and invited her to his birthday party. She said she didn't know. He told her he wouldn't take anything but yes for an answer. She said, okay, she would have to call him in the week with a definite answer, and that was the best she could do because she wouldn't know until then whether or not she would be away on an assignment. Samson kissed her hand, then her cheek, then her luscious lips. He felt an old, half-forgotten pang as he did so and realized, as she left him, that he would never again know peace until he had bedded her.

Samson sat up on the bed, tugging at his moustache. He was feeling more optimistic now. The evening had assumed a most heartening roseate glow.

'Who is she?' he heard Corinne ask, and was brought up sharply by the veiled edge in her voice. Of course, he had yet to explain Jill to his wife. This could turn out to be a little tricky. Thinking quickly, he replied, 'She's a friend of some chap at work. New to London, doesn't really know anyone here, so I thought I'd invite her round, introduce her to a few people.'

He was aware as he said it of how unconvincing he sounded, and he grew angry at himself. It was uncharacteristic of him to be caught on the hop like this. He could not understand how he had failed to provide himself with an airtight invention.

'And what does she do for a living?' Corinne enquired.

Thinking even more quickly, he said, 'I'm not altogether sure. I think she's in the fashion business or something.'

'Will she be bringing this chap from work?'

'I really couldn't say.' Samson felt himself getting into deep water. He picked up his empty glass and stood. 'I think this needs topping up.' He left the room.

Corinne sat where she was, crying silently inside herself. She felt terribly confused by everything. It had struck her, as Samson got up to leave, that since arriving home from work an hour ago, he had not kissed her, nor even touched her once. She was troubled about this Jill. Samson's behaviour had been enough to convince her that he was not telling all he knew – surely she couldn't be a mistress? Not even Samson would go that far, would he?

And she was deeply wounded, too, by the fact that he had not even glanced at her new robe.

●　●　●　●　●

# 3

Richard Pike was preparing himself for his lady.

He had just stepped out of the bath and, having dried his puny frame with a threadbare towel, was now lightly dusting his balls with Pagan Man masculine body talc – a Christmas present from his sister, Deirdre. Not too much – he didn't want to overdo it – just enough to add a little savour, a hint of something exotic and desirable down there. Richard was nurturing high hopes for this evening. His mind was turbulent with images of the sexual extravaganza he and Jill were going to be indulging themselves in when she arrived. Consequently, and to his mounting vexation, he was also nurturing a pretty sturdy-looking erection.

He had first acquired it two hours earlier when Jill had telephoned to say she was free for the evening and could she call around to see him. It had diminished briefly when he was preparing himself for this bath, but, almost simultaneous with his immersion in the piping hot water, it had returned. Now he found himself at a loss as to what to do with it.

Richard wrapped his thin, green towel around his waist. He picked up the saucepan in which he had transported his soap, shampoo, flannel and talc from his room to the bathroom, and held it against his belly so that his rock-hard phallus was both concealed and secured. Then he opened the bathroom door, peeped out, satisfied himself there was no one about, and sprinted, shivering, up the stairs to his room.

Richard lived in a rented bedsitter on the third floor of a four-storey Victorian house in Maida Vale. The house was owned by a couple of petty villains named Ted and Pinky, who had converted the ground floor into a second-hand television retail store and let the remainder off as bedsits. Between Richard's room and the bathroom there were two flights of stairs and three rented rooms.

He arrived at his door with a feeling of relief. The thought of running into someone on the way up had been a daunting one. He was sure that nobody could have failed to notice, or at least surmise, his condition. They were bound to think he was a pervert.

Inside he stood naked, in full priapic splendour, warming his buttocks in front of the gas fire.

His room was small and contained little in the way of furniture. A bed, a rickety table and chair, a wardrobe, a couple of warped boo kshelves, a small kitchen cupboard . . . Tucked into one corner was a Baby Belling, a sink and an Ascot water heater.

A naked light bulb hung from the centre of the damp, cracked ceiling, and the walls were concealed with faded, flowery wallpaper. Richard's own meagre possessions consisted of not much more than a small collection of books, a couple of changes of clothes, a cheap, portable hi-fi and a collection of records, and a battered Fender Precision bass which leaned against the wall in one corner, alongside a tiny, pug-nosed practice amp.

In an effort to bring a semblance of cheer to the place Richard had stuck a couple of posters on the wall. One was of Kate Bush, looking sultry, alluring and rich, and the other depicted a screaming man having a metal spike driven through his head by two cowled figures, as a host of others stood around laughing. Underneath, in garish red letters, was the legend, 'Life Is Not Always A Bowl Of Cherries'.

And that was about it.

He was certainly not wealthy.

There was certainly not room enough to swing a cat.


Richard slipped into a green check shirt, underpants and a pair of faded jeans and picked up his bass. He switched on the amp, sat down on his narrow bed, and began to pluck at the heavy strings. For a minute or so he improvised around a frantic rhythm he had devised a week earlier, then he stopped. He slouched over his instrument and gazed cow-eyed at the wall opposite. He could not concentrate. All he could think about was Jill.

0

Richard was twenty-one and a bass player in a five-piece rock outfit that slotted itself awkwardly somewhere beneath the generic heading of 'punk'. He was also, to his unceasing embarrassment and shame, on the dole. He detested having to tell people this; but he was far too honest to ever pretend otherwise. He aspired to a life devoted to music. He could think of nothing more honourable and rewarding than being a professional musician. But right now his somewhat modest musical abilities were not supporting him, regular jobs were hard to come by, so the State played mother to Richard Pike.

The band he played in had proven itself in the two years since its conception to be monumentally unsuccessful. He had joined three months previously, after answering an advertisement in *Melody Maker*, but already he could see that, despite almost daily rehearsals, it was going nowhere.

They had put together a demo-tape and submitted it to seven record companies, every one of which had rejected it out of hand. Management companies ditto. In the last six weeks they had played only three gigs – two of them, oddly enough, on the same night – and they had just one more lined up, and that was three weeks away.

Richard had not received a penny for his efforts to create beautiful music. None of them had. The only person to pick up a wage was Slider, the roadie. Of the twenty-five to thirty pounds average they were paid for a gig, twelve went into Slider's pocket and the remainder had to pay for each member's beer for the evening, keep them kitted-out in strings, plectrums, drumsticks and the like, and pay for their rehearsal studio. They were operating at a discomfiting loss.

Richard put aside his bass now and got up to place a record on the turntable. He chose Magazine's 'Real Life', then sat down again and began to roll a joint. While he was smoking it, he had decided, he would roll three more for later on, when Jill was here. They would get devastated together and frolic all night in bed. That was his plan. He desperately hoped it would all work out perfectly; he had only ever been to bed with one girl, and that was more than ten months ago.

Richard's big problem was that he was shy. Excruciatingly so. He was also perpetually horny, and the two did not blend well. Not for the life of him could he find the courage to approach a girl, no matter how much he fancied her, and this placed him under considerable stress. He was convinced that all he needed to make his life sublime – apart from a recording contract, of course – was a neat, sexy little girlfriend whom he could rely on, with time, to become his neat, sexy little wife. But his life up to now, if you discount his mother and sister, had been virtually bereft of female company, and he worried constantly that people would think him gay.

That was why he was so excited about Jill. She had just come up to him one night after the gig three weeks ago, and started talking to him. Even when, overcome with shyness, he had found himself unable to do anything more than stammer and blush, she had not been put off. She loved the band, she said, and she really thought he was a great bass player.

Richard still could not believe it. He had not been able to believe it when she bought him a drink, nor when she stayed to help him pack up his gear.

And she was a model! She was gorgeous!

Richard was in love.

He had seen her twice since then, once when they had gone to the cinema together, and then last week when she had accompanied him to the gigs he was playing at Dingwall's and the Rock Garden. They had not made love yet, but that, he was confident, would be remedied in a very short time. Why else would she be coming round?

Following Jill's telephone call he had rushed out to purchase a bottle of wine. After much hemming and hawing over the price he had opted for a litre bottle of Liebfraumilch. The bottle hung on a piece of cord outside his window now, cooling. He had also bought a tin of pear halves and a family-sized block of Double Choc Ripple ice cream. He was nuts about ice cream. He hoped Jill would be, too.

His final purchase on that dismal, damp, dying afternoon had been two packets of three Durex Fetherlite, because he was unenlightened as to Jill's precautionary status. He was broke now. Utterly. Next week, he knew, he would have to forfeit one or two meals and perhaps a day's heating, but, God! it was going to be worth it.

Richard leaned back on his bed and lit the joint he had rolled. He still had an erection. It was straining uncomfortably in his jeans, pining for him to do something about it. He glanced over at the travelling-alarm clock on the mantel-shelf. Almost seven o'clock. She had said to expect her around seven.

He was pleased to note that his bashfulness had dwindled – overridden, it seemed, by his need to get laid. Ever since Jill's call he had been rehearsing the words he was going to say, the way he was going to conduct the evening. He had it worked out to the tiniest detail and it imbued him with confidence.

Earlier that evening, just prior to taking his bath, Richard had eaten twenty-five Liberty Cap mushrooms on a slice of bread and strawberry jam. He had picked the mushrooms himself, two months before on a weekend excursion to Wales. Now he was waiting for the psilocybin in the mushrooms to start mingling with the neurotransmitters in his brain. When it did, he knew, everything would turn absolutely perfect. He would float easily in the world and Jill would be knocked out by his affability, his depth of vision, his adroit sense of humour and his vibrant sexuality.

Richard imagined himself now, having introduced Jill to his room, having poured her a glass of wine, having smoked the first joint, having dipped into a dish of pears and ice cream . . . he imagined himself bringing the subject of conversation around to sex. He imagined himself sliding a hand up her shapely thigh and exploring with his fingertips the creamy flesh above her stockings. She would be wearing stockings, of course. Black ones, with a suspender belt. And he imagined Jill's little sighs and moans of pleasure as he planted tender kisses on her neck and shoulder. He imagined the softness of her tit in the palm of his hand and the tremors of ecstasy that would course through his body as her fingers curled around his rampant tool. She would lower her head and it would be his turn to moan as her shiny, flickering tongue came into contact with his member . . .

He lay back on his bed and smoked his joint, and his prick cried out in mute, throbbing anguish for attention.

0

Richard tried to shift the train of his thoughts onto another track, and failed. He could think of nothing but excessive carnality with Jill. She was a model, she would know what it was all about.

He had fantasies of coming in her mouth, over her breasts, over her face. He wanted her to sit on his face and squirm her juicy cunt all over him. He wanted her to clasp her fabulous legs, still clad in sheer black nylon, behind his back and coax him deeper and deeper into her luscious, clinging love-chute. Then he wanted to have her in the sixty-nine position, and doggie-fashion on the floor – no, perhaps not on the floor; the linoleum was a bit cold.

Following this he wanted to fill her pussy with Double Choc Ripple ice cream and pear juice and slurp it all out of her. Then she could smother his prick in the same and suck him off. Then he would fill her up again and slot himself once more into her welcoming soft tunnel of flesh, glide up and down happily in a divine syrup of melted ice cream, pear juice and feminine secretions.

He hoped she would bring a vibrator so that they could fool around with that, too.

Richard had never partaken of any of these pleasurable activities before. He was aching to try them. He thought about them throughout an inordinate amount of his waking moments, and about ninety per cent of those spent sleeping.

He yearned unceasingly for such an opportunity to present itself. He had endless supplies of jissom just waiting for the right girl.

Or any girl, come to that.

But life had made him so fearful, so abject, that until now, until Jill, his sole knowledge of such delights had been vicariously gained, gleaned with tortured constancy from the pages of softporn magazines.

0

The one girl that Richard Pike had ever performed sexual intercourse with was a sixteen-year-old dope head named Rita, whom he did not even know.

At the time he was one of a floating population of itinerants, down-and-outs, homeless and unemployed occupying a derelict squat in Kilburn. He had left home just a day earlier and coached it to London with the intention of registering himself as unemployed, finding himself somewhere nice to live, buying a bass guitar and amplifier, joining a band and thus launching himself on the first steps of his brilliant career.

He had encountered his first obstacle at the labour exchange.

His claim would take time to sort out, the civil servant told him. He could expect no money from them for several weeks. He was directed to the local Department of Health and Social Security office where, at the end of a two-hour wait, a clerk took his credentials and told him to take a seat until his name was called. One hour ten minutes later he was interviewed by a stern, matronly, bun-haired lady in bifocals. She asked him if he had any money.

Yes, he said, a little.

She asked him how much.

Well, he had one hundred and twenty pounds of his own that he had managed to save, and his parents had loaned him one hundred and fifty – but he could not spend any of that as he needed it to put down as initial payment on a bass and amp, and also to pay the deposit on a flat.

The lady was not interested in that. She simply wanted to ascertain whether or not he had enough to cover his immediate requirements and, as he evidently did, he was therefore not entitled to an urgent needs payment from her office. His claim would be examined and considered by her superior, she told him, and if he was due any payment they would notify him. As he had no address at which they could contact him she made an appointment for him to return in one week's time.

A little disheartened, Richard had wandered the streets of Kilburn. His original plan, to move into a cheap hotel until he could find himself a nice flat, would have to be abandoned, he had realized. If he was to have any chance of succeeding, he would have to conserve every penny.

He questioned several people on the street and eventually found himself standing outside the house where he was to spend the next nine days and nights. It was a tall, crumbling building in the middle of a long terrace. Many of the windows had been barricaded with sheets of corrugated iron. The front door was open to the street, and there was no doorbell or even a knocker, so Richard pussy-footed into the hall.

In a downstairs room that was completely devoid of furniture and fittings, a young woman stood with her back to him, looking out into an overgrown back yard. He cleared his throat self-consciously and asked if it was possible he might stay there for a little while. The woman turned, and he saw that she was breast-feeding a baby. She shrugged and gave a wan smile, saying it was nothing to do with her but, sure, if he could find an empty space he could have it. Richard thanked her, hot with embarrassment, and began to explore the building.

It was filthy. Richard was appalled. He had never lived away from home before, had no idea that people could be reduced to living in such squalor. There was no water or gas or electricity and, apart from a few stained and holey mattresses, very little in the way of furniture. The lavatory was brim full with human excrement. Bottles and discarded food containers littered the floor along with little piles of dog and cat shit. He was severely tempted to forsake his plans there and then and return home, but he managed to resist the impulse.

There was nobody else in the house that day. Richard found a small, apparently uninhabited room at the top and installed himself.

He spoke to nobody during his stay there, did his best to avoid the other people in the house. They in turn ignored him. They acted as if they were totally unaware of his existence, as, indeed, they probably were.

He spent most of his time sitting alone in his bare room, afraid to go out in case somebody usurped his position. When he did venture out, either to buy food or to visit accommodation agencies, he took his belongings with him.

He wrote long letters to his parents and younger sister in Bath. In them he explained that everything was quite all right, that he was ensconced in an inexpensive but respectable hotel, that he had bought a bass guitar and was even now rehearsing with a very promising band. He told them that he had not yet found a job but that it was just a matter of time.

He told them not to worry. He thanked them again for the money they had loaned him and assured them that he loved them very much. He knew they found it difficult to understand his reasons for giving up his job in the carpet shop and upping and leaving them so suddenly, but he hoped they would bear with him for just a little while. He was going to be all right. He would prove it to them very soon.

Richard was sitting in his room early one afternoon, writing the second of these letters home and doing his best to ignore the foetor that pervaded the house day and night, and which he was totally unable to inure himself to, when he was disturbed by a noise on the landing outside. As he looked up the door flew open and a girl lurched uncertainly into the room. She stopped, blinked at him, then sagged against the doorjamb.

'I'm looking for Gary,' she announced in a slurred voice, loving the jamb with a fleshy cheek. She was very young, plump, and dressed in a black sweater, black leather jacket, red-and-yellow kilt and long, black leggings covered with zips. Her feet were naked and dirty. Badges, bits of silver chain, safety-pins and ring-pulls adorned her jacket. Her hair was spiky and dyed black and her face was a violent, painted mess of lipstick and mascara. She was obviously out of her head.

Richard gawked at her emptily. He noticed she had a joint in one hand.

'You're not Gary,' the girl declared. 'Where's Gary?'

'I think you must have the wrong room,' Richard replied. 'There's no one called Gary here.'

The girl hovered in the doorway, seemed about to leave, then changed her mind. She stepped unsteadily into the room.

'He lives here,' she said with a puzzled expression.

Richard shook his head. He felt he ought to apologize.

The girl regarded him with glazed eyes. 'How long have you been here?' she asked him. 'I haven't seen you before.'

'No. I've just moved in.'

'What's your name?'

Richard blushed. 'Richard.'

'I'm Rita.' She approached him and extended the hand with the joint in it. 'Do you want some of this, Richard?'

Richard thanked her and accepted it. He had smoked before, at friends' homes in and around Bath. He tried to avoid Rita's gaze.

'I'll bet the bastard's pissed off,' she said irritably. She performed an awkward pirouette in the centre of the room and wambled over to peer out of the window. Painted across the back of her jacket he saw the name AntiPasti. Beneath this it was just possible to discern Adam and the Ants, who had evidently fallen from favour since having a hit record.

'What are you writing?' Rita asked, turning to face him.

'A letter.'

'Oh.'

She watched him in silence for several seconds, then, 'That bastard!'

Richard feigned interest in his letter.

Rita stared at him meaningfully. 'I want him!' she opined. She tottered over to Richard's side. 'I want him! Give me that joint.'

She leaned forward to take it and, as she did so, appeared to lose her balance. With a little cry she flopped down beside him on the edge of his sleeping-bag, snickering. Her left hand, as she landed, came to rest on his thigh.

Horribly embarrassed Richard stared fervidly at the sheet of paper in his hands. The girl reeked of booze and sweat and he could feel her warm, sticky breath on his neck.

Her fingers shifted slightly on his thigh and she let her head rest against his shoulder, gazing up at him with glassy eyes. She was humming softly to herself, a tune he did not recognize. Richard did not know what to do; he tried very hard to pretend she was not there.

Rita lifted her head. Half singing, half simpering, she said, 'Do you want to fuck me, Richard?'

Richard was astonished. He blushed to his roots. Her hand slid up to his crotch and squeezed him there.

'You *do* want to fuck me!' she cried gleefully. 'I knew you did!'

Richard winced. The idea of intimacy with this sloppy, smelly, drunken tart filled him with revulsion. But at the same time he could not deny that he had an erection, and he was certainly anxious to relieve himself of his virginal bugbear.

Rita pushed herself against him and began slobbering at his neck with her violet-coated lips. With her right hand now she applied rhythmic pressure to his loins.

'Ooh, yes,' she breathed, 'you do! You *do*, don't you!'

Richard sank back and let it happen.

A minute later she was on her back and he was inside her, his jeans and underpants twisted around his knees, humping for all he was worth. She still wore her leather jacket, her sweater and her kilt – only her leggings had been removed.

She thrashed wildly beneath him, calling him a dirty bastard and clawing at his buttocks until she came with a great yell. He carried on and she came again. He humped and humped, until the sweat poured from his belly and back, until his arms trembled with the effort of supporting himself, until Rita's enthusiasm waned and she began to chew idly at a callous on the pad of her thumb. And still he had not come.

He kept going, though, with clenched teeth and aching limbs. He could not understand it. He had never had any trouble on his own.

Eventually he felt Rita's hands pushing at his shoulders. She was crying out at him, 'Oh God, stop! You're hurting me! Stop! Stop!'

He stopped. He collapsed over her, wet, exhausted and

bewildered. Rita shoved him off, sat up and examined herself, told him she had never known anyone to keep going for so long like that. She complained that he had hurt her inside. She picked up her leggings and hobbled like a saddle-sore cowpoke from the room.

Richard lay on his back in the darkening room. His face and neck were smeared with lipstick and his prick, still hard, was red and tender on his belly.

He wondered what had gone wrong. It was certainly nothing like he had expected.

●　●　●　●　●

# 4

Reclining across his bed now, smoking his joint, listening to his music and nursing his erection, Richard noticed that he had neglected to draw the curtains. Christ! He had been wandering about the room, naked and proud, and all the time the curtains had been open! Anybody could have seen in!

He stood up quickly and crossed the room to close them.

In the house across the road, sitting at a table in a lighted window in a second-storey room, was a girl with long black hair. Her curtains were open, too. Richard watched her for a moment. He often saw her sitting there. He wondered what she did for a living.

The girl sat with her hands clasped lightly on the table top, looking out in his general direction. Her room, what little he could see of it, looked warm and inviting. It was predominantly yellow. The wallpaper was pale primrose and the light itself seemed to bathe the room with a rich, citrine glow.

Richard thought the girl looked quite attractive, sometimes he entertained notions of getting to know her. There was no chance, of course. He knew she must think him pretty weird, hanging around in his room all day, not working, and hardly ever going out. She probably had a really good job and a car and an expense account. There was no way she would ever have anything to do with someone the likes of him.

He watched her self-consciously now, partially hidden from view by the angle of his wall. He wondered what she was looking at.

As he watched, the girl began to make sudden, jerking movements with one hand in front of her. She stood up smartly, both hands flapping at the air in some kind of idiot-spastic dance, and backed away from the window, backed into her room full of yellow light. Richard wondered what on earth she was doing.

The girl returned to her window and re-seated herself. A moment later she went through the entire rigmarole again. This time she backed away at an oblique angle and was lost from sight for several seconds.

Richard was entranced. It was not until she reappeared, brandishing a rolled-up newspaper with which she began attacking the air in front of her, that he sussed that she had a wasp. She was being terrorized by a wasp.

But a wasp in November? At night?

All right then, a daddy-longlegs or something. Whatever it was it was giving her a hard time.

Richard drew his curtains closed. He mooned over where the girl's boyfriend could be. He had never seen him, but he presumed he came around later in the evenings and left again before Richard arose in the mornings. He often wished he was that girl's boyfriend. He wished he was not so poor and undesirable and frightened.

As he turned away from the window he caught a glimpse of his reflection in the fly-blown mirror that hung above the mantelshelf. What a weed, he thought, approaching himself and looking closer. God, why am I such a wimp?

There was only one thing about Richard Pike that Richard Pike was not ashamed of, and that was his hair. Shortly after moving to London he had had it cropped, punk-style, and bleached blond. It had been a right decision; he was pleased with the result. His hair tended to get greasy very quickly, like his skin, but when, as now, it was newly washed, it had a pleasing, healthy sheen.

But as for the rest of him . . .

He was five feet ten and tended towards gawkishness. Whenever he happened to notice himself in a mirror or a window he would attempt to improve his stance. He would straighten his spine and thrust his bony chest forward. But generally he was not conscious of how he looked, and then his stooped shoulders, stiff movements, and fearful, forlorn expression would declare the way life had cowed him.

His skin was pale, almost lurid, and susceptible to spots. Seven of them adorned his chin now. Evil little pink volcanoes, brimming with pus, ready to erupt at any moment. There were two more on the bridge of his nose, poised between his sparse black eyebrows. Yesterday he had squeezed them all, but it did no good. They just came back like they were afraid of leaving him.

Richard's nose was long and narrow, his lips were pale and thin. His brow was high and furrowed. His cheeks were gaunt, pockmarked, and his expressive blue eyes were generally wide and

72

startled. All in all he had the mien of a young man apologizing profusely for his existence.

If only he had known that he was far from unique in harbouring feelings of insecurity and inferiority about himself. If only he had known that he was not, on the whole, unattractive to women. If he could just have interpreted correctly the looks in young girls' eyes when he stepped on stage and, wholly absorbed in his instrument, became transformed into a graceful, sensual, soulful animal . . .

But then, if he had known all these things perhaps he would have grown complacent, even arrogant. Perhaps he would have adopted an overconfident outlook on life, been brash and disdainful, offhand and lordly. Perhaps he would have approached girls with assurance and presumption and they would then have recoiled from his spots and his smegma, his poverty and his pride. Perhaps he would have found it virtually impossible to get himself a nice girlfriend.

Or perhaps not.

Who can say?

0

As Richard moved away from the mirror his motion caused a postcard, which was balanced rather precariously on the edge of the mantel-shelf, to topple and fall to the linoleum. He bent and picked it up.

The postcard had arrived that morning in an envelope addressed to him. It bore on its face a colour photograph of the Museumplein, or Museum Square, in Amsterdam. The focal point of the picture was a large, bronze statue, a representation of two human figures, grotesquely distorted. It was called, rather aptly, 'Europeans', and was sculpted by Karel Kneulman, a Dutchman.

People, tourists, who had obviously been in motion when the picture was taken, were now stock-still on the Museumplein, stuck there forever on holiday so that other people might gaze at them and speculate on the prospect of spending time in Amsterdam and visiting the Museumplein there.

Richard was reminded suddenly of an occasion when, as a child, he had accompanied his parents on a weekend trip to London. They had been strolling through St James's park on the Sunday morning. It was Remembrance Day, and as they walked, the muffled boom of ordnance sounded suddenly across the park and everything came to a halt. For a full minute, as Richard stared, hundreds of people all around him had simply stopped whatever they were doing and stood in silence, heads bowed or raised to the sky, unmoving.

Not understanding, he had felt then the strange sensation that they had all somehow become trapped in somebody else's photograph. He had cried out and clutched at his mother's arm, believing himself to be the only one unaffected.

Richard turned the postcard over in his hand now and studied, for perhaps the tenth time, the message that was scrawled on the reverse side.

Having a fucking good time in Amsterdam,
Ralph.

He smiled inside himself, not without a pang of envy. He wondered whether the Museumplein was anywhere near the red-light district. Knowing Ralph it would be. He was unlikely to stray far from where the action was.

Ralph rented the room opposite Richard's. He was a twenty-four-year-old National Car Parks attendant who, two months earlier, had been served notice of his redundancy. Not being one to go down with the sinking ship he had packed a rucksack and set off with his redundancy payment on an extensive tour of Europe. So far Richard had received postcards from Barcelona, Ibiza, St Tropez, Paris and now Amsterdam.

As he studied Ralph's card and the epigram contained thereon there was no doubt whatsoever in Richard's mind that Ralph was indeed having a fucking good time in Amsterdam. Probably, he envisaged, he was right this very moment buried to the balls in the luscious quim of some voluptuous European whore.

Or maybe he was having two at once! That would be more Ralph's style. He had no qualms when it came to fucking.

One of them would no doubt be blonde and slender with massive boobs. Danish, probably, or Swedish. And the other would be dark, maybe Oriental – or maybe even a Negress! Richard caught his breath at the thought.

And she would have long, shiny black hair, and she would be wearing white stockings and a suspender belt. And the other whore, the blonde, would have on black stockings and a red suspender belt, and they would both be beautiful and infinitely unbridled in their passions . . .

Richard squirmed with lust. Sometimes he wished he was Ralph.

The telephone rang downstairs and he jumped.

*Jill! Jill! She was calling to say she couldn't make it after all!*

With his heart thumping wildly he went out onto the landing and stood there. He could not bring himself to go down and answer the phone, he was too afraid of what it might mean. He heard a door open downstairs and someone come out and pick up the receiver. He listened intently to the gruff, male voice, and with a burst of relief heard it greet a familiar. Still clutching the postcard from Ralph, he returned to his room.

He replaced the card on the mantel-shelf and looked around him thoughtfully. His penis still heaved in his jeans. He was beginning to grow a little concerned about it now. He certainly wanted to impress Jill with it later on, but when she arrived, and whilst they were doing away with the preliminary platitudes, he did not want it to be displayed quite so prominently. She might think there was something wrong with him.

He remedied this by pulling on a long, baggy, grey woollen jumper. Its hem fell to his hips and helped conceal his exuberance.

He took a final drag at his joint now and stubbed it out. His head had become detached and effervescent, had expanded so as to contain much of the wisdom of the known universe, which, he cognized, was not worth bothering himself with at the present time. He was possessed of an idiot-grin. His thoughts formed in a rather desultory manner, flitted around in his head, passed on again before he had a chance to trap them, made no sense anyway. He tried to recall what it was that he had to do next.

Ah yes, roll three more joints.

He sat down, placed David Bowie's 'Aladdin Sane' across his thighs and, utilizing it as a worktop, began licking and sticking red Rizlas.

What about the room? he thought. What haven't I done in here?

It was essential to his design that the room be as impressive and as comfortable as possible for Jill's arrival. Everything had to be arranged so that, firstly, Richard himself was revealed as an intelligent, discerning, sophisticated and above all desirable personality, and secondly, one's mind turned naturally to sex.

In a milieu like Richard's this was virtually impossible to achieve.

He had tried, though. His clothes were all stashed away in the wardrobe and his plimsolls were shoved out of sight beneath the bed. A music stand stood in one corner, on it, open, a book of Charles Mingus' exercises for bass. That was important, Richard felt. He wanted Jill to be aware that he could read music.

Four white, wax, household candles were placed strategically around the room. He would light them later. His records were stacked against one wall, those he thought Jill was most likely to appreciate nearest the front, and three books had been dropped with meticulous inattention onto the floor by the head of his narrow bed. They were John Fowles' *The Magus*, *Surrealism* by Uwe M. Schneede, and The Complete Works of William Shakespeare. The latter was a twenty-first birthday present from his sister, Deirdre. He had not read it and did not intend doing so.

Displayed discreetly beneath this triune were two copies of *Penthouse* magazine. That ought to get her in the mood, Richard calculated. She would be bound to notice them and, out of simple curiosity, pick them up and flick through them. He had toyed with the idea of putting a copy of *Whitehouse* there, too, but had concluded that that might be taking things just a little too far.

He would move up close to Jill as she was perusing and they would glance through the magazines together. Casually slipping an arm around her waist he would indicate to her what he considered to be the finer points of each photograph. Then they would move on to the readers' letters.

The readers' letters always gave Richard a big thrill. There was one in particular, from a young married couple who had recently returned from a holiday in the South of France, which drove him wild every time he read it.

The letter was written by the husband and told how, one afternoon, it being chilly and overcast, he and his wife had found themselves at a loss as to what to do. The beach held little appeal and they had already visited the shops several times. So they were sitting in their hotel room, a little bit bored, and, quite naturally, started to doodle around with each other on the bed.

'It was unusual for us to make love at this time of day,' the husband stated in his letter. 'Without either of us realizing it our sex life had grown quite dull of late, almost perfunctory.'

Suddenly, with the two of them half naked and having a wonderful time, the chambermaid had walked in. She had come to tidy the room, believing it to be unoccupied.

'Oh!' the chambermaid said, blushing. She apologized and made to leave, then hesitated and, with a cheeky smile, looked the husband up and down quite unashamedly and said, 'Your husband has a particularly fine weapon, Madame. I can see why you chose to stay indoors today.'

'It's true,' the husband wrote modestly, 'I am rather well-endowed (eight-and-a-half inches, to be precise), and she was not the first girl to remark upon that fact.'

Now, this was where the letter really began to get interesting. To the husband's astonishment and delight, his wife, far from being shocked or embarrassed, actually invited the girl to come over and take a closer look, which she did, promptly. The chambermaid was French, of course, and had a figure like Raquel Welch. And she was dressed in a tiny, décolleté, black-and-white French chambermaid's outfit and black stockings and a suspender belt. Richard really loved what came next.

After commenting some more on the husband's length and girth, the girl positioned herself on the bed and began lovingly testing his penis with her fingers, and then her tongue. His wife, Valerie, watched approvingly, then she joined in too. The two girls happily licked and sucked at his penis and he went crazy with indescribable ecstasy.

After a while he undressed them both and they made love in a variety of positions. And then it turned out that the chambermaid was bisexual and was as attracted to Valerie as she was to her husband. An unexpected twist to the tale came when Valerie discovered, to everybody's unutterable delight, that she was equally attracted to the chambermaid.

'From that day on,' wrote the husband, 'Yvette used to come to our room every day – and not just to make the bed, either! It brought a whole new meaning to our relationship and, far from undermining our marriage, has indeed strengthened it.

'We were both sorry when that holiday came to an end. Valerie and Yvette were in tears when we parted. But we have kept in touch with Yvette, and only a week ago we received a letter from her telling us that she has decided to give up her job and move to England. Needless to say, we have written straight back and told her that we shall be there to meet her at the station when she arrives. She will stay with us, of course, and as the spare bedroom is presently cluttered up with all manner of junk, we propose to have her share ours. Somehow I don't think she will mind.'

Lucky man.

Richard was sure that Jill would enjoy reading that letter as much as he did. And *he* thought it was terrific. He was forever jerking off to it.

A thought from nowhere popped now into Richard's crazily swimming mind. It was something he had read sometime in a magazine article somewhere. It was this:

'At the present growth rate the mass of humanity will exceed the mass of the Earth itself in less than one thousand, six hundred years.'

Richard giggled as he completed his third joint. He giggled because he was blitzed out of his box, because one thousand, six hundred years was an awful long time to wait and see if it was true, because he had a throbbing erection and his underpants were wet and sticky with pre-ejaculatory exudations, and because at any second Jill was going to arrive and do all the things to him that he had ever in his life dreamed a girl would do.

●  ●  ●  ●  ●

# 5

The doorbell rang downstairs and Richard whipsnapped to his feet. This caused the blood to drain from his head and lake in the centre of his body, almost making him faint. With the world churning and flashing around him he staggered to the door and out onto the landing, then lurched jelly-legged down the stairs.

Jill was standing there when he opened the door. She looked divine, smiling prettily, her hands tucked into the pockets of a warm, fitted, black overcoat and her long blonde hair tucked into its collar. A Louis Vuitton bag hung from one shoulder.

'Hello,' she said perkily, a patina of fine drizzle glistening on her hair and coat as she stepped inside. 'I hope I'm not late.'

Richard smiled broadly and opened his arms, inviting a hug and a squeeze and a big French kiss, but she pecked him lightly on the lips and was gone before he could do anything about it, making her way up the first flight of stairs.

'It is upstairs, isn't it?' she asked him over her shoulder. 'I remember you said it was.'

Richard, his mind still swirling slowly, replied in the affirmative and followed her. He eyed her backside as they climbed, took note of her slender white fingers as they curled around the banister, savoured the dizzying assault of her perfume in his nostrils. He hoped somebody might come out of their room now and see what a beautiful girlfriend he had.

Nobody did.

Inside his room Jill tossed her bag onto his bed and unbuttoned her coat. She did not remove it but stood rubbing her hands briskly in front of the fire. Then, with an elegant, backward motion of her hands she released her flowing hair and turned to face him.

'How are you?'

'Oh, fine. How are you?'

'Okay.'

'Good.'

'What have you been doing?'

'Oh, not much. Is it cold out there?'

'It is a bit. It's not too bad, though.'

He noticed she was casting her eyes around the room as she spoke, and felt suddenly ashamed. He hoped she would not be too disenchanted now that she was witnessing the true extent of his poverty.

She stood three or four inches shorter than he, her weight balanced evenly on both feet. Golden earrings in the shape of five-pointed stars hung on slender chains from her ears. Beneath her overcoat he could see her slim figure clad in tight blue jeans and a dark green, woollen cardigan, interwoven here and there with tiny flashes of gold lurex. His eyes took in furtively the swell of her breasts beneath the thick wool.

'What a day I've had!' Jill announced with an indignant sigh.

'What happened?'

'Oh, I had to do a photo-session this morning for some Italian beachwear manufacturer. I went all the way over to Greenwich – I had to be there by nine – and the studio they were using was a horrible, dank little basement with faulty heating. There was nowhere for me to change or make-up properly, and the photographer was a horrible, brutish Italian who thought he was God's gift to women. All he wanted to do was grope me. It makes me so angry when that happens. Usually they're all right, most of them are very professional. They're there to do a job and they respect the fact that you are, too. They're usually quite polite and friendly and don't keep making grabs at you every five seconds. But every now and then you meet one who's got nothing but sex on his mind. This one, today, instead of telling me how he wanted me to pose, or just signalling, which is all some of them do, he kept coming over and grabbing me, pushing me into the positions he wanted, mauling me with his horrible, sweaty hands. And his fingers were disgusting! All brown with nicotine stains. He even tried to kiss me, you know! I told him to get lost. And he was plastered in after-shave. He smelt like a poodle-parlour. And his breath was like an ashtray. He was awful! I don't know why they think that just because you're a model you're fair game for everyone. This job really pisses me off sometimes.'

Having delivered her tirade Jill stared hard at the linoleum. Richard swallowed. He was not quite sure of how to interpret her words. He was beginning to feel a little uncertain of himself. At the same time he adored her precise, slightly bourgeois accent and the way her green eyes flashed and darted and her hands made little impotent, passionate gestures in front of her. And when she swore he was enchanted, though he was careful not to show it. He tried now to think of something comforting to say.

'Still, I shall be on location in the Seychelles soon,' Jill added, brightening. 'That's something to look forward to.'

'Yes,' Richard said, though he did not agree. 'When did you say you are going?'

'The fourteenth, provisionally, but I'm still waiting for confirmation from the company.'

She looked up at Richard now appealingly. He took this as an indication that she wished to be kissed, and stepped forward to embrace her. At the same moment she shifted her body, turned away from the fire, and he ended up with his nose in her ear and one foot on hers. He pulled back, snuffling stupidly. Jill said, 'Oh, sorry,' and sat down on the bed.

Richard's eyes fell to her feet and the Paris green stock heels she wore. As she sat, the hem of her jeans rode up an inch and revealed, to his disappointment, white cotton socks. He supposed that stockings and a suspender were a bit impractical beneath such tight jeans. She was still very lovely, though. His lust had not diminished one iota.

Jill leaned forward and picked up *The Magus* from the floor. She glanced at the blurb on the rear cover then asked him if he had read it, and was it good. He replied that he had read some of it and, yes, he was enjoying it. He watched her carefully as she replaced it and his heart skipped a beat as she slid a copy of *Penthouse* from beneath it.

'Do you buy these?' she asked, almost incredulously. There was something slightly withering in her tone.

'Er . . . well, yes,' he confessed.

'What for?'

Richard did not have an answer. This was not what he had expected. This should have been his big moment; the Great Seduction was to have started here, but Jill's response stymied him and made him crumple a little inside. She flicked through a few pages and discarded the magazine, and Richard forlornly stood and watched his moment pass.

'I really don't understand men,' Jill said. 'They have such one-track minds.'

'It's quite natural to feel physical attraction towards the opposite sex,' Richard offered desperately.

'Yes, I know it is. Of course it is. But men always take it so far. Sex, sex, sex . . . It's all they think about. It doesn't matter when or where or with whom – or with what, even – just as long as they get their little thrill. It's sickening, sometimes.'

Slightly shattered, Richard turned away. Some rapid rethinking was called for, he realized. It was back to the starting-line, without a pistol. He still had his wine, his hashish and his pears and ice cream. Regarding the latter, though, it was glaringly obvious now that he would have to bow a little more to convention than he had planned.

'Is that damp on the ceiling?' Jill asked.

'Er, yes.'

He looked at her sitting on the edge of his bed. She appeared suddenly to be a long way off – an invisible presence seemed to fill the space between them. She looked small, like he was seeing her through a reversed lens. Somehow he found it difficult to imagine himself making love to her.

He pulled the hem of his jumper down, worried about what to do next. He would have to take it more slowly, that was it. Appease her with wine and hashish and good music. Lavish her with affection and ice cream. They would sit and chat for a while, get to know each other better, slowly forget about the outside world. She was bound to come around, she had urges like everybody else.

At a perfectly chosen moment, when they were sitting close to one another, conversing in subdued tones, relaxed and *en rapport*, he would whisper her name and lean forward, press his lips tenderly to hers. With gentle pressure of his hands on her shoulders he would push her back onto the bed, slowly peel the clothes from her body.

A sudden thought dropped now like a live hand-grenade into the crowded prison cellar of his mind: *What about her clitoris! What if I can't find it!*

0

Richard's earlier aplomb was now non-existent. The confidence he had experienced when he was alone had dispersed itself rapidly like dust in a bitter breeze. As he stood before the girl he loved and feared he felt like a gangling, inept buffoon. He felt as though his clothes had all shrunk and his limbs were hanging out like oversized hunks of meat. He felt like a little boy who was about to mess his pants, who knew he was going to do it, and who could do absolutely nothing to prevent it.

'Do you fancy a joint?' he enquired timidly.

Jill wrinkled her delectable nose. 'Not really,' she said with an insouciant air.

'But I thought you smoked dope?'

'I do . . . sometimes. Not very often, though. Especially lately. It makes me lethargic and I get very irritable afterwards. And I don't think it does much for my looks, either. You can always tell on a photo when I've been smoking the night before.'

'I rolled a couple up,' Richard said, showing her.

'Oh, I'm sorry.' She smiled up at him apologetically. 'Maybe later on.' Then she added, 'I thought you were broke?'

'Oh, Slider gave me this,' he replied. It was a lie. He had bought the hashish from an urchin who had approached him in the street some days earlier, offering half an ounce of fresh Moroccan for three pounds. The child could not have been more than ten years old and had presumably lifted it from his parents' stash. Still, such an offer was far too good to refuse and Richard had paid up, consoling himself with the certain knowledge that had he not done so somebody else, probably far less deserving, would have.

Immediately afterwards he had experienced the icy suspicion that the deal had been a set-up. Instead of crossing to his front door, less than one hundred yards away, he had taken to the backstreets, wandering for almost an hour in the freezing cold until he was reasonably assured that no casually dressed members of the Drug Squad were on his tail.

'Did he give you the magazines, too?' Jill asked, knowingly. Richard blushed. She reached out and took his hand. 'I'm sorry. I'm wicked, I know I am. My mother is always telling me off about my sense of humour.'

Richard exploded silently at her touch. The contact was brief, though. She let her hand fall back into her lap.

For the first time Richard noticed the ring that sparkled on the third finger of her left hand. He sat down beside her. 'Is that a diamond?'

'Yes. A diamond cluster, actually.'

'Who gave you that?'

'Oh, some chap I used to know.'

'It looks like an engagement ring.'

She laughed briefly. 'Oh no, nothing like that. He was just a rich Arab who wanted to impress me. It didn't work, though. He bought me all sorts of presents then asked me to go back to Kuwait with him. I told him no. He got very upset.'

'Why do you wear it on that finger? It looks like you're attached.'

Jill shrugged. 'I don't know. I just put it there, that's all. It seems as good a place as any.'

0

Richard and Jill made small talk for a while, interspersed with periods of uncomfortable silence. Richard put a record on. It gave them something to talk about, and when the words ran out he was able to feign absorption in the music.

His ice cream still floated in a bowl of cold water in his little kitchen cabinet. His wine still hung on a cord outside the window. His candles remained unlit and his joints unsmoked. He could no longer decide what to do about these things. He could no longer decide about anything at all.

The psilocybin, the memory of which had been driven from his mind, had begun to supercharge his cannabis high. It was effecting subtle changes in his world that he was not yet fully conscious of. He sat and gawked vacuously, plundered his mind for something intelligent to say. He remarked mentally upon the geometric exactitude of a small area of linoleum that had been worn bare by years of scuffing feet. It reminded him of a donkey. He wondered why he had not spotted it before.

Jill was telling him about her family. She was telling him now, with a fond smile, about her pet Afghan hound, Jason, whom she missed so much. 'He curls up on the lawn in summer,' she was saying, 'and he just lies there like a big, woolly snake. And when you call him he opens one eye and lifts his tail just once, just one wag. But whenever I go home now he goes mad! You should see him. He leaps all over me and runs around in circles, barking with joy. He has such a funny voice, too. Deep-throated and low, as though his lungs are filled with cobwebs or something.' She tittered. 'He loves me so much, Jason does,' she said with sincerity. 'I wish I could bring him with me to London, but it would be cruel because he's used to the open countryside and the sea. He loves the sea!

Sometimes I take him out for a long walk along the coast to a little cove I know just a mile or two beyond Hastings. He loves it there – there's hardly ever anyone about . . .'

Richard goggled enraptured at her smiling, red lips. He filled his gaze with her wide, tanned cheeks and quick green eyes. He loved the way her slender nose wrinkled when she laughed and her expression could change so suddenly from merriment or exuberance into wistful sadness, and vice versa. He adored her shining blonde hair as it rolled and twisted about her shoulders. She had it parted on the left, and at times it would fall forward and completely obscure her face. Then she would toss her head back and sweep it behind one ear with a graceful movement of her hand. Richard longed to touch her hair. He longed to caress its fine texture with his fingers, press his lips to it and inhale her intoxicating feminine fragrance, but he did not dare.

Presently, at the end of a silence lasting perhaps twenty seconds, Jill turned to him and asked gaily, 'Do you want to go to a party?'

Richard did not want to go to a party. The very thought of walking into a room filled with strangers was enough to make him quail, could make him turn all foetal. Come to that, so could the thought of walking into a room filled with friends.

'A party?' he echoed querulously.

'Yes, a party,' Jill's countenance reflected amusement and a hint of petulance. 'There's no need to look like that! It isn't such a dreadful prospect, is it?'

'No, no.' He covered himself quickly. There was no way he could explain to her how he felt about parties, and neither could he tell her about his preparations earlier that evening. 'No. It's just that, well, I just . . . I hadn't thought about going out this evening.'

'What had you thought about doing, then?'

He glanced away at the opposite wall, which seemed somehow more imposing than it had ever done before. 'Oh, I don't know. I thought we could just stay here and listen to some records. You know, just sit and chat.'

He did not catch Jill's expression, and if he had he would not have understood it.

'Well, I would like to go,' she said. 'I haven't been to a decent party for more than a week. And I did say we would be coming.'

'Oh. Well, yes, that's all right. Let's go,' he blathered. 'I would quite like to go, too, if that's what you fancy doing.'

Jill smiled and stood up. 'Great. Come on, then.'

'What, now?'

'Yes. I said we'd be there by eight.'

'Whose party is it?'

'That chap Samson, remember? The one I told you about who was trying to chat me up at Dingwall's.'

Richard was stunned. 'Why do you want to go to his party? I thought you said you didn't like him.'

'I did not say I didn't like him, I said I thought he was a lecher. He was just out looking for someone to screw. I'll bet you anything he's married. You can always tell.

'But I think it might be quite a good party. He's very high up in the music biz, and he obviously enjoys a good time. And that's another reason why I think you should go, Ricky. I think you ought to get to know him. He could be a very useful contact for you.'

Richard winced at the name Ricky. Nobody else called him that. He did not like it. He thought it sounded a bit poofy.

He was very uneasy about this Samson. He harboured suspicions as to Jill's true relationship with him. And he dreaded to think how he was going to cope in a room full of trendy executives and business-types. He knew they would all dislike him.

Jill was tucking her hair back into her collar. She chuckled to herself, remembering a comedian she had heard on the radio a few days earlier. 'I'll bet he's seen more romance than a policeman's torch,' she quipped, referring to Samson Tallis.

Richard, tying his plimsolls, was too caught up in his thoughts to laugh. 'Do you fancy a joint before we go?' he asked, almost weeping. His three neglected joints lay on the mantel-shelf and he was praying for a brief respite.

'No thanks,' Jill replied, then added, 'Why not bring them with you? I'm sure they'll be appreciated.'

Richard had not considered this, but, in order not to appear mean in his girlfriend's eyes, he decided he would do just that. He picked them up and, lifting his jumper, slipped them into the breast pocket of his green check shirt. Jill was already on her way out. He crossed the room and took his brown leather jacket from behind the door. This was a jacket that Ralph had once described as being 'something that no self-respecting cow would have admitted to being the originator of'. It was true. It was undeniably

86

a hideous piece of hide, ravaged and stained with age. Neverthe-less, it was all he had.

He wrestled his way into the jacket, turned off the fire and the light, and followed Jill out of the door.

In the road outside, illuminated by street-lamps and the lights from shop windows, it was cold and drizzling steadily. The girl across the way had drawn closed her curtains.

Standing outside the television shop and watching the pro-grammes being broadcast on the second-hand televisions was the deaf guy. He came down most evenings. He would stand at the window and lip-read Crossroads, then, at its end, transfer his gaze to another set and catch the news with subtitles. Sometimes, when the weather was fine, he would stay there all evening, until an automatic time-switch in the shop turned the screens blank at around nine-thirty. Then he would wander slowly back up the street, disappear into whatever world he inhabited when he was not watching television. He was always alone.

Richard had no idea who he was or where he lived. They were on nodding terms but they rarely spoke – it embarrassed Richard when he could not understand the fellow's garbled intonations, and he always did his best to hurry by with just a nod and an implied 'hello'.

As he and Jill emerged into the street now the deaf guy did not notice them. He stood huddled, back to the rain, in a khaki trench coat, engrossed in the American presidential election. His lips were writhing in agitation as he watched a quavering ex-president James Earl Carter announce to the world that he had been trounced by a senescent actor from Illinois. They passed by without acknowledg-ing him. None of them could possibly have foreseen that, the very next time the deaf guy came to watch television, it would be Richard he would be seeing on the news. It's doubtful whether he would recognize him, though.

'How are we getting there?' Richard asked, shivering.

'Oh, we can walk. It's only about ten minutes away. I like to walk when it's like this. The rain is good for your complexion, you know. Ooh, look!'

She pointed to the sky where a rocket splashed a fiery trail as it sped upwards into the blackness. It burst into a shower of glowing vermilion stars which sank slowly back towards the earth and vanished. Another followed a little to their left.

'I had almost forgotten it was Bonfire Night!' Jill cried. 'We ought to be going to a bonfire!'

Richard would have preferred that, but he realized by her tone that she was not serious. He was aware that the air was thick with smoke and the smell of gunpowder. It stung his eyes slightly and caught in his throat. He did not recall it ever having been like this before. He wondered if there was a building on fire nearby.

'We ought to get something for Samson,' Jill said as they passed an off-licence. 'It is his birthday, after all. Don't worry, I'll pay for it.'

Richard hovered outside as she went in to buy a bottle of something. He did not want to go in, it looked too bright. He thought about the bottle hanging from his window. He thought about the ice cream and pears. He felt terribly emotional.

He was disturbed by the smoke. It was hanging in the air all around him and it seemed unnatural. Richard looked around to see how other people were coping with it. They seemed to be doing all right, seemed to be ignoring it, in fact. Maybe it was just him, then? Was that a possibility? Was the smoke there just for him? Was it a warning? He wondered whether he ought to cry out for help.

He thought, for no particular reason, of Ralph. No doubt Ralph was having himself a good time right now. No doubt he was having himself a *fucking* good time!

But here's something about Ralph: He was not, at that moment, having a very good time at all. Far from it, if the truth be told. He was sitting in an interrogation room of the Amsterdam Gemeente-politie nursing a pair of cracked ribs and a messed-up face, and endeavouring to explain to two Dutch detectives how it was that he had been discovered in the early hours of that morning lying face down and unconscious in a dumper truck alongside a dead, homosexual wine-waiter from a nearby Korean restaurant. The answer was beyond Ralph. He did not have the faintest idea. The events of the previous evening were a total blank.

And, in fact, time would fail to provide either himself or the politie with a satisfactory explanation. And when, weeks later, he was to discover a venereal sore inside his rectum, he would stamp and curse and tear his hair and still the memory would elude him. It was to remain a mystery for the rest of his days.

Ralph's troubles did not end here. When he was later escorted to the youth hostel where he had been bunking, in order that he might pick up his things, it was to find that some scumbag had ripped off his rucksack – passport, wallet and all. Ralph was not too happy with his current state of affairs in Amsterdam. He was beginning to wish he had never set foot in the place.

0

When Jill came out of the off-licence and handed him a bottle wrapped in white tissue paper Richard almost cried out with relief. He had come close to seeing something in the thick smoke. Something had almost stepped out of it and touched him.

They carried on along the street, with Richard endeavouring to adjust his stride so that he was not always several paces ahead of her. His erection made walking uncomfortable. He was sick to death of being sexually aroused.

More rockets whizzed into the heavens and exploded with dazzling displays of coloured fire. Richard tried to think of things to say, things profound, or at least witty, that would endear him to Jill. He sensed that she was growing weary of his company. He could feel her impatience like an inflexible aura, pushing him away. He longed to slip an arm around her waist but could not conceive of a reasonable excuse for doing so.

They passed a school. On the wall outside the school some enterprising child had painted in white letters several inches tall the words, 'Simon Buryfield eats warm poo and worms,' Richard considered this for a moment or two, concluded that it was hilarious. He was hard put to contain his mirth and had to turn away, swallowing forcefully, for he sensed that Jill would not share his opinion.

Thinking along humorous lines now he recalled a joke he had heard a while back.

'Do you know –' he began. At the same moment Jill said, 'Who do you –'

They both broke off.

'Sorry,' Richard said.

'Sorry,' Jill said. They both made apologetic laughing noises.

'What were you going to say?' Jill asked.

'Oh, nothing. Go on, what were you going to say?'

'No, tell me yours first.'

'It was nothing. Really.'

'Oh, all right then. I was going to say, Who do you think I met the other day?'

Richard was stumped. 'Humphrey Bogart?'

'No, silly.' She turned to him with a jubilant expression. 'David Essex!'

'Where did you meet him?'

'Well, you remember that chap Terry I told you about, the one who I met at dance class? He's a sound technician in a recording studio, and he invited me down one evening because I was bored and had nothing to do. And when I got there David Essex was there doing some recording!'

Richard was jealous. He resented Jill's high lifestyle. He wondered whether she had gone to bed with David Essex. Or with Terry the sound technician.

'What's he like?' he asked.

'Ooh, he's lovely. Great singer . . . and a really nice personality, too.'

Richard fell silent. Presently Jill said, 'What were you going to say back there?'

'Oh, nothing. It was just a joke I heard.'

'Tell me. I like jokes. It isn't filthy, is it?'

'No. Not at all.'

'Tell me, then.'

'Okay. Do you know what they are going to do with Idi Amin when they catch him?'

Jill smiled, then giggled.

'You're not supposed to laugh yet,' he said. 'I haven't told you the funny bit.'

'I know. I always laugh before the end of a joke. Go on, then. What are they going to do with Idi Amin when they catch him?'

'They're going to bone him and present him to Cyril Smith as a wet suit.'

'Ugh, that's grotesque!' she cried, but she laughed and told him she would have to remember that one and Richard was happy for several seconds. He was about to try and put his arm about her and ask her if she knew any good jokes herself, when they turned into a narrow street and Jill said, 'Here it is!'

He looked up to find himself standing outside the entrance to Kimberley Mansions.

● ● ● ● ●

# 6

Only minutes earlier, as Richard Pike and Jill Richmond were leaving Richard's cruddy bedsit in Maida Vale, the doorbell rang in the Tallis's apartment.

Or rather, the doorbell *sang*.

Samson had introduced an electronic chip into the circuitry, transducing and synthesizing the sound so that the familiar Avon chimes were now possessed of all the essential qualities of the *vox humana*. At the press of the button outside, the 'bell' rendered itself in resonant, adenoidal, tin-can tones –

'*Door-bell*,' it crooned. '*Doorr-belll . . .*'

The effect upon unsuspecting persons inside the apartment was invariably well worth the trouble it had taken to install the device.

Samson, in a frivolous mood now, was shaking his head, hands and hips to Blondie and adding discordant accompaniment as they performed 'live' on video-tape on his television screen. At the announcement by the 'bell' of the arrival of his first birthday guests, he called out, 'I'll get it!' and pranced with frolicsome steps to the television and video-recorder and switched them off.

He adjusted his tie, smoothed his hair and winked at himself in the mirror. He tra-la-la'd over to the travertine table and relieved his whisky glass of its contents. Humming a merry tune he smoothed his trousers. Then, with one hand resting loosely on his hip and the other hanging limply at shoulder level, he puckered his lips and minced like a fey hairdresser to the front door.

He opened the door with a flourish and threw his arms wide.

'Darlings!' he cried with ebullience. 'How sweet!'

On the threshold, wrapped up warm in winter wear, were Gerald and Margaret Bailey. They both wore broad beams of greeting as the door opened, and the two beams froze for an instant as they contended with the loud, cruciform figure in red that filled the doorway. Then Margaret, a petite, wiry woman in a blue raincoat and green-and-white woollen hat, stepped forward.

'Hello, Samson,' she said, smiling tolerantly, and kissed him on the cheek. Gerald, tall, lean and bespectacled, followed as though affixed to her.

Behind them and between them, trailing like an old, bedraggled son, came Rogelio Ramon Reyero.

0

'Oh, how wonderful! How divine!' Samson gushed. He closed the door with an exaggerated sweep of his hands, then swung round to clasp Margaret by the upper arms.

'Margaret!' he said, and kissed her again.

Margaret kept her smile and pushed towards him a large, box-shaped, brightly wrapped parcel. 'Happy birthday,' she said.

'A present? For *me*?' He took it and raised it to his ear, shaking it. 'Whatever can it be?'

He turned to Gerald, who grinned sheepishly and held out a hand. 'Sam,' he said, by way of greeting.

'Gerald!' Samson cried. He grabbed the hapless fellow and hugged him, kissed him, and hugged him some more.

Corinne came out of the bedroom and swept down the hall in her new robe.

'Margaret!'

'Corinne!'

They embraced, as old friends do who have not set eyes on one another for a lengthy period. Then Corinne turned to embrace Gerald, who was bearing-up with a stoical grin and making uncertain chortling noises as Samson continued to hug him.

'Samson, stop making a fool of yourself,' she said, slapping his shoulder and turning to Margaret with a strained look. Margaret made a commiserative face.

Samson released Gerald and grabbed Margaret once more and kissed her. Gerald kissed Corinne. Everybody made it awfully plain that they were overjoyed at seeing one another again. Then Corinne turned to Rogelio and extended a hand.

'Hello, Rogelio,' she said warmly, courteously. 'How are you?'

The diminutive artist, swathed and hooded in a big buff duffle-coat, had paid no heed to the effusion around him. He had been staring at the carpet. Now he raised his blue eyes to hers.

'I am well,' he said in a half-strangled, oddly accented voice. He removed a hand like a little bag of bones from his pocket, and placed it in hers.

'We're very pleased you could make it,' Corinne said.

The little man nodded with a remote smile. 'Yes,' he said.

'Yes, we are,' Samson agreed, tearing at his parcel. 'We are indeed.'

'You remember Corinne and Samson, don't you, Rogelio?' Margaret asked.

Rogelio looked at Corinne. His face bore no expression whatsoever but his gaze was searching, and vaguely discomfiting. He looked at Samson and his gaze seemed almost to dilate somehow, as though he was taking in something other than Samson the man.

At length his eyes softened and he said, distantly, 'I have not met these . . . persons on a previous occasion.'

'Yes you have,' Margaret said. 'Don't you remember? They came to both your exhibitions and we introduced them to you quite some time before that. Corinne is quite an admirer of yours.'

Rogelio shrugged, pulled at a wispy black side-whisker, and turned away. 'Yes,' he said.

'Well, come on everybody,' Corinne said. 'Coats and hats off and let's go inside and have a drink, shall we?'

Margaret removed her hat and shook free her short, mousey hair. A rather plain-faced woman of thirty-two, two years younger than her husband, there was normally nothing in her appearance that would excite one's attention. But now, as she slipped out of her raincoat, it was to reveal beneath it a pure-silk, calf-length kimono, printed with cranes and clouds on azure. Loosely knotted around her waist was a wide, matching sash, and on her feet, blue high-heels.

Corinne, in the middle of a word to Gerald, stopped mid-sentence. 'Margaret! What a beautiful kimono!'

Margaret beamed delightedly.

'Thank you. Gerald bought it for me – didn't you, darling – a present for our ninth anniversary. This evening is the first opportunity I've had to wear it.'

'Oh, it's exquisite!' Corinne reiterated. She collected the three coats from Margaret, Gerald and Rogelio, and clasped them to her. 'You look absolutely radiant.'

Even Samson was impressed. 'You ought to get one of those,' he told his wife.

'You mean you ought to buy her one,' Margaret corrected him.

'That'll be the day,' Corinne said. She moved away to hang up

93

the coats. As she returned to guide her guests towards the lounge she endeavoured to keep Gerald and Rogelio between herself and Margaret, feeling that her own robe looked quite dowdy alongside the elegant blue kimono.

'Clogs!' Samson cried suddenly, bringing up the rear. He had succeeded in ripping apart the parcel and was holding up a pair of wooden-soled clogs with dark green leather uppers. 'Who would have guessed?'

0

The five entered the lounge.

The Tallis's lounge was a spacious, comfortable affair, approximately fifteen feet by twenty-five. At one end was a French window which let out onto the balcony and commanded an impressive view over much of London, and alongside this was a large casement window, making the room pleasantly light and airy during the day.

Corinne had carpeted the floor in soft, deep-pile, beige Axminster, and the walls were of pastel shades, enlivened here and there with oriental and occidental prints.

In shallow alcoves set around the walls shelving systems in chrome and-smoked glass had been fitted. One of these was the domain of Samson's Sony hi-fi system and his records and tapes. The others held books, pot-plants, and ornaments, artifacts and knick-knacks of varying kinds.

The centre of the room was taken up by the travertine occasional table and an armchair and two comfortable sofas, coloured ecru and delicately printed with pale orange leaves and fronds. Beyond these, beneath the window, was a small dining table, also in chrome and glass, and three chairs. A large, stained glass bowl filled with fruit sat in the centre of the table. Along the adjacent wall stood the drinks cabinet and another shelving and utility system.

Full length, pale orange curtains had been left open to facilitate a view of the bonfire and firework displays as the evening progressed.

Arranged in tactical locations about the room were framed photographs of Samson fraternizing with pop stars, male and female, many of whom had long since become extinct.

And, of course, there was now a variety of birthday cards.

'Mind if I have a look at your cards, Sam?' asked Gerald, who was standing wearing a slightly abandoned look as Corinne and his wife engaged in quickfire comments and enquiries into each other's welfare.

'Go ahead,' said Samson, and Gerald pursed his lips and grinned, bobbed his head and shoulders, shoved his hands into his pockets and moved off to simulate interest in the birthday cards.

'This *is* a beautiful room,' Margaret was saying. There was a tiny trace of a northern accent in her voice, although she had striven hard to erase it. Twelve years earlier she had moved down to London from Lancashire. She had taken a job in a boutique in Soho and found a small flat which she shared with two other girls, one of whom had been Corinne.

'Of course, you haven't seen it before, have you?' Corinne replied, fiddling a little nervously with the neckline of her robe.

'No, this is the first time we've seen you since your move. Time flies so, doesn't it. Oh, but it is lovely, darling. You've designed it so well.'

'Now then, what about drinks?' Samson demanded, clapping his hands together.

'Oh, just a small, dry white wine for me, please,' said Margaret.

Gerald looked up. 'Yes, I'll have the same, please.'

Rogelio had separated himself slightly from Corinne and Margaret and was standing gazing around the room. He cut a spavined figure in his stained green tee-shirt, his ill-fitting, faded blue jeans held up by an old, red-and-white striped school tie, and his worn pink ballet shoes. He was sallow skinned and knobby limbed and had neglected to shave for several days. His curling black hair massed chaotic about his head, like something constructed there by a sick rook, and his eyes were bloodshot and loco.

His age was a matter of guesswork, on his part especially, but mid-thirties would be not too far off the mark. Slung over one shoulder he had a black-and-white cloth bag embroidered with a South American design. There was a look of perplexity on his little screwed-up face and he scratched abstractedly at his left shoulder.

Margaret, throughout her conversation, had been casting solicitous glances in his direction. Now she bowed her head slightly towards him as he began to speak.

'It is, yes, a beautiful room,' he murmured. 'There is space.'

'Why, thank you, Rogelio,' Corinne said, much pleased.

'But there is something else,' he added, and his look of perplexity deepened. He shook his head once and his eyes flashed. 'There is something else . . .'

Samson returned with drinks.

'Two dry white wines, as requested,' he said. He handed one to Margaret and one to Gerald.

'I hope this won't make me tipsy,' Margaret said, 'Gerald and I rarely drink these days, you know.' She sipped the wine and looked up with a smile. 'Mmm, lovely.'

'Yes, quite a cheeky little vintage,' Samson quipped. 'I'm rather taken with it myself, I must admit. Impudent without being insolent, wouldn't you say?'

Margaret and Gerald both laughed.

'That's a good one, Sam,' said Gerald. 'I've not heard that before.'

Samson grinned and nodded, saying, 'I don't consider myself to be a connoisseur of wines; I'm not into all that pretentious, upper-class cat-crap, but, the thing is, I know what I like' – he nudged Gerald with an elbow – 'and that's what counts, isn't it.'

'That's right,' Gerald agreed, looking into his wine. 'Yes, it is.'

Samson crossed back over to the drinks cabinet and returned with the bottle. 'Well, come on, drink up and you can have a refill.'

'Don't be silly, you've just this minute poured them,' Corinne admonished him.

'Well, they can have another, can't they?'

'Oh no, one glass is quite enough, thanks,' Gerald said. 'We won't drink any more this evening, will we, darling? We're really only drinking this because it's a rather special occasion.'

Samson looked affronted. 'What! I'm not having any of that. This is my birthday party. None of this teetotal rubbish here. I expect you both to get roaring drunk. Come on, knock it back. By the way, you haven't brought any dope with you, have you?'

'Oh no, we don't touch that either.'

Samson sagged. He took his cigarettes from his pocket and proffered the pack. The Baileys both declined. He took one for himself and placed it between his lips, lit it, then said to Gerald, 'I understand you can kill inadvertently these days.'

Gerald's expression made it obvious that he did not know what he was talking about, so he went on, 'Corinne told me. She said you've turned yourself into a Kung Fu marauder.'

'Oh,' said Gerald, letting off a quick, self-conscious laugh. He looked at the floor, pushed his large, steel-rimmed glasses up his nose, looked up again and grinned like a chump, shuffled his feet, put his hands in the pockets of his thick brown cords, then removed one and picked at a piece of lint on his dark blue jersey. 'Aah.'

'Is it true?' asked Samson wryly.

'Well . . . yes.'

'Am I safe, then?'

'Oh, I think so, Sam.'

'I'm not on your hit-list?'

'No.'

'But if I was would you tell me?'

'Yes.'

'Honestly?'

'Yes.'

'You're that confident, then?'

Gerald didn't look very confident. 'I only started taking classes a few weeks ago, actually,' he said. 'I'm hardly what you would call an expert yet.' He snickered apologetically. 'And there's a lot more involved than simply self-defence, you know. There's really a whole philosophy behind it . . .' He hesitated and brushed a lock of light brown hair from his forehead.

'A whole philosophy?' echoed Samson. 'I didn't know that.'

'Oh yes, and one is taught from the outset not to abuse it in any way. The point of learning it, really, is that the more proficient you become the more your awareness increases and the less likely you are to find yourself in a situation where you need to use it – if you see what I mean.'

'I see, yes. But at the same time, you must feel infinitely more self-assured in the knowledge that, for instance, were you to be set upon by a gang of muggers as you made your way home this evening, you could deal with them all without so much as batting an eyelid.'

Gerald's laugh almost choked him. 'I wouldn't say that, Sam.'

'You wouldn't? Well . . . In all honesty, then, will you tell me, have you or have you not come here tonight with the intention of inflicting bodily harm upon my person?'

Gerald laughed again. 'No, Sam.'

'You're sure of that?'

'Yes.'

'Promise?'

'Promise.'

Samson wiped his brow. 'Phew, that's a relief!'

'Well, why don't we sit down?' put in Corinne, anxious to put an end to her husband's befoolment of their guests. 'Samson, why don't you put some music on?' She turned to Gerald. 'I think it's absolutely fascinating. I've seen these chaps on television, these Chinese and Japanese masters and such, breaking bricks and tiles and huge blocks of ice with their hands. Even with their heads! However do they do it without injuring themselves?'

'Yes, it's quite remarkable,' Gerald agreed. 'Perseverance is the key, I think. Single-minded devotion. They build themselves up both mentally and physically over years and years of constant training.'

'But don't you ever get hurt when you're training?'

'Not so far,' he grinned. 'Touch wood.'

I'd rather you didn't,' said Samson, who was enjoying himself immensely, 'We don't want anything broken.' He had selected a cassette tape and was about to rejoin the others when he noticed Rogelio. He stopped still and stared.

The little fellow seemed to have entered a light trance. His eyes were glazed and his nose twitched, rodent-like, as though testing the air for something. At the same time his arms hung quite rigidly a few inches from his side.

'Something else,' he whispered hoarsely. The others looked up. 'I do not have it yet.'

He took a step towards Corinne, hovered, hesitated, then shook his head and moved away. 'I am uncertain,' he said. 'I am not happy.'

Suddenly his expression cleared.

'I have it!' he exclaimed. He turned triumphantly to Margaret. 'Yes! I have it!'

Margaret sat forward. 'What is it, Rogelio?'

'Fornication!'

'I beg your pardon!' Samson cried.

'Fornication,' Rogelio repeated with certainty. He sniffed at the air. 'It is here!'

Samson turned with a laughing, disbelieving face to Gerald, then back to the artist.

'No, no, I think you've got it wrong,' he told him. 'I think what you are referring to must be my wife's cooking. She's been experimenting with something oriental.'

'No,' Rogelio insisted. 'I have made no mistake, but . . .' He re-acquired his puzzled expression and his nose crinkled again. '. . . it is not here . . .'

He turned and moved towards the hall.

'Ah, yes, it is stronger here.' He wheeled suddenly and fixed Samson with a piercing blue stare. 'It is not occurring yet! This is why I am so confused.'

'My God!' said Samson.

Rogelio veered away again. 'It is not in this room . . . but it is this home.'

He muttered something else quite incomprehensible and stepped out into the hall, bee-lining towards the main bedroom. Samson moved swiftly to intercept him.

'Just a minute! Hang on!' He caught him and steered him back with one arm. 'Enough's enough, you know.' He turned to Gerald and Margaret. 'I say, you two, if you really must bring your livestock everywhere with you I think you ought to have it under better control than this.'

'Samson!' Corinne cried angrily, rising to her feet. The Baileys exchanged apprehensive glances. Margaret put an arm around Rogelio's shoulders and led him to the sofa and sat him down. The artist's features were blank now, as though whoever lived inside him had gone out suddenly and switched off all the lights.

'Sorry about that,' Gerald said in an undertone, so that Rogelio would not overhear. 'He's very preoccupied. Very unpredictable, but he means no offence. The thing is, he has such a finely tuned mind. And since he had that . . . that mental collapse thing, he's been rather frail. We have to be very careful with him. It's a bit of a problem at times because people just can't seem to understand how different he is. But he does sense things that other people are unaware of. It's happened before on several occasions. It's quite uncanny at times. It's a kind of prescience. It's almost like with some animals, you know, you must have noticed it with dogs – and with cats especially – how at times they seem to sense things that we can't. He really does have that kind of, umm, *a priori* sensitivity, I suppose you might call it.'

'Well, yes, fair enough,' whispered Samson, 'but couldn't you have brought him something to play with?'

'I'd like a drink, please, Samson,' Corinne said sharply.

'Fine.' Samson returned to the drinks cabinet and fixed drinks for himself and his wife. Back at Gerald's side he asked good-humouredly, continuing to whisper, 'How about Rogelio? Is there anything I can get him? A bowl of water, perhaps? A saucer of milk? A few acorns?'

Gerald looked embarrassed. So did Margaret, who had over-heard. Corinne looked irate. Rogelio made no discernible response whatsoever. The seconds ran out and they were saved by the doorbell.

'*Door-bell*,' it cantillated evenly. '*Door-bell, door-bell.*'

'I'll get it,' said Samson as the Baileys looked bemused. He put aside his drink and quickly left the room.

● ● ● ● ●

# 7

Samson opened the door to find Jill and Richard standing there. His features brightened perceptibly as his eyes fell on Jill and he invited her in with a welcoming smile, 'Jill . . .,' taking her hand and raising it to his lips, utterly charmed and charming. 'I'm so pleased you could come. I was beginning to think you had forgotten me – I hadn't heard from you.' He kept her hand in his as she stepped inside.

She gave him a cheerful grin, telling him, 'I didn't know until the last minute whether I would be able to come or not. I've been awfully busy. Everything's been all up in the air lately.'

'Well, I'm very pleased you did. It's so nice to see you again.'

'This is Ricky,' Jill said. 'He plays bass guitar in the band you saw at Dingwall's the other night. Remember?'

Samson eyed the quailing youth. He was somewhat less than over the moon at his presence. He had not anticipated a boyfriend. Jill had told him at the nightclub that she was with a member of the band but he had naturally assumed that it was a one-night stand. He would never in a month of Sundays have dreamed that she would bring him with her.

'Hi,' he said drily. 'What's your Weltanschauung?'

Richard's face registered instant distress. He did not understand the greeting and felt that, incredibly, he was already committing some heinous social blunder. He looked to Jill as if for support and, receiving none, back to Samson. Attempting a smile he managed hello and half-made to shake hands but, finding no hand proffered, was obliged to continue the motion and busy himself with a non-existent itch on his neck. His eyes dropped, unable to deal with the hostility in Samson's gaze. He knew he had made an awful mistake in coming here. He felt he ought to say something in explanation but for the life of him he could not think what.

'I see,' said Samson with cruel satisfaction.

Jill took the bottle of wine from Richard. 'Happy birthday,' she said. 'We've brought you this. We didn't really know what else to bring, but you can't go far wrong with wine at a party, can you. I hope it's all right. I rarely drink wine but my friends seem to like this one.'

'Oh, you shouldn't have,' Samson said, 'I wasn't expecting you to bring me anything. The fact that you're here is more than enough for me.' He unwrapped the tissue paper and swiftly appraised the label, smiled. 'Ah yes, a fine wine! A fine wine indeed! Quite a cheeky little vintage, if I remember rightly. Impudent without being insolent, I seem to recall.'

Jill laughed and he laughed with her. 'That's lovely,' he said. 'Thank you very much indeed.' He slipped an arm around her shoulder and gave her a hug. 'Come on, let me take your coat.'

Jill slipped out of her overcoat and handed it to him, retaining her Vuitton bag. Samson hung it up and returned to her side. Ignoring Richard he guided her towards the lounge with one arm around her waist and his mouth close to her ear, telling her, 'You look absolutely stunning. You're going to bedazzle everybody here, you know. I don't think I'll want to have anything to do with anybody else now that you've arrived.'

Jill smiled knowingly and told him that she didn't think it was true, really, and that she had met his type before.

Richard stood where he was, abandoned in a stranger's hallway. He watched the door as it slid to behind Samson and his girlfriend, and he wondered whether or not he ought to follow. Something told him no. Something told him that he had been excluded quite intentionally, that he was not a welcome guest, that nobody in that room would like him.

Extraordinary things were occurring in Richard's world now – slow, silent explosions of colour and light, inside him and out, pullulating, efflorescing streamers of vision and thought. He could detect noises coming from the lounge – the twitter and drone of conversation and the thumping, piping, rising, descending tones of music. It reached him and passed him, one swift river of sound. It came out of the room and enveloped him like a liquid sheath and it was impossible to know whether it was loud or soft, fast or slow, happy or sad . . .

The room was congested, he knew. Crammed to the wallpaper with pop stars and executives, models, dancers, punks, punkettes, journalists and jeunesse dorée, all of whom were far better off than he, all infinitely more successful. With small steps he approached the green door and listened. The gloss paint gleamed at him, hard and impregnable, offering no succour, no leniency. He could not enter that room. He sensed that beyond that door lay Hell for Richard Pike.

Tiny beads of sensation popped quietly in Richard's brain, showering his innards with dancing, tingling flights of uncertainty. What was he to do? He could not go in there, and yet at the same time he could not leave. He could *not* leave. Could he?

No, for, he reminded himself, Jill was in there. And she was in there with another man – a good-looking, successful, intimidating man in a brick-red suit whose intention it was, beyond any shadow of a doubt, to get her as quickly as possible into his bed. Richard stood impotently at the door. He willed himself to step forward, to push it open and enter, to seek out Jill and demonstrate to all and sundry that she was with him and him alone.

His attention was captured by the green paint on the door. It was not, he now perceived, as hard and implacable as he had originally believed. Staring at it now he found he was able to peer into it. It was a mysterious green, deep and endless, and as he gazed he felt drawn, as if he were being pulled, gently but inexorably into its depths. He felt it was bathing him, absorbing him, welcoming him.

He inclined his torso so that he might examine with greater ease this wondrous greenness. His whole being was taken up with it; he sensed that there was something intrinsically meaningful in its vernal luminescence, something which he had yet to fully grasp. It struck him as odd that he had never before noticed how colour was imbued with personality, how it possessed life and character of its own like something sentient. All his life colour had been little more than an adornment to him, a property afforded objects in differing degrees, dependent upon their susceptibility to the bombardment of light particles upon them – not that he had really thought about it in those kinds of terms; he had always been aware, it seemed, that it worked something like that, and he had always taken it for granted. Colour had always been, well, just colour.

He pushed his face even closer to the door. The greenness was miraculous, ineffable. It flowed outwards, or he flowed in, and embraced him, merged with his consciousness, brought him towards a realm of understanding that he had never previously experienced. Now he could not only see it, he could feel it. He could taste it and smell it. It was smooth like velvet, it vibrated pleasantly against his ear-drums, it danced lightly on his taste buds like nothing had ever danced before, and it rendered ecstatic his olfactory bulb.

Richard squeezed the greenness within himself and his mind turned green. He shivered elatedly and his body turned green. Everything was green. The world was green. *Life* was green!

*My God!* Richard's jaw dropped slack in wonder. *My God! Life is green!*

Momentarily he was stunned by the vastness of this cognizance. He blinked rapidly in order to assimilate it more fully. He could not understand how he had failed to see this until now, it was so blindingly conclusive. It was momentous! *Life is green!* It threw light upon a lifetime of misunderstanding!

He straightened. His head buzzed wildly. He was overcome with the need to impart his new-found knowledge to humanity – beginning with the persons in the room before him. But how was he to expound upon a concept so abstruse? Words did not seem a suitable medium. It would require a moment's contemplation. His heart pounded in his chest – how he longed to enter that room and inform everybody! He envisaged the looks of awe and admiration on their faces as he divulged his revelation.

But then he thought, *God, what if they already know? What if, in fact, this is something that is common knowledge, something so banal, so utterly self-evident to everybody except myself that nobody has ever considered it worth mentioning? What if I am the only person on the entire planet who has never until now caught on to this?*

He grasped that this was a distinct possibility. And, if it was indeed the case, then by entering that room he would be setting himself up for complete ignominy and calamitous consequences. By what means, then, was he to ascertain the truth?

He turned away to ponder and realized that he no longer knew what it was that, only seconds ago, had been so earth-shattering. He ransacked his mind and came up with, Life is green. That couldn't be it. He tried again and the same words reappeared. He regarded them with a puzzled frown. They were meaningless. They were three tiny, stupid words drifting inanely far to the rear of his mind's eye. He discarded them and looked at the door. There was nothing remarkable about it at all, it was just a door.

He peered hard at the green and it was just green. He looked up. Life, once more, was achromatic. He felt terribly let down.

0

Richard thought about making his exit now. The lounge still hummed with activity. He was unable to gauge the amount of time that had elapsed since his arrival, it seemed like an eternity he had spent staring at the green door, but he wanted to leave. This was no place for him. Forget the party, forget Jill, she wasn't right for him anyway. He would go home and bury himself beneath the covers, play some music.

He was about to move towards the front door when he heard a sound behind him. He turned as the lounge door opened and an attractive brunette in a long, loose, colourful, oriental robe came out.

● ● ● ● ●

# 8

Whilst Samson was absent from the room Corinne had been making apologies to her guests for his behaviour. She was infuriated, but she attempted to play it down, feeling that it was better to contain her own indignation than to create further embarrassment and discomfort by giving full vent to her emotions. At the same time, though, she let it be known that she considered her husband's deliberately boorish attitude to be something quite reprehensible.

The Baileys were sympathetic and did not appear unduly offended. Margaret in particular seemed to understand Corinne's predicament. She had been acquainted with Samson since soon after he and Corinne had first met, and from the very beginning had not been favourably inclined towards him. When she had learned of Corinne's intention to marry him she had expressed her apprehension, but to no avail. Now she appeared anxious to reassure her friend that she was on her side.

The Baileys main concern, however, was for Rogelio. They were hoping that, once he had acclimatized himself, he would settle down with the drawing materials he carried with him in his shoulder bag.

'Once he becomes absorbed in his art,' Margaret said, 'absolutely nothing in the world will disturb him, will it, Rogelio?'

The ragged artist twitched perceptibly at the sound of his name. He issued a sibilant, 'Yes,' which apparently meant no, and then asked, without looking at anyone, whether he might have a glass of aerated water. Corinne promptly provided him with one and was in the middle of putting to him a question concerning his work when Samson reappeared. He sauntered into the room with his arm around a beautiful, slender, smiling blonde, and Corinne froze.

*This must be Jill!*

'This is Jill, everybody,' Samson announced with a sweeping gesture of his wine bottle. His face was ruddy now, his bloodstream agreeably suffused with alcohol. He introduced her to each in turn.

Corinne nervously lit a cigarette then rose to shake hands with the girl, telling her she was very pleased to meet her. Jill smiled enchantingly and said how pleased she was to meet Corinne, too.

There was something very likeable about her, even at such immediate acquaintance, and this confused Corinne for she had as good as convinced herself that they were rivals.

'What'll you have to drink, Jill?' enquired Samson.

'Oh, just an orange juice, please.'

'Oh, come on now. You're not still stuck on that fruit juice kick, are you? Can't I tempt you with something a little stronger? Tell you what, why don't you let me knock you up a cocktail? One of my specials. I'm pretty damn hot when it comes to fixing cocktails, you know.'

'No, really, an orange juice is fine. That's all I drink.'

'Good girl!' Margaret Bailey pursed her lips approvingly.

Samson shrugged. 'Oh well, an orange juice it is, then.'

He poured her the orange juice then deftly splashed more wine into Gerald's and Margaret's glasses.

'I say, steady on, Sam,' said Gerald, grinning and bobbing in his seat.

'Don't give me that,' Samson retorted. 'You need to loosen up a bit, both of you. Knock it back, come on. Get with it. Enjoy yourselves.' He turned to Jill. 'These two profess to being tee-totallers, too, but I reckon it'll do them the world of good to get pissed. Bring them out of their cocoons a bit.' He turned to Corinne. 'What about you, my wife? Could you handle another drink?'

Corinne nodded. 'Yes, I think I could.'

'And what will it be?'

She hesitated, then, 'I think I'd like a brandy, please.'

'A brandy! I say, that's a little bit reckless for you, isn't it?'

'Well, party spirit, you know,' she replied unconvincingly. 'You'd better put something in it, though. I don't think I would enjoy it on its own. What can I have?'

He sucked in air. 'Ooh, I don't know . . .,' he said, then, grinning and winking at Jill, continued, 'You leave it with old Samson, eh? I'll fix you something that's just guaranteed to make your toes curl.'

Corinne pulled on her cigarette. She felt stifled and uncertain of herself. She felt she had to get out of the room. She needed to be alone for a few minutes to collect her thoughts.

'Will you excuse me a minute,' she said. She opened the door, and as she stepped outside was startled to find a young man in jeans and an old leather jacket hovering in her hallway.

'Oh!' She halted abruptly and her hand flew to the neckline of her kaftan robe.

'Oh,' said the unexpected youth, and writhed stiffly. 'Er – hello.'

They stared at each other for a moment.

'Er – I'm Richard,' the youth said. 'I came with Jill.'

'Oh,' Corinne sang, relieved. 'You're her boyfriend?'

He looked away shyly. 'Yes.'

'I'm sorry,' Corinne said. 'You gave me such a start. I didn't know there was anybody out here.' She held out her hand. 'I'm Corinne. Corinne Tallis.'

Her hand was electricity in his. Richard gawked and inhaled involuntarily to his belly. He did not understand.

'You work with my husband, do you?' Corinne asked.

'Pardon?'

'My husband, Samson. You're the chap he works with?'

Richard shook his head, his gaze transfixed by the shimmering, iridescent lights that glinted like tiny rainbows in her brunette hair. He did not have the faintest idea what she was talking about. His eyes met hers. She was beautiful.

'I don't think so,' he said.

'Oh, I thought Samson said Jill was coming with a chap from work. From *EMI*. You don't work for *EMI*? No. Oh, I must have got it all wrong as usual. That's typical of me. Sorry about that.'

He travelled deeply in the hyaline pools of her hazel eyes, her voice echoing somewhere quite far off, but he did not hear what she was saying. He was rooted to the spot, agog in a sweet, poignant, rhapsodic emotion that he could not explain and did not wish to lose hold of. His eyes fell to her robe, to the mandala design printed upon it, and he almost cried out. His body sang, the very cells enchanted. A voice he had never heard before spoke from somewhere deep within himself, disclosed to him that here, in this beatific vision of womanhood that stood now before him, was something numinous, something quite sublime. Here was Aditi, here was Nut. Here was Nammu, Demeter and Ge. Here was Shakti and Persephone, and Venus-Aphrodite risen out of the

sea. Here was Godhead personified in its purest, holiest, quintes-
sential female form – and he knew he had to worship.

He sensed himself gravitating towards her, weak with devotion,
needing to lay his head in submission upon her warm and bountiful
bosom. This was not sexual, this was not lust; it was something
that far transcended things physical. It was Love, in its truest,
deepest, most spiritual sense. His lips trembled as her lips moved
and her words caressed his insides like a velvet tongue,

'What is your line of work, then?'

'Oh!' He snapped back suddenly with a feeling of intense panic.
What had he said? What had he done? 'I – I play in a band.' To his
relief he had not moved, he was still facing her. He studied her
face for any intimation that he had committed something unto-
ward, but she was smiling at him quite pleasantly. 'I'm on the dole,
though, actually,' he added forlornly.

'Oh dear,' said Corinne, 'you have my sympathy. I was unemployed once myself. A few years ago now, mind you, but I know
how soul-destroying it can be. And I think it's probably worse
these days than it was then, from the point of view of finding a job,
at least. The figures just keep rising, don't they.' She shook her
head. 'I don't know. I'm not at all sure about Maggie and her
policies. Do you have a profession?'

'Not really. I just want to play music.'

'Hmm, that's a tricky one. It's an incredibly competitive business, you know – well, I expect you do know. You ought to have a
word with Samson. He works in A & R. You never know, he
might be able to help you.'

Suddenly Corinne gave a brief laugh.

'Look, what are we doing standing here in the hall? Why don't
you come in and meet the others and have a drink?'

With some trepidation Richard followed her. He was vaguely
astonished to discover that there were few people in the lounge.
He was conscious of a strange ambience pervading the room –
an inertness, an oppressiveness that disquieted him further.
Nobody looked particularly happy. Was it because he had
entered?

Jill was sitting on one of two comfortable sofas, a glass of orange
juice in her hand. Samson was perched casually on the arm,
preening the ends of his moustache as he monopolized her
attention. She looked up and smiled when Richard walked in.

Corinne introduced him to the others and poured him a drink and he edged into the seat beside his girlfriend.

'I wondered where you'd got to,' Jill breathed during a pause in Samson's conversation.

'I had to go to the toilet,' he said. He wanted to give her hand a squeeze but couldn't. He sat rigidly, trying very hard to retain a hold on his shifting, scattering, fraught and tangled, stretched, drugged and dreamy, schizoid, paranoid, blitzed and wasted, utterly fucked-up mind.

●　●　●　●　●

# 9

Small talk and platitudes prevailed now in the Tallis's lounge as old friends, acquaintances, and total strangers strove to be at ease in each other's company. Margaret Bailey sat next to Rogelio on one sofa. She engaged Corinne in reminiscence or related the success she and her husband were having with their Clog Shop, sniffling a little as she did so and dabbing her nose from time to time with an embroidered handkerchief, for she was suffering from a slight cold. Gerald sat on the other side of Rogelio, his elbows resting on his long thighs and his fingers intertwined in front of him. When not adding to or agreeing with something his wife had said he would smile meaninglessly, wipe his spectacles, snuffle to himself, sip at his wine, tap his feet or make some inaudible remark to the minikin painter. Rogelio himself was cross-legged and largely oblivious. His eyes travelled the room – now roll, now hurtle – but his body remained in stasis.

Samson, in the main, concerned himself with Jill – chatting, wisecracking, and making subtle probes in an effort to divine her liability quotient. He had developed a system whereby, through sharp observation and a series of resourcefully posed questions, he was able to determine, rapidly and with a pretty remarkable degree of accuracy, a woman's sexual responsiveness to him at any given time. The system worked on a scale of zero to one hundred. Anything below fifty he would discard instantaneously. Fifty to sixty was generally not worth the effort. Sixty to eighty signified promise, and above this the scale ranged from walkover to absolute bliss. Jill he had initially placed around the seventy to eighty mark, but now he was off-balanced somewhat by the diamond cluster ring that adorned her third finger. He felt rather affronted. It was hard to give it credence. How could she possibly have had the bad taste to go and get engaged to such a scruffy, spotty wimp?

Jill, expecting to find more people at the party, asked Samson whether she and Richard had arrived earlier than intended. He assured her that *she* had not.

Richard wanted to go home, but he could not say so; and Corinne flitted anxiously from person to person, desperately passing pretzels and struggling to break her own and everybody else's ice.

But the full complement for this fateful evening had not yet been arrived at. On the floor below, for instance, one further presence was preparing to ascend, to make its personal contribution to the chaos that was soon to ensue.

It was dark in the apartment beneath the Tallis's. And cold – both electricity and gas having been cut off some days earlier. The air was thick and stale with smoke. On a threadbare sofa a woman was sitting, a huddled, shapeless figure, her heels drawn up to her buttocks. She was wrapped for warmth in an old, coarse woollen blanket, and she drew endlessly on a chain of hand-rolled cigarettes.

She had been sitting like this for some hours, pale and virtually motionless, and though she was cold her body refused to shiver. The cigarette she held close to her mouth. In its brief glow, as her lips perpetually tightened and drew, her eyes were illumined. They were narrow and hopeless and hard like glass, and they burned with the madness of contained and bitter hostility.

Now, slowly, the woman began to straighten her frozen legs. She lowered her feet gingerly to the floor. Unwrapping the blanket from about her body she stood stiffly and stretched her brittled limbs. In the darkness her eyes turned to the ceiling and she scowled at those above, whom she was about to join. Bending, she picked up her foil-wrapped tobacco, papers and matches, and crossed the room. Taking her keys from the sideboard she left the apartment.

The bright neon strip in the corridor made her squint. As she pulled the door shut behind her she caught the knuckle of her forefinger painfully on the jamb – not for the first time. In silence she yelled with pain, aimed murderous imprecations at the world and those in the apartment overhead. The knuckle was bloody and throbbing, a slice of flesh gouged away. She sucked on it as she made her way up the stairs.

At the top of the stairs she paused for a moment. Then she walked directly up to the door of number seventeen.

When the doorbell butted in everybody reacted. This time it was an impatient, staccato interruption.

'Doorbell! Doorbell!' it snapped.

'Ah, I expect that's Julia,' Corinne said. 'Good.'

She looked over to Samson, but it was evident that he had no intention of answering the door again. So she went herself, to return a minute later with a tight-faced, straw-haired woman in her mid-thirties, dressed in a dark brown tartan jumble-sale skirt and a brown jumper.

This, then, was Julia. Responding with curt nods to Corinne's introductions she was furnished with a drink by Samson – at Corinne's request – then seated herself on a dining-chair near the French window and rolled a cigarette in silence.

Rogelio, whose mad blue eyes had turned madder and bluer the moment she arrived, watched her now intently.

● ● ● ● ●

And so it was that they were all gathered together in the same room. Now something quite bizarre was set to take place. Something which, although nobody there was actually aware of it, had already, insidiously, begun . . .

# PART THREE
# An Accumulation of Space

'It is generally only amongst groups of animals which are confined in zoos that fights to the death occur.'

Iddio E. Scompiglio
from
*The Book Of Imaginary Hauntings.*


and


'Old ghosts never die,
And never fade away entirely, either.'

Iddio E. Scompiglio
from
*The Book Of Imaginary Hauntings.*

# 1

Minutes passed.

'Ooh, there's another one!' Margaret Bailey cried. She was standing looking out of the French window. 'Gerald, darling, come and look.'

Gerald joined her and they linked hands and peered together out into the damp evening where squibs, rockets, Roman candles and Catherine wheels were making brief, bright bangs and flashes of colour amidst the gloom.

'There!' Margaret cried. 'Oh, that's gorgeous!' She turned to Julia, who still occupied her seat by the window, 'Some of them are quite spectacular, aren't they!'

Julia leaned forward and pulled up one of her grey woollen socks. She gave a negligible movement of her head and twisted her pale, thin lips in agreement, turned to look dourly at the night, then turned back and began to roll another cigarette.

'You've certainly got a splendid view from up here,' Gerald commented over his shoulder.

'Can't complain,' Samson replied.

Jill got up and joined the Baileys and together they expressed their appreciation as more fireworks burst outside. Samson placed himself staunchly at their rear, his hands deep in the pockets of his trousers, gazing at Jill's pert rump and happily contemplating the prospect of taking her from behind.

Richard had remained seated where he was, on the sofa opposite Rogelio, grappling intently with his own private firework display. And Corinne, who had been out of the room for some minutes, re-entered, turning down the dimmer as she did so – for which Richard threw her a grateful look.

'It's a bit bright,' she said to no one in particular. She smiled at Richard and crossed the room to join the others.

Presently there was a lull in the action.

'Do you think that's it?' Jill asked.

'It looks like it, for the moment,' Margaret said. 'But no doubt there will be more later on. I should imagine they will go on for most of the evening.'

Jill brought her eyes closer to the windowpane, made a circle around them with her hands. 'What's that?' she said suddenly. 'Look, down there!'

Everybody looked.

'What? Where?'

'Down there. Look!'

'Where? I can't see anything?'

'What is it? What are you looking at?'

'On the roof of that building! Something's moving! Look! There's somebody moving around! What are they doing?'

They all peered hard –

'Oh yes, I see it!'

'Where? Where?'

– and eventually Corinne straightened and said, 'It's only children.'

'But what are they doing there?' Jill wanted to know.

'Playing.'

'Playing? On the roof?'

'Yes. It's a playground.'

'A playground?' she said, astounded. 'A playground on the roof of an apartment block? Four storeys above the street?'

Corinne was amused. 'Yes. What's so odd about that? You've seen them before, haven't you?'

'No. Never.' She looked back outside. 'That's incredible! What a strange concept. It's so dangerous!'

'No, there's no danger. It's fenced off quite securely so they can't fall off or climb over. It's really the safest place for them to play.' She shrugged. 'I mean, where else can they go in a place like this?'

Jill shook her head. 'I don't know. I'd never thought about it. I've never come across them before; we don't have them down my way – at least, I don't think we do. No need for them, I suppose.' She brushed her blonde hair back behind her ear and laughed a little self-consciously. 'How silly of me. I thought I'd caught a gang of cat-burglars red-handed, or something. What a crazy idea, though – playgrounds on the roofs of apartment blocks.' She was silent for a moment, then she looked up at Samson and added, reflectively, 'I don't know, life is really strange sometimes, isn't it?'

Samson smacked his lips and nodded sagely. 'It's the strangest experience I've ever had,' he said.

'Corinne, darling!' Margaret cried suddenly, 'you've changed your robe!'

– and she had. During her absence from the lounge she had changed into a loose, plain, pale grey dress. A turquoise brooch was pinned above her left breast and a slender gold chain adorned ner neck.

'Oh – yes,' she said.

'But why?'

'Oh, I just didn't feel comfortable in the other one. It's a ropey old thing, really. I've had it ages, you know. I really don't know what made me decide to put it on. Something possessed me to drag it out of the wardrobe – God, I can't think what!'

'I disagree. I thought it was rather attractive. In fact, to be honest, I thought it was new.'

Corinne laughed. 'Oh no!'

Margaret was about to add something else but was prevented by a sneeze.

Grabbing at the opportunity to shift the subject of conversation away from herself, Corinne said, 'That's a nasty cold you've got. Are you taking anything for it?'

Margaret shook her head, poised, mouth half-open and eyes half-closed, for another sneeze.

'Well, you ought to. Would you like me to get you some Codis or something?'

'No thank you,' Margaret said. 'I never take anything like that. I believe it's best just to let it run its course. Gerald and I don't believe in contaminating our bodies with drugs, do we, darling.'

'No, we don't,' said Gerald.

'And anyway, it's nothing. It's just a common cold.'

'Yes, but didn't you say it's been hanging around for some time?'

Margaret blew her nose. 'A little while.'

'I think you ought to go and see your doctor. You can never tell, you might have a chill or something, and it could easily develop – '

'Oh, don't be silly, darling. It's just a cold, that's all. I'm certainly not going to pay my doctor a visit because of it. That's another thing we're not in favour of, isn't it, Gerald? General practitioners these days are not the most advisable persons to call upon when you have an illness. They're overworked, for one thing, because so many people go trotting around to see them over the most trivial of ailments. And generally all they can do is palm you off with a few chemicals to get rid of you. Have you any idea how many millions and millions of tablets and medicines are prescribed each year? It's astronomical! And a good percentage of them are nothing more than placebos.

'No, that's not something Gerald and I are in favour of.'

'Yes,' Gerald inserted. 'A good doctor should proscribe rather than prescribe.' He grinned, pushed his glasses up his nose, swept a lock of hair from his brow and looked very pleased with himself. Samson turned on him with a look of disbelief.

'You what?' he demanded, 'What did you just say?'

Gerald repeated the statement, appending it this time with a couple of brief, snuffling chortles.

Samson expelled air contemptuously. 'Well, that's deep, that is, Gerald,' he said. 'Christ, that's really bloody deep. I think that's about the deepest thing I've heard all year. Have you got any more like that?'

Gerald laughed, and Samson, cupping one hand to his mouth and leaning sidelong to Jill, said, 'What a prat! And he's only just getting started, too. You wait till later on . . .'

'It's true, though, Samson,' Margaret insisted, 'drugs are prescribed at the drop of a hat these days. Doctors really don't have the time to examine you properly, and even if they did – '

Samson ignored her. He walked away with his hands still in his pockets, shaking his head, and sat down next to Rogelio.

'Hello, Rogelio,' he said loudly, and dug him in the ribs with an elbow. 'Everything all right?'

The little artist jumped, squirmed and unravelled his skinny legs. He turned to Samson with a piqued look. 'Yes, it is all right.'

'Be sure to let us know if you catch a whiff of anything, won't you?'

Rogelio nodded and punted himself along the sofa a couple of feet. Margaret eased into the space between him and Samson. Meticulously smoothing the hem of her kimono she asked, 'Did you get many presents, Samson?'

'Nope,' Samson replied.

'I promised him a new suit, but it won't be ready until Friday,'

Corinne said. 'It's so irritating. I specifically asked for it to be finished by today, and they assured me it would be.'

'Did you hear from your mother?'

'Nope.'

'Hmm.' Margaret concentrated on her kimono. Samson chewed the ends of his moustache.

'I was looking for a card from her,' Margaret said.

'Patricia sent a card – his eldest sister,' said Corinne.

'You have two sisters though, don't you, Samson?'

'Well, we haven't really been in touch with Eleanour for quite some time,' Corinne said.

Margaret nodded speculatively to herself. Samson looked over at Jill, grinned amiably and raised his eyebrows. 'Having a good time, Jill?'

'Oh, yes thanks,' Jill said.

'Good,' said Samson. 'So am I.'

0

'What kind of things do you paint, Rogelio?' Jill asked, having been apprised earlier on of the small man's station.

Rogelio had the side of his neck towards her. He was gazing over his left shoulder at one corner of the lounge. He turned and focused upon her, dull-eyed. At length, when he seemed about to fall asleep, a spark of animation returned, his lips moved and a faint sound emerged: 'Space . . .' he said.

The sound trailed away, dissolving into the room like a sparrow's turd in an ocean, and as it did so the artist's head came forward and his attention was gone. Jill was somewhat at a loss.

'Space? – what, you mean like Outer Space?'

The little man scrutinized her blearily and his thumbs began to twiddle in his lap. He turned and looked back over his shoulder, and when he returned his gaze to her his expression was pained. One hand rose slowly and slid over the top of his head. It grasped the hair at the rear of his crown so that his face was almost completely obscured in the crook of his elbow. Then the hand came slowly forward, mauling his unruly mop with bony fingers and leaving red trails on his skin as grubby nails descended over his forehead and cheeks.

'Not . . . Outer . . . Space,' he said, and shook his head from side to side in a tired and exasperated manner. He turned away again to the corner. Jill looked questioningly at the others.

123

'Perhaps I can explain,' offered Gerald, pulling up a chair and seating himself diametrically opposite her. He touched a crooked forefinger pensively to his lips and furrowed his brow, then asked, 'Are you at all familiar with Rogelio's work?'

'I'm not sure. I don't think so,' said Jill. 'I'm not really very up on modern art, I'm afraid.'

'Well, he has had two exhibitions at private galleries here in London,' Gerald said. 'And some of his paintings are beginning to command quite considerable sums of money. One of his pictures, "The Journey From Ylem", was the subject of a discussion on Nationwide some months ago. Did you see it?'

Jill shook her head guiltily. 'I'm very busy, actually. I don't watch television very much.'

'I remember that,' said Samson. 'Wasn't that the canvas that was reckoned to have been used for several months as a replacement for a broken windowpane in a council tenement flat on the Isle of Dogs, and then chucked into the Thames where it drifted for days before being stumbled upon amongst the mud and detritus at low-tide by Rogelio, who merely added his three R's in the bottom right-hand corner and then claimed it as an original work of art?'

Margaret threw him a withering look. 'In the words of one obtuse and narrow-minded critic, yes,' she hissed, 'but you certainly can't claim that that was a representative opinion. Not by any means. The man who wrote that was an ignorant, jaundiced bigot.'

'I thought he was quite an influential voice,' Samson said, goading her. 'Wasn't he writing for the *Sunday Times* or something like that?'

'He was a Philistine!'

'All the same, though, I could see what he was getting at.'

'Pah! He's like you, he knows nothing about the subject. Like so many of these so-called cognoscenti, these "connoisseurs" and "aesthetes" he has no appreciation whatsoever of real art. Have you ever read his columns? He is an ofay, half-blind fool who finds change unacceptable and who would be unable to recognize genius if it walked up to him and bit him on the ankle!'

'Which, in Rogelio's case, is not such an unlikely prospect,' Samson laughed winking at Jill. Margaret clenched her teeth but said nothing.

'Now the crucial thing about "The Journey From Ylem", Gerald continued, leaning forward and making emphatic framing gestures with his hands, 'is that it is not a painting that is intended to have a direct and immediate appeal to the objective senses. By this I mean that, when the, so to say, uninitiated observer first casts his or her eyes upon it he or she is apt to – well, misunderstand it and in some cases even dismiss it. You see, it speaks to you somehow subjectively – in fact, it is designed to encourage an awakening of the subjective faculties to which so little attention is generally paid. The essence of the painting is something to be grasped by the feelings alone, intuitively. It is not a painting to be looked at, it is a painting to be assimilated.'

'That's why, to certain people who have absolutely no recourse to the higher realms of sensitivity, it can appear to have no value,' Margaret said pointedly.

'Yes, I would recommend that you try to get to see it as soon as possible,' said Gerald. 'Like all of Rogelio's work it is most impressive. And I think that this one is really the *pièce de résistance* of his output to date – wouldn't you agree, darling? It's an extraordinary *oeuvre*. There is something – well, there is something quite disturbing about it.'

'It has received considerable acclaim,' Margaret said proudly. 'Do you know that at this very moment it is short-listed for a display in the Museum of Modern Art in New York?'

'Oh, well, I'll try to get to see it, then,' said Jill. 'What's the name again?'

'Rogelio Ramon Reyero,' said Gerald. 'We are both quite sure that it's a name to watch out for.'

'And, if possible, avoid at all costs,' added Samson.

Jill lowered her head so that her hair fell forward and helped conceal her smile. She looked over at Rogelio, who was paying no heed to anybody, then back to Gerald. 'But what is this Space thing that he was talking about?'

'Aah,' Gerald narrowed his eyes and looked knowledgeable. 'This is Rogelio's most recent artistic project, the one that he is at present engaged upon. It is an attempt to convey in a visual medium the space between objects, as opposed to the objects themselves.

'Let me try and explain that. You see, the space that surrounds us all, the atmosphere, the Void, if you prefer, is as real and as palpable as anything else in existence. It is an integral part of reality. But we – mankind – have been conditioned by centuries of rationalist, deductive and scientific thinking not to look upon it as such. Compare it to dreams, if you like. Dreams are something that, from childhood, we have been taught to believe are unimportant, unreal; simple conjurings of the sleeping mind that are superfluous to our daily lives. We are taught to pay very little attention to our dreams. Yes, I know we sometimes stop and think, "Oh, that was a strange dream I had last night," or "I wonder what that was all about," and I know that psychologists have written whole books on the subject, but on the whole we rarely take our dreams seriously or give them our full attention for any length of time. They are too elusive, too fragmentary – do you see what I mean? Whereas the truth is that dreaming is as much a part of your life as is, let us say, making the bed, or brushing your teeth, or playing the piano . . .'

'Or making love,' said Samson.

Gerald gave a twitch. His eyes darted nervously. He removed his glasses, studied them and put them back on. Recovering himself he went on, 'And so it is with space. Space is not empty, space is not "nothing". It is full, it is alive, it is a part of our existence. We have to learn to experience it as such, that's all.'

'Hmm, I see,' said Jill, who did not look as though she saw. 'But, I mean, well, how is he going to show this? I mean, how do you paint space?'

'Ah. This is what he is experimenting with right this very moment. And I have no worries whatsoever that he will discover the method he is searching for. I have every confidence in Rogelio. You can see, even now, how he is concentrating almost all of his energy upon observing and calculating the amount and diffusion of space within this room – or outside, or wherever he happens to be – in an attempt to discover the most satisfactory means for transferring it onto canvas. You must understand that the mind of the true artist is not like the minds of we "mere mortals". The artist knows things inherently that we are hardly able to grasp at. And Rogelio, in particular, has a very finely attuned mind. He perceives almost effortlessly what we cannot. Many years ago, whilst he was still a child, he was able to reject all attempts to indoctrinate him. He has not been conditioned as we have. He has, so to speak, shed his yoke of objectivity, and now his desire is that, by means of his art, he might demonstrate how we may shed ours.'

Jill pulled a face and looked a little dubiously at Rogelio, who was now on his knees on the sofa and still peering intently at the corner behind. Feeling obliged to make a comment of some sort, she said, 'I'm glad I'm not artistic.'

Samson chuckled and stretched his limbs, eyeing her thighs quite unashamedly. 'There's art and there is art, Jill,' he said, 'and Rogelio, I believe, resides permanently in the latter category – And I think it's about time we had another drink.'

0

Corinne rose from her seat in order to go and see how the food was getting on. Half way to the door she hesitated, frowning slightly. 'Samson, what's this music?' she enquired. 'It isn't very good party music.'

'Well, it isn't a very good party, is it!' he retorted. 'I mean, Jesus Christ, it's a bit bloody subdued in here! I think the music quite suits the mood.'

She smiled waveringly. 'I think it's more likely to have engendered the mood. It's a bit funereal. Can't you put on something a little livelier? Put on something we can all dance to.'

'But you don't dance. I haven't seen you dance in years.'

'Perhaps that's because you have never taken me dancing.'

'You don't like dancing. You know you don't.'

'Well, perhaps I've changed my mind. And I wasn't referring solely to myself. What about everybody else? They might all like to dance.'

'All right then, who wants to dance?'

Margaret gave a thin smile. 'I don't really think so, Samson. Gerald and I don't dance, as a rule.'

'Fine. I'd guessed as much. Jill?'

'Well – there isn't a lot of room, is there?'

'That's no problem. We can easily clear some space. Would you like to dance or not?'

'I don't know really. I suppose I might do. It depends.'

'Right, that's two no's and a don't know. How about Rogelio? No. Obviously not. If he stood up and shook his body his bones would fall out. Julia, then? Ricky? No. You see?' he said to Corinne, 'none of them wants to dance, and I don't want to dance.

127

We would all much rather sit here and glumly discuss illnesses and the merits of modern art.'

Corinne faced him resolutely. 'I don't think you really gave anybody a chance to voice their true opinions. And I still think you might change the cassette. I would like to listen to something a little more cheerful.'

'Very well, my darling wife,' he said, rising, 'despite the fact that you are about to disappear into the kitchen where you will not be able to hear it, I shall put something a little more cheerful on just for you.'

'I shall only be away a few minutes,' Corinne said. 'And I can still hear it out there.'

'Actually, I rather liked that music,' Margaret said. 'I do agree with you, Corinne, that it is hardly conducive to a party atmosphere, but it's very restful all the same. What is it?'

'It's a recording somebody lent me,' Samson said as he removed the cassette. 'It's called "Music For Airports" by some new group called Eno.'

Richard, who had just passed seven epochs maundering in his own eidetic Erewhon, had been drawn back onto the track by the sound of a voice calling 'Ricky'. Now, as the subject of the conversation turned to music, he found himself re-converging with some semblance of a previous reality. He gazed blankly at Samson. 'It isn't a group,' he said diffidently, in an effort at being helpful. 'It's a man.'

'I beg your pardon?'

'Eno. It isn't a group, it's one man. His name is Brian Eno. He's been around for a long time. He was a founder member of Roxy Music and he has made a lot of solo albums; he has worked on albums with David Bowie, Robert Fripp – '

'I see,' Samson said, cutting him short. 'You know a lot about these things, do you?'

Richard faltered, startled by his tone. 'I don't know. I wouldn't – I mean, well, I've been a fan of his for a long time.'

Samson glared at him, highly resentful at being shown up by such a weedy youth in front of his wife and Margaret and, most of all, Jill. As if to compound the insult, Gerald chipped in.

'Ho ho,' he chortled, clasping one knee with his hands, 'I'd have thought you would have known that, Sam. I thought you were supposed to be an expert on the music scene.'

Samson looked up, saw both Margaret and Corinne smiling to themselves. He looked at Jill. She, mercifully, did not appear to have caught on.

'You know, that brings to mind something I was reading a little while ago,' Gerald went on quite innocently, 'I can't think where I saw it, since I never read those music journals, but there was an article somewhere or other concerning a tape recording that was submitted to all the major record companies. Apparently the music on the tape was from a long-playing record by a group that were already internationally famous, and had been for some years – I believe it was The Eagles, or some such group – but whoever sent it in submitted it under a different name. They claimed it was a demonstration tape by a new, unknown group. You know, they were pretending it was from a group looking for their first recording contract. And, do you know, not one of the companies recognized the music. Not even the company to whom The Eagles are contracted! And not only that, but every single record company turned it down. They all said it was not a commercially viable sound! Can you believe it!'

'Oh, I can believe it,' said Margaret. 'It sounds quite typical to me. Do you know anything about that, Samson? Did the tape turn up on your desk?'

'It's news to me,' Samson muttered darkly. His eyes fell burning on Richard – how *dare* he set him up like that! – and his mind swam thickly with images of revenge. He was irate with himself for having been caught out in such a manner. The wimp would pay for that. He would pay in triplicate – and Samson, believing he had gauged his personality fairly completely, knew precisely the method by which to go about making him pay.

Richard, understanding that he had tripped something terrible, but not knowing quite what, sank back into the sofa. His body, tortoise-like, made an involuntary attempt at retracting its extremities. Failing in this, it wrapped its arms tightly about its middle and pressed its calves hard against the base of the sofa. His mind cringed as it struggled to comprehend what it had done wrong.

Samson curled his mouth grimly and turned away to select a new cassette from the cassette rack.

● ● ● ● ●

# 2

'How about Abba?' Samson asked, slotting a cassette into the deck. He was cheerful again, his anger flushed away by the sweet waters of impending revenge. 'That's good dancing music. Know anything about them, *Ricky*?'

Richard produced a timid smile. 'Well, yes, I think they're quite good.'

'Good. Good. Well, why don't you get up and dance, then?'

'Oh. No thank you. I don't think so.'

'Oh, come on. Don't be a stiff. Get up and jive. Why not?'

Richard gulped. 'I – Well – There isn't much room.'

'No problem. I've already told you we can easily push the furniture back. Come on. There's nothing to be frightened of. Get with it!'

'I don't really want to, thanks,' Richard said. He writhed and looked fearfully at Jill.

'Suit yourself,' said Samson curtly. 'If you want to spend the whole evening sitting there that's up to you – but that isn't my idea of having a good time.' He swept around the sofa, both arms raised. 'Jill, your stuffy pal is not inclined; might I have the honour?'

As he moved in on her his hand caught Richard's glass, toppling it and its contents from the arm of the sofa into his lap. At the same time he stepped heavily on his toes.

'Oh shit!' Samson cried as Richard squirmed and fluttered. He did not remove his foot, acting as if unaware that he was stepping on him. 'Corinne! Can we have a cloth, please? Ricky's drink has gone for a burton!'

Corinne, who was in the kitchen now, tossed him a dishcloth through the serving-hatch and he fussed over Richard, at the same time leaning his weight heavily on his toes. Then, having thoroughly upset the sorry youth, he left him. Taking Jill's hands in his he said, 'Come along, Jill. Let's dance, shall we?'

'Well . . .' Jill looked a little uncertain.

'Oh, this is a great song!' Samson cried, pulling her to her feet. 'I love this one! It's a real smoocher!'

He led her to an uncluttered area of carpet near the window and began to rotate his hips lasciviously in time with the music. They danced close together, there being limited space to move in, and though their bodies did not make contact, Samson still touched her fingertips lightly with his. As they danced he murmured things in her ear that were calculated to make her smile, and he cast frequent glances in Richard's direction, hiding his satisfaction as he observed the youth's wretchedness.

Four songs later Jill returned to her seat. She undid her cardigan, remarking that she was hot, and dropped it over the back of the sofa. Beneath it she had on a loose, lime green, camisole top. The skin of her shoulders and back was smooth and tanned and naked; she wore no bra and her nipples pushed pertly against the flimsy silk of her garment.

She laughed as she sat down. 'That was fun! I love dancing. Did I tell you I've been going to classes?'

'No, you didn't,' Samson said as he lit a cigarette. He was breathing heavily and perspiration glistened on his skin, for he had not intended dancing for quite so long. 'I thought you might, though,' he continued. 'You dance so well.'

His eyes shone covetously as they roamed over her body. He leaned across her, on the pretext of taking her glass in order to refill it, and let his gaze drop into her naked teenage cleavage. Her perfume mingled with her perspiration and he inhaled deeply as the scent rose to his eager nostrils.

Richard, too, turned goggle-eyed as Jill sank onto the sofa beside him. Despite his unmitigated bewilderment and despite his hallucinosis, he found himself suddenly re-possessed of a sizzling erection. He glanced furtively at his crotch but it was well concealed by his jumper. An embarrassing stain had spread, though, where his drink had landed. He was roasting hot but had not been able to pluck up the courage to remove either his leather jacket or his jumper. He sat and squeezed his sweaty hands together unhappily.

'Here you are, Jill, my love. One orange juice on the rocks,' Samson announced.

'Oh, fabulous! Just what I need.'

As she took the glass from him he allowed the backs of his

fingers to brush lightly up her slender arm. She looked up at him sidelong and smiled demurely.

'Now then, anybody else for a refill? Julia?'

Julia, silent and morose in the corner, nodded, drained her glass and held it out to be taken.

'That's the spirit! And Gerald, how about you?'

'No thanks, Sam. I've still got plenty. Margaret too, thanks,' Gerald replied, speaking for his wife who was in the kitchen giving Corinne a hand.

Jill leaned forward and tapped Gerald's knee. With a questioning look she directed his attention to Rogelio.

The little chap had left the sofa. He was standing behind it now. He appeared to have re-entered the trance he had occupied earlier. There was something reminiscent of awe on his face and his hands floated, palms out, in front of him at about shoulder level. His eyes were fixed upon the same corner he had been staring at twenty minutes earlier and his lips moved in a barely audible whisper.

Gerald left his chair and lowered himself onto one knee on the sofa, facing him. 'Rogelio, how are you feeling?' he whispered.

Rogelio's head inclined towards him but his eyes did not waver. 'It is beautiful,' he breathed.

Gerald glanced at the corner. 'Is there something there, Rogelio? Have you found something?'

Rogelio's little hands took one of his. His features changed and he seemed almost about to burst into tears. 'It is . . . It is close,' he said.

Gerald squeezed his hand and smiled reassuringly. 'Good. Good.'

Rogelio spread his lips poignantly to reveal two rows of uneven yellow teeth. 'I must . . ,' he breathed. 'I must . . .'

'Yes, of course,' Gerald said. He turned to Samson. 'You won't mind if Rogelio does a bit of drawing, will you, Sam?'

Samson, tongue in cheek, crossed the room. 'What's he going to draw?'

Gerald pointed.

'But there's nothing there,' Samson said.

'That's not quite true,' Gerald replied in a low voice. 'To your eyes there is nothing there. To Rogelio – to the artist – it is replete. He has chosen it. It seems to be ideal.'

Rogelio came out of his trance. He shuffled his feet, scratched his shoulder, full of perplexity. 'You did this?' he asked Samson, blue eyes imploring.

'What?'

'Ah!' Understanding dawned. 'Of course. I was uncertain.'

'What? What are you talking about?'

'He means, did you arrange that area yourself?' said Gerald.

'What do you mean, "arrange" it? There's nothing there to arrange. It's just blank wall and carpet!'

'Yes, but has it always been like that?'

'Well, no. The rubbish bin generally stands there, but I took it out earlier to empty it and I haven't got around to bringing it back yet.'

'Yesss,' Rogelio hissed. 'He is true! It is auspice!'

Samson clapped a hand to his brow. 'My God!'

'Well, will it be all right if he just sits here quietly and draws?' Gerald asked.

Samson blew out air. 'I can't personally think of any reason for objecting – providing he doesn't make a mess, of course. But, just a minute, I'd better check with everybody else.' He turned. 'Will anybody raise any objection to Rogelio's situating himself here behind the sofa and spending the rest of the evening sketching the empty area where the rubbish-bin used to be but isn't any more?' he asked loudly.

Jill spluttered into her glass. She hid her laugh with her hair and hand and shook her head. Julia glared at him and shook hers minimally. Richard smiled like a man up to his neck in quicksand.

'Fine. You have the field,' Samson said.

'Thanks,' said Gerald.

Rogelio sank to his knees behind the sofa. He lowered his body so that his weight rested evenly between his heels. Keeping his eyes on the space in front of him he took his cloth bag from his shoulder and laid it by his side. He removed from it some coloured pencils and an artist's sketch pad and placed them on the carpet on his other side. Then he placed his hands together in an attitude of prayer and closed his eyes. He remained this way for a few seconds, whispering soundlessly, then put his hands flat on the carpet in front of his knees so that the thumbs and forefingers formed a triangle. Now he leaned forward from the waist and placed his forehead in the triangle.

Samson bent over him. 'Becoming as one with the carpet, are you?' he asked.

Rogelio paid him no heed. He straightened, took a deep breath, picked up his pad and pencils and laid himself full length bellywise on the floor. He looked up at Gerald, smiling. 'It is good,' he said, and Gerald smiled back.

Samson, shaking his head and laughing to himself, returned to the centre of the room and sat down.

● ● ● ● ●

# 3

'Corinne, darling,' Margaret asked in a voice laden with concern and a need to be fully informed, 'how *are* things with you and Samson?'

They were in the kitchen. Corinne was at the cooker, emptying chopped kelp and pork slices from a saucepan into a dish, and Margaret stood at her side, sniffling a little as she spooned sauces, relishes and dips into a lazy Susan. Corinne stiffened.

'Don't think I'm prying,' Margaret said. 'It's just that I can't help wondering whether everything is all right between you.'

'Yes, of course everything's all right,' Corinne lied. 'Things are fine. Why do you ask?'

Even as she said it it struck her that she was, behind the words, stating something quite definitive about her life and about her relationship with Margaret. Not so long ago they had been intimate friends and confidantes. There was virtually nothing she would have kept from her. But with the passing of time, and almost without her being aware of it, her affections had undergone a change. Margaret was no longer a close friend, she was no longer somebody that Corinne wished to have privy to the vicissitudes and nuances of her personal life. In fact there was no longer anybody in the entire world that she would have felt at ease in confiding her troubles to. Her life and her thoughts were her own. They were private and confidential, and though her troubles beset her from all sides, and though she longed for some form of even momentary release, she knew that she could rely upon nothing but her own inner resources to bring about an improvement in her situation.

And, she perceived, Margaret was really no longer a person she would particularly want to have as a close friend anyway. She could not place a finger directly on the reasons for that, but . . . well, things change. People change. Neither she nor Margaret were the same people. In fact, she realized with sudden finality, they really had very little in common at all these days. She found herself resenting Margaret's questions, looking upon them as an attempted intrusion.

Margaret's narrow, fine-boned features held a dogged benignancy. 'There seems to be such a lot of tension between you, that's all.'

'Well, it has always been like that to some degree, you know that. Samson is not the easiest of persons to live with, and I know I can be difficult, too. We clash from time to time, but – no, everything's fine. Really.'

'Oh, that's good then,' Margaret said, her tone a trifle petulant. 'Gerald and I think a lot of you, you know. I know we don't see very much of each other these days, but I still regard us as being close friends. I would like to think that, if there was something upsetting you or something you needed to talk over with somebody, that you would still think of me as your friend. I'm always there; I'd always be glad to help. We both would.'

Corinne turned and began loading platters of food onto a dumb-waiter, ready to wheel through into the lounge when everything else was ready. She glanced briefly in Margaret's direction. 'Thanks. I know you would,' she said. 'The same applies for me, too, you know.'

Margaret transported the lazy Susan to the serving-hatch. 'How do you find not working? Don't you get bored sitting around all day long in the house on your own? You can always come over and visit us.'

'Oh, I'm not sitting around all day! Not a bit of it! More often than not I find there is so much to do around here that the day has gone before I've even started!' She wondered what was making her say these things. What prevented her from confessing the truth? 'No, I'm never bored. It's fine.'

'Whose idea was it that you leave the job? Samson's?'

'No. Mine. At least, Samson did encourage me to leave, it's true. He felt there was no point in my carrying on. But the decision, when it came down to it, was mine. I was getting fed up at ClimbDown. It was getting to be too much.'

Margaret said nothing for a few moments, then, 'Well, it doesn't look as though it's doing you any harm, I must say. You've put on weight since the last time I saw you. It suits you.'

'What! Margaret, how can you say that? It's awful! I've grown so fat!'

'Nonsense. You're not fat at all. You needed a bit more flesh on you. You were too skinny before. You were almost as skinny as I

136

am. A couple of extra pounds has done you the world of good. It's put a nice, healthy glow into your cheeks.'

Corinne glazed her exasperation with a sharp laugh. 'A couple of pounds! Margaret, I've put on well over a stone in just a matter of weeks! I've been doing all I can to lose it again but I can't. Look at me, it's horrible. I can't even look in the mirror any more. I'm immense!'

'Not at all. You're over-reacting. I think you look marvellous. I'll bet Samson does, too, doesn't he?'

She was tempted to reply that Samson could not bear the sight of her, but she held back, saying instead, 'I haven't asked him.'

'You shouldn't need to.'


'You're very lucky, you know, not having to worry about your weight,' Corinne said.

'Yes, it's true. I can eat whatever I like,' Margaret chirped. 'I have a very fast metabolism. I could eat an elephant and it wouldn't show.' She paused, then added a little hesitantly, 'Darling, I must say, you've really done us all proud this evening. This is a magnificent spread you've prepared, but I was just wondering . . . there seems to be rather a lot of meat in most of the dishes.'

'Yes,' said Corinne, puzzled. 'Why?'

'Didn't I tell you? I'm sure I did. Gerald and I are vegetarians.'

'Oh.' She looked at the array of food she had put so many hours into preparing. 'Oh. No, you didn't tell me. I don't think so, anyway.'

'I'm sure I must have,' Margaret said apologetically. 'It's something I always try to make a point of. We haven't touched meat for more than six months now. Didn't I mentioned it on the phone?'

Corinne shook her head. She was sure she would have remembered if Margaret had told her. She felt deflated and pained, and could not think of anything to say. Tears welled suddenly behind her eyes. 'What about the fish?' she said quickly. 'Can you eat fish?'

'No. No flesh of any kind. We're a terrible nuisance, aren't we. I feel so guilty. I can't think how I could have forgotten to tell you.'

'I'm sorry,' Corinne said, as if it were her fault. She somehow managed to force a cheerful smile. 'Never mind, there's plenty of salad. And cheese – I can cut you some cheese if you like, and some bread.'

'Oh yes, that'll do us fine,' Margaret said. 'We're neither of us terribly hungry, anyway.'

0

They had almost finished in the kitchen when Margaret took Corinne conspiratorially by the arm and asked her in a hushed voice, 'Who's that girl, darling?'

She was referring to Jill.

Corinne felt herself growing tense again. She looked into Margaret's eyes. They were dark, almost black, and glassy, and there was something almost vulturine in the expression on her face. Corinne recoiled momentarily with genuine dislike. Why was she asking such pointed questions? What was she getting at?

'I'm not exactly sure,' she said, feeling that this was somehow the reply that Margaret had been hoping for. She moved away. 'She works with Samson or something.'

Margaret nodded shrewdly and Corinne said, 'Is the business still thriving?'

'Oh, yes thanks. It's really thriving. It's doing marvellously, in fact. Things are going very well for us at the moment. We're both extremely happy.'

'Yes. You look very well.'

'Mmh,' she agreed, shining brightly. She lifted her short mousey hair with the backs of both hands and let it fall, continuing the motion of her hands upwards and outwards, and stepping forward lightly like a ballerina. She laughed to herself, then said, 'I've just completed a Dead Sea Mud skin therapy course, for one thing. That has really done my skin the world of good. It's a pity about this stupid cold, though; it's made my nose so red, otherwise you would be able to see more clearly. You ought to try it, darling. It's well worth it.'

Corinne gave a barely perceptible wince as, for the umpteenth time, Margaret called her 'darling'. She wished she would not do it, it was so irritating, and so affected. When she had first known her she had spoken with a broad Lancashire sprawl and had referred to everyone as 'luv' and 'duck'.

'I'm pleased everything is going so well for you,' Corinne said.

Margaret smiled happily, her eyes sparkling into the middle distance. 'Yes. For Gerald and I, and for Rogelio, too, despite his illness.' Her body gave a little quiver of pleasure, adding emphasis to her next words: 'Oh, life can be so *good*, darling!'

138

Sensing that she had not yet finished Corinne remained silent. She was a little wary. This euphoria that Margaret was now evincing so dramatically struck her as being somehow not quite genuine. As though to prove her wrong Margaret turned to her and said, 'I must tell you! Oh, I must!' She gripped Corinne's forearm tightly with both hands and gazed at her beamingly. 'I'm – I'm going to have a baby!'

Corinne gaped for a second, astonished. Then, remembering herself, she hugged her. 'Margaret! That's wonderful! Congratulations!'

Margaret laughed and hugged her in return.

'But I thought – ' Corinne began, pulling back. Her voice trailed off as the words caught somewhere inside her. Margaret completed the sentence for her.

'You thought Gerald was sterile?'

Corinne nodded. She was well-apprised of Gerald's sexual history (at least, she had thought she was) for Margaret had never made any secret of it. Quite the contrary, in fact.

It was, sad to relate, a tale of woe. Gerald had been impotent from the very beginning of his relationship with Margaret, and they had been wed for two years before he was able to satisfactorily consummate the bond. On that evening, almost before she had had time to regain her breath, Margaret was on the telephone to Corinne, acquainting her with the good news.

Gerald's ability to sustain an erection had then held good, with only minor lapses, over a period of months. At the end of this time, however, they discovered that he was sterile. This had come as a crushing blow and it reduced him overnight once more to a state of unremitting flaccidity. And, as far as Corinne was aware, the malcondition had not subsequently improved.

Margaret lowered her eyes. 'Yes, he is,' she said.

'What?'

She nodded.

'But then – ?'

She lifted her eyes again and stared directly into Corinne's. 'It wasn't Gerald.'

'What!'

'It isn't what you are thinking,' Margaret stressed. 'You are allowing yourself to jump to conclusions, I can see by your reaction, and it isn't like that. It isn't like that at all.'

'Well then, what is it?' Corinne urged. 'I mean, *who* is it?'

'Calm down. Just give me a minute and I'll explain everything.' She took a deep breath. 'Yes, the baby is not Gerald's, but Gerald is fully aware of that. And he is delighted. He is as delighted as I am.'

Corinne stared at her. She obviously was delighted. She obviously was very, very happy indeed. Corinne was confounded.

'Well who *is* the father then?'

Margaret's features stayed very calm. Her lips were parted with a hint of a smile and her eyes shone, penetrating and jubilant.

'Rogelio,' she breathed.

'ROGELIO!!'

'Darling, shush! This is between you and I.'

'But,' she raised a hand to her chin. 'Margaret, I don't know what to say. I – I don't understand.'

'I know you don't,' Margaret said in a quiet voice.

'How did it happen?' Corinne asked, still not fully able to grasp what she had been told.

'It was one afternoon just before he was discharged from the hospital. He was staying with us on a weekend release.' Her face turned mellow with reminiscence. 'It was lovely . . .' she cooed.

Corinne felt almost sick. 'But Gerald . . . Margaret, how could you?'

'I've told you, Gerald knows! He has known all along, he knew at the time. He is overjoyed.'

A bizarre image splashed suddenly into Corinne's mind. It sprang from a discussion she and Samson had had one evening some months earlier. They were in bed and Samson, as was his wont, was expounding on the subject of other people's sex. Somehow or other the conversation had veered to include Gerald and Margaret and, presently, Rogelio. Samson was lying back and chuckling to himself, his head cradled in his hands on the pillow and his face crinkled with mirth.

'I remember when I was a kid,' he had said, 'there were some people lived down the road and they used to have a pet terrier, a tiny, long-haired, yapping thing. An odious little beast it was – whenever it saw you standing still it used to come up and try and fuck your ankle. And the people next door had a bitch, a large mongrel, and she was on heat, and this terrier, as was to be expected, got himself horny as hell. He got through into the garden and went berserk trying to fuck this mongrel and the mongrel just acted like he wasn't there. I'll never forget it, it was one of the most pathetic things I've ever seen – that titchy little dog, all pink tongue and hot eyes and little red cock jerking, trying to mount an indifferent female ten times its size. And nowadays, whenever I see that little out-to-lunch artist friend of yours, that's always the first thing that springs to mind.'

Corinne shook her head and turned her face away from her friend, but the image stayed with her. True, Margaret was not ten times Rogelio's size, she was a slightly built woman – and her attitude now seemed to infer anything other than indifference. But, this notwithstanding, she was still some inches taller than he, and the whole idea of the two of them making love was something that Corinne found a little tricky to contemplate.

'Are you sure you're pregnant?' she asked.

'Yes, the doctor confirmed it this week.'

Margaret's manifest bliss was a little hard to contemplate, too.

0

Margaret took Corinne's hand and held it fondly in hers. 'I can see I have a lot of explaining to do, don't I. Don't look so depressed, darling. It isn't as if I've committed some unspeakable felony!'

'I know. I'm sorry. It's just that it's a bit of a shock. You know. . . . I don't quite know what to think.'

'No, I know you don't. I know it must seem a little confusing to you – I would have preferred some other way of telling you, but I didn't know how. You see, you have to understand that Gerald and I, and Rogelio especially, are no longer bound by those rigid conventions and customs that society has created in order to regulate all of our lives. We have found something different, something utterly marvellous! that has given us the freedom and strength and understanding to enable us to step beyond all that. We are no longer fettered.' Her voice and features grew suddenly earnest. 'Society has always been structured in such a way as to suppress us and control us whilst at the same time feeding us the illusion that we are free. The populace is subordinated and coordinated by those who consider themselves to be in power, and yet we believe that we have freedom. And this is especially true of the Western world. We think we have freedom. We believe that *this* – ' she spread her arms expansively, 'is all.

'So called "Christian" ethics, dreamed up and enforced by men who had the audacity to set themselves up as ambassadors to a God they themselves had created and adapted . . . False conceptions of reality; dogma and inculcation; science, technology and religion; mental conditioning and enslavement, all fed ingeniously into us over hundreds – thousands – of years to convince us that this is all, to prevent us from stepping beyond and realizing our true consciousness . . .

'But it isn't all. It can't be – sheer logic will tell you that much. For if it was, then surely we would be happy? Surely we would not need to resolve our differences by means of strikes and wars, surely our prisons and mental institutions would not be overflowing with persons incapable of integrating into society, surely we would not all be so alienated from one another, banging our heads against metaphorical walls and screaming within ourselves to know what is really going on, what all this is all about, why we are here . . .?' She paused to collect herself and to examine her words. Her cheeks had grown flushed and her eyes glittered like diamonds. She appeared a little disorientated, as though surprised at the vehemence of her own outburst. 'I'm not explaining myself very well, am I?' she said at length. 'I know you probably think you've heard all this before. Perhaps it sounds trite to you, or perhaps even naive. Maybe you think it is just some paranoid, leftist ravings, but that is not the case. What you have to understand is that there *is* something else. It *is* possible to experience true freedom. We *can* be happy. I know this, because I have found it. But it isn't something that is easily put into words. What I am talking about is a new culture, a new morality, something that takes you way beyond the confines pre-set for us by "civilized" society; and it is a morality that cannot at first be intellectually conceived. It is subjective, it speaks to you from inside. It comes to you and it fills you with strength and knowledge and love, and you feel it inside and you know, you just *know*, that it is right.'

She paused again, her breathing rapid and deep, to measure Corinne's response.

Externally, Corinne's response was negligible, but within herself there was turmoil. Though she believed she had caught the gist of what Margaret was saying, the words themselves had come across to her as garbled and confused. She was at a loss as to how to respond. It was evident by Margaret's manner and tone that she

142

was deadly serious, and yet what she was saying did not, somehow, appear very sound. And it was uncharacteristic of Margaret to allow herself to become so impassioned. Certainly, she had always been one to take up a banner when there was one around to wave, but not to this extent. Not quite. She had always remained somehow apart, slightly aloof, very much in control. Something here did not ring true. It was as if it were somebody else speaking, or as if her words were not entirely her own.

Corinne, Gerald, Rogelio and I have discovered something very beautiful,' Margaret went on. 'Rogelio introduced us to it some time ago. We have joined the Sons and Daughters of Scompiglio.'

Corinne remembered vaguely, and something went cold inside her. 'That's that religion thing you mentioned last year, isn't it?'

'Yes. You remember, I showed you a pamphlet? But please don't dismiss it so disdainfully, darling. "Religion thing!" indeed! It is more than that. It is much, much more than that. Iddio E. Scompiglio tells us in his writings: "Religion is the way we have to strengthen ourselves against ourselves, love is the way we have to strengthen ourselves against others, and Iddio E. Scompiglio is the way we have to strengthen ourselves against strengthening ourselves."'

Corinne raised a hand to her eyes, her lids had grown heavy.

'Iddio E. Scompiglio,' Margaret continued in a reverent voice, 'has given us freedom through understanding. He teaches us that it is wrong to love only one, to possess only one, to need only one. He tells us, he *shows* us, that we must give love to all, and that we must give love to ourselves. We must not possess others, we must give. That is our duty. Without that we cannot hope to gain a true understanding of our purpose here on this planet. Rogelio brought this to us, Gerald and I, and we shall be forever indebted to him. He has enabled us to see, through Iddio's teachings, what we are here for. You must see, Corinne! Before Iddio our lives were meaningless! We had no direction, no motive. Everything seemed to lead directly to emptiness, frustration and disillusionment; there was nowhere to turn, no way out. But now we are happy. Now we have a task to fulfil. I want you to understand this. I want you to see it so that you can share in it too!' Margaret clasped her hands before her and stood in a posture of joyful resolution. 'Oh, Corinne! Scompiglio reigns!' she declared. 'Scompiglio lives for all mankind! We must all live for Scompiglio!'

Corinne regarded her blankly. Her mind reeled as she tried to take all this in. *Margaret pregnant? Rogelio the father? Gerald overjoyed? False conceptions of reality? Subordination, coordination, dogma, inculcation? Mental conditioning and enslavement? A new morality? The Sons and Daughters of Scompiglio?* What did it all mean? What was happening?

She felt uncomfortable, threatened. Something told her that she did not want to hear any more. There was something unreal about it. Something unnatural. Something *weird*.

She had time to realize, suddenly, that she was in a state of shock, then the room lurched, undulated, and her body shifted away beneath her. An arm flew out like liquid for support.

'Corinne! What's wrong?' Margaret cried. She caught her and helped her as she slumped onto a stool. 'Are you all right?'

Corinne nodded weakly as the kitchen slid slowly back into focus. 'I'm all right. I just went a bit dizzy.'

'Do you want anything? Some water?'

She shook her head, then nodded. 'I could do with a drink.'

'Did you bring it with you?' Margaret asked, looking around the kitchen.

'Yes, but I emptied it.'

Margaret called through the serving-hatch to Samson and asked him for another drink for his wife. A moment later he passed one through and she handed it to Corinne.

'I'm all right,' Corinne said, sipping at the drink and pursing her lips. 'Really. It was just a momentary dizzy spell.'

She reached for the pack of cigarettes that lay on her worktop, lit one and inhaled the cool smoke deeply. She was anxious not to resume the topic of conversation – at least for the moment. She glanced at her watch.

'Goodness, time's getting on! We really ought to be eating by now.'

Rising unsteadily, under Margaret's solicitous gaze, she began to place the last few items onto the dumb-waiter. As she was preparing to wheel it from the kitchen she caught sight of the trifle which she had earlier moved along the sideboard. She slid it back now, so that it was in front of the serving-hatch where she might reach it later, when the savoury courses were finished.

● ● ● ● ●

144

# 4

'Nacreous Sheene and the Slug Pellets.'

'I beg your pardon?'

Richard winced. He did not want to say that name again. He hated it. He had not wanted to say it in the first place, but Jill, in an effort at promoting his interests, had asked Samson for his opinion of Richard's band the other night, and whether or not he thought they had potential. Samson had been thoughtful for a moment. Then he replied that there were one or two songs that did stick in his mind, and he had asked Richard to remind him of the name of the band, for he claimed to have forgotten it.

It was Leon, the lead vocalist, who had come up with that name. Leon had been to university.

Leon dreamed of being a rock star. He wanted to have young girls falling at his feet, fighting to touch his garments, and lubricating copiously in their bedrooms at the very thought of his name. He wanted money, fame, fast cars and high living. He dreamed of making love all day and all night – beautiful women, the most beautiful women in the world.

He tried very hard, too. He dyed his hair several colours and wore outrageous clothes; he strutted, pouted, wiggled and spat on stage; he held the microphone in provocative poses; he made lewd and suggestive movements with his hands, hips and tongue; he struck poses and visages contorted with angst; he had even, on one occasion, slipped his pink satin pants to his knees and full-mooned at his audience.

But sadly for Leon, despite his agonistic approach and despite his two:two degree in social studies, he was never going to make it as a superstar. Something about him was not quite right. It had to do with his physique – he was too muscular and stout – and with the tattoos that wreathed his biceps and triceps. And it had to do, too, with his face. When he posed before his audience there was something in his expression that did not speak of insolence or rebellion, not even of moodiness. Nor was it sorrowful, sexy or strange. What it was, quite simply, was goatish and depraved. At the same time it was pathetic and inadequate. Leon just did not make it. There was something uninteresting and faintly ridiculous about him when he stepped onstage. He tended to remind one of nothing so much as a grossly misplaced matelot.

And, in fact, Leon rarely succeeded in making-out with the opposite gender. It was Slider, the roadie, who got all the girls. At virtually every gig (for he worked with other bands besides Richard's), after he had helped the members set up their gear, and as they were all sweating it out on stage, Slider could be found outside, tumbling some eighteen-year-old darling in the back of his Bedford van. He rarely failed – in fact he rarely even tried. He just had the knack somehow.

Richard wavered beneath Samson's laser gaze. He did not want to have to repeat that name.

'Nacreous Sheene and the Slug Pellets,' he said again.

Samson nodded, pulling at his moustache. 'So you're a slug pellet, are you?'

'Don't you think some of their tunes are really catchy?' Jill asked. 'I'm always finding myself singing them in my head.'

'Ye-es,' said Samson with a twinkle. 'There was one, I remember, that did stand out. The lyric, particularly. What was it now . . .? Something about eating out . . . Going into town for dinner, or something. Was that it?'

Richard went suddenly wide-eyed and his heart gave a lurch like he had been kicked from inside by a cart-horse.

'Is that the one?' Samson persisted. 'You must know the one I mean?'

Richard blushed crimson. He looked frantically about him, all eyes had turned to him. He looked at Corinne, who had just re-entered with Margaret in tow and a dumb-waiter loaded with food. He looked back at Samson. He looked at the floor, and at his dirty old plimsolls.

'Come on,' Samson said. 'What was it called?'

Richard cleared his throat. He said reluctantly, in a hoarse voice: 'Going Downtown to Lunch.'

'What? Speak up. What was it?'

'Going Downtown To Lunch.

'That's the one.' Samson sank back on his sofa. ' "Going Downtown to Lunch". Yes, I liked that one. It had an immediate

146

chorus, and I thought the lyric was particularly good. How did it go again?'

Richard was hot and prickly. This was a song penned by Leon. The words did not bear repetition in respectable company.

Samson was tapping his feet and clicking his fingers. 'Come on, Ricky. I've forgotten it. How did it go again?'

Seeing no alternative, Richard began to hum the tune in barely audible tones in time with Samson's beat.

'No, the lyric,' Samson insisted. 'How did the lyric go?'

'I can't remember it properly,' Richard croaked. 'I'm a terrible singer, anyway.'

'No you're not, I heard you singing harmony. And if you were able to remember it then you must be able to now. Come on, stop hedging. I'm trying to help you. I think that song is a potential single. With the right producer and arranger I can even envisage it being a hit.'

So, strained and squeaky with embarrassment, Richard began to sing. This is what he sang:

> 'Well, there ain't no stoppin my baby
> When she knows what she wants to do.
> It's no good tryin to dissuade her,
> And anyway, no sane man would want to.
>
> She says she wants to go out to dinner,
> And I know she means she wants to stay in.
> She says she sure likes eatin together,
> And you know, it puts my mind in a spin.'

He stopped there.

'That's it,' said Samson, grinning malevolently and continuing to tap his feet. 'I remember it now. What about the chorus? How does that go again?'

Half-choking, Richard began again, as quietly as possible:

> 'We ain't goin out nowhere tonight –
> I'm actin on a hunch.
> We're stayin where we are tonight –
> And I like it a whole bunch.
> Cos when my baby got appetite on her mind,
> She treats me good and she treats me kind,
> She don't wanna move, 'cept a way downstairs,

147

And she keeps me dancin like I'm Lionel Blair.
Cos my baby,
Yeah, my baby,
Ooh, my baby likes goin downtown to lunch.
I said, my baby,
Yeah, my baby,
Ooh, my sweet baby likes goin downtown to lunch,
Ooh yeah, she likes goin downtown to lunch.'

He fell silent, praying that he would not be made to continue. A huge, embarrassed silence had turned the air brittle. He could not speak. Everybody was staring. He was close to tears. He could not look at anybody.

After a suitable period had elapsed Samson clapped his hands and cheered. 'Love it! Great! Might have to rewrite parts, though, if you plan on getting it airplay.'

Richard's body twitched. He wanted to flee but his limbs had ceased up. He had become rigid – fixed and mute like a statue. Like a statue in bronze, a statue called 'Europeans' that stood in the centre of a stone square in Amsterdam. All around him were people, unfriendly, who did nothing but stare and speak in undertones, or throw unkind remarks his way. It was only a matter of time before they would move in and physically abuse him, and then they would pass on, laughing, and he would be left behind, alone on the Museumplein, forgotten.

0

Corinne, understanding something of Richard's discomfort, and incensed with her husband for subjecting the boy to such humiliation, said, 'Come on, everybody. Help yourselves to the food. There's plenty here for all.'

She was still feeling a little faint, but she tried to conceal it with a show of conviviality. 'Richard, do help yourself. Here's a plate for you. Julia, Jill, feel free to make yourselves at home.'

'I'd better not, actually,' Jill said. 'It looks delicious, but I've already had my full intake of calories for today. I dare not allow myself to go over the limit.'

Richard turned gratefully to the food and was startled by what he saw. It was so bright. He had to blink several times to make sense of it, and even then he was not fully able to convince himself of its validity. Was this for eating?

148

He saw Gerald leave his seat and found himself sufficiently in control of his body once more to be able to rise and follow suit. Together they approached the food. His stomach was shrunken like a prune, tight with fear, and he knew he was not going to be able to eat. Nevertheless he felt he had to. But surely this was a joke? Surely this was not real food?

He leaned forward a little to examine a bowl of colourful lumps that bobbed slowly in a lake of turbid liquid. From the liquid a cloud of hot steam arose and collided with his face. Deep within the liquid he thought he saw murky forms swimming. He frowned, then sniffed. The smell that he picked up was distinct and rather personal, and he shrank back, deciding that this was not for him.

He looked up. Corinne had her eyes on him. He could not read the expression on her face. When she saw him looking she glanced away. He liked Corinne. He liked her a lot. He hoped he was not being a great disappointment to her.

There was a game in progress. Richard understood this suddenly, and everything became much clearer. He looked at the food in a new light, found himself wanting to play.

Now his eyes came to rest on a plate piled high with variform white, pink and green things. They had been arranged precisely to resemble something, but he was unable to determine quite what. He sensed, though, that whatever it was it was not intended for the human digestive tract, and he was pleased with himself for having surmised this so quickly.

The next dish to catch his attention gave a slight shudder as he watched, and the one following seemed a mass of writhing pink tentacles. No, this was not for him, either. He gave a little laugh. He was enjoying this game. He noticed that none of the others were taking anything from these dishes, so he knew he must be right.

But he was still faced with the dilemma of what to choose. Obviously, something here had to be selected and the art lay in guessing which one. He watched Julia. She was gripping a plate in one hand and hovering over the food as though in a quandary not dissimilar to his own. But he could see that she had not fallen in with the spirit of the game. Her face was sullen and tight and she looked as though she might come in handy for putting out a small fire with.

'Would you like to try some *tempura*, Julia?' he heard Corinne say. It was obviously a trick question and he liked Corinne even more for having posed it. Julia signalled no with a stiff movement of her head. Then she pounced with her free hand onto a small, soft, flat, yellow object and a scoop of green cubes, dropped them onto her plate, and moved away back to her corner. Richard smiled; that was her out of the running.

Gerald and Margaret were standing next to him and conferring quietly, and he wondered if that was allowed. Then Margaret reached down and removed something that was on a lower shelf of the dumb-waiter, not within his line of sight. So that was it! How sneaky! Richard watched with the corner of one eye.

The things Margaret was putting on her plate were recognizable. They were the only things that were. There was cheese, for example, and bits of green salad. Gerald crouched by her side and began to help himself to the very same items. Neither of them took very much, but they seemed happy with what they had taken, and they both moved away and sat down.

Richard stooped to see what was on the bottom shelf of the dumb-waiter. There was a large bowl filled with green salad which tempted him momentarily, until something rustled deep within its foliage. He cocked his ear and listened. It rustled again and he decided to leave well alone. Cheese in triangular and rectangular segments lay on a plate. He reached for a small piece, not sure whether he would be able to cope with it or not. Then his eye fell on the bread.

The bread had been broken into hunks about the size of a woman's fist. It was white and fluffy, like clouds, like cauliflower . . . like ice-cream. It looked homely and familiar and there was an aura of friendship about it that was enough to convince Richard that this, indeed, was the choice to make. Ignoring the cheese, the thought of which filled him now with revulsion, he took the smallest piece of bread, laid it on his plate and returned to his seat beside Jill. There was a smile on his lips, for he was feeling suddenly very pleased with himself. This was a triumph. It was the first thing he had done right all evening and it filled him with hope. Perhaps he could make himself fit in after all.

He leaned towards Jill and indicated his piece of bread with a finger. 'Look,' he said. 'I got it.'

Jill's eyes travelled from him to the bread and back again. 'Pardon?'

Richard broke into a smile that seemed to him to extend way

beyond the boundaries of his face. 'I got it,' he said, and sniggered, covering his mouth in case his smile went too far and caused Jill some damage. Then he heard Corinne's voice addressing him: 'Is that all you're going to have, Richard?'

He turned to her, and was shocked by the appalling sadness that lay across her features. It filled him immediately with confusion and remorse. He glanced at his bread, then back at Corinne again. What had he done wrong? The bread looked fine. It looked perfect. What was she suggesting? Had he, after all, made the wrong choice? No, he couldn't have, the bread suited him so well. It was Corinne, then. Ah! She was playing a joke, trying to mislead him. But her face told him no. Corinne was not joking. Then it must be she who had made the mistake, surely? Yes, that had to be it.

So he stuck to his guns.

'Yes, thank you very much,' he said, and almost burst into tears when he saw the way she looked at him.

'How about you, Julia?' Corinne asked. 'Won't you have something more?'

Julia, crunching noisily on a mouthful of celery cubes, shook her head.

Corinne turned to her husband, and her jaw was trembling slightly. 'Samson?'

'Nah, I don't think so,' Samson drawled. 'I'm not hungry at the moment. Maybe later on. Right now I think I'll just make do with another drink. Anybody else care to join me?'

Richard watched Corinne as she picked up a plate and crossed to the sofa where she placed herself heavily opposite him. She sat hunched forward, staring silently at her hands, which she held, fingers linked tightly together, on the empty plate on her knees.

Samson poured drinks for those who wanted them, then returned to his seat. He placed his feet, ankles crossed, on the travertine table in front of him, and laid one arm along the back of the sofa. Casting a wry eye around the room and at the dumbwaiter still piled high with untouched food, he said, 'Oh well, anybody for an After-Dinner Mint?'

0

'Richard, what instrument do you play in your group?' asked Margaret, because there was a definite lull in the conversation.

151

She and Gerald were sitting on dining-chairs one each side of the dining-table, a little forward from centre so that they were able to link hands beneath the table. Their plates had been relieved of their meagre morsels and both sat now wearing identical smiles. Their eyes were glassy and there was something distinctly null and void about the two of them.

'Bass,' Richard answered, without looking at her. He was intent on his hunk of bread, wondering what possible significance his choosing it could have held for Corinne. He was absolutely shattered by the knowledge that he had hurt her somehow.

'Bass guitar?' Margaret asked.

'Yes.' Remembering himself Richard looked her way and offered a smile.

'Do you play many concerts?'

'Concerts?' Richard said. 'Oh, well, no, not many, really. Not at the moment, anyway.' He was having a lot of difficulty focusing on her. Her bright blue kimono dazzled him and her hair shone like a twisted halo about her head.

'I imagine it must be very difficult,' she said. 'You can't make very much money.'

Richard took this as a veiled criticism of his appearance, and he blushed. He was still sweating profusely and his clothes clung to his skin. His crotch, in particular, was soggy with spilt liquids. He was aware of a strange smell in the room. It was a personal smell, similar to the smell that had arisen from the bowl of lumps a few minutes earlier. But this smell was even more personal than that one had been, and Richard was almost certain that he was the cause. He was under the distinct impression that he was emanating foul, pungent odours and that everybody else was being too polite to remark upon it. He attempted to sit very still, knowing that the slightest movement was liable to waft great streams of b.o. into the air around him.

Thinking very hard and fast he said to Margaret, 'Money – ' and then found that he had nothing to follow it up with. He frowned and looked at his bread.

'They don't make any money at all,' put in Jill. 'It's a rotten business to try and make a living at. You need to have a manager or a record company behind you, and even then you're liable to starve. When you're just starting out it's really terrible. Gigs are awfully difficult to find, and they pay such piffling amounts of money. They seem to expect you to play simply out of love. They don't care that you're trying to make a living out of it.'

'There must be a fairly substantial outlay too, initially, I would imagine, isn't there?' Margaret asked. 'Your equipment and things?'

'Oh yes,' piped Jill. 'And then there's transport on top of that. None of the band members make any money. It's only the roadie that gets paid.'

'Oh, that's awful,' Margaret said. 'Do you mean you have to pay a chap to carry you to and from your concerts, and yet none of you who actually play get any?'

Richard nodded, clutching his plate. 'In a way, though, the roadie is the most important member of the band. We'd be really stuck without him. None of us has any transport.'

'Actually, they've got a bit of a problem at the moment,' Jill said. 'Slider – their roadie – his van had broken down. As it happens they don't have any gigs for the next couple of weeks, so we're hoping he'll have it fixed by then. It's been off the road for about ten days now. He's got it parked on the pavement outside his house and he can't move it.'

'What's the problem?' Samson enquired.

Jill shrugged. Richard said, avoiding Samson's eye, 'I don't know. I don't know much about engines and things.'

'It was very lucky, actually, because he had just moved house,' Jill said. 'He used to live right out in Collier's Wood, which made it terribly difficult for him to do all his gigs and things – he more or less makes his living out of that van – so he's bought a flat nearer the centre. Just off Portobello Road. It sounds as though he got it very cheap, somehow, from what he was telling me. He worked some kind of deal with the previous owner – which is quite typical of Slider – and he had just finished moving all his things into the new place when the van conked out. If it had been a day earlier he would have really been stuck.'

Richard listened, went owl-eyed with suspicion and astonishment. How did she know all this? He did not recall having told her. She must have seen Slider at some point. A throb of jealousy ran through him. Why had she not mentioned it to him? Was she having an affair with Slider?

Samson leaned forward, suddenly interested. 'Just off Portobello Road?' he said. 'Do you know the name of the street?'

'Layfield Road,' Jill replied.

Samson smiled. 'What kind of van does he have.'

'A Bedford. A blue one.'

'Ha!' He laughed out loud and slapped his leg. 'The twat!'

'What?' said Jill, bewildered.

'Corinne!' Samson cried. 'Corinne, did you hear that?'

Corinne looked up. 'What's that?' she said, dully.

'Arlo!' Samson exclaimed.

'What about Arlo?'

'The police! You said he suspects he's being watched by the police . . .'

'Yes, that's what he said.'

'Well, haven't you been listening?'

'I'm sorry, I was miles away,' Corinne said. 'I wasn't really following your conversation.'

'What's Arlo's address?'

'Layfield Road. Number twenty-three, isn't it?'

He turned to Jill. 'What number has this Slider bloke moved into?'

'Eighteen.'

'Almost opposite!' Samson fell back, laughing. 'The stupid, paranoid, freaked-out twat!'

He stood and crossed the room to the telephone.

'You mean it isn't the police?' asked Corinne.

'Of course it isn't! It's this Slider bloke – his van's parked outside and he can't shift it.' He rubbed his hands gleefully. 'Just wait till I tell him!'

He reached for the phone, then hesitated, thoughtful. 'On second thoughts, I think I might let him stew for a while' – replacing the receiver – 'it's too late for any dope now anyway.'

Corinne, noting the expression on her guests' faces, felt obliged to explain. 'Arlo is a drug dealer,' she said. 'He was supposed to deliver some dope yesterday for Samson – for the party – and he telephoned to say that he felt he ought to stop dealing, for the time being at least, because he thinks the police are on to him. There was a Bedford van parked across the road. He thinks it's a police-van, keeping an eye on him.'

Jill crinkled her adorable nose and gave a little cry of amusement. Richard, who was not too sure what was going on, laughed with her.

'So haven't you been able to get any?' Jill asked Samson.

'Nope. Not a whiff.'

'And a good job, too,' Margaret said. 'There must be something wrong with you if you need that stuff. You're far better off without it.'

Samson snorted and sat himself down again. 'Bollocks,' he said.

Richard, at this point, began to experience a strange sensation. It was a kind of gentle, buffeting feeling and it seemed to be affecting a certain portion of his anatomy. But, at first, he had difficulty in pinpointing the precise location, for he was becoming increasingly uncertain of where exactly his own body ended and the rest of the world began. He traced it, eventually, to his midriff, turned, and discovered that Jill was nudging him there. Her beautiful face and clear green eyes told him that there was something he ought to be aware of.

She leaned towards him and whispered in his ear, 'Your joints.'

A spasm of intense unease stirred his innards. He turned anxiously to see what it was about his joints that was so remarkable, and found nothing. As far as he was able to make out they were perfectly okay; and he did not think they were causing him any pain, either, although his hands were trembling quite noticeably.

He lifted his arms and examined his wrists from all angles, then his elbows. He wondered if there was something unspeakable happening to him that he was simply incapable of perceiving.

'What about them?' he asked.

'Your joints,' Jill repeated. 'In your pocket. You can have a smoke.'

And suddenly he understood. And suddenly he saw a way of redeeming himself in everybody's eyes. He reached gladly into his grey jumper, delved around, located the three joints lined up like little soldiers in his breast pocket, and pulled one out.

'Ricky's got some smoke, if you would like some,' Jill said brightly.

Richard smiled shyly at Corinne, showed her the joint. 'Would you like some?'

'Thank you,' Corinne said. 'That's very kind of you. I don't smoke it, though – but please go ahead. Samson's been complaining all evening because he couldn't get any.'

Richard fumbled in the pocket of his jeans and withdrew a

155

small, gold-coloured cigarette lighter – a Halloween present from his sister Deirdre some years ago. He flicked it with his thumb and touched the orange and blue flame to the tip, pulled the harsh smoke into his lungs.

After taking a few long drags he offered it to Jill. She shook her head, she was still not keen. He made to offer it to Gerald and Margaret but it was plain that they were not interested. He swivelled on his seat to face Julia. She still occupied her seat in the corner and was looking away, out of the window, where the occasional burst of colour still brightened the night. Her expression was so grim that he did not dare disturb her.

Finally he offered it to Samson.

Samson, instead of accepting it, eyed him cannily, stroking his chin with thumb and forefinger. 'No thanks,' he said.

Corinne turned to him curiously. 'You what?'

Without taking his eyes off Richard, Samson said, 'No, I don't really feel like any at the moment.' He folded his arms, smiling behind his moustache, sinking himself more comfortably into the sofa, and wallowing in *schadenfreude* as he mused over the possibilities of what was to come.


Richard fell back, slayed by the weight of his monumental faux pas. He stared at the joint in his hand. It was long. It was very long. It was longer than any long and dusty road he had ever travelled down in his life.

And it was fat. It bulged like a bantam's thigh. It was fully laden with prime Moroccan, too, for he had been far from sparing when it came to rolling it – his aim had been to get Jill bombed.

*But he could not possibly put it out now! Not in front of all these people! He would look such a fool!*

He raised it self-consciously to his lips and took a little puff. Already he could feel its effects. Only inches from his face a silent avalanche had begun as his vision began to disintegrate. It was as though the already shredded fabric of his universe was finally collapsing altogether. He felt himself to be on the verge of seeing something he would have no idea how to cope with.

● ● ● ● ●

# 5

Meanwhile Rogelio, sequestered behind the sofa, was gazing with a rapt expression at a piece of air in front of him. His sallow features had grown lightly flushed. His hands lay twitching slightly in his lap. He was cross-legged and almost cross-eyed.

He was undergoing something transcendental. He was passing through that joyous, soaring, suffusive rapture known solely, rarely, and then only fleetingly, to artists, lovers and psychopaths. He was being temporarily beatific.

Minutes earlier, as he had been happily tracing outlines on his artist's sketch-pad, he had become aware of the strange vitality contained within the emptiness that confronted him. He had raised himself from his prone position, had curled his little legs beneath him, and had sat, watchful, with quiet intensity.

A poignant smile had then cracked his wizened face; he felt himself stirred by an inner excitement. He put aside his pad and his coloured pencils and had forgotten himself as he witnessed the miracle that began to unfold before his eyes.

All manner of weird and wonderful cogs had been grinding in Rogelio's mind at that point – unfortunately not all in synchronicity. One by one, though, their revolutions had grown smaller. They had continued to diminish, little by little, until finally a point was reached where there was no longer any motion there at all.

Then came stillness. The emptiness that had transported him from without had shifted to transport him from within. It had become the essence of his very being.

This was what was going through Rogelio's mind at that particular moment:

And this is what life meant to him just then:

But gradually, by degrees, something was once more beginning to impinge itself upon his consciousness . . .

0

The first manifestation of Rogelio's imminent return to self-awareness came in the form of a barely discernible tic above his upper lip, which caused a tiny movement amongst the wisps of black whisker sprouting there. This was followed by a wrinkling and stretching of the nose. His bloodshot blue eyes focused on the world again, and a glint of wariness stole into them.

Something was not right.

It had to do with the space in front of him, but at the same time it could have nothing to do with it, for to him the space was a source of ineffable delight, and the notion that it might be that which was troubling him was something he could not possibly entertain.

Nevertheless, there was something.

Rogelio peered into the space. He retrieved his pad and examined the sketches he had made, peered at the space again, shook his head.

He eased himself forward a little way on his hands and knees so that he was able to see around the corner of the sofa. What he saw there caused his features to alter drastically, firstly with astonishment, then with purest pleasure.

The space had grown! During his rapture it had spread, expanded so that its volume was now more than twice what it had previously been!

Rogelio goggled enthralled. He sat back on his heels and tensed his buttocks with joy.

As his initial excitement abated he began to consider how best to deal with this new development. He shifted himself back to his original position, studied again his drawings.

But as he studied them he began to sense something else. He became greatly agitated within, loath to accept the information filtering through from his higher faculties. But it grew too insistent to ignore, and with a sigh he closed his eyes and became receptive. He opened them again with a feeling of unease. He scratched at his shoulder. It was true. He had not been mistaken. The room was flooded with 'malcontent'.

He dwelt upon the likely causes of this and knew within seconds that it was issuing from those persons with whom he was sharing his evening. And without any doubt it was issuing with a greater puissance from some than from others . . .

Rogelio listened to the voices. They told him much but not enough. He raised himself to his knees so that he was able to peer over the top of the sofa.

The primary cause of the emissions, he saw at once, was the woman Julia. She sat rigid in the corner, coiled like a spring, and her face was ashen and taut. She looked to Rogelio as though she might burst into flame at any moment.

Her emanations disconcerted him quite profoundly. They crowded around her like cornered beasts, barbed and serrated, with a ferocity that almost made him yelp. Some darted from her like needles, with a swiftness and voracity that was staggering, and others sawed and stabbed, ravaging without surcease the space she occupied. Rogelio looked away, squinting.

He turned his head to the man he knew as Samson, who was seated with his back to him only inches away.

Samson's emanations were of a comparable strength but marginally less harmful in their essence. They gave the impression of being held beneath a greater discipline than Julia's, for he had an

161

outlet: he was able to inflict hurt at will, on a mundane, social level. His pathological need to cause pain and disruption wherever possible was assuaged somewhat by his ability to accomplish this by means of words and actions. Julia possessed no such skill, and consequently her emanations raged unappeased.

Samson's emanations had a specific character too, Rogelio perceived: they hung heavily about him, swathing him, few travelling far beyond his physical presence. In fact, as Rogelio had come to understand on a previous occasion, Samson was trapped by his radiations. They moved everywhere with him, their smothering density varying from moment to moment, but never leaving him – rather, turning around and radiating back upon him. Rogelio had attempted to warn him of this. He had awareness of how this type of emanation could cause great and incomprehensible suffering to its emanator and how, as an unconscious form of displacement activity, he or she might be compelled to try to redirect this suffering, aim it outwards at the world which they mistakenly believed to be its cause – but he had known immediately by Samson's response that it was too late. Samson was trapped far too deeply to ever be capable of insight into his predicament, or of effecting any measure that might help counter it.

All this flashed through Rogelio's mind in less than a second, then his attention was drawn to a disturbing phenomenon that was occurring above his head. That soupçon of radiations that was able to percolate fully away from Samson's physical presence was, upon encountering the emanations of Julia, clashing with a great deal of discord. They were generating much disharmony in the upper reaches of the room.

Rogelio knitted his brow and raked his hairy little jowls with his fingernails. These two, then, were the most obvious progenitors of the malcontent – but he was fully aware that they could not be held entirely responsible.

For instance, there was the strange young man with the long cigarette.

Rogelio surveyed him now with a sensation of bewilderment. Never in his life had he witnessed emanations like this. They were extraordinary. They were unique.

Richard was like a sun going nova. His emanations burst from him in spasms; they chased around him, spiralling about his

162

person, or shot off without rhyme or reason into nowhere. They pulsed energetically, danced and shimmied, or curled back into themselves, shrinking until they were barely perceptible. At times they vibrated with a near paralysing intensity, and at others they held still, seemed almost frozen.

Malcontent there most certainly was in Richard's radiations, but it was the unfamiliarity of their nature that caused the gravest doubts within Rogelio's mind. Baffled, and more than a trifle unnerved, he shifted his attention to Corinne.

Corinne Tallis's emanations, as he had discerned on former occasions, were susceptible to fluctuation. At times they could shine quite brilliantly, radiating healthily into her space, but frequently they ebbed, collapsed, until they were no more than a feeble evanescence huddled desperately close to her flesh. They were like that now. In fact they were more faint than he had ever seen before, and he knew with consternation that unless something were done they were in danger of fading altogether . . .

And the blonde girl, Jill, sitting alongside the inexplicable young man . . . ah, she had lovely emanations. Rogelio cocked his head to one side, smiling tinily. They were vibrant, full, auroral – they were a pleasure to behold.

But, Rogelio was cognizant, hers was the form of emanation that was most susceptible to adverse influence. He perceived this and was sad, for he knew that the adverse influence that was pervading the room was indeed capable of exerting maleficent pressure upon her. And he was aware that this influence, for the most part, had assumed the specious form, and that the girl was young and inexperienced, that she in fact attracted such influence, would almost certainly be unable to recognize it for what it was and consequently would have little or no defence against it.

Rogelio shook his scraggy head, mauling his hair and raking his jowls once more. He knew that the intensity of the emanations being directed towards Jill had the potentiality, ultimately, of destroying her. They would rape her spirit, turn her onto the Downward Drift from which it was unlikely she would find an escape. And due to her innocence and vanity she was liable to misinterpret their intent from the very outset. She would not begin to understand the real motive until it was far too late.

He felt that he should be helping her; that he, as a Son And Daughter of Scompiglio – as one of *the primary* Sons And

163

Daughters of Scompiglio – should be making definite steps towards her protection. And not only hers, for it was glaringly obvious that the others in the room were also in direst need of guidance.

But how? What method was he to employ?

He sat back on his haunches and dipped into his cloth bag with the black-and-white South American design. He pulled out a small, green leatherette-bound volume entitled *The Book Of Imaginary Hauntings*, by Iddio E. Scompiglio. Closing his eyes and holding the book in the cupped palms of his hands, he allowed it to fall open at random. Then he opened his eyes and read what was printed there:

> 'The fish must (never) be allowed to
> leave the deep.'

Rogelio closed his eyes tight again and went into deepest meditation. How to apply this? In what manner was it meaningful within the context of this particular situation? What was the fundamental truth behind these immortal words of Iddio?

At length he roused himself and turned again to investigate the goings-on in the room. This time his mind came to rest upon his two good friends – or rather, upon his *three* good friends, for it was true, they had now formed a trinity.

Rogelio shimmered with happiness. He loved his good friends so very much. At times he was overwhelmed by the warmth of feeling he had for his good friends.

Margaret saw him looking and gave a little finger wave and a smile, emanated in his direction. Her emanations were pure and kind and strong. Gerald, catching her example, followed suit, and Rogelio beamed happily, flexed his little body with pleasure and was bathed in emanations of tenderness and love.

But a question mark floated now into his consciousness, irking him once more. He sensed the need for further illumination. Taking out his book again he repeated the little ritual and this time read:

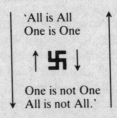

'All is All
One is One

One is not One
All is not All.'

His countenance cleared. This was one of his favourite passages, and somehow he had known that this would be the page at which the book fell open. Profound understanding poured into him and caused him to place the palms of his hands upon his breasts.

A sudden loud voice cut rudely and unexpectedly through the atmosphere of the room. Rogelio glanced up, startled. Conversation died and everyone looked unsure.

It was the room that had spoken. Now it spoke again: 'Door-bell,' it said. 'Dooorrr-bell.'

Rogelio saw Corinne and Samson exchange glances. Corinne said something about not expecting any more guests. She rose and left the room.

She returned almost immediately. With her was a large, sandy-haired man in a light grey suit, white shirt, open at the neck, and red carpet slippers.

'It's Hugh,' Rogelio heard Corinne say to her husband. 'He wants to borrow your hammer.'

Rogelio stared at the newcomer and his eyes widened in alarm. His voice rose involuntarily to his throat and caught there, emerging as a tiny, strangled, gargling sound which nobody heard. He gripped the denim of his baggy blue jeans and his limbs started to tremble. What was this? What could it possibly signify?

In appearance there was nothing about the man to give rise to such a reaction, but this in itself was a cause of great agitation to Rogelio, for he knew that the others could not be conscious of it. Because what was so utterly mind-shattering about Hugh was the fact that *he had no emanations at all*!

● ● ● ● ●

# 6

Hugh was a freelance journalist.

He was an amiable, droll, slightly eccentric though somewhat fiery-tempered Scot, who, with his wife, Angela, and their two teenage daughters, occupied an apartment on the floor above the Tallis's. He was forty-four, ruddy-faced and freckled, clean shaven, six feet tall and just a shade on the flabby side. His fair sandy hair was thinly distributed and liberally tinged with grey. His eyes, adequately supplied with crows' feet, were brown and bright and his expression was usually one of subtle, secret amusement.

He wrote articles and, less frequently, short stories for a variety of publications, and was an occasional offscreen contributor for current affairs programmes on independent television. Earlier in his career he had published, under different names and off his own back, as no publisher would touch them, a series of four books. All four were failures; they sank into instant oblivion, leaving him with considerable debts to pay off. The income he derived from writing now was modest, largely due to an unfortunate tendency he had at times of allowing his enthusiasm for a subject to override his actual mastery of it. When this occurred it could prove difficult to discern where the strict facts of a matter ended and Hugh's probably unwitting extrapolations began. For this reason discerning editors were wont to be otherwise engaged when a manuscript of his arrived on their desks.

Be that as it may, Hugh was successful in publishing a steady stream of his work.

The larger part of his income, however, came from a series of sound business investments he had made whilst still a young man in his twenties, with money left him by a dead godmother. It was this, not the typewriter or pen, that kept him in the lifestyle he had grown accustomed to.

Politics and the human mind were Hugh's pet subjects. He liked to think of himself as something of an authority in these fields – and no flyweight when it came to philosophy, either. Had circumstances not turned him into a family man he could have seen himself being a bit of a *primum mobile* in world affairs.

In conversation he generally spoke slowly and emphatically, and enunciated precisely – with his Caledonian lilt, almost quaintly. But again, he was apt to grow over-excited when caught up in a subject. Then his ruddy cheeks would deepen in colour, little flecks of spittle would gather in the corners of his mouth, and his speech would grow rapid and his elision unclear.

Oration, he firmly believed, was his forte. He practised regularly in front of his bedroom mirror and treated his family to lengthy mealtime discourses which, though their subject matter generally interested them little or not at all, often ended by rendering them near helpless with mirth. His unpredictable sense of humour and eccentric views of life made him popular with most people he came into contact with.

In short, Hugh was an engaging loon.

0

'I hope I'm not interrupting your little gathering,' he said as he followed Corinne into the Tallis's lounge. 'I didn't realize you had company. It's just that I'm putting up some shelves in Katrina's bedroom and I've gone and split the haft of my hammer.'

'Not at all,' Samson said, rising. He liked Hugh – he was possibly the only person he did like. He liked his wit and his cynicism and his spirit. He had spent some enjoyable hours sinking whiskies in Hugh's company. 'You must stop and have a drink with us. You can drink my health. It's my birthday; did you know?'

'I wasn't aware of the fact, but aye, you've persuaded me. I'm not one to say no to a drop of whisky – providing, that is, that you're sure I'm not being a nuisance.'

Corinne reassured him that he wasn't. She was experiencing a pang of guilt at having somehow not thought to invite him. 'We're always pleased to see you. Would you like something to eat? There's plenty. Help yourself.'

'Ah, thank you, no. We've eaten only an hour ago.' Hugh patted his belly with his hands.

Samson poured him a large Scotch, then left to look for a hammer.

'A good solid one, if you've got it, Samson! With a claw!'

When he returned, a gleaming, steel-hafted, twenty-ounce clawhammer in one hand, Corinne was introducing Hugh to the other guests.

'Beware of that one!' Samson warned him as he shook hands with Gerald Bailey. 'He might look like a hamster but there's more to him than meets the eye.'

'Oh, and how's that?'

'His feet and hands have been classified as lethal weapons. Isn't that so, Gerald?'

Gerald sniggered foolishly. 'Not yet, Sam. Not quite.'

Samson explained about Gerald's Kung Fu classes, at which the Scotsman raised an appraising eyebrow. He commented drily that that was all very well, but in his opinion there was no real substitute for the traditional Glaswegian method of a broken bottle in the face. Gerald fidgeted and squeezed Margaret's hand more tightly, and Samson laughed.

'Well, come on then, Hugh. Drink my health,' he said, raising his glass.

'Oh aye, happy birthday!' Hugh knocked back a mouthful. He swilled it around and swallowed. He smacked his lips. 'Aye, not bad. Not bad at all, though you can't beat the real thing. How old are you, by the way?'

'Thirty.' Samson spread his arms. 'And never been kissed.'

'Aah, you don't know what you've been missing, lad. Still, it's not at all a bad age to be – and I guess there's hope for you yet.' He was moving towards a seat when he spied the small head of Rogelio projecting above the back of the sofa. 'Och, and who's that?' he enquired, for they had not been introduced.

'Oh, this is Rogelio,' Corinne said quickly, before Samson had a chance. 'He's an artist. Rogelio Ramon Reyero.'

Hugh stepped over and extended a hand, obviously not quite sure what to make of the little man. 'And I'm very pleased to meet you!'

Wild-eyed, Rogelio gave him a bag of bones, then withdrew it quickly and sank back out of sight. Hugh took a seat on the other sofa, beside Richard and Jill.

'So what's new, Hugh?' Samson said, sitting down opposite Jill and smiling at her. He tinkled the ice in his glass and his gaze lingered on her mouth, shoulders and breasts.

Hugh shook his head lugubriously. 'Not much. Not much at all.'

'Oh, come on. That's not like you. You must have something you can tell us?'

Hugh placed his glass on the travertine table in front of him. He sat forward with the palms of his hands resting on his thighs, just above the knees, and his elbows akimbo. He stared at the steel clawhammer that Samson had laid in the centre of the table. He seemed to have something on his mind.

Eventually, without looking up, he said, 'Have you heard the terrible news?'

Silence.

'What's that?' Corinne asked.

Hugh raised his eyes to hers. 'They've done it.'

'What? Who have done what?'

He gave a grim sigh. 'They've done it. I never thought they would, but they have.'

'What? What have they done?' Corinne cried in exasperation.

'They've gone and elected that crazy old cowboy president!'

'Oh God, yes!' exclaimed Jill. 'I know! It's terrible! I never thought he would win.'

'I can't believe it,' Hugh went on quickly. I mean – ' he spread his hands and looked around appealingly. ' – how? How can they do it? What's the matter with them all? Can they not see that the man's completely unsuited to the job? For God's sake! A crumbling old actor like that and they go and make him boss of the world! You couldn't have a worse choice!'

'What's so bad about Ronald Reagan?' Samson asked, less because he favoured him – his knowledge and interest in politics were basically zero – than to egg Hugh on. He knew from experience what an enlivening, not to say enlightening, event a debate of this nature with the Scotsman could be.

Hugh turned on him. 'What's so bad about him! What's so bad about him! Oh Jesus Christ, man, do you really need to ask me that question? Can you not see for yourself? Don't you read the newspapers or watch the television? Do your own eyes and ears not tell you?'

Samson shrugged. 'I've seen the news, of course; but I can't say I've noticed anything particularly alarming about him. He seems like quite a decent old stick to me.'

'Aye, well he would to you, I suppose. You've no knowledge of human beings. That's half the trouble with the world today – no

169

insight, and too much apathy to be bothered about anything. You just want to sit around and let it all drift by, wait for somebody else to come along and sort out all the problems. But then you're the first to moan when they start sorting them out in ways that don't suit you. You can be sure of that. And the only people who do have it in them to get up off their backsides and start trying to put things in any kind of order are always the wrong ones! I mean, look! Look at the specimens we've got governing us now! Can you honestly say they inspire you with confidence? Can you? Oh Jesus Christ, I've never seen such an ill-trained bunch of monkeys! And we do it all the time! Look at history, man! It's the same story all the way down the bloody centuries!'

Samson pulled a dubious face and Hugh collected his breath. 'And Ronald Reagan, he's the worst rum monkey yet!' he resumed with a vengeance, rolling r's like he had them to spare. 'The man's an actor! A second-rate one, I'll grant you, but he's nevertheless adept at disguising his true feelings. Oh God, I can't believe it. I just can't believe it!'

'I do agree with you, I must say,' Margaret cooed. 'Apathy is a problem. There are few people with the right idea, and those that do make any attempt at changing things, as you say, Hugh, are invariably the wrong ones. And he worries me to death, too. How anybody could vote for a man like that I can't imagine.'

'Well, at least you've got the sense to see it,' Hugh said.

'I feel sorry for Jimmy Carter,' said Corinne. Her speech was just a little slurred and her glass just a little unsteady in her hand. 'He's been so unlucky lately, with the hostages in Iran and his helicopters crashing and everything . . .'

'But you still haven't told me what's so bad about him,' Samson said. 'I mean, you're not really condemning him simply because he's old and he's an actor, are you?'

'A failed actor, that's the vital point – ' Hugh began, but he was cut short sharply by Margaret: 'His bombs, Samson! Surely you don't support that? He wants to bring them over here!'

'Well, we've got to have some protection, haven't we?'

'Protection from what?'

'From the Russians, of course!'

'And you think Reagan's bombs will protect us? Samson, you're crazy! He just wants to site them over here so that if there is a war it'll be in our back garden and not his!'

'Aye, "Maggie Thatcher's would-be wedding present from the hero she wished she'd married", that's what I call 'em,' Hugh said, more than a little put out at having been cut short at such a critical point in his argument, and anxious to regain control immediately.

Samson frowned, laughed. 'What?'

'It's the psychology of the thing you've got to get a grasp of here,' Hugh told him. 'That's the all-important factor – and for some reason it's the one that's paid the least attention to in political affairs. I mean, have you not spotted the way she's been craftily kow-towing to him all through his campaign? Have you not noticed that look that comes into her eyes whenever the subject of Ronald Reagan is brought up?'

'No, I can't say I have.'

Hugh stretched his lips across his teeth. 'Aah, there's a lot more than politics involved here, let me tell you . . . And it's only the beginning, too. You see. Now that he's made president there'll be no holding her. It'll be, "yes Ronald, no Ronald, do with me as you will, Ronald . . ." You see, you've got to have an understanding of the workings of the female mind. And you've got to try and see the situation from Maggie's point of view: She's risen to a position more powerful than any woman has held in the history of this country – barring the queens, of course. She's a pioneering spirit, a woman with guts and determination who has toiled and sweated to reach her pinnacle. It's a remarkable accomplishment, there's no denying that. It's little short of miraculous.

'But what does she do now? She's made it to the top, and when she stops and takes a look around she sees that she is up there on her own, and there is nowhere else to go. There's weight, she sees, in the old saying that it's lonely at the top. There's no one left to respect now, no one for her to look up to – she's left them all behind.

'Now, this is not by anyone's standards a desirable state of affairs, for, believe me, every woman needs a man she can look up to, even one as hard-headed as Maggie.' Hugh paused here, anticipating a cry of protest from at least one of the females present. But nobody said a word, and seeing that he had their undivided attention, he went on, his eyes bright and earnest: 'But then! Suddenly! What does she see?' He part-raised himself dramatically from his seat, shading his eyes with one hand and peering into the middle-distance. 'Yes! There he is! Look! Striding

171

out of the sunset, six-guns toting and dewlap wobbling in the breeze – it's the man of her dreams! It's a shining, no-nonsense hero!

'And what a fine figure of a man he is too! He's mature and he's vigorous; he's flamboyant, but he's certainly not impetuous; he's charismatic, but always humble; influential, but affable and benign. And he's handsome, too, and quite remarkably successful. Oh my God! He's a father, a brother, a husband and a lover all in one. He's just about perfect!

'And as from this very day he's the most powerful man on the planet! Good Lord, he's more than perfect, he's little short of a god!

'So what does she do about it?' Hugh's voice, which had grown quite hectic, now fell to a more controlled level. He sucked errant spittle back into his mouth. 'Well, I'll tell you. She does what any woman would do, she sets out to get her man. And this is where the troubles begin, because, of course, it's a dream. There is no way she can ever have him, and she knows it.

'But a woman like Maggie is not to be dissuaded; the rituals of courtship must proceed – but they must also be retained strictly within the bounds of decency and protocol. So she begins by letting him know that she is there. She gives him her support, she lets him see that in her he has a staunch ally, an admiring friend, and – if he plays his cards right, who knows what else?

'And Ronald, well, he's no dummy when it comes to the ladies. He's been around a bit, he knows the signals. So he responds. But he responds symbolically, and so does she. They have to; their fantasy can only possibly be played out by use of symbols. And this might even be subconscious, I don't know. Whatever . . . it's a classic textbook syndrome; except that the symbols they have chosen to express their affections with happen to be the most potent and destructive playthings ever conceived of in the history of the human race.

'Look: Ronnie tells her about his missiles. He lets her have a glimpse of them. He tantalizes her. He waves them in her face. He tells her he would like to give her a few. And she is mightily impressed. She's weak at the knees. She wants them. Oh God, how she wants them!

'And she lays herself submissive (figuratively, that is). She gives him her body (in this case, England). She accepts with joy his projectiles. "Oh yes, Ronald! Put them here! Put them here!

Sink them deep into England's virgin soil!"' Hugh inhaled deeply, hissing through his teeth, shaking his head. 'Aye. Aye. It's the most blatant and unequivocal use of symbolism as a representation of the sexual act that I've ever come to witness. Freud would have given his right hemisphere to be alive today to see it!

'And what's so bloody incredible,' he added, 'is that nobody else has even spotted it!'

Samson sniffed pensively. He smiled to himself, chuckled and said, without malice, 'You're mad, Hugh.' He stood up to pour more drinks and change the tape cassette which had run out some time ago.

'That's as may be,' Hugh replied. He reached for the clawhammer and began slapping it rhythmically in his hand, 'but if I am I'm glad of it, because I'd hate to have to admit to being sane like the rest of you.'

At length Margaret said, dabbing her nose with her handkerchief, 'That's fascinating. I hadn't looked at it in that way before. It sounds, well, a little far-fetched at first, but when you give it some thought it's really quite plausible.'

'Of course it's plausible!' Hugh snapped. 'It's common sense. Plain, everyday, common or garden sense – and that's the thing the world's most lacking in these days.'

'Yes, I agree. But that is because the vast majority of people give their allegiance to the wrong leaders. The wrong *type* of leaders. I think you're absolutely right in that respect. And it would certainly pay dividends if it were made compulsory for the persons we elect into power to undergo a thorough psychological examination *before* they are allowed to take a position of any influence or make any important decisions. We don't know a thing about their backgrounds or their mental conditions, it's true. They could be anybody! I mean, look at Hitler!

'And what's worse is that they don't actually know anything about why they are there, what their real purpose should be. They're so wrapped up in their dreary, never-changing, day-to-day political humdrum that they can't see anything beyond it. They don't give any attention to our spiritual nature . . .'

Hugh nodded, missing her gist. 'Aye, and I'll tell you something else: Reagan's mental condition is bordering on the precarious in my book. He's no politician, he's a demagogue and a warmonger masquerading as a benign old gentleman; a mad cowboy shooting it out in the O.K. corral – and he wants to use our O.K. corral! It's fitting you should bring in Adolf Hitler there, because if you want my opinion the two are of like mind.'

'Oh, come on, Hugh,' Corinne objected. 'You can't go making sweeping statements like that. I know the man might be less than desirable as a world leader, but to glibly compare him to Adolf Hitler without anything to back it up with . . .'

'And who says I've got nothing to back it up with?'

'Well, have you?'

'Aye, I have. And if you'll refrain from interrupting me I'll tell you what it is.'

Corinne looked doubtful. 'All right. Go on, then.'

Hugh cleared his throat. 'Right. Now, the first thing to take into account is that the man is a failed actor – '

'What!' Corinne was incredulous. 'Hugh, how can you say that? He's made dozens of films! He's a millionaire!'

Hugh exploded. 'Jesus Christ Almighty, woman! I'm about to explain things if you'll only let me get a word in edgeways!' He turned to Samson. 'Can you not keep your woman under control, Samson? She's going to drive me to violence in a minute!'

Samson chuckled. 'Corinne, be quiet or I shall have to have you ejected.'

'Sorry,' said Corinne with a faint smile. She too was fond of Hugh, although she saw him rarely, and she too found him amusing. 'Carry on, Hugh. I promise not to interrupt again.'

'Very well. Now, the point I want to impress on you is that, although by our standards Ronald Reagan might appear to be an immensely successful man, I believe that in his own terms the opposite is the case. He conceives of himself as a dismal failure, no matter to what heights he may soar.' He paused, surveyed the others hotly to discourage any possible intercession on the new president's behalf, 'You see, Ronald Reagan, being of an artistic inclination – and I'm going to be using the term artist here in its broadest sense – possesses, or is possessed by, an artistic mind. And the mind of the artist, be he actor, painter, musician or whatever, is not like that of the average human being.' (The Baileys turned to one another at this, exchanged small congratulatory nods and smiles.)

'It is susceptible to certain bents and strivings, certain internal

174

stresses that the majority of us are only minimally aware of, despite your thoughts to the contrary. The true artist is psychotic, bordering on the psychopathic. You see, in psychological terms the distinction between the mental processes of the artist and those of the psychopath is extremely tenuous. Both feel themselves to be social misfits, and their concomitant insecurity and inability to integrate themselves with society makes them miserable. It compels them to seek other ways of self-expression and recognition.

'It's a gross form of egoism, if you like; but it's an egoism with a double edge. For no matter how aware they might be of the irrationality of their thoughts and feelings they remain slaves to them. They must do as they direct. If you want a more authoritative opinion on this you can take a look at Freud's *Paths to the Formation of Symptoms* if you like. You can't get much more authoritative than that without approaching God.

'Now then, virtually the only distinction between the artist and the psychopath is the means they are driven to choose by which to try and appease these feelings, these "powerful instinctual needs", to borrow Freud's phrase. The artist, through his or her chosen art form, stands a chance of achieving the recognition and even the mass adulation he craves. And depending upon the individual concerned it may or may not be enough to satisfy him.

'But the psychopath has no such outlet. His frustrations are vented in other, socially unacceptable ways. They can drive him to blind hatred, to murder and destruction. And it goes without saying that this, ultimately, does not bring him the contentment he seeks.

'But to get back to Reagan. It's my belief that he went into acting solely in search of wealth and fame and adoration. And I'll not deny you that to a large degree he achieved this. But he was never a great actor. He was never a John Wayne, or an Olivier. He was, for the most part, a B-movie star. And I think this rankled, deeply. For within himself I'm in no doubt he needed to be number one. And I think his ego was thwarted so badly that, upon reaching an age where he knew he could never attain to the heights he aspired, it compelled him to opt out, to move into a profession where he might still have a chance. It compelled him, in fact, to press for the ultimate: to become ruler of the planet, where he might be idolized by the population of the entire world. And look you!' Hugh exclaimed loudly, 'he's very nearly done it!'

His face was outraged and contemptuous. 'He won't stop there. He won't be able to. In his own eyes he is not a success. He's a failed artist. And there is truly no more dangerous personality for a leader than that.

'I said he had a mind like Adolf Hitler, and I've no need to tell you of the destruction he brought on the world – and that was when he was winning! When Hitler finally came to face up to the fact that defeat was inevitable he passed the order that Germany be razed to the ground. He wanted nothing left behind for the Allied forces to find. He ordered that the civilian population be shot and that his soldiers commit suicide. That's how bad Adolf Hitler felt when things got a little bit out of hand.

'And did you know,' he concluded in ominous tones, 'that Hitler too was a failed artist?'

There was a silence lasting perhaps ten seconds (which Rogelio, still accumulating space behind the sofa, received with near reverential awe).

'Aye,' Hugh said, pleased with the response. 'As a teenager he tried twice to enter the Vienna Academy of Fine Arts. He failed the entrance examination both times.'

It was Samson who broke the silence. He expelled air noisily and pulled a sceptical face. 'That's stretching things a bit, Hugh, isn't it? What kind of wine did you have with your dinner this evening?'

'It might sound a little simplistic, true enough,' Hugh conceded, 'but that's only to help me get it across to the likes of you who knows nothing about the subject. In point of fact it should be obvious to you. But I'm writing an article, as it happens – have been for some months now – and all the relevant psychological, historical and political data are in it. I recommend you have a look at it sometime.'

Samson was not bowled over by the idea but Corinne and Jill, and the Baileys especially, were agreed that it would make an interesting read.

A mischievous glint came to Hugh's eye and he placed the haft of the clawhammer beneath his chin, smirking. 'It's a big problem we have here,' he mused, 'but it's not insurmountable, for the essence of any problem is like that of time.'

'What?' demanded Samson.

'Time. The essential nature of time, according to Einstein and modern-day physics, is that it is not constant and neither is it absolute. It's relative. It varies according to the point of view of the observer.'

'And what the hell's that got to do with anything?'

'Well, you can apply the same principle to any problem you might be faced with. Just change your own position in relation to the problem. Lateral thinking – shift your viewpoint so you see it from another angle.'

'You've lost me there, Hugh,' Samson said peevishly. 'What are you talking about?'

'What I'm saying is if you look hard enough and in the right direction it's always possible to find a more optimistic view of any problem. Including Ronald Reagan.'

'Such as?'

Hugh grinned. 'Well, why not try looking upon him as America's answer to the world population problem?'

Samson stared at him blankly. Hugh chuckled, then Gerald chipped in with something he had been wanting to say for some time but had been unable to find an opportune moment for. It was something he had seen on a lavatory wall recently. 'Lee Harvey Oswald,' he said, 'where are you now that America needs you?'

0

'Maybe someone will assassinate him soon,' Samson suggested airily, 'before he has the chance to do too much damage.'

The Scotsman smiled. 'Aye, it's always a possibility.'

'More a probability, I'd have said. Are American presidents in season right now?'

'They've been in season ever since John Wilkes Booth popped Lincoln way back in 1865. I think it's generally accepted that they're fair game at any time. But, you know, presidents are notoriously shy beasties. They might be seen quite frequently from a distance, but it's nigh impossible these days to get close enough to one to shoot him, even with a good sniper's rifle.'

'Shut up, you two!' Corinne cried. 'That's horrible. You shouldn't joke like that about murdering another human being.'

'How should we joke about it then?' asked Samson.

'It's wrong,' she protested, clearly upset. 'Don't say it. It could so easily happen. It's . . . immoral!'

Hugh turned to her now with a reproachful expression. Slowly, gravely, he said to her, 'Surely it's better for two men with neither the intent nor the power to speak jokingly of killing one man than it is for one man with both the intent *and* the power to speak with certainty of putting in jeopardy the lives of millions?'

Samson raised his eyebrows and gave an approving nod, impressed by this. He turned to Gerald and remarked, sarcastically aside, 'I'll bet you wish you'd said that, don't you?'

Gerald beamed and looked at the insides of the lenses of his spectacles.

Corinne fell silent. She could not think of a reasonable counter. In fact, she could no longer think very clearly of anything at all. She was pretty drunk. She was not used to alcohol and she knew she had already gone over the limit this evening. Her head had become quite muzzy. She was unable to hold her attention on anything for any length of time. The voices and music around her buzzed and whined and she drifted into them and away again with little control over her mental faculties. She could feel herself sinking inexorably towards a stupor.

She hardly cared. She had struggled so hard to try and hold herself together, but now it didn't seem to matter anymore. She felt so let-down, so bitterly disappointed by everything. All her effort, all her organization . . . all for nothing.

Nothing.

She sipped her brandy. So what did it matter if she was drunk? Samson was drunk. Samson was acting like a pig. He made her so angry. And Margaret and Gerald . . . Rogelio . . . it didn't make sense. It was all so crazy.

She looked dazedly at Richard. He was a strange young man, but she liked him. She felt a gentle, sisterly, even motherly kind of affection for him. And when they had met earlier, in the hall . . . how strange, the way he had looked at her . . . She could not recall a man having looked at her quite like that before. It had been a little disconcerting. He was much younger than her. It had made her feel quite shy.

Richard had finished his joint – Corinne wondered that he had smoked it all on his own – and he sat now with the smouldering roach on one hand and his bread in the other, his plate balanced on his knees. She held out an ashtray for him. He had been using one to flick the ash into but he seemed unsure of what to do with the roach. He raised his eyes blearily to hers and she smiled. He stubbed the roach into the ashtray. He smoothed his hand over his short blond hair. He looked shattered. He gazed at his bread once more.

Corinne watched him till her mind drifted away again. She remembered Tamasin and she lowered her head to hide her eyes.

'A problem here, I think, is that when you start talking about death in terms of millions it loses all meaning,' Margaret observed. 'You can't really envisage it. That's how politicians can get away with such appalling ideas. I mean, Corinne is right, it is wrong to talk like that about murdering someone, but I think she is reacting because, when you talk in terms of one or two human beings, it is real. You can imagine it and it offends you, whereas she can't really envisage the effects of a nuclear exchange.'

Hearing this Corinne was indignant. Her protest had been misconstrued. She certainly was able to envisage the consequences of a nuclear exchange – as much as was anybody, that is – and she felt she ought to put Margaret in her place for suggesting otherwise. But she didn't trust herself to say it. She was too taut. And she didn't dare raise her head. And she felt so *heavy*. She just wished they would all leave her alone.

Hugh bristled at Margaret's words. 'Aye, that's a problem right enough. But the real problem is this: What the hell is wrong with the lot of us that we can allow a lunatic like that to become boss of the world?'

He slap-slap-slapped the gleaming, steel-shafted, twenty-ounce clawhammer menacingly in his hands.

'I don't understand how *anybody* can listen to a man like Reagan,' Margaret said. 'And how we can allow him to Lord it over us here in Britain is beyond me. We're supposed to be so proud of our heritage . . . and we're just letting America rule us.

'What's needed is a revolution. On the continent they would have revolted. In Italy or Spain. They would never allow it to happen over there. Still, you never know, I suppose,' she added as an afterthought, 'perhaps there will be when the time actually comes.'

'Revolution is no longer a revolutionary act,' Gerald waxed philosophically. 'Not anymore. Not in this day and age. It means nothing. It's become too commonplace.'

Margaret looked at him curiously and Samson rolled his eyes as though in pain. He nudged Jill's toe with his own and wailed, 'Oh Christ, he's off! I told you!'

Hugh admonished him. 'Just a minute, Samson. There's no need to be so scornful. That's a pertinent observation he's made there.' He was distant for a moment, rolling Gerald's statement around in his mind. He took a mouthful of whisky and savoured it in the same way, then held out his glass for Samson to refill. 'Aye, I like it,' he said. 'It has a ring to it; a ring almost of familiarity, although I don't recall ever having heard it before. Have you just thought it up?'

Gerald nodded happily and a look of amusement once more lit Hugh's features. 'You might compare it to farting in respectable company,' he said. 'The effect would be more or less the same. Some people will tut-tut a little and others will turn up their noses. One or two might even laugh, but most will prefer to ignore it if they can, try and pretend that it didn't happen, or that if it did they didn't notice.'

He chuckled merrily, highly appreciative of his own wit, and Margaret turned to Samson with a smile and remarked, sarcastically aside, 'I'll bet you wish you'd said that, don't you?'

0

'So you're a psychologist, are you?' Margaret enquired politely of Hugh.

'No, not exactly,' he replied. 'I'm a writer. A journalist.' (And Rogelio, who had been listening intently to the discussion, let out a great sigh of relief as cognition flooded his soul – for it was written in the works of Iddio E. Scompiglio that journalists don't emanate. At least, not always. This, according to the sage, is a quality they have in common with psychiatrists and soldiers. He goes on to state that, although a similar tendency might be expected of most politicians, Christian fundamentalists and others of an affinitive bent, such is perceivably not the case. 'There is nothing anomalous here,' he explains: 'those in the latter categories are possessed of inchoate minds whilst those in the former are merely primitive.'

Rogelio, of course, ought to have seen this the moment Hugh walked into the room, but so much was happening, and all at once, that his brain was having difficulty unscrambling it all.)

Hugh said, 'I read psychology when I was a student, though, and it's a subject I like to keep myself in tune with. If there's ever going to be any kind of change for the better in the world it's going to be necessary to educate the mass of humanity in matters of the mind and human behaviour. It's obvious to me that we're all of us bloody demented, and in fact I wrote some books about exactly that some years ago, though nobody understood them – I think they got taken toc seriously – and before we can hope to make any kind of positive progress there's going to have to occur a radical change in the attitudes we hold towards ourselves and each other, as individuals and as a species.'

Margaret pursed her lips. 'That's interesting,' she said, smiling obsequiously. 'My husband's a bit of a writer, aren't you, darling.'

Hugh scowled. He had been hoping she would ask him to continue, give him the opportunity to expound upon his long-term scheme for the salvation of mankind.

'Are you, Gerald? I didn't know you wrote,' Corinne said, her attention momentarily aroused, for no particular reason, by this piece of information.

'Well, I don't, really,' said Gerald uncomfortably.

'Yes you do. Don't be silly,' Margaret scolded him. 'You're always writing something or other.'

'Just scribbling. Nothing of any importance,' Gerald apologized.

'He's getting very good,' Margaret said proudly. 'His latest story is very clever. It takes the form of a letter to the Prime Minister, written by a worried mum whose son has – well, I won't say it, because there's a brilliant twist at the end and it would spoil it for you if I gave it away. I have it here with me somewhere, would you like me to read it to you? It isn't very long. Where is it, now? I'm going to send it off to a magazine for publication. In fact, it's very fortunate you're here, Hugh. Perhaps you could give us some idea of where to send it, being in the business yourself?'

'Aye, perhaps,' said Hugh, without enthusiasm.

'Here it is!' She withdrew from her handbag two sheets of notepaper, both sides of which had been written on in a thin, blue-inked scrawl.

'Don't you think Gerald should read it, as he's the author?' Corinne suggested.

'Oh no!' said Gerald, and Margaret added that, as the letter was supposed to have been written by a woman, it would sound more authentic if she read it. 'It's called "What Has Happened To The Son I Knew?"' she announced. She held the two sheets in front of her and looked around with a sparkle. 'Are we sitting comfortably?' She cleared her throat, took a deep breath and began:

'"What Has Happened To The Son I Knew?" by Gerald R. Bailey. "Dear Mrs Thatcher, I feel it beholden upon myself to bring to your attention a scandalous perpetration that has been rife within this country, and indeed within the whole world, for many years now, and which is causing distress and heartbreak to persons from all walks of life, including myself.

I am a widow. Three years ago my husband, Clyde, succumbed to cancer of the liver. Soon after that my eldest son, Rolf, was tragically killed in an horrendous car accident, which meant that my sole remaining joy in life, my only comfort and solace, was my youngest son, Eddie. And now I no longer even have him because it has transpired that he has been cruelly wrested from me. But he is not dead, Mrs Thatcher. Not yet. He has fallen prey to the evil organization of which I speak.

This organization into which he has been sucked by subtle techniques of brainwashing and mental suggestion and persuasion, has no qualms about teaching him to relinquish all his former values and to leave his family and his home. They are bent upon turning him into a moron. He has been compelled to swear blind obedience to their cause and to devote himself wholly and with total disregard for anything, *including his own life*, to the furtherance of their aims.

And this organization proclaims that, in accordance with the wishes of its leaders, *the lives of others may be of no consequence either*!

Mrs Thatcher, I ask you, how can it be that my son has been drawn into the clutches of such an organization? How is it that an organization such as this one can be allowed to operate in a country like ours? You may ask yourself, What is happening in the world today that persons both young and old can be drawn under the baleful influence of such a malignant, insidious power?

No doubt you will be shocked and moved as you peruse the contents of this letter, Mrs Thatcher; but will it shock you further when I inform you that this organization holds a legal standing in Britain, and that it operates under so-called Christian ethics? I hope and trust that it will.

But what I have to tell you next will shake you even more. For not only does this organization have legal standing but it is openly supported by your government! And its ultimate aim, Mrs Thatcher, under *your* leadership, is total subjugation of any who might attempt to stand in its way.

I am sure that you will agree with me that this is an appalling and unbelievable situation that must be set right. I am sure that, once you come to understand the full implications of what is occurring within this fiendish organization which you control, you will agree with me that something must be done and that my son, along with those thousands of other innocents, must be released from its iron grip.

And so I appeal to you with my heart and soul to lend me your wholehearted support in this matter of utmost urgency. As a mother yourself I am certain you can understand and sympathize with my feelings, and will agree with me that something must be done post haste to secure an end to the furtherance of this terrible perpetration. My son will almost certainly die without your intervention, but before that occurs he is liable to be used as an unwitting instrument to bring about the deaths of others.

You must help because, yes, Mrs Thatcher, I am sure you have recognized and understood already the organization of which I speak. Eddie, my only remaining child, has joined the army.

Yours sincerely,

0

Margaret laid aside the sheets of paper and looked up with a slightly haughty expression. At first nobody said anything; nobody seemed quite certain of how best to express their feelings. They were all waiting for someone else to begin.

Hugh stared at the carpet. Samson touched Jill's ankle again lightly with his toe and pulled a mocking face. Jill averted her eyes, trying to keep her smile a secret. Richard had not heard a word; his expression was one of bewildered blankness. And Julia just looked disgusted.

It was Corinne who spoke first. 'Well done, Gerald! What a clever idea! That's very thought-provoking!' – but even as she said it she was aware, through her drunkenness, that her tone was far too effusive. She glanced at Samson, praying that he would not make any comment.

Gerald bobbed and shifted lankily, grinning like a baboon, but making no sound other than a series of erratic snuffles. Margaret was evidently very pleased with him, and she told the others so: 'He has an author's approach to life,' she said, one hand brushing some flecks of dandruff from his shoulder. 'I've always told him that. I noticed it years ago and I've always tried to encourage it. Now I believe it's really beginning to blossom forth. He's becoming quite intent upon it, aren't you, darling. He often disappears for hours at a time into the bedroom so that he can write.'

'Are you sure he's not just playing with himself in there?' enquired Samson, and Jill's shoulders shook.

'Samson!' Corinne cried.

Margaret chose to ignore him, turning instead to Hugh and smiling sweetly. 'What do you think, Hugh? Speaking as an expert in the field, where would you go to get it published? Do you think we should send it away?'

'Aye, I think you should,' Hugh said, poker-faced.

Not catching on, Margaret asked, 'Well, to whom would you send it?'

'Och, I don't know. Fiction isn't really my field. I'm a journalist in the main these days.' He tickled the claw-peen lightly with two fingers, then, unable to resist the impulse, added, 'Why don't you try sending it to the *War Cry*?'

Samson creased up at this, and Jill spluttered into her drink and turned away, her body convulsed with silent laughter.

'I see,' said Margaret. She folded the sheets of notepaper in offended silence and returned them to her bag.

'It's an interesting idea,' Corinne said quickly. 'However did you think it up?'

Gerald was in the act of removing his pullover. He folded it and laid it on his lap, resting his arms upon it and twiddling with the left-hand cuff of the pale blue nylon shirt he had on underneath. 'Well, it's interesting, really, the way it came about,' he said with some hesitancy. Nobody attacked him so he went on, 'I was meditating one afternoon . . .' he paused again '. . . reflecting on a passage I had just been reading from the works of Iddio. It was a particularly difficult passage and its true meaning was not at first at all clear to me. But gradually, as I concentrated upon it, I began to see what he was saying, so to speak, behind the words. And then my thoughts seemed to take on a volition of their own. They moved on, in a logical sequence I suppose, but somehow without my consciously generating them. It's very difficult to explain, but it was as if I were simply observing them as they flowed across my mind. And I became inspired. This idea began to germinate within me, growing, with a feeling of mounting excitement, and I found myself stimulated to creativity.'

'Who was that you said?' Hugh asked. 'The works of who?'

'Iddio. Iddio E. Scompiglio.'

Margaret returned to the conversation with some animation. 'You recall what you were saying a few minutes ago, Hugh? About there being a need of some kind of radical change in the world if things are to improve? Well, did you know that this change is actually already taking place? And that it is being brought about by one man?'

Hugh shook his head. 'No, I wasn't aware of that.'

'Well, it's true! He is with us now, working for the good of mankind!'

Samson sat forward, indignant. '*Who?*'

'Iddio E. Scompiglio.'

'Who the hell,' demanded Samson imperiously, 'is Iddio E. Scompiglio when he's at home?'

*Author's Intervention*

It becomes expedient, nay, imperative at this point to interrupt the narrative in order to advance a few elucidatory items concerning this controversial and enigmatic figure, Iddio E. Scompiglio. For this reason inserted here is a short biographical conspectus entitled –


## IDDIO E. SCOMPIGLIO: LEGENDS, MYTHS AND CERTAINTIES.
### (i)

Firstly it has to be said that where Iddio E. Scompiglio is concerned there are *no* certainties. The man is an enigma from head to toe. No records of any kind (other than his own published works) can be found under that name and there is no known documentary evidence to prove he even exists, although his followers will deny this quite fervently.

A religious cult, its members numbering some several thousands worldwide, has been founded under his name and has established 'centres' or churches in some twenty or so countries around the world. Its administrative headquarters are based in Rome and Southern California. The purpose of this cult, known as the

Church of the Sons And Daughters of Scompiglio, is, to quote their own literature, to 'apply the teachings of the Founder in order to bring about a significant advancement in the evolution of human consciousness', to 'restore peace and sanity to a disunited world', and to 'liberate the individual from the all-pervasive thralldom of Not-Know, thus bringing him or her to a real and glorious understanding of the true spiritual nature of mankind'.

These teachings, however, are delivered not by Scompiglio himself but by certain 'Proclaimers' – high-ranking officials of his church, supposedly appointed by him to convey to the world the knowledge contained, somewhat cryptically, in his written works. These works are three in number, *The Book of Imaginary Hauntings*, *The Telic Scrawls* (so called because it has been reproduced in its entirety in the original longhand script – something, acknowledged wryly by the author himself, that does not make for a particularly easy read), and *The Pronouncements To The Scions*. This last volume, not available to the general public, is said to contain rules and regulations for fulfilled living, various ceremonies, rituals, hymns, prayers and obeisances to be performed in honour of Scompiglio, and certain esoteric essays not printed elsewhere.

Perhaps one of the most surprising things about Iddio E. Scompiglio is his sense of humour. Evident in the extreme in much of his work, it is not a quality one normally associates with mystics, sages and religious leaders. It is this (though not only this) that has led some critics to argue that he is nothing more than a practical joker, intent on causing confusion and making money out of it. His work, they say, is misleading, deliberately obscurantist, and ultimately meaningless. He is a charlatan, a lunatic or a clown, or perhaps all three, for he writes in such wildly divergent styles that one cannot help but question whether it is all the product of the same mind.

I do not hold with this argument, however. Having studied his works quite intensively I am inclined to give him more credit. He admits himself that his work is 'demanding', and he recommends that in order to gain a true and full understanding of his writings they should be read at least three times. And, this aside, I find it hard to accept that so many thousands of sane and educated persons throughout the world can be duped so completely as to run their entire lives in strictest accordance with the precepts set down in a couple of volumes containing nothing but a load of obscure, arcane gobbledygook. And gobbledygook moreover, written by a practical joker or jokers, lunatics or charlatans who may not even exist!

Recent years have seen several allegations levelled against the Church of the Sons And Daughters of Scompiglio to the effect that it employs 'nefarious methods' of recruitment and conversion into its ranks. Cries of brain-washing, hypnotism, drugs, black magic and other forms of skulduggery have been heard, as well as claims that the church has been coercing its members into coughing-up exorbitant amounts of money as a condition of continued membership. None of this, as far as I can ascertain, has ever been attested in a court of law.

My own introduction to Iddio E. Scompiglio occurred some years ago. I was browsing in a pokey, secondhand bookstore in Hackney, East London, and happened to come across a pile of dusty old books left unshelved in a corner. Sifting through them I discovered the two aforementioned works. I had not heard of Scompiglio at this time, neither was I familiar with the Sons And Daughters of Scompiglio. The titles caught my eye and, as I was vaguely on the lookout for a guru at the time, a quick perusal was enough to persuade me to buy them.

It was not only the contents that intrigued me; the publishers, Scion Press, were unknown to me; their address was not given, nor was a date of publication; there were no biographical notes nor a photograph of the author; and one of the books, as already mentioned, was printed entirely in longhand.

I enquired of the shopkeeper as to further information concerning Scompiglio. He was a flabby, wheezy, squint-eyed septuagenarian with wild grey hair and florid cheeks. His briar pipe transformed his shop into a hazardous reminder of London at its worst during the pre-clean air bill days. He told me he had never heard of him. Those books, he said, had been lying in that corner for as long as he could remember. He had never got around to sorting them out.

I asked him how much he wanted for them. He said thirty pence each – a steal as far as I was concerned. Then he tried to sell me some of his poetry. He had had it xeroxed that morning. He seemed to think it would benefit me to read it.

I declined as politely as I could, paid him his money, and left.

At home I sat down and began to study my two new acquisitions; and having done so I was left with a feeling of bemusement. I did not have the faintest notion of what to make of them. Scompiglio's writings are both perplexing and bizarre. At times it is exceedingly difficult to take him seriously, but at others one begins to suspect that one is studying the thoughts of a true genius. His style is sometimes so steeped in abstruseness as to be virtually impenetrable and, conversely, can at times appear so naive that one is tempted to dismiss him and relegate the book to the waste-paper bin.

He makes frequent and often incomprehensible use of allegory, occasionally loses himself in bombast and pedantry, has little jokes at his own and his readers' expense, and contradicts in one essay things that he has gone to great lengths to explain in another . . . And all of this, one cannot help but be convinced, is deliberate. But why? To what end?

The emotional tone of his writings varies to a considerable degree. He will ask questions of you with the innocence of a child, advise you with the patience of a kindly schoolmaster, lull you or arouse you with the dexterity of a playful lover, persuade you with the tenderness and understanding of a protective parent: And sometimes he will rave with all the venom of a thwarted dictator.

And through it all, unmistakably, comes a message. The message is this: Iddio E. Scompiglio holds our future in his hands. He is a purveyor of great knowledge, a man of infinite wisdom, a man unlike other men, to whom the secrets of the Cosmos have been entrusted. He is the New Redeemer, the Saviour of mankind. He has the power to release us. He brings enlightenment and spiritual fulfilment to all who are prepared to follow his Way.

Now all this might sound like so much guff, but the fact is that Scompiglio is gifted with an extraordinary degree of literary virtuosity, and despite – or perhaps even because of – the unorthodox and at times quite outrageous manner in which many of his discourses are delivered, he remains throughout the larger part of his work, at the least, *convincing*.

I found this hard to come to terms with. Being then and now of a sceptical turn of mind I was surprised to find that his work was having a quite marked effect upon my thinking. It was as if, by the very act of reading him, some latent, unperceived part of me was being rekindled and was responding quite forcefully to what I had read. And I have to confess, reluctantly, to being unable to put my finger on the element in his writing responsible for this.

What I wish to do here is to attempt an objective and impartial assessment of his two books, *The Book of Imaginary Hauntings* and *The Telic Scrawls*. This is hardly an easy task, for his cogency will, I fear, be dissipated in a synoptical review of this nature. Many of his claims are, I feel, to be taken with a pinch of salt, but at the same time one should attempt to look beyond the words and not allow oneself to be blinded by scepticism.

*The Book of Imaginary Hauntings* is a slender volume of precepts, dictums, epigrams and aphoristic verse. It is Scompiglio's *vade mecum* – a handbook for his Sons And Daughters to carry on their persons at all times and to turn to frequently for inspiration and advice.

Many of the entries contained herein may be, at first glance, distinctly lacking in meaning. A degree of familiarity with the ways and practices of the Sons And Daughters of Scompiglio, and with the jargon employed by them, is a prerequisite to the book's being of any kind of value.

It is interesting to speculate on the sources of Scompiglio's ideas. Much is owed to traditional Eastern thought. Elements of the Vedic scriptures can be found, for example, and traces of Buddhism, as well as more than a sprinkling of wisdom culled and adapted from Taoist texts such as the Lao-Tzu and Chuang-Tzu. Sufism and Zoroastrianism have left their mark, too, and nearer home, the influence of such luminaries as Immanuel Kant, Henri Bergson, Helena Blavatsky and the twentieth-century Russian mystic, George Ivanovitch Gurdjieff, is quite marked. Noticeably absent is any form of indebtedness to the distorted modern-day Judaeo-Christian or Islamic dogmas.

But perhaps by attempting to trace origins in such a way I am doing Scompiglio an injustice. His followers claim that his doctrine is universal, and as such is bound to contain elements of the teachings of masters who went before. But more importantly, they insist, he brings a new message, a new freedom, a new method of deliverance. Iddio E. Scompiglio is the one true Father of All. He is Exemplary. He is Unique.

And with this latter I cannot help but agree.

*The Telic Scrawls* is a much meatier tome. It comprises a series of more than thirty lectures and dissertations of a philosophical and mystico-religious nature, all of which are purportedly designed to be of immediate practical value to the serious student. As far as I am able to make out the ultimate aim seems to be to persuade and convert the reader in the shortest time possible.

Some of the titles attract the attention, viz. 'The Third Coming Of Christ', 'The Journey From Ylem', and 'The Connection Between Man And Consciousness And The Failure Of The Two To Interact In Accordance With The Cosmic Design', to name but three. The essays are generally quite lengthy – certainly too long for ungelded reproduction here – and so I have selected a handful which I present now in precis form.

A convenient one to begin with is 'The Ages of Being'. It is shorter than most, it is representative of the rest of Scompiglio's work, and it is fairly straightforward, if somewhat bizarre. It is intended as a guide to those treading, or just contemplating treading, the uncertain path to enlightenment.

A human lifespan, according to Scompiglio, is divided into seven distinct ages or periods through which all of us must pass – though not everyone will necessarily pass through all seven. (Any apparent debt to Jacques' celebrated speech from *As You Like It* is not, upon fuller investigation, upheld. Interestingly, though, Scompiglio does pay tribute to Shakespeare elsewhere in his work, referring to him almost reverentially as a 'Conscious Mind'.)

The first of these periods is called the Period of Innocence. Its duration can vary, depending very much upon the developing consciousness of the individual concerned. Throughout this period no responsibility or blame may be laid upon the individual, for he or she is of course a mere infant, and as such is wholly reliant upon others. Any choices or actions made by the individual during the Period of Innocence are the outcome of impressions received from the outside world. For this reason, Scompiglio says, parents should be pupils of their children as well as teachers, for in the behaviour of the infant are mirrored in their most pristine form the attitudes of the adults with whom it has no choice but to associate.

After the Period of Innocence comes the Period of Confusion and Discovery. This can last for anything from five to fifteen years. It is the period during which the individual first begins to form an independent consciousness. During this time come the first ink-lings that the data absorbed from the parents or guardians over the preceding years may not necessarily be correct or true. This can be a source of great and often unconscious inner conflict for the individual, for he or she is still very much dependent, physically and emotionally, upon the parents. His inner response to this situation will colour and often determine the course the rest of his life will take.

Those persons who emerge from the Period of Confusion and Discovery after only a relatively short time, say five to eight years, will generally pass on into the Period of Insignificant Attainment. This is a dangerous period; spiritual development hangs here in the balance. Specious bounties and objective enticements tend to lure and sway the individual. Immediate gratification of the senses takes paramountcy; the inner voice, if heard, is usually silenced or disregarded.

Generally, what happens now is that as a natural consequence of the actions taken and the choices made during the Period of Insignificant Attainment, the individual enters into the Period of Complacence and Eventual Acceptance. The vast majority follow this road, Scompiglio says, and for them there is little hope. Unless arousal can be generated by external means this period will mark the end of their spiritual development.

There are, of course, exceptions to this rule, as there are to all the examples given. Scompiglio discusses these in some detail but space does not permit more than a mention in passing here.

It is far better, Scompiglio states, though infinitely more distressing at the time, for the Period of Confusion and Discovery to be allowed to run its full course – say twelve to fifteen years. Some – but sadly not all – who survive this lengthy ordeal will emerge from it into the Period of Real Attainment. For them life holds no bounds, they are firmly set on the Spiritual Path, and providing they hold fast and do not falter or fall foul of the numerous pitfalls along the Way, they will move on into the final stage, Knowing and Seeing. Knowing and Seeing is not referred to as a Period, for, although it has a beginning, it has no end. Knowing and Seeing is the realm of the sage; Knowing and Seeing are the two points that form the angles at the base of the symbolic Triangle of Perfect Understanding, at whose apex is Illumination.

The percentage of persons arriving even so far as the Period of Real Attainment is, unhappily, minimal. More often the individual will emerge from a prolonged Period of Confusion and

Discovery only to fall into the Period of Despair, and thence the Downward Drift. Once there, as with those trapped in the Period of Complacence and Eventual Acceptance, little hope remains. With the passing of each day spent on the Downward Drift the possibility of success or attainment diminishes considerably and proportionately. In reality, says Scompiglio, this period is nothing more than a further prolongment, though highly intensified, of the Period of Confusion and Discovery.

Each of these periods is subdivided into several 'mini-periods', detailed thoroughly by Scompiglio, and it is only through being made aware of all these that one can hope to evolve along the True Path. According to Scompiglio the number of persons alive today who are currently evolving along that path without the benefit of his guidance is precisely nil.

'The Nature of Up' and 'God' are two dissertations rolled into one, dealing with the bloated sense of importance we humans attach to ourselves when attempting to comprehend such basic questions as the nature of existence, the universe and God. Though guilty of somewhat incomplete logic Scompiglio approaches the subject in a scientific and philosophical manner, but delivers it in quite indignant tones.

'Who dares to presume,' he begins, 'that anything *is* anything other than in relation to anything else?' He takes as an example our conception of direction. 'What is up? What is down? A ceiling is said to be up, but only for as long as you are beneath it. Build the ceiling on the floor and it is no longer up and no longer a ceiling. Nothing *is*.'

He continues a mite discursively in this vein for some time before coming up with, 'How can the moon be above? It can be "overhead" – but only in relation to you who are observing it. In relation to the Earth, or to the Sun, or to any other of the heavenly bodies it has no position. It can't have, for to claim that at any given moment the moon rests in a particular position relative to the Earth, is to claim knowledge of the Earth's position in relation to the Universe, which is absurd, for to do that necessitates postulating the position or state of the Universe itself. And how can we do that, for it is beyond the scope of human ingenuity to know the position or state of the Universe. We have nothing relative with which to compare it.' '. . . (it follows that) the

Universe in our understanding is relative to nothing. Therefore nothing can exist within the Universe in relation to anything else.'

This is all rather confusing, and might be deemed callow were it not for the fact that confusion, of a type, seems to be Scompiglio's primary aim at this point. He is trying to jar us, to bring us into a new mode of thinking. He is preparing our minds for something that is still to come. He concludes this section with the (I believe) deliberately ambiguous statement: 'There is no direction.'

From here he passes on to the subject of God. God exists, he says, but it is pointless for any living (sic) human being to endeavour to come to know God, for It (he invariably refers to God as It) is unknowable. It is also indifferent.

He defends God's indifference in the following way: This tiny planet is approximately four and a half billion years old; man has been on it for only one million years. There are currently more than four billion human beings living here as well as countless trillions of other living entities. The Earth forms part of a solar system, making a regular elliptical orbit around the star we have named the Sun. At its perihelion the Earth comes to within 91,341,000 miles of the Sun; at its aphelion, 94,448,000. Light travelling at 186,000 miles per second takes an average of 8.3 minutes to cover the distance from the Sun to the Earth.

The Sun's nearest neighbour, outside of its own solar system, is called Alpha Centauri and lies at a distance of 4.29 light years. A light year measures somewhere in the region of six trillion miles.

The galaxy in which our Sun and Alpha Centauri lie is known as the Milky Way and it contains about one hundred billion stars. It is one galaxy amongst millions. Modern instruments are able to detect galaxies and other, unknown objects, at distances of more than *twelve billion light years* from Earth. This distance does not mark the edge of the Universe, it is simply the limit of man's ability to perceive it . . .

In this matter Scompiglio continues for several thousand words, setting down almost *ad somnum* an impressive array of facts, figures and dimensions etc. discussing theories and certainties and seriously testing the reader's boggle-threshold until one finds oneself struggling in a mental whirlpool, searching desperately for some kind of meaning to it all. How he achieves this I have been unable to fully determine; the facts he produces may for the most part be looked up in any good, up-to-date encyclopaedia, and yet

Scompiglio, with remarkable literary virtuosity, succeeds in involving the emotions of the reader to an astonishing degree.

And it is here that Scompiglio performs what is probably the most ingeniously contrived 'sleight of pen' that it has ever been my privilege to read. For, somehow, suddenly, with an abrupt and totally unforeseen about-turn, he points a wrathful, accusing finger at the reader and demands, with searing tones, 'How dare you, or anybody, assume that in all this there exists somewhere some divine entity, some beneficent deity, some awesome ancient being who has nothing better to do with Its time than keep a constant regular check on how you are getting along?'

'You are nothing!' he declares. 'You are less than nothing! God had no awareness of your birth; It has no awareness of your continuance; and It will care nothing when you die. Your contribution is not even worthy of derision!'

The effect upon the mind of the reader of this dramatic about-turn is startling, and it is impossible to convey its full impact here. One experiences a sudden sense of isolation and loss, a feeling that all is one's own fault, an onset of guilt and shame and a humiliating feeling of insignificance. It is a truly brilliant piece of writing.

Scompiglio then deftly proceeds to soften the blow. He informs us that, although it is not possible to come to know God Itself, it is possible to know a manifestation of God. Each inhabited planet, he says, manifests from time to time a 'Christ Form', which is an attribute of the Ultimate Unknowable. This Christ Form will adopt the form common to the most highly evolved species on that particular planet. It will act as a catalyst in the psychic or spiritual development of this species.

Those who are sufficiently advanced (those in the Period of Real Attainment?) will be capable of recognizing the Christ Form and they will accept it. They will be guided by it and will permit it to help them onto the next rung on the ladder of their evolution. And those who have truly evolved in accordance with the designs of the Cosmos will be guided by the Christ Form to a point beyond anything experienced on the physical plane. They will be shown the true nature of being, they will shed their material bonds and step into the bosom of Immanence, where God is no longer unknowable and where Heaven exists for all.

This again is a masterful example of literary engineering. Having already been subjected to the lengthy and exhausting preamble and then drastically 'unmanned' by the denunciation, the reader is left feeling so deflated, so devastated physically and emotionally, that he or she is in direst need of reassurance. And reassurance is there, delivered in such a warm and comforting way that by the end one has regained one's footing and is filled with an overwhelming sense of excitement and wonder. And what is more to the point, one *believes* – for the time being at least. Only by studying this essay personally can its brilliance be fully appreciated. It is not difficult to imagine how an 'instant conversion' of the reader might take place on the strength of this piece alone.

It is interesting to note, incidentally, that although Scompiglio does not go so far as to openly assert that he is the Christ or Christ Form of which he speaks in this essay, one is left in little doubt that this indeed is what is being implied.

'The Third Coming of Christ' is a curious piece of work, meriting inclusion here because i) its claims are, on the surface at least, preposterous, and ii) it illustrates beautifully Scompiglio's tendency to contradict statements he has made elsewhere. In regard to both of these points, I was able at a later date to enquire personally of various Sons And Daughters of Scompiglio why it was that their master indulged in such practices. I received the unedifying reply that Iddio E. Scompiglio follows the Way of Malamat, of which I shall have more to say presently.

The Third Coming is a lengthy piece, and at the risk of making it sound even more outrageous than it appears in the original text, I have reduced it here to its barest essence. Obviously it is not intended to be taken literally, its true meaning being hidden by the actual words – at least, so say the Sons And Daughters. My own recommendation would be to endeavour to get hold of a copy of the original and then follow the advice of its author – read it three times. Perhaps then your first opinion will be changed.

The Second Coming of Jesus Christ, for which so many pious and not-so-pious Christians the world over have been in attendance for so long, has, according to Scompiglio, already occurred. It happened on the afternoon of June 30th, 1908, in a remote region of central Siberia known as Tunguska. However, due to erroneous calculations (on the part of whom? God? Jesus? Scompiglio does not make this very clear.) nobody was around to witness it.

His 'evidence' is this: there occurred there on that day an event which has been a source of mystery to scientists and laymen alike ever since. An explosion of truly gargantuan proportions knocked down every tree in the area for thirty kilometres in all directions and wiped out a herd of five hundred reindeer in its entirety. Local villages were flattened and villagers found their clothes burning on their backs.

A whole host of theories was put forward as to what might have been the cause. The most tenable – that it was a large meteor striking the Earth – had to be abandoned after an examination of the area revealed no craters and no meteor fragments. Another suggestion was that it was a particle of anti-matter colliding with the Earth. Anti-matter is known to interact with matter and a particle colliding with the Earth would disintegrate into energy, taking with it an equal mass of normal matter and causing an explosion comparable to that of a sizeable hydrogen bomb. Again, there is no evidence available to substantiate this.

A further idea was that a mini-black hole had struck the planet, producing a vast explosion as it entered the atmosphere and passing right through the Earth itself before proceeding on its way back into space. The properties that a black hole is believed to possess would account for this up to a point; but upon its emergence on the other side of the planet it would have caused another explosion of equal size. Or, were it to have emerged somewhere beneath the ocean, in the North Atlantic, say, a gigantic water spout as well as the explosion would have been the result. Nothing of this kind was observed or recorded by man.

Suggestions grew more and more bizarre as one after the other theories were disclaimed. Some investigators believed that the explosion was caused by the wreck of a nuclear-powered, inter-stellar spacecraft manned by aliens! But by far the most outlandish is the one put forward by Iddio E. Scompiglio.

Scompiglio says that the cause of the explosion was Jesus Christ making His long-awaited return to Earth. He came in a burst of glory unparalleled in human history, but (and here I am cutting a long explanation very short) having been away for so long He completely mis-appraised the situation and chose entirely the wrong place and time to make His appearance. Not only that but earlier signs and portents that He had sent down were either misinterpreted or totally ignored by the populace. Finding nobody there to witness Him but a handful of charred peasants He was left, therefore, with no option but to make His way, hangdog, back to that from whence He came.

Now, Scompiglio tells us, it is the Third Coming of Christ for which humanity unknowingly waits. And again, he claims, it has already occurred. Christ is here, now, on the planet, working to restore sanity and order where all has gone amok. Having profited from His humiliating experience in 1908 He has opted for a more subdued approach this time, returning as a normal human baby and thus allowing Himself many years in which to study us and familiarize Himself with our ways. He has attained adulthood now and has already declared Himself to a select few; and when the time is right He will reveal Himself to all.

In this essay too Scompiglio refrains from making any direct claim to being the Saviour of whom he speaks. He seems, moreover, to be enjoying a harmless joke at Christ's expense. But beneath the apparent absurdity his words are pregnant with hidden meaning. A deeper study of the work can reveal much that was not perceived before.

Or maybe not.

'The Journey From Ylem' is a mystical treatise dealing with the evolution of life, specifically mankind, and the universe. It is a particularly difficult essay to come to grips with and one can only assume that it is largely allegorical in content, although much of the allegory is lost on me. It opens rather grandly with the splendid *ipse dixit*: 'You, who have evolved from the Ylem of this world, be aware; your work has only just begun!'

In the same manner Scompiglio proceeds to inform us that the world is constantly expanding and that life has evolved in order to maintain this expansion. As humans, we are a prototypical life-form, being the first to be equipped with consciousness of self in order that we might be aware of the purpose of our being here. One of man's primary reasons for existing is to ensure that the planet be allowed to continue its expansion. (Long-winded examples of 'evidence' are given in support of this, but due to their incomprehensible nature I have not bothered to quote them here.) One day the Earth will fill the entire Cosmos (What will become of the other planets, stars etc. is not gone into) and then all can begin again in accordance with Cosmic Purpose.

One significant point he makes concerns the evolution of

consciousness of man. As already stated, one of our main reasons for existing is that we continue the expansion of our planet. However, this is something we do more or less in passing. We have other reasons for being alive. A time is coming, Scompiglio asserts, indeed it is very close at hand, when certain signs and portents will be made manifest to all. Those who have been Awakened (through Iddio) will know, when these signs appear, that a great change in human consciousness is occurring. Some, the chosen ones, will be ready to cast off their shackles of material necessity. They will know who they are, and when this Time comes they will know that the Gates of Heaven have opened to receive them. They will all step forward singing, with joy in their hearts, to be accepted into the bosom of the Immanent One.

It is difficult to know how to interpret this latter section. No precise instructions or explanations are given and, short of actually committing oneself to membership of Scompiglio's church, none will be forthcoming. Reduced here once more to its bare essentials it is, however, a concept that the Sons And Daughters of Scompiglio set great store by. Make of it what you will.

The final essay I wish to discuss here is one called 'The Intrinsicality of Over-Development and Decay'. This one is interesting again for its *outré* assertions, once more disconcertingly at odds with statements that have gone before; and also for the furious, megalomaniacal tones in which it is deliverd, viz. the opening sentence: 'Verily I say unto you that I am your scourge. I am your terror. I shall compel you to look more closely at yourselves, for only then will you see that, truly, mankind is the cancer growth of the Universe!'

In that opening sentence is captured the gist and thrust of the essay. Employing vivid, though, one suspects, specious comparisons, Scompiglio launches into approximately twelve thousand words of almost pure vitriol, likening the development of the human species on the planet Earth to the development of cancer in a single biological cell. 'Just as the cancerous cells, their over-development ungovernable, divide and spread throughout the body of a man,' he says, 'so does man divide and spread across the planet; and so will he continue until he has covered the Universe itself.' '. . . it is because mankind has lost touch with Purpose and Meaning,' he goes on, offering a glimmer of hope, 'that it has defiled its planet in such a manner, and will go on to defile the entire Universe unless Purpose and Meaning can again be instilled into its collective consciousness.'

Much use is made of medical and scientific facts and theory to give weight to this argument, covering in intricate detail the manner in which cancer invades the human body. How well this stands up in the light of current medical research I am not qualified to say. Cancer, he says, is a warning, and in order to obtain the cure we so desperately and pitifully seek we have only to stop. 'Stop destroying,' he tells us, 'and the destruction within you will also stop. Stop giving pain and your own pain will be dissolved. Stop defiling and you will no longer be defiled. Stop treating the planet as your expendable plaything – it is not expendable, it is not a plaything, and above all, IT IS NOT YOURS!'

And you can't say fairer than that now, can you?


(ii)

Though somewhat uncertain of Scompiglio's work after examining it for the first time, my curiosity was nevertheless aroused and I was prompted to find out more. With this in mind I made enquiries at my local library. Scompiglio, it turned out, was unlisted and unheard of; not only was there no reference to any other works by him, but those I had just read were unrecorded also. In an old edition of Whitaker's *British Books In Print*, however, I came across the following: '*Scompiglio in Asia* – three months spent working with a very great man,' by Timothy Pendicott, p. Port and Herman, 1957.

This book, again, was unlisted and unobtainable through the libraries system, further investigation revealing that it had been out of print for some years. I telephoned the publishers. They, at first, had difficulty in recalling either Pendicott or his book. When eventually they did remember him they informed me that they had no plans to reprint and had no idea of the author's whereabouts, having had no contact with him for ten years or more.

This only served to further whet my appetite, and I was eventually successful in tracking down a copy in the British Library archives.

Since that day, incidentally, I have come across only one other reference to Scompiglio, and that is contained in Vanessa Field's recent book, *Men of Mystery of the Twentieth Century* ('feminism forsaken for alliteration's elegant allure!' cried one reviewer gleefully without even a glance beyond the cover). This pocket-encyclopaedia-sized volume purports to being the most comprehensive reference book available on the subject of the 'unknown'. 'After years of painstaking research,' reads the blurb in part, 'Vanessa Field has succeeded in compiling a world-spanning dictionary of groups, societies and individuals etc. currently involved in practice and/or research of an occult, mystical, religious or quasi-religious, paranormal, philosophical, psychic or spiritual nature.' A remarkable achievement – if only it were true.

The most charitable comment I can make concerning her book is that it is unusually unreliable and biased in the extreme. For instance, under the heading, Scompiglio, Iddio E. we find: self-proclaimed religious leader; founder of the Church of the Sons And Daughters of Scompiglio. Date and place of birth unknown. Author of two volumes of obscure arcane gobbledygook.'

This would not be quite so condemnable were it not for the fact that such haloed figures of world renown as, for example, George King, George de la Warr, Bubba Free John, Phyllis Schlemmer and Marjorie Kawin-Toomin are each allotted several paragraphs, as are Matthew Manning, Doris Stokes and Uri Geller. And old Bhagwan Shree Rajneesh gets an entire four pages to himself – which I think says much for where Ms Field's head is at.

Timothy Pendicott's book, as the title suggests, is an account of a part of the author's life spent travelling, mainly in Asia, in the company of Iddio E. Scompiglio. It is rather shoddily written, and after only two or three pages it becomes obvious that Pendicott is, or was, a committed follower of the sage. This is unfortunate in many ways, for it tends to make the reader question with a greater scepticism the veracity of his claims and, in fact, serves to prejudice one's opinion from the outset.

Pendicott tells of miracles of healing performed by Scompiglio, of feats of levitation effected whilst in a meditative trance, of the great man's ability to go without food or drink for days on end without suffering any adverse consequences, and of the words of ineffable wisdom that poured from his mouth whenever he opened it to speak.

Scompiglio was a man in his mid-thirties at this time. He was travelling the East, accumulating wisdom, preaching his gospel to those who would lend him an ear, and gathering disciples in preparation for what he called the Day of Declaration. This was the day he would choose to announce himself to the world and establish his church, which was to be set up by his followers in the meantime, as the one, true religion of the world.

Little is given in the way of biographical details, largely because, as Pendicott confesses, little is known. Scompiglio offered no information concerning himself, preferring to hold himself somewhat aloof, even from those closest to him, and relying upon his undeniable personal magnetism and an impressive assortment of miracles to keep everybody happy. He was, says Pendicott, a swarthy fellow, small in stature though with a presence that dominated any gathering of which he might be part. His hair was jet-black, quite long and curly; his eyes bright blue and his teeth brilliantly white and even. He radiated an aura of peacefulness and immense self-confidence. He spoke several (Pendicott says 'most') languages fluently and without a trace of an accent, so it was not possible to discern which was his native tongue. His features, however, indicated a Southern European origin and, in fact, the last time he was seen, when he gathered his followers together and delivered to them his valedictory speech and blessing, was in the north of Italy. This scene is movingly described in the last chapter of Pendicott's book.

On that day, says Pendicott, Scompiglio called together all of his most devoted disciples – or his Sons And Daughters as he was now preferring to call them – by the side of a lake in a secluded valley deep in the Dolomite mountains. It was a warm and pleasant day and Scompiglio, dressed in white as was his custom, sat cross-legged on a large flat boulder and spoke at length to his followers.

He told them he was going away. He had done all that he was able to do for the present and it was time for him to bid them all farewell. From now on it was up to them; he would wait whilst they continued with his work, doing what had to be done, preparing the world for his Coming. When that work was completed he would return in such a way that all would know who he was.

His followers, about twenty-five in all, were stunned, horrified. Some, indeed, were prostrate with grief; but he spread his hands and told them not to mourn. They should not be afraid, he said, and their tears should be of joy not sadness, for had he not promised them that he would return? If they went away now and applied all that he had taught them over the past few months then their reunion would not be long in coming. They would all meet again in a far, far better place.

And in the meantime, though he was leaving them, he would still be with them in their hearts. He would be guiding them and from time to time he would make them aware of his presence, they would see that he had not deserted them.

He then gave to each of those assembled a specific task to complete. These tasks, for the most part, involved the setting up of spiritual centres or churches around the world where people might come in order to be initiated into the ways of Scompiglio. When enough of these churches had been set up and a sufficient, unspecified, number of persons had been adopted into them he would return. Pendicott's task, in company with several others, was to take Scompiglio's teachings to the United States of America.

Having delivered this speech Scompiglio stood up on his rock and led the faithful in a hymn, penned by himself and praising the wondrousness of his doings. When this was over he walked amongst them, smiling beatifically, and gave a silent benediction to each in turn. Then he turned and walked away.

His Children watched with tear-filled eyes as he stood with his back to them at the water's edge, gazing at the sun reflected in the lake's mirror. To many it must have seemed that he was preparing himself to step out onto the surface of the water, to part with them in a manner befitting a being of his magnitude, but this was not to be. Perhaps he found the water a trifle chill that day, or perhaps he had spotted some stray patches of oil that might have soiled his sandals . . . whatever his reasons, he turned away from the lake and made his way with slow and dignified steps along the pebble beach that bordered it, disappearing eventually into the lush green forest that covered the slopes of the surrounding mountains.

Pendicott ends his book with the words, 'And so He was gone; but we all of us knew with utmost conviction in our hearts that He would not be long in returning as He had promised. Until that time, though, it was up to us. We were His prophets, His Proclaimers. We each of us had a task to fulfil, and when that has been accomplished He will be able to return, bringing with Him the true eternal liberation of which He has spoken so often, and which, to some of us, He has actually already revealed.'

It was here, in Pendicott's book, that I first learned of the existence of the third volume of work accredited to Iddio E. Scompiglio, *The Pronouncements To The Scions*, which, as previously stated, is not generally available. It remains the jealously guarded property of the members of Scompiglio's innermost circle and no one outside of this circle may so much as cast an eye upon it. To gain entry into this circle one has to prove oneself, by longstanding membership of the Church of the Sons And Daughters of Scompiglio, and by certain acts of devotion. The nature of these acts is not known.

It so happened that at the time of my first becoming acquainted with the works of Iddio E. Scompiglio I was scheduled to make a trip across the water to the United States of America. Realizing that this was too good an opportunity to pass up, I hastily rearranged my programme so that a visit to the California base of the Church of the Sons And Daughters of Scompiglio might be included.

## (iii)

The California headquarters of the Church of the Sons And Daughters of Scompiglio lies in the countryside about two hundred miles north of Los Angeles. You take the scenic coastal route to a point about six miles short of Guadalupe, then turn off down a narrow, unsignposted dirt track. Follow this for about a mile into a deep canyon and then up onto a large plateau above the ocean. Here, hidden amongst the trees, is a big old house surrounded by outbuildings and several acres of private and mostly uncultivated grounds.

It is an idyllic setting. With its natural forest, pools and streams, its abundance of wildlife, its tranquillity and its near permanent sunshine it seems the perfect place to come to find inner peace and contentment and to commune with one's spiritual master, even if he happens to be elsewhere at the time.

I was expected and was greeted by a tall, bronzed, smiling, silver-haired man in his early fifties, who squeezed my hand firmly and introduced himself as Father Ken. Father Ken was Chief Proclaimer of the California branch. He was Iddio's main man in America. With his counterpart in Rome he reigned supreme until Iddio should choose to return. His word was law. I was honoured.

He was an affable fellow, though, exuding self-confidence

without being overbearing. He seemed genuinely pleased to be talking to me. He took me to a small office where we chatted for about half an hour, and then gave me a guided tour of the place. I was able to put to him many questions concerning his community and its beliefs and practices.

He had been largely responsible for the setting up of this branch, he explained, as well as many of the others scattered across America. It had been purchased with his own money and with donations from devoted members of his 'family'. It was these donations plus course fees that kept the church going.

People came here mostly to study and to learn about themselves and their relationship to the world; some came simply in order to be. Various study courses and exercises were available, devised for the most part by Iddio, and aimed at heightening spiritual awareness, instilling strength and calm and understanding into the individual, and preparing him or her for the work that was to be done on the planet. The courses and exercises were all set forth in *The Pronouncements To The Scions* and were carefully graded so that the member came slowly to an awareness of self and of the full nature of Iddio's mission. They could last anywhere from a few hours to several weeks and when one was completed the member was usually only too eager to sign up for the next.

From time to time as Father Ken and I strolled through the grounds, we came across other Sons And Daughters – tending the vegetable garden, perhaps, picking fruit, holding informal seminars beneath the trees, or meditating. I spoke with several of these, discovering their response to Scompiglio to be quite uniformly exuberant.

Carole, for instance, was an attractive, auburn-haired, thirty-year-old ex-real estate agent from New York. She told me she had been introduced to the community three years previously: 'I met this guy at a party in LA where I was on vacation,' she said, bright-eyed and smiling. 'We got on pretty good and he invited me back here. I was pretty open to suggestions at that time, you know, I just wanted to have some fun. So I made him promise that he wasn't a Moonie and I thought, hell, why not? Well, we got here and I thought I'd maybe stay a day or two, and I ended up staying three weeks! And when I got back to New York it was just too much. I couldn't handle it any more. So I quit my job and got the first flight back again. I had money and a car and a nice apartment and security, you know, taken out to dinner every night – the works. And I was screwed up. I was so screwed up I didn't even know it. I just knew there was something wrong. And now, when I go back there and I see my friends and they're all still caught up in that same trip, I think, oh wow . . . *oh wow*! . . . I've tried telling them, persuading them to take a trip down here just to see what it's like, but you know how it is. They're still clinging. They just can't experience anything beyond all that.' She turned to Father Ken with a repentant shrug. 'I guess I'm just not trying hard enough.'

Jim was an LA cab-driver. He was a jovial, down-to-earth, working-class American, who was hired by Father Ken one day to drive him from the airport to the big house. On the way Father Ken had talked to him about Iddio E. Scompiglio and the work they were doing. 'At first I thought he was a nut,' Jim smiled. 'You get so many freaks and weirdos round here you just learn to humour them. But we got talking and after a while I found I was beginning to like the guy. And when we got here he offered to show me around, and they gave me a meal and, shit, I signed up for an introductory weekend course!' He laughed. 'Now I'm head chauffeur, I teach yoga, and my wife, Candy, she runs the crèche. And we've still got our apartment in Santa Monica but we use it mostly as a stopping-over place now, for members and new members.'

And so on . . .

All of those to whom I was introduced were polite and friendly and seemingly very much at one with their world. I did detect, though, a certain wariness when answering some of my questions and they all exhibited a rather aggravating air of superiority, as though they knew something I didn't. They were at pains to assure me that they were all free to come and go as they pleased.

'We don't need barbed-wire,' one woman explained, 'nor guards nor coercion of any kind. The power of Scompiglio is all that brings us together. We come to love Scompiglio. We are free agents with our own minds and we are working to build a free world. Most people who come here choose not to leave – they might leave this centre but they never leave Iddio. They recognize His Truth straight away; in their souls. They return to their homes with a new awakening and the resolve always to help Him in His work.' Her words were greeted with warm approval by the others.

No signs of coercion, mental, physical or other, were in evidence, it's true; but then, if any such means were being employed they would hardly have been included as an integral part of my tour. I asked about rules and regulations and Father Ken told me that they were simple and few. No alcohol or drugs of any kind (other than medically prescribed) were permitted. Sex outside of marriage was frowned upon but not actually banned, and marriage outside of the community was not recognized. When a married couple became members of the Sons And Daughters one of their first duties was to undergo a second wedding ceremony, presided over by Father Ken or one of his deputies, in order to be officially recognized as wed in the eyes of Scompiglio. Any person coming to stay at the centre was expected to work without pay for a minimum of four hours per day, outside of course time, to help maintain the centre's upkeep. This was also an excellent way of making the member feel that he or she was actually a contributory part of the organization and not simply someone calling in for services. Sundays were kept free, though some courses were held in the morning. Rules of a more personal nature were learned by the member as he or she progressed.

As I have said, answers to my questions were given readily, if a hint warily; but some of them did tend to fall some way short of being entirely satisfactory. I was often left with a certain fuzziness of mind, as though my attention had wandered briefly and I had missed some essential point, whereas whoever was speaking seemed under the impression that my query had been answered quite lucidly. A good example of this is the reply I received from Father Ken to a whole series of questions I put to him concerning the convoluted and cryptic nature of some of Scompiglio's work, the apparent contradictions, the bizarre tones in which some of his essays were delivered, the sometimes incongruous sense of humour he often manifested, and the highly elusive nature of the man himself. Father Ken's answer was that Iddio E. Scompiglio followed the Way of Malamat.

To the questions, Why did he not declare himself to the world several years ago when, according to Timothy Pendicott, he was performing quite remarkable and convincing miracles, and Why does he not declare himself now in order to put off sceptics and to bring order into a world seemingly gone insane, I received the same reply. And when I raised the topic of the allegations of improper conduct etc. that had been levelled against the Sons And

206

Daughters of Scompiglio, Father Ken assured me that they were all without foundation and that they had been spread, to begin with, by none other than himself and his fellow Proclaimers. Nonplussed, I asked him why and he told me it was because, yes, Iddio E. Scompiglio follows the Way of Malamat. He then launched into a detailed explanation of this.

Malamat is an ancient Sufi term meaning way, or method, of Blame. Persons who adopt the Way of Malamat represent themselves to the outside world under a deliberately bad light in order to discourage praise and admiration which they might otherwise attract, and also as a means of personal protection. The intention is to put people – or certain people – off rather than to draw them.

To the Sufi mystics of old the Way of Malamat was always held in great esteem. Their most eminent spiritual masters are said to have adopted it. It is a method that has been largely lost to sight in more recent times, although it is reckoned to have been followed, probably under other names, by the masters of all the great religions. Jesus Christ, for one, is said to have followed it in order to fulfil his Mission on Earth, and Father Ken quoted me numerous examples from the New Testament and other Christian texts which he believed bore this out.

Malamat is not very well understood in this day and age, he told me. Society has progressed in such a way that we have virtually lost sight of our original spiritual nature. The prevailing, materialistic view is that one should strive within society to seek the approval and praise of others. The deliberate attraction to oneself of blame rather than praise or respect cannot be comprehended by the ordinary mind.

Father Ken went on to tell me that there is a specific reason for adopting the Way of Malamat. The old Zoroastrian scriptures teach that there was a certain 'mark of kingship' always to be found on persons who were destined for high eminence in the world. This mark might be physical in nature, in the form of a blemish, a birthmark, or a certain recognizable characteristic; or it might be manifest in the power of attraction or other psychic powers the person had. Anyone possessing this mark or power, or 'hvareno' as it is known, would be destined for very high advancement. Whether this meant that he would become a great king or ruler, or whether he would become a great spiritual leader, it was not possible to tell.

I asked Father Ken for a description of these marks or this mysterious power. He was evasive, saying that it was not for him to reveal and that knowledge of this kind, when placed in the wrong hands, could be extremely dangerous. 'Only those of the highest and purest spiritual attainment can know how to use this power rightly,' he said. 'For others the power of personal attraction can be a terrible temptation, difficult to resist, and when utilized wrongly harmful to an inestimable degree.'

What he did tell me was that the Buddha had this power – it was recognized when he was still a child – as did Jesus and other great Redeemers whom he did not name. And, predictably, Iddio E. Scompiglio has it too.

Any man bearing these marks or possessing this 'hvareno', he said, if he desired to follow the spiritual path, had to protect himself from the hero-worship and outward exaltation of his person that this was bound to attract, and against being eventually drawn into Messiahship. And any man who adopts this method of blame is, to the uninitiated, extremely hard to understand in terms of his external behaviour.

'But surely,' I objected, 'all that you and the Sons And Daughters are doing is drawing Scompiglio into Messiahship?'

'Not so,' Father Ken replied, 'for we are the ones He has chosen. He came to us, selected us specifically, though none of us know why, and demonstrated to us that He was the Christ. At that time too He was following the Way of Malamat. It was only to a very select few that He chose to reveal His powers. And He gave us certain gifts and He gave us certain tasks and then He left us. When we have fulfilled our tasks – when we have proven our worthiness to Him – he will return. But you must not think that He has abandoned us, for He has not. He is always in our consciousness and He "visits" us from time to time to see what our progress has been and to give us further guidance.'

Noticing the inflection Father Ken gave to the word 'visits' I enquired as to the nature of these visits. 'Do you mean he actually visits you in his physical form? I mean, does he just roll by in his car now and again and stop for tea, or are you hinting at something a little more miraculous?'

Father Ken smiled a mysterious smile and said, 'You are an outsider, a newcomer to our church, and as you have not been initiated into the ways of the Sons And Daughters of Scompiglio I am prevented from disclosing to you certain things concerning our Master and the ways He has taught us. I can assure you, however, that when He comes to us He is not bound to rely upon those forms of tranport to which you and I might be accustomed.'

He seemed to think that this was enough, that with this all my questions had been answered. I pressed him further, but to little avail. Handing me a selection of leaflets and a programme of church events he urged me to consider enrolling on an introductory weekend course or attending an afternoon workshop or at very least a seminar. I promised to give it some thought.

My next question evoked an interesting response. I asked Father Ken about Timothy Pendicott, saying that I had hoped to meet him whilst in the United States and, in fact, had been more or less expecting to find him here. At the mention of Pendicott's name Father Ken's face darkened and the three Sons And Daughters who were with us at the time grew noticeably edgy. Father Ken covered his confusion quickly, however, glazing it with a smile and the words, 'Timothy Pendicott is no longer with the church. We have no knowledge of his whereabouts.'

I would have liked to have questioned him further but he politely but firmly veered away from the subject, ushering me towards the communal dining-room where I was treated to a delicious meal of lentil soup, mixed salad and vegetarian quiche Lorraine, fruit juice and fresh fruit trifle. The mood at the table was one of levity and strong camaraderie – perhaps I should say brotherhood – and it was impossible not to be caught up in the atmosphere of optimism and exuberance that pervaded the room. All were anxious that I postpone my departure so that they might instruct me further in the teachings of Iddio E. Scompiglio.

Time was tight, however, and I had to be on my way.

Father Ken accompanied me to my hired car and bade me a warm farewell, telling me he hoped and believed with the fullness of his heart that he would be seeing me again before very long. I wasn't so sure about that but I thanked him for his hospitality and promised to look in again next time I was passing.

As I drove away my feeling, in spite of my good humour, was one of dissatisfaction and a certain amount of perplexity. I had spent several hours in the company of Father Ken and his Sons And Daughters, discussing their Master and the organization he had founded, and yet both he and it remained as big a mystery to me, if not bigger, than before. Several fundamental questions remained unanswered, the most fundamental of all being Who *is* Iddio E. Scompiglio? Does he actually exist or is he a figment, some phantom godling invented by Father Ken and his fellow Proclaimers as a means to further their own dark ends? If he does indeed exist is he truly the new Messiah as is their claim? To arrive at an answer to these questions seems to entail becoming a fully-fledged member of the Church of the Sons And Daughters of Scompiglio; and even then, I suspect, illumination would be patchy.

Of Timothy Pendicott I know nothing. Obviously he fell from grace, but as a consequence of what heinous crime, and of what has befallen him since, I cannot say. Perhaps in time answers to all these questions will be forthcoming. Perhaps the Day of Declaration will reveal Scompiglio to be the great avatar he claims to be and perhaps he will succeed in putting the world to rights. Anything's possible, but don't hold your breath.


And now, before returning to the narrative, here is a little nugget of information concerning Hugh, the irrepressible Scotsman and freelance journalist, and an indulgence he was wont to take pleasure in during certain moments known only to himself.

There were occasions in Hugh's life, not so frequent of late, when he found himself obliged to spend time away from home. This might be at the behest of a magazine editor or it might be other. It might involve spending one night away or perhaps several; but the fact is that Hugh always regarded it as something of an imposition. He was not happy when deprived of the company of his loved ones; he was easily bored and grew lonely very quickly. Although he liked to pretend otherwise, in his heart of hearts Hugh was a family man and he floundered when far away from the comfort and security of his own home.

An essential item of luggage on these excursions, then, a soothing, consoling reminder of everything he held dear, was a pair of black silk panties belonging to his wife, Angela. Securely bolted in his hotel bedroom Hugh would remove all his clothes and stretch out on the bed with the panties in his hand. Then he would proceed to caress himself from head to toe with the flimsy negligee. He would pamper and cosset himself, press the panties to his face and rub them gently over his belly. He would tickle his scrotum with them and drape them over his erect penis. And as he did so he would imagine his wife lying naked before him, smiling, her thighs spread, her fingers parting the plump lips of her vagina.

After only minutes of this treatment Hugh's excitement would build to a pitch. Then he would wrap the panties tightly around his phallus and pump himself vigorously with his fist until he came into the skimpy material.

Hugh had been doing this for many years. He saw it as a demonstration of his devotion to his wife and it afforded him considerable joy. When he had first hit upon the idea he had approached Angela, offering her a pair of his jockey shorts with the suggestion that she do likewise. It would be romantic, he told her, and so erotic, making love whilst separated by the miles. They could even do it over the telephone!

But Angela was having none of it. Ever practical, she told him not to be so immature. She told him he was a pervert. And so Hugh was left to carry on his practice alone, in secret. He still enjoyed it, it was still a lot of fun, but now it was tinged with a modicum of guilt – which sometimes actually served to add to his enjoyment of the experience – and he regretted being unable to tell her about it.

Now this might seem like a pretty strange thing to do, when you think about it – a forty-four-year-old man behaving like a guilt-ridden teenager – but the truth is, it did keep him true to his wife. Not once in all their seventeen years of marriage had he been unfaithful to her. Not even in his thoughts.

Now, back to the narrative . . .

'Who the hell,' demanded Samson imperiously, 'is Iddio E. Scompiglio when he's at home?'

'He is a great avatar,' said Margaret.

'He is a custodian of the secrets of the universe,' said Gerald.

'He is a man who has seen his original face,' said Rogelio, whose head had reappeared above the back of the sofa.

Samson pulled a face. He looked remonstrative, disbelieving, without hope. 'I think you three have got your ley-lines crossed,' he said at length.

'What's an avatar?' asked Jill.

Hugh explained. 'It's a Hindu term meaning a god who returns to earth in human form in order to teach the faithful and guide them along the spiritual path.' He seemed troubled, strangely ill at ease.

'Oh,' said Jill.

'Well, where is he? Who is he? What's he done?' Samson demanded. 'I mean, is he the new Christ? I've never heard of him.'

'He is here among us,' Margaret replied. 'He is Scompiglio, and he has come to forge a change – a peaceful change. He is effecting a change in our consciousness. He will unite the whole of mankind. He will deliver us safely through our crises. He is showing us the way to true spiritual freedom. He will build a kingdom here on Earth and he will point us to the gates of Heaven. And those of us who recognize him, who believe in him and who devote ourselves to him and help him will be taken on the path to Heaven. We will be set free!'

'And he is not *the* Christ, Sam,' Gerald stressed, 'he is *a* Christ. He is *the* Christ for now, for this age, but he is one in a long, long line of Christs. Jesus too was *a* Christ, as was Krishna, as was the Buddha, as were others throughout all of history. It is very important to understand this, Sam. Christ, as a word, is a description, not a name. It means a presence, an aspect of a far greater Truth, a facet of the Divine Presence that is everywhere and which Iddio E. Scompiglio calls the Great Pervader, or the Immanent One. This Truth, this Glory, pervades all of space, and in its essence it lies within every single one of us; but we have lost it. We have lost our knowledge of it and our ability to become aware of it, and so it lies dormant within us, almost forgotten. From time to time, though, it becomes incarnate, manifesting as one particular individual, a great teacher who will have the power to make us realize the potential we all possess and to bring us to a full awareness of it within ourselves. Do you see? Christ is everywhere at all times, but in order that we do not lose sight of it it becomes one man for one lifetime. And that man, now, is Iddio E. Scompiglio.'

'Well, why haven't I heard of him if he's so bloody influential?' Samson said.

Margaret smiled quite patronizingly. 'It is because he has not yet chosen to reveal himself to all.'

'What?'

'The world is not yet ready. He is waiting for the right moment. He has declared himself to a select few whose task it has been to prepare the way for him, to create a safe and expectant environment for him.'

Samson snorted. He stood up, helping himself to a sliver of Brie. 'And you're among the few, I suppose?'

'We are not among those to whom he has revealed himself directly,' Margaret said, 'but we are certainly committed to preparing the way for him. We are Sons And Daughters of Scompiglio. We have been shown the Truth and we recognize that it is Eternal. Scompiglio is here to deliver us. We will follow Scompiglio!'

'What? You mean you've never even seen him?' Samson was incredulous. His eyes travelled from one to the other of them and his lips twisted into a sneer. He was quite drunk now, though still lucid, and the Baileys made him angry.

Hugh said to Margaret, 'Tell me, if this new Christ chappie has so far only revealed himself to a very select few, how do you know that he actually exists? And by what means do you interpret his intentions?'

'By various means,' Margaret replied. 'For instance, Rogelio, who is one of the primary Sons And Daughters of Scompiglio, is able to communicate telepathically with our masters, the Proclaimers. From time to time he enters a trance, often quite involuntarily, during which he may pick up psychic messages being transmitted to him from the headquarters of our church. When he comes out of the trance he is invariably exhausted and confused – it is no easy process, by any means – but often he has a message to pass on to us all. And, of course, we use more conventional means to keep in touch with our brothers and sisters, such as the telephone and the post – '

At this point in the conversation Julia very loudly cleared her throat. Everybody turned to see if she had anything to contribute. She hadn't so they carried on.

'Yes, okay,' said Hugh, frowning, 'but in order to carry out the will of your master, or these "Proclaimers" as you call them, you must surely have something a little more concrete?'

'Yes, of course. There are his writings.'

'His writings?' Hugh enquired.

0

'Yes. There are two volumes of his work – well, there are three actually, but the third is only available to the highest ranking

213

members of the church. His books contain some of the most beautiful, profound and inspiring words imaginable.'

'Hmmm,' Hugh rubbed his jawbone with finger and thumb. 'So am I right in saying, then, that his teachings, or the major part of them, are contained in these books, and that these are the source from which you draw your inspiration and faith?'

'Not entirely. There are courses, seminars and prayer meetings which we attend – but these are all centred around his writings or deal with the new messages that he has lately passed on to his Proclaimers. I have the handbook with me – we carry a copy everywhere we go, don't we, darling. Would you like to see?'

'I would indeed,' said Hugh.

'Let me have a look at that,' said Samson rudely. He snatched the book from Margaret's hand as she took it from her bag to pass to Hugh. He studied the cover. *The Book of Imaginary Hauntings*, he announced out loud. 'I feel better already!'

'This book contains the thoughts of Iddio in their purest, most concise form,' Gerald explained. 'It was originally issued as a small volume of aphorisms and short poems to be studied and meditated upon and passed on to others. Many of them are allegorical in form and many appear deceptively simple at first reading. It is really necessary to study them for some time before their true meaning becomes clear.'

'Why, it's just a book full of smartass one-liners!' Samson declared, standing in the middle of the lounge and flicking the pages. He screwed up his eyes. 'There's nothing to it! It's a lot of obscure arcane gobbledygook as far as I can make out. Listen to this, page twenty-four: "Do not judge another by the opinions of others. Do not judge self by the opinions of self." Now what the hell is that supposed to mean?'

Without waiting for an answer he thumbed to another page. 'What about this one, then? This one is really deep. Listen: "You are the living evidence of Cosmic Intelligence. The ability of the Universe to produce forms through which It may be consciously aware of Itself is repeated, in you, over and over again."' He turned mockingly to the Baileys.

'It is intended to be meditated upon, Samson. And it is not always to be taken absolutely literally. Just think about it,' Margaret said patiently, retaining her smile. 'As Gerald explained, it can appear over-simplistic or extremely hard to grasp. The words themselves are not always as vital as the image they project, the feeling they implant in your mind; and that is something it takes time to understand. That is Iddio's intention. He writes allegorically, or simplistically, or cryptically, but always with purpose. He wants to discourage the dilettante element who might be attracted to him for the wrong reasons. He only wants people drawn to him who are prepared to work, to help him. That is why it is necessary to study his words, to dig deeply for the real meaning contained in them, to spend *time* and *effort*. If you do this then gradually there will occur an awakening within you and his real meaning will become clear. It's like a seed that has to be planted deep in the soil before it can begin to germinate and eventually burgeon forth; but when it does you will find yourself communing directly with Iddio. It is one of the initial stages on the path leading to enlightenment. It is a very beautiful experience, but it requires work to develop and appreciate it, Samson. Hard work and application.'

Samson ignored her. 'Oh, here's a good one! Listen to this one, everybody. This is what Iddio E. Scompiglio has to say on the subject of life. "Life," he says, " – rise above it before it rises above you".' He looked up. 'Well, at least he's got a sense of humour.'

'Samson! Stop it!' Corinne cried, but nobody heard her.

'And here's another good one!' Samson crowed. '"Give thanks to any person who makes you fight with yourself." Hah! Yes, I think it's working. I can feel myself becoming enlightened! One more ought to do the trick – ah yes, here's the one: "He who believes he is, is not. He who believes he is not, can be. But he who neither believes nor holds forth with any opinion will shine like a beacon amongst his fellow men. His life force will mingle with the life force of the Universe." Oh yes! Oh God! I think I see the light!' He stopped and laughed out loud.

'Page thirteen,' came the half-strangled voice of Rogelio.

Samson turned enquiringly. 'What?'

'Page thirteen.'

He turned to page thirteen, and what he saw there killed his laughter dead. He read it quickly and in silence: 'When the obtuse man reads my words he will laugh out loud.'

Samson closed the book. He glared at Rogelio, incensed. Rogelio returned his gaze with a look of glazed innocence; the Baileys looked smug.

'I've never read such a lot of fucking crap in my life!' Samson announced savagely. 'You're fucking weird, you three. You're fucking bananas!'

'Samson!' Corinne cried.

Margaret's smile turned to one of indulgence. 'Oh Samson, if only you knew,' she said.

'Knew what?'

'If only you knew how much you are limiting yourself by adopting that attitude. Don't you understand? Don't you see that unless you allow yourself to change, unless you allow yourself to open your heart and mind, you are doomed? There is no hope for you. You must give yourself willingly to Iddio so that he can guide you, Samson. He will embrace you and you will be accepted as part of the Immanent One. Otherwise you will die. It's as simple as that. Do you want to die? Don't you desire immortality?'

Samson's eyes widened. 'Immortality! Oh my Christ!' He turned to Hugh, hoping for support, but Hugh seemed strangely unwilling to meet his eyes. Instead he said, 'Could I have a look at that, Samson?' and he reached out to take the book.

'There is a Time coming, Sam,' Gerald said. 'It is close upon us even now, Iddio tells us. It will be recognizable when it comes by certain signs and portents personal to each one of us separately. Now, there will be those of us who are ready for it, who have been cleansed and prepared and who will know it when it is here. We will be able to join hands gladly and step forward singing into the bosom of the Immanent One. The doors of Heaven will be open to receive us. But there will also be those who refuse to accept the signs for what they are, and inevitably, those who, through never having become Awake, *will misinterpret them entirely*, or ignore them and do nothing in consequence. This is what our work entails now – to prepare as many as we can. It is crucial. And that is why Iddio came – to show us how. Because all those who are not prepared, who have not accepted the Ways of Scompiglio, will be left behind. They will have to suffer the awful consequences. This is not bullshit, Sam; this has been demonstrated to me. I have seen the Heaven that awaits us and I have seen what it will mean to ignore it. And that is why it saddens me to see you taking this stance. I don't want you to be left behind.'

'Oh yeah, and I suppose I'm going to burn in hellfire for all eternity?' Samson mocked. 'I've heard it all before, Gerald. I've heard it since I was a kid and I've had it up to here. You religious nuts are two-a-penny. How can you be so naive? How can you be so gullible? You talk about truth – well, here's some truth for you: there's a new messiah in every fucking shop-doorway and they're all of them just hanging around waiting to empty the pockets and minds of suckers like you. You're a prat, Gerald. You're a dupe. You're a fucking do-do's ass-hole.'

Gerald smiled sadly to himself and Samson, his fists clenched stiffly in front of him and his body contorted like a Billy Graham, proclaimed scoffingly, '. . . and there shall be wars and there shall be famine and there shall be much gnashing of teeth – as a consequence of which the humble dentist shall arise to occupy a position of great esteem throughout the land!' He stopped, wiped his lips, laughed. Then he went on: 'And the rich shall be banished and the strong shall be put down, the unbelievers shall perish for all eternity and the meek shall inherit the earth . . . but, Christ! Not until we've finished with it!'

He laughed again and turned to Jill to see if she was laughing too.

Jill, like Hugh, was a little unsure of where to put herself at that moment. She gave a wavering smile because she felt she ought to, and leaned forward to pick up her orange juice from the table in front of her. As she did so her camisole top slipped forward a little, affording Samson, from his position above her, a glimpse of her smooth breasts and of one soft, pink nipple pressing snugly against the green material. She caught him looking and for a second their eyes locked.

And then Corinne stood up.

0

'Samson! Shut up!' she shrieked. Her face was red, her eyes blazing, her features distorted and pained. It had suddenly all burst through. She was hysterical. 'Shut up! I can't stand it! I can't stand you behaving like this! Why must you always be so rude? Why do you have to act like such a pig?'

She glared at him, trembling – and then she seemed to lose her balance. Her knees buckled and her arms flew out, and with a surprised 'oh!' she flopped backwards heavily into her chair. Confused and humiliated she glared first at her husband and then at her hands shaking on her knees. Her face changed. Tears flowed suddenly from her eyes. 'I can't stand it anymore,' she sobbed. She covered her face with her hands and wept.

Margaret was at her side in a second, dealing out soft murmurings of comfort and support.

Samson was lost for words; for a second he seemed almost contrite. Then he sat down angrily and folded his arms, chewing at the tips of his moustache.

He looked across at Jill. She had her head lowered and was examining her fingernails. Becoming conscious of his gaze she raised her eyes and gave a quick, timid smile, then looked away again. The Pink Floyd sang 'Tear down the wall', Corinne continued to sob and Margaret soothed her and looked daggers at Samson.

Jill stood up suddenly, her Vuitton bag over her shoulder. 'Where's the loo?' she asked.

Samson directed her. He watched her as she left the room. He realized suddenly how much he wanted her. He bit his upper lip. I'm going to have you, he told himself. And fuck decorum, he wanted her tonight. He glanced briefly at Richard – and engagement ring or no engagement ring there's no way I'm going to share the same pussy with that little prick!

He was distracted by an unexpected sound. The tape had just ended and somebody had begun to sing. It was Margaret. Kneeling on the floor beside Corinne's chair and still holding her hand, she had begun to chant softly. There was a jubilant, infuriating smile on her face and her eyes were bright and wide.

With her free hand she reached behind her, underneath the table until she found Gerald's. He too began to sing, though a little more self-consciously than his wife. The words they sang were not very clear, but it was evidently some kind of paean to their messiah.

A third voice joined them, a thin, sorry, bleating voice. It came from just behind Samson's head. It was Rogelio.

As they reached what was obviously the chorus Samson was able to make out some of the words: 'We will follow, for we believe. We will change the world. Scompiglio comes to us this day, to lead us on to Heaven.'

He regarded them all with bitter contempt.

'Jesus Christ it's like a bloody madhouse in here!' he complained

218

to Hugh. Hugh gave an embarrassed shrug, stared at his book. He looked shaken. 'I don't believe it,' he said quietly.

Samson decided to put another cassette on. As he stood Margaret broke off for a moment. 'Oh Samson, if only you could see your face!' she laughed.

Samson almost shook with fury. 'You fucking wankers!' he spat, and then his eyes happened to fall upon Richard. He stopped where he was and stared at him in astonishment.

Richard was sitting hunched forward on the sofa, totally unmindful, it seemed, of what was going on around him. He was holding his piece of bread in his right hand – he had still not eaten it – and he was lapping at it dreamily with his tongue, licking it like it was an ice cream.

And suddenly all of Samson's anger and resentment and frustration was re-directed.

'Hey!' he called. 'Hey you! Ricky! What the fucking hell do you think you're playing at?'

❋   ❋   ❋   ❋   ❋

# 7

Richard had no idea what was going on anymore. His world had turned pretty damn ga-ga. Nothing existed other than thought and his everlasting ice-cream.

He was lost in a whirling, swirling, parodoxical universe where reality seemed to be a fish that darted silver in the gloom a little way ahead. Always just beyond his grasp, it enticed him on, beckoning and teasing, beautiful and unique, taking him ever downwards, down down down.

On the other hand, though, he could see that reality was not necessarily a fish. Reality might conceivably be pure thought, pure mind. It might have nothing at all to do with solids. Reality . . . perhaps reality was harmony – or at least harmonious. Or then again, perhaps it was . . . the thought came to him out of a thick, soupy fog. He only glimpsed it for a split second before it had turned around and disappeared again back into the fog. Like it was naked and scared and on display. He did not get a chance to see what it was.

Reality might be diffident, then? Or just prudent? Or was it actually terrified? Unattainable. Yes! Unattainable! That was it! Reality was unattainable! With a feeling of satisfaction he licked his ice-cream.

But then he thought back on how the thought of reality had appeared out of the fog and then disappeared again, and he was reminded once more of a fish darting silver just out of reach. Logic described a perfect circle and brought him back to his original conclusion: reality was a fish.

Or was that an analogy? Was reality an analogy for a fish?

Or was a fish an analogy for reality? Or did it require both of them to form the analogy? If that were the case, what would be the analogy that the two of them formed? In fact, what *was* an analogy?

He thought hard on the word 'analogy'. What was its meaning? It had something to do with comparisons, he thought, but he couldn't quite get it straight in his mind. He looked at it. It spun like a boomerang around the great Outback of his head and it was senseless. He frowned and it decomposed instantly into a shower of spinning fragments that slipped off somewhere and left him with Nothing.

Something griped in Richard's stomach, pulled him painfully into familiar territory, into places where he had no desire to be, and it filled him with a feeling of melancholy and of deepest isolation.

Richard had a theory about himself. It was something he had first conceived as an infant. He had continued to nurture it and watch it grow throughout his childhood and into his adult years. To begin with he had not paid it a great deal of attention; it was just something dreamed up as a diversion, a cold, though indispensable comforter in moments of distress. But it became an integral part of his everyday fantasies and with the passing of time it had grown more cogent until a point was reached where he found he could not help but take it seriously. It made sense where previously there was none.

His theory was this: he believed he was not of this Earth. He believed that, due to some minor cosmic miscalculation (minor in purely cosmogonal terms, that is) he had been deposited in the wrong body, on the wrong planet, in the wrong galaxy, and in all probability in the wrong universe. The original version of this theory had been that he was simply misplaced in time, but a cursory study of human history had been enough to convince him otherwise. There was not a period in the entire evolution of mankind that Richard Pike could have comfortably fitted into. Not even a short one.

From this he had inferred that somewhere, on another planet, perhaps, in an unknown, parallel universe, there existed another individual, another Richard Pike, who was as alone as he was, who was equally bewildered and equally misplaced, and whose sanity was likewise being shredded and scrambled by a world in which nobody liked each other and everything that happened was contrary to the way he knew it should be.

Richard often thought of the other Richard Pike. Sometimes he would be depressingly amused trying to imagine what the other Richard Pike looked like. Would he be the complete opposite of himself, for instance; would his thoughts and feelings, his whole physical, mental and emotional make-up be directly opposed to

221

Richard's? Would his world be perhaps ordered and sane whereas he was unkind and dislikeable, more suited to this world? Would his hair be dyed black? Would his complexion be smooth and blemish free? Would his name be Ekip Drahcir?

These were the kind of questions that occurred to Richard during his lighter musings. More often, though, his thoughts would take on a far more sombre hue. Then he would become immersed in schizoid imaginings, endeavour to communicate telepathically with the other Richard Pike, try to project himself out of this world and into the world where he really knew he ought to be. And sometimes – when he was walking along the street, say – he would burst into tears just thinking about what that other person was having to undergo.

Richard gave all of this total credence. He had to; it explained so many things. But he had no idea what he might do about it. It was not as if, for instance, there was anybody he could write to.

0

Richard was thinking in terms of the other Richard Pike now, when Samson shouted at him after noticing him licking his piece of bread. He was wondering whether, out of sheer malice, the other Richard Pike had been deliberately refusing all this time to respond to his efforts to get in touch telepathically. He was wondering whether the other Richard Pike might be gleefully aware of his torment. He was imagining that, along with every other human being in existence, the other Richard Pike was part of some unthinkable cosmic conspiracy, of which he, the earthbound Richard Pike, was the solitary victim.

So it took a little time for Samson's words to penetrate his haze, and when they did it was their timbre rather than their meaning that came through clearly. This was enough, though, to disconcert him. He looked up, blank and fearful.

The room and everything in it swirled dangerously. Through his submarine images of things Richard made out Samson, a satanic figure, angry, menacing and garbed in red, glaring down at him. Richard was afraid. He did not understand why Samson was being so unkind to him. He assumed that everybody else liked Samson and that, ergo, they all disliked him. Somewhere outside a dog began to bark. There was a bang as a firework exploded, and the dog fell silent.

'I said, what the fuck are you playing at?' Samson repeated, tapping the knuckles of one hand with a tape cassette.

Richard did not know. He did not understand. A vacuous smile was clinging to his face and he decided to keep it there whilst striving to find an answer to the question. Little by little, as he ransacked his brain, the smile began to freeze until he had grown conscious of every muscle, every tight tendon and raw nerve end that was involved in keeping it there.

His eyes rolled onto his ice-cream and as he stared at it he became aware that there was something odd about it. 'Oh!' he said suddenly, and it turned back into a hunk of white bread. 'Oh. I thought it was ice-cream!'

He laughed – and then he realized what he had said. A rush of confusion and embarrassment made his body writhe and push itself hard into the sofa. He turned to Jill looking for support – and to his shock discovered that she was no longer there!

Sitting alongside him on the sofa was nothing; just empty space. He looked quickly around the room – she was nowhere to be seen – and back at the space. He gawked at it, unable to believe it was there, looking for Jill who might be somewhere hidden inside it.

On the far side of the space, looking at him curiously, was Hugh. He seemed a long way off. Richard's face said imploringly to Hugh, 'What's happened?' and Hugh turned away, back to a book he was studying in his lap. Richard's head began to shake. Where was Jill? Where was Jill?

He saw Gerald and Margaret Bailey. They were looking at him. And he saw Rogelio's scraggy, wizened monkey face peering at him from over the back of the other sofa. He had a strange suspicion that a minute ago they had all been singing, but he knew that couldn't be true.

'It's very hot in here, isn't it?' Margaret said.

'Well, open the window then,' Samson replied curtly, not taking his eyes from Richard.

She did. She got up and pushed open the French windows, letting in a waft of cool air and a faint smell of potassium nitrate and sulphur. Outside, two more fireworks detonated loudly in quick succession. Hugh glanced to the window. 'It's like Belfast,' he muttered, though he had never been there.

Samson was not letting up. 'You thought it was ice-cream?' he said sarcastically to Richard. 'Ah, yes. Of course.' – but for a moment even he seemed lost for words. He turned to slip the cassette into the recorder. And Richard's eyes fell on Corinne.

When he saw Corinne he collapsed inside. She was slumped in her chair, one hand raised uselessly to her cheek and brow. The other lay like a dead thing in her lap. Her eyes were heavy and downcast and her face was blotched and streaked with make-up where tears had run. Her beautiful brunette hair was all dishevelled and her cheeks were still wet. Richard gaped at her. *It was him! What had he done that had made her cry?*

Richard could not get a hold of it. He could not make sense of what was happening. He wanted Jill. Where could she possibly be? He wanted her to explain it all to him. He wanted to call out, Jill! Jill! Come back! Jill! Help me! Please help me!

He dared not look at anybody now. He fixed his eyes on his hands on his knees and stared at them. Harder.

And harder.

And harder.

● ● ● ● ●

# 8

'Well, I think I'd better be making my way,' Hugh said, ashen-faced, placing his hands on his knees and rising ponderously to his feet. He bent forward to pick up the hammer he was borrowing from Samson, eyeing it with some discomfort, not knowing quite what to say or how to bid farewell without making it obvious he was attempting an escape.

'So soon?' Samson exclaimed, leaving aside for a moment his progressive annihilation of Richard as a person. 'No. Hugh, stay and have another drink.'

Hugh shook his head. 'Noo. I've got my shelves to be finishing off. And they'll be wondering where I've got to up there.'

He shuffled his feet but made no move towards the door. Casting a solicitous glance in Samson's direction, he stepped over to him and said in an undertone, 'Is there anything I can do before I go, Samson? I mean, do you need any help, or anything at all?'

'No, no-o,' Samson assured him. 'I've got it all under control, don't you worry.'

Hugh grimaced. 'Are you sure? It's just that – och, I don't know, I feel as though I'm a bit responsible.'

'Nonsense!' Samson laughed. 'You. Why should you feel responsible? What's all this got to do with you?'

He looked at the Baileys. They were holding hands and had begun to sing again, quietly. Margaret had her eyes closed. She was smiling. Her face, turned heavenwards, was flushed, aglow with religious ecstasy. Or perhaps it was her cold – whichever it was its effect was evidently highly salutary as far as she was concerned.

Gerald sang slightly more into his shirt. His free hand lay uneasily in his lap, flapping occasionally on his thigh like a beached cuttlefish. Hugh shrugged.

'Some people just don't know how to behave when they're in company, that's all,' Samson said. 'But there's no need for you to concern yourself. No need at all. I'll have it all back to a civilized state in no time. I'm going to throw them out in a minute.'

'But what about your wife?' Hugh asked.

'She's all right! She gets like this sometimes. It's one of those woman's things. You know. She'll be as right as rain in the morning. Look, are you sure you won't have just one more for the road?'

'No, I mustn't. I must be on my way.'

'Oh well.' Samson pursed his lips. 'I'll see you to the door then.'

He took Hugh's arm, in truth as anxious as his guest to be elsewhere – though for not entirely the same reasons. Hugh bid everybody a constrained good night.

At the door Samson paused for a moment. He looked back and surveyed the room, shaking his head in disbelief. 'Freaks!' he said.

With a look of wry amusement he followed Hugh out into the hall, closing the door behind him as he did so, and leaving Corinne, Richard, Gerald, Margaret, Rogelio and Julia all alone together in the Tallis's lounge.

● ● ● ● ●

PART FOUR

# The Great Pervader

## or

# A Continuing Accumulation of Space

'Death is only life without a body.'
Iddio E. Scompiglio

WARNING – Persons easily distressed, of a nervous disposition or delicate constitution are advised not to read beyond this page.

# 1

Rogelio had a memory. He was not aware that he had it, and neither was anybody else; it was suspended somewhere deep in the cages of his mind, held secret and safe from the light of day.

It was a particularly unhappy memory, pain-filled and deeply distressing. Had it been made into a film it would have been cut to ribbons, a book unmercifully abridged, a stage-play banned. Only in real life could it have passed the censor untouched.

Sometimes, without warning, without any ostensible cause, this memory would be restimulated. It would irrupt into the mainstream of his consciousness like some self-willed predatory nightmare, raging through his mind like a tiger on acid, dragging him away from wherever he might be and compelling him to relive it once more from beginning to end.

This was happening now.

Unnoticed by anyone he had fallen back helpless behind the sofa. He was sitting like a stone, staring into the contents of his engram, his eyes glassy wide and his face blanched and frightened.

He was four years old. He was in a tree, an old walnut tree in front of the house where he lived with his mother and father. It was a small frame-house, the yellow-brown paint flaking and the woodwork warping, but it was nevertheless superior to the wood and tin shacks that formed the jimtown down the road. There lived the other braceros, the immigrant agricultural workers who came to California in their droves from Mexico and beyond, desperately seeking work and willing to put in long hours for little pay.

Rogelio was privileged. His father held a position of foreman on an orange grove belonging to one of the major landowners in the region. His great-grandfather had come to Los Angeles in 1884, had eked out a living peddling tamales, had married a poor Mexican girl and taken her to the country where they found work in the orchards. He had stayed, worked hard, proven trustworthy, risen to foreman, been given the little house outside of the jimtown, had produced a son who took over when he grew old and feeble.

The son had worked hard, had married, had inherited the house and the job, had produced a daughter, then another daughter, then a son, who was Rogelio's father, and so on . . .

Rogelio's father was ill. For the first time in his life he was unable to work, and his mother, who usually took Rogelio to work with her in the fields, was home for an hour tending to him.

Rogelio knew little of all this. He lay in the arms of his tree, four years old, hidden from the world, playing with a wooden doll his father had made.

It was a hot, torpid afternoon and little was being done in the fields. Only in the orchards where there was some shade, or indoors, was it possible to do much work. Rogelio grew drowsy as he played. He day-dreamed and dozed, woke up and played again.

In the distance a car was approaching. He looked up at the sound, for few vehicles passed this way. It came rapidly into view, spewing a plume of pink dust in its wake, passing him. It was an old Plymouth, pale green, rusting in places and dented. Just beyond his tree it was slowing down suddenly and coming to a halt. Rogelio watched it. It was reversing a little way towards him. It was pulling in and disappearing around the side of the house.

The boy heard car doors slam, heard male voices, a strange, high-pitched laugh. He heard his dog, Popo, barking. A loud bang made him jump, sent a flock of sparrows skywards, and Popo fell silent. He thought on this for a moment, listened, heard nothing more and soon lost interest, returning to his doll and his dreams.

He played, he dreamed, he dozed, and later – he did not know how long – he was roused by two more bangs in quick succession, muffled slightly this time, coming from inside the house. He was shifting himself and peering between the branches and leaves.

There was the high-pitched male laughter again. There was a second voice, car doors, and an engine starting. The pale green Plymouth was sliding out from behind the house. It was rolling by his tree and away up the road in the direction from which it had come.

Minutes passed and Rogelio was growing bored. Hs was lowering himself out of the tree and going around to the back of the house.

He noticed Popo. She was lying outstretched on her side in the dust in the back yard. Rogelio was laughing at her, for he knew she never slept in the direct sunlight. He was walking over to her, calling her name, dimly aware of the flies that buzzed around her. She did not raise her head or open an eye, and when he bent down to clasp her his hands came away red and wet and sticky with her blood and hair.

He was pushing open the screen door into the kitchen now. He saw his mother sitting on the floor, propped against a cupboard door. Her head was over her chest, her face hidden behind her long black hair. Her skirt was rucked up to her hips and her cotton blouse torn open. It clung wetly to her skin, bloody and glistening.

Rogelio spoke to her. He went over to her and tugged her by the arm. Flies were swarming. There was broken glass on the kitchen floor and a strange smell, unknown to the child, of gunpowder and whisky. He saw his father lying face down in the doorway to the bedroom, his life's blood forming a large puddle on the floor beneath him.

Rogelio sat down beside his mother and waited patiently.

0

Evening was approaching and Rogelio had grown hungry and tired. He had left the house and was wandering along the road under a still scorching sun, out towards the open country.

A gang of braceros was at work in a nearby orange grove. He was leaving the road and crossing between the trees to speak to them. He was telling a man on a ladder that his Mama and Papa were lying on the floor. He was pointing back the way he had come.

The man he was addressing was turning and peering down at him. Clearly he did not understand.

'They don't get up.'

The man gave a snort of amusement and passed on some remark to his neighbour.

One or two others were gathering around. Rogelio was trying to make them see but they looked nonplussed, or grinned as if there was something vaguely comical about him. They made comments he did not understand. The foreman came to see what was the matter and a woman gave Rogelio some water and a dry tortilla and pointed him back towards the road.

He was walking some more, no longer sure of the way home. He found other workers but failed each time to make them understand. They assumed, for the most part, that he was a stray member of their own community; they assumed, as had the others, that his Mama and Papa had got drunk, had made wild love and passed out. None of them commented on the blood that had dried on his hands and arms; it was barely distinguishable from walnut stains.

The sun had lost its glare. It hung red over the horizon and Rogelio had spotted a car. It was some way ahead, parked off the road in the shade of a cypress windbreak. He could see two figures. One leaned against the roof, the other was crouched alongside the front offside wheel. He was hesitating a moment, his child's mind unsure of what came next. The car was familiar to him, it was an old pale green Plymouth. He was stepping forward now to approach it.

0

'My Mama and Papa are lying on the floor and they don't get up.'

The man resting against the roof of the car was tall and lean. He was dressed in wide brown pants, brown shoes and a grubby white shirt. He turned, sleepily surprised, to look down at his visitor. He was aged about twenty-two, with a gaunt face, pale skin, thick red lips and lifeless, red-rimmed eyes. His chin was covered in honey brown stubble and his hair, almost blond, was greasy and astray, one lank forelock dangling over his brow.

'Hey now, what's this? What's that? What we got here?' he was saying. His lips slid back into an unpleasing smile, giving a glimpse of uneven grey teeth. He had turned right around and was leaning with his elbows on the roof of the car now. 'Watchoo doin out here, boy?' In one hand was a bottle of whisky, three quarters full. Lying along the roof was a shotgun.

Rogelio was tugging at the man's pants in exasperation. 'My Mama . . .'

The man was laughing – a weird, high-pitched sound that Rogelio recognized. His companion by the wheel grinned. He was about the same age, of heavier build with dark hair, cut – almost shaved – crew-style, and a chubby pink face. He wore jeans and a black sweatshirt with a red and yellow Babe Ruth emblem on the front. He was sweating heavily and his sweat stained his shirt. He said nothing.

'Hey, Pachuco, you gettin mad at me?' the lean man was saying through his laughter. He was swigging the whisky and passing the

234

bottle to his friend, lolling against the car. He was wiping his lips
with his wrist, smirking.

The two men were talking to each other. The lean one was taking
the shotgun from the roof and lowering himself onto the balls of
his feet beside the boy. 'Hey, Pachuco, listen to this. What do you
say we go for a ride in the automobile?'

Rogelio looked at the big pale green car. The man was opening
the rear door. 'We'll go find your Mama and Papa! We'll go see
what they been doin!'

He climbed inside. He was tired and troubled. Looking up, he
saw the lean man straighten and wink at his friend before climbing
in beside him.

They were driving and the two men were laughing and passing
jokes and passing the whisky bottle back and forth between them.
Rogelio was sitting small against the door, shrinking from the
stale-smelling bulk of the lean man.

'Pachuco, you know what this is?' the lean man was saying now.
Between his legs he was caressing the length of the dull black
shotgun barrel. 'You know what it does?'

He was giggling and lowering the muzzle so that the tip was
touching the boy's cheek. Rogelio innocently returned his gaze.
The lean man was scrutinizing his face closely, leering, making a
clicking sound in the back of his throat, curling a bony finger
around the trigger. Babe Ruth was watching eagerly through the
rear-view mirror.

'Okay. I'll show you. I'll show you what it does.'

He was shifting the barrel suddenly, pointing it out of the
window and squeezing the trigger. There was a deafening boom
and the gun barrel leapt into the air. It banged the top of the
window-frame and flew backwards at the same time, ramming the
lean man in the chest. 'Fuck! Fuck! Motherfucker!'

Sharp smelling blue smoke stung Rogelio's eyes and throat.
Babe Ruth was laughing, tears in his eyes. The lean man glaring at
him furiously, rubbing his breastbone, then relaxing. He slumped
back against the door and began to giggle. Rogelio's ears were
ringing. He watched him. The man giggled helplessly, drunkenly,
an insane, wire-strung, yapping sound that screwed up his eyes
and shook his shoulders and chest.

Now he fell silent. He sucked at the rim of the whisky bottle. His head was swaying and his red eyes were on Rogelio. 'Hey, Pachuco, you know what this is?' He was squeezing himself between his legs. 'You ever seen one of these before?' He was starting to undo the buttons of his pants. 'You know what it does?'

He was rubbing himself vigorously now, snickering. He stretched his lips and sucked in air through his teeth. His free hand reached out suddenly and grabbed the boy by the hair, yanking him over. 'Hoo! Look boy! Know what it is? Huh? Huh?'

Rogelio was pinioned by the man's arm. He was lying still, hardly able to breathe. His face was pressed against reeking flesh. The lean man was twisting his fingers in his hair. He was pressing him against himself, grunting.

Suddenly Babe Ruth's voice. His hand over the back of the seat was thumping the lean man urgently. 'Hey! *Hey!* Looka here! Hot tamale! Looka!' The pressure of the man's arm eased.

Rogelio was thrust aside. The lean man craned forward to see through the windscreen. He sat back and stuffed himself inside his pants. Babe Ruth was slowing the car, pulling it to a halt.

Rogelio saw a girl, aged about fifteen or sixteen, appear at the front nearside window. She was thin-faced and dark, a Mexican peasant girl, her long hair tied behind her head. Babe Ruth was asking where she was going, leaning over and unlatching the door. The girl did not understand. He repeated himself in Spanish. She said she was on her way home, to the next village.

'We're headed through there,' he was pushing open the door. 'We can save you a walk.'

The girl backed away a step and shook her head.

'Me and my brother, we're just takin the boy back there. His folks are there. I reckon you must be familiar?' He invented some name and the girl shook her head again, but seeing Rogelio in the back seemed to ease her mind a little. A few more words and she nodded. She was climbing in the front beside Babe Ruth.

He was driving, and he was taking the car off the highway and down a dirt track. They had been talking with the girl, making jokes and suggestions. She was shy. She replied with quick smiles and frightened rabbit eyes and few words. Now she said suddenly, 'No! It is not this way!'

236

The lean man was giggling again. 'Senorita, you ever seen one of these?'

She was turning, her eyes widening with shock.

'And you ever seen one of these?' In his right hand the shotgun was pointed at her head. He was grinning delightedly. He was letting go of the gun suddenly to seize her by the hair, as he had done Rogelio. He was hauling her bodily half over the back of the seat, forcing her head down. 'Suck, senorita. Suck!'

Babe Ruth was pulling the car over to the side, killing the engine. He was sliding over behind the girl and pushing her cotton skirt up over her back. 'Jeez,' he was saying, 'Jeez.' He was undoing his jeans and ramming his fingers into her vagina.

Rogelio watched them. He watched them as they got out of the car and dragged the girl into an adjacent field. He watched her face, crazed with fright, blubbering, praying as she fell out of the door.

He was very tired. He laid his head down on the seat and curled up his legs. The sun had dipped behind the hills now and there was only darkness beyond the car door. His mind was dazed by the things that had happened to him. He was troubled by the sounds coming to him from outside. He was thinking suddenly of his parents.

He sat up. He could see no one, they were on the other side. He wanted to leave them. He was climbing out of the car and walking away.

0

It was back on a main road, perhaps half-an-hour later, that the car lights picked him up. They turned the invisible asphalt beneath his feet an eerie, mottled grey, lifting it, shifting it, making it grow with a life of its own. They gave him a black shadow which stretched away before him, flying giddily into the darkness ahead. He stopped and turned. The car was approaching rapidly, the headlights full in his eyes.

He watched it for a second. He knew that he did not want to be back with the two men and the girl. He did not like them, and for the first time that day he was afraid. He ran.

He was in vines. He was stumbling blindly between the ranks over loose clods of dry earth, down an incline.

The car pulled up on the road behind him. He heard the door open and a man's voice was calling after him. He ran on, losing his footing, crashing into a vine and tumbling to the floor, his face and forearms scraping on the hard soil. He was scrambling up again, heedless of any pain. Breathless, panicking. He dashed headlong, feeling he was making no headway.

He was aware that he had been spotted. In the darkness to his rear he sensed a presence, huge and distinct. He was darting beneath the wires of the nearest rank, the leaves shaking violently as his pursuer did the same. The beam of a torch touched him, lost him, found him again.

There were footsteps. Close behind. Heavy and crushing hard soil; the sound of laboured breathing. He was ducking beneath another rank, and another, knowing instinctively that he had the edge in that direction. He heard his pursuer curse and he sped on, gaining inches – until the ranks came to an end.

Rogelio halted, ran forward, and fell with a cry into a shallow ditch. He landed heavily and lay still, winded and gasping, his limbs paralysed. The torch flashed only feet away. It vanished, reappeared and flickered over him. A figure, dark and towering, was stepping down into the ditch.

A massive hand fell on his shoulder and pulled him upright. He screamed, but the scream caught somewhere in the back of his throat and no sound emerged. The torchlight blinded him. It shifted and he blinked his eyes. He was staring into the gleaming, quizzical face of an officer of the highway patrol.

⊙　⊙　⊙　⊙　⊙

# 2

When he had seen Hugh off at the front door Samson hung around in the hall for a minute. He took off his brick-red tie and dropped it over the hallstand. He leaned against the wall, his hands deep in the pockets of his trousers, musing and attentive. Presently he heard the bathroom door open. He stepped forward alacritously, in perfect time to intercept Jill as she made her way back towards the lounge.

'Ah, Jill!' He spread his arms with a surprised and delighted smile, placing himself in her path and effectively barring her passage. '*Quelle coincidence!* Where have you been? No, don't answer that. I missed you. You know, it's been unbearably dull in there these last few minutes. I had to get out to reassure myself I was still alive!'

'Dull?' Jill said. She halted in front of him, looking up at him with questioning, smiling eyes. Her earrings winked at him as they danced in the light. The little stars twinkled on the ends of their slender gold chains. Her Vuitton bag hung from one shoulder and she had re-applied her make-up.

'Well, perhaps not dull, exactly . . .' he said with a grin. She looked divine. 'Calamitous might be a better word.' He slid his eyes over her with a quickening of his breath and a distinct stirring in his loins. His mind raced stealthily ahead, shaping in earnest his next few moves.

'Look, I feel I owe you an apology for all this,' he said, swaying a little and turning his hand vaguely towards the lounge. 'I mean, I invite you here to my party, promising you an entertaining evening, and then these – *cuckoos* turn up and ruin everything for everyone. And what with everything else I feel I've really let you down.'

'No you haven't. Of course you haven't, Samson,' she replied warmly. 'I've enjoyed myself. I've had a good time. Really.' There was a glimmer of sardonic humour in her eyes as she added, 'It wasn't quite what I was expecting, exactly, but . . . I'm glad I came.' She nodded towards the lounge. 'Aren't they friends of yours, then?'

'Friends of mine? God! No way are they friends of mine. They're friends of my wife's. She has a penchant for collecting bits of human debris.'

Jill twisted her mouth in a contemplative manner. 'I think we ought to be going quite soon, though.'

'Going? What, already? No, don't go yet. The party hasn't even started yet. Listen, I've had enough of this; I'm going to throw this lot out in a minute. I've got a few friends turning up' – he glanced at his watch – 'ooh, any time now as a matter of fact. They're a great bunch. They'll get this party on its feet. You'll see. Things'll really start to move when they get here.'

'But what about Corinne?' Jill said. 'She isn't very happy with it all, is she. Wouldn't it be better if we went?'

'No. No-o. Don't worry about Corinne. She gets like this sometimes. She gets these turns. But she's fine, really. I expect she'll go to bed in a minute.

'Listen,' he slipped an arm about her waist, allowing his gaze to plummet into the front of her halter-neck top, 'What do you think of my apartment, anyway? Would you like to have a look around? You haven't really seen much of it, have you. And there's nothing happening in there at the moment. If you like I'll show you around and we can rejoin them in a few minutes, when the others arrive.'

Jill considered this for a second. She seemed to think it would be a good idea. 'All right,' she said, 'if you're sure. I would like to see it, actually. It's a nice flat. I'd like a place like this. I could do with a bit more room where I am. Have you lived here very long?'

'No, not very.' He propelled her gently away from the lounge door. 'Prior to this I was working in the States. I had an apartment in New York for a while, and before that I was in LA'

'Really?'

'Yes.'

0

Rogelio stayed with the police for one and a half days, until they succeeded in locating his home. He was able to tell them his name and that he had found his mother and father lying on the floor, but little else.

On the first day he was taken in a patrol car around the villages and jimtowns in the region, and driven out to the local farms to make enquiries of the landowners. Nobody could place him. It was midway through the following morning that the cop happened to drive past the little frame house where he had lived with his parents.

The house was silent and still. There was no breeze and not even the leaves on the walnut tree moved. Rogelio led the cop around to the rear of the house. In the yard Popo lay as he had last seen her, her body food now for a living carpet of insects. There was a putrid, palling odour in the heavy air.

Rogelio was pushing open the screen door and entering the kitchen. The air came alive, dark and loud and angry with flies. The smell here was worse but he did not notice. He was crossing to where his mother sat. He was pushing at her body. She did not move.

'You see!'

He turned to the cop, but the cop was no longer behind him. Frowning, he went back over to the door. The cop was outside in the yard. He was on his hands and knees, throwing up into the dust.

0

Julia had been sitting since her arrival on the chair in the corner of the room, observing the evening's proceedings with a feeling of increasing aversion and estrangement. She was wondering when the party was going to begin. She was asking herself why she had come.

In her mind a process of consolidation was underway. She was bolstering her opinions – opinions which she had formulated earlier, much earlier – concerning the people in whose company she now found herself. The majority of these persons she had never set eyes on in her life before. Nevertheless she was reflecting morosely on the way these people, all people, and men especially, had mistreated her.

Time and time again she had allowed them, unwittingly, to exploit her. She had been younger then, of course, and incapable of seeing through their veneer; she had been gullible and green and they were all statesmen in the art of dissimulation. It was not until later, having been discarded so many times like an empty cigarette carton, that comprehension had begun to dawn.

With abhorrence now she was recalling, as she ever recalled, those years of climbing on stages and catering to the appetites of beer-sodden males. She recalled the wolf-whistles and the cat-calls

241

and the prurient, ghoulish leers. She recalled the cynical hunger in their eyes as she removed her outfits piece by piece, as she jiggled her tits and rolled her hips and put her fanny on display like a fillet of boiled bacon.

She recalled with bitterness and anger the men who had inveigled their way into her life; their disarming smiles, their glib, seductive promises and assurances of love and security and a future. She recalled how she had swallowed it all then. In those days she had believed that love could be a reality, that sincerity was a genuine human trait, that dreams were attainable. It was only after she had married, had got pregnant, had found herself suddenly abandoned and obliged to seek out a back-street abortionist that she had begun to seriously question her beliefs.

Four years later she had fallen again; and history had repeated itself: two years of wavering uncertainty, then desertion and the discovery that she was pregnant once more. For the second time she had murdered her unborn child.

And that was when she had begun to grow indurate. Something inside her had bared its teeth. She had entered into a contract with herself: It would never happen again. Never. She had learned her lesson. It was better to be alone than preyed upon.

And one day she woke up and she was thirty-five. Life had passed her by like a sandstorm. And it still went on, long after her desire and use for it had waned. It embraced her like a straitjacket, clinging tenaciously, heedless of her attempts to extricate herself from it.

All this she held inside herself now, clamouring to yell it in their faces. But she couldn't. She remained mute, for she was so *tight* inside. Her guts were tight, her limbs were tight. Her hands were tight like arthritic talons. Her lips were compressed like they'd been stapled together with steel wire. Nothing could get out. Nothing could get in. Her thoughts bombarded her, crashing around inside her skull, winding her tighter and tighter. She was like a steel mainspring that had been wound beyond its limit and was about to let go.

0

'I was thinking . . .' Jill was saying, '. . . some of the things Hugh was saying, about nuclear war and everything. It's true, isn't it.' She stood by the kitchen window, looking out, two fingers sliding abstractedly back and forth along the edge of the stainless-steel draining-board.

Samson had arranged himself close behind her. He was nibbling at the ends of his moustache, appreciatively observant of the fact that, were she to shift her weight backwards by a mere inch, her left buttock would come into contact quite piquantly with the unfurling monster in his trousers. 'What's that?' he enquired softly.

'Well, it's something I think about a lot. You know, it really worries me.'

'In what way?'

'Well . . .' She turned to him with a look of troubled introspection, her shoulders raised. 'I mean, sometimes – when I'm walking down the street, say, an aeroplane will fly over. A forces jet, not a passenger plane. And without even realizing I'm doing it I find myself thinking: Oh God, could this be it? Could this be the one? It's like a reflex. I feel myself tensing up, anticipating the flash. And it's so *real*. Sometimes I'm almost paralysed with fear. It's horrible. At any second I know I could be frazzled.

'We live in this age . . . it's *incredible*!' she went on, her green eyes flashing and her hands tense by her sides. 'I don't think there's anyone on this planet today who can really claim to be sane. Not with a threat like this hanging over us every second. It's so big. So insidious. It creeps into every corner of your life. It reduces your life to nothing. It makes everything so meaningless.'

Samson shrugged.

'Doesn't it get to you like that?' she asked.

'Not really.'

'But you must be worried by it?'

'Well, I do think about it, sure. I know that it's a very real threat. But at the same time, I'm not going to allow it to dominate my thoughts. I can join the CND and go on demos and things if I feel it'll do any good; but I keep it all in proportion. It's no good living in constant dread of something that might well never happen. I live to enjoy myself. That's what I think we're here for.'

'But they could drop the bomb at any second! We could be wiped out!'

'True. But equally, we could spend our lives locked away in a cell somewhere underground, too afraid to go anywhere or do anything in case they chose that moment to launch an attack. And where's the sense in that, now?

'Small point:' he added lightly, ' – it wouldn't be a forces jet, it would be a missile. Or a bunch of them. So you can rest easy next time you spot a plane.'

She was exasperated. 'I'm nineteen!' she protested. 'I've got all these things I want to do! I should have my whole life ahead of me still!'

Samson suppressed a sigh, wishing she would shut up. These young girls, they were so fickle. They wandered off the track so easily. Where was the point in getting het-up over a subject like this? You were never going to solve anything. It just put the dampers on everything.

And it was so remote from the matter in hand.

Still, she had to get it off her chest, he supposed. He wasn't going to make much progress until she had.

He put his hands on her shoulders. Light-heartedly he said, 'Well, if it came down to it I think I would rather be frazzled than survive a nuclear war, anyway. I mean, the only other survivors would be Margaret Thatcher and her minions, bits of the army, the police and an assortment of blistered, starving lunatics. Just think of that.'

She half-smiled, tautly, out of politeness. Then she said, 'How can it be like this? How can these people be given the power to do these things? This is *my* life. Why aren't I given a say in what happens to me?'

'Jill. Jill. Come on,' he said, squeezing her shoulders gently and drawing her to him, inhaling deeply as he felt the ends of her breasts depress softly against him. 'Don't let it get on top of you. You have to enjoy life. Have fun. Be nice to yourself.'

'Yes, I know,' she said. 'But it just makes me so angry sometimes. You know. It just gets to me. I wonder what's wrong with us all that we can entrust our lives to some egomaniac like Reagan or Thatcher. It's crazy, isn't it. It's unbelievable.' She shook her head, hooking her blonde hair behind one ear. 'Everything. It's all so bloody bewildering.'

He raised his eyebrows, mildly surprised. 'Yes, bewildering's the word,' he agreed, opting for a jocose rejoinder now. 'Bloody damn bewildering if you ask me. God, I haven't been this bewildered since travelling down the birth-canal.'

0

From the pocket of her tartan skirt Julia took a crumpled packet of

244

tobacco wrapped in gold foil, and some cigarette papers. She rolled another cigarette, her eyes alternating between glaring balefully at the others and staring out of the window. It was very warm in the Tallis's lounge. Even with the French windows open it felt close.

Julia's odium irradiated silently into the room as her nicotine fingers performed automatically the delicate operation with tobacco and paper. Though deep inside her fugitive tears still formed they were vaporized before they could penetrate the substrata of her thoughts, were debased and dispersed beneath the layers of thick armour she wore. Her loathing reached out to touch all men, all of humanity, all of existence. It reached in to maul her beleaguered soul.

More than anything else these days Julia despised herself – for having allowed herself to be taken in so easily. And so often. For having allowed herself to fail.

Screwing up her face now she put the completed cigarette to her lips, struck a match to the tip and drew hard. She had neglected to dampen the tip, and as she pulled the cigarette away it caught, dragging a piece of her lower lip with it. She winced and cursed inaudibly. Taking a paper tissue from her pocket she dabbed at the lip, examining it for blood.

Across from her the Baileys were still carolling their preposterous hymn. She scowled at them – and at Gerald especially. She plastered her lungs with tar from the newly-wetted cigarette.

Why on earth had she come here tonight?

For a second she drew a blank. For a second she was uncomfortably disoriented. She had known what to expect, the kind of idiots she would have to meet. She had known that she was incapable of enjoying it, that it would not change anything, that she would still be herself at the end of it.

She had known too that Samson would be here. Samson, who was the embodiment of all the men she had ever hated, who had ever wronged her. So what had made her come?

She thought now, with a chill ripple of emotion, of a vague notion she had entertained earlier. A half-formed plan she had hatched whilst sitting alone in her flat in the dark. It was designed to bring emphatically to the fore, in a manner that nobody could possibly avoid taking notice of, her preoccupation with the way life had treated her.

It involved Samson. In fact, its success would be largely dependent upon his being there. And she was coming to realize now, with mounting frustration and anger, that Samson was not likely to be returning to the room for some time.

Julia was distracted from her sullen meanderings quite suddenly by a curious noise – a wingeing noise that seemed to come from somewhere close by, actually within the room. Though not particularly loud it was piercing. It cut eerily through the Baileys chanting and through the soft music that played through the stereo system. It aroused Corinne momentarily from her stupor and even caused Richard to raise his head.

It ceased a moment, then resumed. 'Mmmmaaaaaaaaaaa!' it went. 'Mmmaaaaammmmmmmaaaaaaaa!'

She glanced about her, trying to locate its source. It was disturbingly obtrusive, an anguished ululation, like that of some wild creature in deep distress.

She half-raised herself from her seat, feeling the hairs on the back of her neck rise as she recognized a certain quality in the sound: it was not issuing from the throat of an animal. Its origin was distinctly human.

She located its source at last. It was coming from behind the further of the two sofas. It was Rogelio.

0

'Do you really know all of those people?' Jill was asking now, referring to the photographs Samson had on display in the lounge.

'Ye-es,' he replied with nonchalance, grateful that her *weltschmerz* was only fleeting.

'What, on a personal level or just business?'

'Both. Some of them are my closest friends. You know, you approach them initially on a business level – or they approach you – but the nature of this business involves getting to know them quite intimately. It has to, if you think about it.'

'Yes, I can see that. But people like Paul and Linda and –'

'Oh yes, I see them quite frequently. When they're in town, that is. In fact, I had dinner with them only a couple of weeks ago. I invited them along here tonight, as a matter of fact.'

'Really?'

'Yes. But they can't come. They're off to Jamaica, working on a

246

new album.' He waited a second, then added, 'Debbie might be coming, though. Debbie Harry. She and Chris are in town doing some promotion. They said they'd try and make it later on. They're a great pair. I like them a lot. And they're bound to bring some friends, so who knows who might be turning up?' His voice took on a confidential air and he nodded towards the lounge. 'That's another reason why I want to get rid of that lot in there. I can just see them trying to lead Debbie and Chris and everyone in a rousing session of Songs of Praise. They'd probably have them converted by the end of the evening – and what the hell would that do for their record sales?'

She tittered and stepped over to the cooker to investigate the contents of various pots and pans Corinne had left behind.

'They are pretty weird, aren't they,' she agreed, dipping into one and withdrawing a sliver of carrot. 'I mean, sometimes I can laugh about it, that kind of thing. It's just a joke, in a way. But at the same time it's a bit sinister, too. Don't you think? It gives me the creeps.'

'Ye-es,' he said vaguely.

'There are so many of them,' she said. 'And they manage to get such a hold on people. They become so powerful.'

'Mmmh,' he concurred. He was only half-listening now. He was contemplating the fine profile of her left breast and the nipple, forming a perfect peak beneath the green of the halter-neck top. His mind was occupied once more with the task of assigning her a precise rating on his liability scale.

Initially, at their first meeting, he had placed her quite categorically around the seventy to eighty mark; and since then he had reaffirmed that assessment several times. And now all her signals told him she had risen by several degrees. She was ripe for the plucking, so to speak – were it not for one crucial thing. The ring. That damned diamond-cluster ring that she wore on the third finger of her left hand.

'You'd think that you would never get involved with something like that,' Jill went on, 'that it's only people who are really gullible or inadequate or something who get taken in by it. But it's surprising, sometimes, the people who do . . .'

The ring was the one point of contention still extant in his mind as far as Jill was concerned. It was causing her to fluctuate on the scale. It was a nagging uncertainty, a perplexing conundrum.

Mentally he had compared it to discovering a dry rat's turd in his Sugar Puffs.

'I suppose if it fulfils a need,' she said. 'But they always get so fanatical about it. They always insist that theirs is *the* way. The one "True Path". They blinker themselves, I think. They never allow for anything else.'

He was undecided as to the wisdom of at some point broaching the subject with her. She and the wimp hardly gave the impression of being besotted with one another, it was true. But then again, it was hard to be certain. They were young, he reasoned, in a group of strangers. Things like that. Their behaviour would naturally be a little restrained.

On the other hand, though, it might prove more expedient to simply forge ahead regardless. He could always change his tack if she did not respond accordingly. It was only really the time factor that was unresolved, after all. Other than that she was a dead cert.

He slid up beside her on the pretence of joining her in fishing around in the pans, and placed a hand lightly on the small of her back, peering over her shoulder.

'It's a fine feast,' he murmured.

'It's the same with the established religions,' she said, ' – with Christianity. They just limit themselves to a set of basic rigid ideas and never try to look anywhere else. And if it were true, if theirs *was* the "True Path", then there would be no need for the others, would there? I mean, surely, if one group had the answer then word would get around and everyone would flock to them. Don't you think? The very fact that there are so many groups all setting themselves up in opposition to one another seems proof to me that they've all got it wrong. They're all a load of wallies.'

Samson blew air covertly, wondering at her ability to prattle on. He leaned over the cooker – and as he did so he stopped short suddenly. He turned away so that she would not catch his expression. He had just noticed something. He had just noticed that the diamond-cluster ring was no longer on Jill's finger. He put his hand over his mouth, hard put to prevent himself from throwing back his head and cackling out loud at the irony of it all.

● ● ● ● ●

248

# 3

Corinne opened her eyes.

They were heavy, languid. They passed no messages back to her brain. Of their own accord they closed again.

She fell away behind them. Dark seas, gently swirling, inexorable, washed over her, drawing her with them. She drifted like flotsam, like jetsam, pulled slowly with the spiralling drag of an unfathomable whirlpool.

It was all so pleasant. This feeling, this calmness, this soft smile on her lips, she could feel even as her tears welled and her sadness threatened to flood. Knowing that whilst this sensation endured, whilst she made no attempt to fasten, to belong to anything, she would be detached from the world, could bid farewell to her knowledge, all her connections were dissolved.

Anybody desiring to speak with her now need not receive an instantaneous reply. Any event that might occur need not demand her attention or participation. Any crises would simply pass on by without her. She was random. She was elsewhere. She was no place in particular. Nobody could intrude upon her now – they all lacked the means of locating her.

But something *was* intruding. Though she resisted it, though she denied it and struggled against it, something external had succeeded in perforating the frail walls of her token world. She could feel a part of herself fastening on to it, reluctantly, acting on instinct. It was lifting her, pulling her, reeling her in, and now she had to, wanted to, go with it. She was being hauled back out of the whirlpool. She opened her eyes.

The room slid gradually back into focus. It hovered, then lurched unsteadily, the light making her feel a little nauseous. In front of her she made out her hands. They were far away, hazy, little to do with her, disembodied white things on the wide grey expanse of her thighs.

She was aware of the mess she must appear. She felt huge, lifeless – an unsightly mass of useless flesh, a prisoner of her own corpulence. She was confronted with an image, something from a

249

television documentary the other day: the queen in a colony of termites – a bloated, bulging tube of pulsing jelly encased within a soft, semi-translucent membrane, unbelievably massive, disgustingly alive, mindless, unable to move, totally dependent. She shuddered. She was turning into a figment of one of her own worst nightmares.

Now something else was making her uneasy. It was the same thing that had drawn her back to consciousness. A strange sound, a human cry, so plaintive as to cause her to react against her will, and bring her rushing to try and do something that might help alleviate the distress its originator was so plainly suffering. She was confused. She could not decide where the sound was coming from. For one terrible moment she thought it was herself.

She groped for the cigarettes and lighter which lay on one arm of her chair. Her limbs responded like plasticine to her efforts at coordination, her torso so cumbrous she could barely move it forward the required distance. The attempt seemed to take an age.

She succeeded in grasping the pack then slumped back heavily. The strange noise still continued. She sensed rather than perceived a flurry of movement to one side, and understood that Margaret had darted behind the sofa, that there was something the matter with Rogelio. A part of her strove to stand up, to offer some kind of assistance, but she knew she was incapable of rising.

After several fumbling attempts with the lid of her cigarette packet she succeeded in coaxing out a cigarette and lighting it. It came to her now that she had just glimpsed her husband through the serving-hatch, in the kitchen. And he was with Jill. She understood what must be going on in there but found it impossible to summon up an appropriate emotional response. It didn't seem to matter any more. Nothing did. Her eyes were filling with tears again but that no longer mattered either.

She took a feeble puff of her cigarette, too far gone to inhale the smoke. Her eyelids were once more leaden and warm, insisting they be allowed to come together. There was a marble ashtray on the other arm of her chair. She let the cigarette drop into it, still alight. Her hands fell into her lap. Her head lolled back against the chair. For a second she was looking at Richard, hunched forward like some strange unhappy statue on the edge of the sofa. She felt a moment of immense pity for him. Then her eyes closed and she slid away for the last time.

0

Samson was thinking back, trying to remember when he had last noticed Jill wearing the ring. Was it in the hall? He thought so but he couldn't be certain. In the lounge, though, definitely. How about since they'd been in the kitchen? Again, he could not quite recall – but really, what the hell did it matter?

He smoothed the ends of his moustache and watched her as she talked on. He was relaxed and assured, no longer speculating. He understood now the reason for this sudden spate of nervous chatter. It was a front; a self-conscious and over-compensatory attempt to mask – more for her own sake than his – the glaring univocity of her move.

In a hurried voice she was telling him now about some friend she had known who had got himself mixed up with a religious group. Samson would have been surprised, she said, because he didn't seem the type. He was young and intelligent. He was studying economics at university. He was well off, too, and really good looking. You'd have thought he had everything going for him.

But they picked him up on the street one day. She couldn't remember which lot it was now . . . It wasn't the Hare Krishnas, she didn't think. Nor the Moonies. But it was one of those sects.

Samson interrupted her with an indulgent twinkle. 'Is that all you ever think about?'

'What?'

'Sects.'

For a second she was abashed. Her eyes darted, avoiding his, and her cheeks pinked a little. Then, recovering herself quickly, she said, with a foxy smile and a certain aplomb, 'Religious sects?'

He just smiled and settled himself comfortably back against the worktop, leaving her to tread water in the little pool of silence he left behind. He was enjoying this cat-and-mouse charade immensely.

'Do you ever take anything seriously?' Jill asked.

He folded his arms and looked her up and down. 'One or two things.'

She formed her lips into a cute, thoughtful little pout. Then,

251

irrelevantly and seemingly out of the blue she said, 'Tell me something about you.'

'Like what?'

'Well . . . Don't you have any children?'

He snorted amusedly. 'Children?' he joked, 'Nah. Never. Can't stand 'em. Nasty, noisy little brats, shitting and pissing everywhere, breaking everything in sight, coming home covered in blood and expecting you to go out and beat up somebody's six-foot, ex-wrestler dad . . . God, I wouldn't have them in the house unless they were tied up and gagged. You know, I even hated myself when I was a kid.'

She laughed and he felt a little of her tension slip away. He had been going to add that there was no point, anyway, because Corinne and he were getting a divorce, but he changed his mind. He reached for her hand. 'What about you?'

'Don't be silly. Of course I haven't.'

He let his fingers slide lightly up the smooth skin of her arm, coming to rest on her bare shoulder. 'You're beautiful,' he murmured. His other hand went up to her right shoulder and drew her gently to him, delighting in the pressure of her belly as it collided softly with what had now developed into a very serious erection indeed; revelling in the knowledge that she had felt it too.

She showed no inclination to pull away. His lips touched her cheek, her hair, then back to her cheek again. One tentative hand began to roam the velvet smoothness of her back. She let out a little sigh. 'What are you doing?'

'I want to make love to you.'

'But Corinne. She can see.'

He glanced beyond her, to the serving-hatch; Corinne was in view but her eyes were closed. He planted two kisses on Jill's shoulder, let his lips brush her neck. 'Don't you want to?' he said huskily.

She was silent a moment, a ghost of a frown on her brow. Her green emerald eyes were shining, looking directly into his, then dropping, her lower lip held between her teeth. She seemed about to reply, then her attention veered suddenly, caught by something.

'What's that noise?'

It was Samson's turn to frown. A curious, incongruous sound was filtering through to them from the lounge.

'What the hell – ' He let go of her and strode over to the serving-hatch to peer through.

The moment she had realized what was happening Margaret Bailey had darted from her seat and rushed to Rogelio's side. She found him sitting in a small, rag-doll pile of wavering limbs, crying out tragically, bright tears squeezing through his tight-shut eyelids.

She dropped to her knees and cradled his head to her bosom. She held him tight.

Unconscious of her presence he was reaching out with one little hand and pawing floppily at her kimono. The other gripped the leg of his baggy jeans.

'Mmmmaaa-mmaaaaaaaaaaaa!' he wailed. 'Maaaaaamm-mmaaaaaaa!'

She rocked him. She soothed him. She pressed her face into his chaotic hair. 'It's all right! Rogelio! It's all right, my baby!'

He continued to cry out, his face all contorted, like a man with a fragment of burning shrapnel in his belly. His eyes opened suddenly and the tears tumbled out like panic-stricken sheep.

'Mmaaaammmmmaaa!'

'I'm here!' Margaret told him. 'My baby! Rogelio. Mama's here! Mama's here!'

She squeezed him tighter to her. She kissed away his tears. She whispered words of comfort. She hugged him and soothed him – and gradually his cries began to abate. His body relaxed against hers, and his wild blue eyes rolled upwards to stare uncomprehendingly at her. Then suddenly he tensed. He drew a great, gasping, struggling breath and sat half-upright, his body rigid.

'*Mama!*' he shrieked, his eyes on a space above and before his head, then fell back, barely sensible, and stared blindly at the back of the sofa. Margaret bent over him, quietly sobbing.

Gerald had stationed himself at her side, one hand laid supportively on her shoulder. Now his fingers gave her a gentle squeeze. She looked up at him.

'I didn't know,' she wept, her voice laden with self-reproach. 'He was here all alone and neither of us realized it was happening.'

Gravely Gerald lowered himself onto one knee beside her. 'We can't blame ourselves,' he said. 'You know that. We've always been aware that one day it might happen when we weren't there.

And we *were* here. We were here in time. That's the important thing.'

She nodded, unconsoled, stroking Rogelio's head in her lap, and Gerald gazed at the carpet, seeming to wrestle with something deep inside himself. Presently, with some hesitancy, he said, 'Margaret . . .'

She bowed her head.

He took her hand. 'Darling, I must.'

She nodded weakly. 'I know,' she sniffed, without looking up.

Now, in a sudden transformation of character, Gerald assumed the airs of a solemn man, a figure of great authority, someone bowing beneath the load of a heavy burden. He shifted his body until he was facing Rogelio. He took his lifeless hands in his.

'Rogelio,' he whispered. The artist did not stir.

'Rogelio.' He gently patted his cheeks. 'Rogelio, it's me. It's Gerald.'

A tiny spark of life came gradually into Rogelio's eyes. The eyelids quivered and he focused slowly on the man before him, seeming to show a ghost of a glimmer of recognition. Gerald smiled. He gripped Rogelio's hands more firmly.

'Rogelio,' he repeated urgently, 'you have to tell us. We have to know. Is there a message?'

0

'Hah!' Samson guffawed, moving away from the serving-hatch. He had been able to see little other than the top of Margaret's head rocking back and forth and her husband positioned anxiously at her shoulder, but he had heard Rogelio's pathetic cries. 'Hah! Would you credit it? He's already beginning to distinguish Mama from Papa!'

'What is it?' asked Jill.

He shook his head, chuckling. 'Nothing,' he said. 'It's just that loopy little artist again. I think he's giving birth to a new creation.'

The mood of a few seconds ago broken, he took her hand. 'Come on, I'll show you the rest of the place.'

He led her out of the kitchen and into the hall. 'All the best bits are still to come.'

• • • • •

# 4

'We have to know, Rogelio. Is there a message?'

As Gerald's persistent, repeater-technique interrogation succeeded in hacking a path through the depredation that had seized the minute limner's mind, his body began to show signs of a return to life. His features were grey and twisted, his eyes dulled by pain. He was facing into an abyss. There was emptiness, reachlessness, above him and all around him. He was staring into the chasm where his mother and father should have been.

The memory that had rocked him was almost dispelled, though not entirely. Residual, hypnopompic images were still swimming before his mind's eye. His pupils were dilating and contracting in an attempt to focus on them: myriad tiny creatures swarming and clustering, intangible but alive, tantalizing and repulsing. In his solar plexus a volcano of emotions had erupted, racking him and making him sob convulsively.

The images shifted desultorily. He made sweeping, clearing motions with his hands, trying to remove them from his vision. They were disconnected, apart, and yet they came together like one, formed a living, moving carpet.

And he was aware that in the atmosphere behind them there was something else. He sensed a presence, something huge and distinct. And he understood that the myriad creatures were not separate from this presence, and that at the same time they were. They were manifestations of it, and it was a manifestation of them. They were apart but never disconnected. There were a million, a million million, and at the same time they were One. He closed his eyes for a second, striving to elicit some meaning from it all. His hands went to his breast, trying to quell the unbearable flood of emotion there.

And now his mind was being fuelled by Gerald's questioning. It began to revolve with a vengeance. The message. What was the message?

At first he did not understand what was being demanded of him. He began to whimper, entreating his inquisitor to leave him be;

but Gerald was not letting up. Though he was not conscious of it, Margaret's arms were around him. Her tears, from time to time, were splashing his cheeks or falling into his hair.

And still Gerald persisted. The same question. The same tone of voice. *The message. What was the message?*

Rogelio sank deeper into himself. He retreated into that region where, sometimes, tranquillity reigned. And gradually something began to clarify. It came like a cloud forming, spreading, deepening, and then suddenly parting to reveal the blinding orb of the sun. In a stab of pained recognition, that crippling memory now obliterated and forgotten, he realized what had happened to him. He had been in trance! He had been away somewhere in a telepathic communication of minds on another plane!

And this time something momentous had occurred.

He racked his brain to try and recall what it might have been. The message! The message! And with a strangled gasp it came to him now just what had occurred. He had been communing just now, but this had not been one of the customary communications he was used to. There was something far more compelling about it. This time – and he understood this now with terrifying certainty – for the first time ever, he had been communing *directly with the mind of Scompiglio!*

He let out a cry. He opened his eyes.

'Rogelio! Tell us!' Gerald's voice was imperative. 'Tell us!'

And listen. This wretched, tragic mite of a human being was now poised on the verge of precipitating himself, finally and irretrievably, into total madness. He was about to say the words and perform the actions that would bring about utter chaos. In that room filled with loneliness and fear and sorrow and hate and confusion and religious fervour and specious emotion and misdirected love, he had become the catalyst which would be the direct cause of the deaths of three persons. Indirectly he was going to cause the deaths of five, even six.

Gerald and Margaret Bailey, those two ludicrously, *criminally*, misinformed imbeciles he was unfortunate enough to regard as friends, had steadily and systematically annihilated him with their 'love'. And now he, in turn, was about to do the same for them.

0

Meanwhile Samson switched off the light and closed the door to the first bedroom as he and Jill stepped back out into the hall.

'Like it?' he asked.

'Yes. It's lovely. It's really nice.' She paused to admire an oriental print on the wall. 'You've got so many nice things.'

He stood with his hand on the doorknob to the main bedroom, slouching slightly, a little drunk, his eyes smouldering.

From a low table nearby she picked up an ornament, a smiling dolphin in coloured glass. She turned it over in her hands, examining it with care. Throwing him a sidelong glance she said, unexpectedly, 'You were a bit rotten to poor Ricky back there.'

'What?'

'Back there. In the lounge. You were being really cruel to him.'

'Was I?'

'Yes, you were. You know you were. You were doing it on purpose. Knocking his drink over, and getting at him like that. Making him sing that song.'

'No, not at all,' he said. 'I liked that song. I needed a refresher, that's all.'

'Liar.'

He hesitated. He had not anticipated rebuttal at this stage of the game; it was all going like clockwork. He was momentarily taken aback.

She was looking at him sidelong again, with a mischievous glint in her eye this time. Then she threw back her head and laughed, a musical sound. Samson frowned.

'It's all right! I'm joking!' She replaced the dolphin on the table and nimbly stepped over to him, taking his free hand with both of hers and giving it a squeeze. 'I always do that. It's my sense of humour. I'm wicked, I know I am.'

He damned her silently. She was still scrutinizing him through narrowed, laughing eyes.

'You don't like it when someone gets at you, do you.'

'Oh, it's not that,' he said. 'It's just that . . . well, Ricky . . . you know, he seems a decent enough young bloke and everything, but he doesn't really strike me as being quite right for you, Jill. I'm a little bit surprised at seeing you with him, that's all.'

She smiled quickly but averted her eyes. Her thoughts went to Richard and the impression he had made on her when she first laid eyes on him.

She had been smoking that night – one of the few occasions she had indulged – and she had picked up quickly on the thrumm of his bass. As she danced she had watched him, the way his fingers chased lightly over the fretboard and he hugged his instrument to his body, swaying his hips slightly, his eyes closed. There was something quite fascinating about him, she had thought. Something sensual and contained, an alluring, animal quality that she was unable to quite put her finger on.

She had gone up to him after the set and told him how much she adored the band. She had seen immediately how shy and withdrawn he was, but that had not discouraged her. It had even kind of added to the attraction. She thought it was rather sweet.

Since that time, however, she had found herself beginning to wonder. Offstage he was rather dull, and rather gauche. He was terribly difficult to talk to and when he did he was always so serious about everything. She thought he was a bit weird. And this evening, for example, there had been several instances when she had found herself wishing she had not been with him.

Richard's image had undergone a change then in Jill's mind. She was coming to the conclusion that he was really a bit of a dickhead.

And she no longer thought his band was particularly good either.

Samson pushed open the door with a veiled smile.

'This is the main bedroom,' he announced.

0

And Rogelio's eyes were huge; deep blue lagoons surrounded by wide beaches of white sand, the sand broken up by streams of blood. His pupils now were pinpoints.

He had wriggled free of Margaret's arms, was sitting erect. His hairy little jaw was shuddering and his limbs were all jerks and spasms.

He felt himself to be witnessing something presageful, something awesome and profound which he could not quite grasp a hold of. He knew that the vision he now beheld was somehow inextricably bound up with the experience he had undergone whilst in trance. And he recalled the strange man, Hugh; the so-called journalist, the man *who had no emanations*! There was a connection there also, he was sure.

He became aware once more of the space he had been observing earlier, which had caused him such great joy and consternation. It was a seething mass, hovering about him, filling almost half the entire room. He was astonished and alarmed at the extent to which it had grown, at the sheer virulence of the malcontent it now contained.

And he noticed that three persons were no longer in the room. *One of them was Hugh!* The space had moved into the places they had occupied, had undoubtedly been the agent which had inspired their exits. *But where did Hugh fit into it? What was his role in all this?*

Rogelio's mind began piecing two and two together now, linking the terrifying actuality within the room with Hugh's unheralded arrival and his premature departure, seeing a connection between these and the events that he had experienced in trance and which he was still not fully able to recall. Brittle panic was rising within him – he sensed himself to be responsible for what had occurred. He knew he should have been able to prevent it, if only he had known what it was.

And Gerald's voice was still clamouring in his ear. *The message! The message! What was the message!*

Weakly lifting a hand he waved towards that monstrous manifestation that he alone had cognizance of. He began to mouth some kind of a reply, but from his throat there came a series of constricted hiccoughing sounds. 'Uk! Uk! Uk!'

Gerald held his shoulders. 'Rogelio, what is it?'

'Uk! Uk!'

'It's all right. We're here. You can tell us.'

'Uk!'

'Rogelio, calm your mind. Remember your training!'

'Uk! Uk! Uk! Uuuuugghh! Uk! Uk!'

And finally a word came through.

'It . . .'

The Baileys leaned closer.

'It is . . .'

'Yes?'

He struggled. For a second his eyes swivelled to focus like needles on Gerald. 'It . . . is here!'

'What?'

His face was a study of dread. 'It is here!' he croaked. 'I have summoned It.'

Gerald was exasperated. 'What? Rogelio. What is it?'

The artist suddenly shrank back. He raised an arm as though to protect his head and let out a scream. 'Aaarrgh!'

'Rogelio, what's happening?' Margaret cried.

'Punishment!' he shrieked.

Gerald crouched nearer to him. 'Rogelio, what is it?' he demanded. 'We don't understand.'

'Don't understand!' Rogelio screamed, hiding behind his arm. 'Don't understand! It was me! I have done wrong! Iddio! Iddio!'

0

'It's a bit bright!' Jill said, blinking.

Samson reached behind her and dimmed the lights. 'We can soon alter that.'

She stepped into the centre of the room, taking in the coral wallpaper and carpet, the lilac curtains and candy-pink ceiling, the huge bed with its crimson coverlet and black satin sheets, the David Hamilton prints, the video system, the hi-fi system and the wall-to-wall mirrors.

She paused in front of the mirrors and studied herself. Presenting herself obliquely to the glass she struck a pose, surveying her reflected image with a critical furrowing of the brow.

She tossed her bag onto the bed and, hardly aware that she was doing it, lowerered her body, bending one knee forward and leaving the other leg trailing. She lifted her hair gracefully with the backs of her hands and let it cascade around her face and shoulders.

Samson, his warhead fully primed, sauntered over to the sound system and slipped a cassette into the deck.

She stood with her feet apart, her arms akimbo, her breasts pushing provocatively forward. She took stock of herself then dropped in a feline movement into a crouch. Her arms were between her supple thighs, her fingertips sinking into the deep pile of the carpet. She narrowed her eyes and formed her lips into a pout, vampish.

Now she rose again. She pushed her fingers into the tight pockets of her jeans and raised her eyebrows and grinned at Samson's reflection in the mirror. 'Hmm,' she said.

Samson had removed his jacket, dropping it over a chair-back. He slid up behind her now. He placed his hands over the curve of her hips and lowered his head to kiss her shoulder. 'God, you're beautiful,' he breathed.

She smiled and tilted her head slightly to one side, watching him in the mirror.

'You know, you still haven't answered my question,' he murmured.

'Haven't I?'

'No.'

'Which question was that?'

He eased himself forward, his rearing live weapon pressing itself snugly, though not too presumptuously, into the cleft of her perfectly rounded backside. His lips caressed her neck, nibbled at her earlobe. He smiled with satisfaction as he heard her sigh, as he felt her buttocks press reflexively back onto him.

0

Rogelio suddenly spun around on his knees and dived across the carpet to where his black and white cloth bag lay. He scrabbled inside it, pulled out his dog-eared, green leatherette bound *vade mecum*.

Locating the page he sought he scanned the words he now knew could only confirm the worst. They were underlined in red. They were these:

> There is One in Existence
> Who cannot be reduced to less,
> In Whom decay is not inherent,
> And Whose Connection
> Is entirely dissolved.
>
> The One Transcends Awareness
> Yet still Awareness
> Recalls the Specious Form.
> Knowing this we must accept
> And know the Great Pervader.

He looked up, aghast. The room was so congested now, so threatening, so perilously malcontented. Its space was crowding in his direction. He shuffled back several inches until his shoulder blades came into contact with the wall.

'I have summoned it!' he wailed. 'Me!'

Gerald and Margaret followed the direction of his gaze. They exchanged apprehensive glances, turned back to him.

'Rogelio,' Gerald exhorted him once more, 'please try to explain.'

Rogelio slowly raised his arm.

'Look' he said.

They looked.

'You see?'

They didn't.

'The Great Pervader! The Immanent One!'

●　●　●　●　●

# 5

Samson Tallis and Jill Richmond were getting along quite famously now. They were still clinched before the mirror. She had turned her head so that their eager mouths could meet, so that their tongues could snake out and explore.

With one hand he had slipped down the upper hem of her camisole top. He was gently fondling her naked left breast, rolling and tweaking the hardening nipple with finger and thumb. His other hand lay across her belly, pulling her against him.

She had grasped his hair, forcing his lips against hers. With soft sighs and moans she was rotating her buttocks, a slow undulating motion causing sweet friction against his hardness. They weren't talking very much.

She turned suddenly, straining up against him and sucking his tongue deep into her mouth. His hands went to her bottom, in his excitement all but lifting her off the ground.

Then she pulled her mouth away, breathless. 'Samson, no! Not here!'

0

'What!' exclaimed Gerald in a hoarse whisper, thunderstruckedly.

0

Ignoring her he bent his knees and took her full weight, his mouth finding her firm young breast.

'Oh God! Samson! Someone might come! Corinne!'

He teased the smooth flesh with his tongue, made circles around her distended nipple. 'She won't come.'

'How do you know?'

'One, she's out cold.' He planted kisses around her flushing aureola. 'Two, she doesn't sleep here any more, she uses another room.' He gently stretched the nipple between his teeth. 'And three, I've put the catch on the door.'

'But – '

'Shh . . .'

0

The madman was shrinking into the wall, struggling violently with the contents of his mind. He flapped his hands to take in the entire room.

'The Immanent One!' he wailed. 'See! See!'

0

Turning his hips slightly he availed himself of the opportunity to glance sideways at his reflection in the mirror. The sight afforded him immense pleasure.

Jill was half sitting on his hands. She had wrapped her legs about his middle and her head was bowed, her blonde hair obscuring her face. The perfect globe of her naked breast hung over him, flattened slightly to his mouth, and with her hips she was still making slow, sinuous movements, writhing her loins against his.

Acknowledging himself with a cheery wink he neatly flipped her around, bent from the waist and let her drop gently onto the bed.

0

At the sound of these words a change overcame Margaret. Her troubled face turned suddenly radiant. She looked again in the direction Rogelio was indicating. Her hand slid across the carpet to find that of her husband.

'Oh!' she said. 'Gerald. Oh Gerald.'

And Gerald took her hand. He pulled her closer to him. He pushed his glasses up his nose and raised one hand to his brow, which had broken into a sweat. 'Oh my,' he said, staring. 'Oh my. Oh my.'

'Do you see It? Margaret said. 'Do you?'

0

He went down with her, freeing her other breast, gluttonizing the heavenly flesh with lips, tongue and eyes. He laid his full weight on her and squirmed his anguished prick against her thigh.

Now he kissed and caressed his way back up to her mouth. He rolled himself off her slightly so that he might unfasten the stud and zipper of her jeans. As he did so her hand snaked over his belly, finding his outstretched penis and giving it a squeeze through the material of his brick-red Fiorucci trousers.

0

And listen once more. This is incredible.

Rogelio scrambled to his feet, pressing himself to the wall, yelling at the top of his voice. 'Me! Me! I have summoned It! Oh Iddio! Iddio!'

In front of him the Baileys, holding one another, rose slowly like two persons mesmerized. They were still gazing in wonderment into the air in front of them.

'Go!' Rogelio yelled, rushing forward and pushing at them. 'Go! You must be not here now!'

And they took a step in the direction of the door.

'NO!' he shrieked. They were walking right into the Great Pervader. 'NO! NO!'

He grabbed them and tried pushing them towards the French windows, glancing fearfully over his shoulder as he did so.

0

'I'll do it,' Jill said as he failed to tug her tight jeans over her hips. She slid from the bed. He lay back and watched her as she wriggled them down her tanned legs and stepped out of them. Then, in an elegant movement, she arched her body and pulled her top over her head.

His eyes travelled hungrily over her lissom form. 'Not those,' he said as she made to peel off the tiny white panties she wore. She looked at him quizzically. 'I want to take those off.' He reached out and found the volume control of the amplifier, turned it up a notch.

She sat down on the edge of the bed in order to remove her white anklets. Samson kissed her back. 'Those too,' he said.

0

The Baileys were in transports. They had taken three steps then halted, and Margaret, her face passionately aglow, was passing a hand rapturously around the room. 'Gerald. Oh Gerald. *Look!*'

And Gerald looked – at Richard Pike sitting petrified on the edge of the sofa, at Corinne slumped untidily in her seat, dead to the world, and at Julia, who was clutching the edges of her chair, literally vibrant with rage, her lips drawn back like a hydrophobic dog, the epitome of apoplectic fury. At that very same moment a firework burst outside the window, showering the room in shimmering viridescent light.

And at that same moment again something went haywire in the electrical circuitry of the doorbell Samson had installed. It commenced to give utterance of its own accord.

'*Door-bell, door-bell,*' it said. '*Door-bell, door-bell, door-bell.*'

Margaret gasped. 'Oh! Do you see it? Do you?'

Gerald was slack-jawed. He nodded. 'The signs!'

'It's the Time!' she cried. 'Oh darling, rejoice! *Rejoice!*'

0

She returned to him, lying alongside him, supporting her weight on one elbow. With teasing fingers she brushed the length of his erection. 'What about you?' she said.

'Be my guest.'

She smiled and began to unbutton his shirt, running her hand over his broad chest and down to his stomach. He craned upwards to roll his coarse cheek against the fullness of a pendent breast, worrying the teat with his tongue.

Now she undid the flies of his trousers. She lifted aside the flaps and his bulging member, confined within the taut fabric of his dark brown St Michael briefs, impressed itself proudly like a chocolate Yule log.

0

'The Time!' Rogelio screamed, leaping frantically up and down at their side. 'The Time! The Time!'

'*Doorbell,*' the doorbell said without any trace of emotion whatsoever. '*Door-bell, door-bell, door-bell.*'

0

She gazed upon it for a moment then laid her hand on it and curled her fingers around it. She gave it a gentle squeeze, rolling the pad of her thumb around the sensitive area at the base of his glans.

She smiled at him teasingly and he pressed upwards against her hand, avid for pleasure.

'Does he want more, then?' Her eyes were dilated like she was drugged; but she had taken nothing. He was her drug and he knew it and it excited him further.

0

Margaret turned suddenly anxious to the hysterical artist by her side. 'Rogelio, you are coming too, aren't you?'

'No! My friends. No. It is not me!' His face registered great distress. He could not explain why he was not going to accompany them. He was not even certain himself. But something deep inside him had spoken through his madness, had told him he was to remain behind.

'Oh Rogelio!'

For a second her eyes were brimming with tears again, but she smiled, waveringly but resolutely. She stooped and embraced him. He wriggled briefly in her arms, turning his head in anxious glances over his shoulder.

Margaret straightened and Gerald extended a hand and laid it on Rogelio's bony shoulder. 'Rogelio!' he said, by way of goodbye. The tiny fellow took his hand, took one of Margaret's, and pressed them to his cheeks. Then, releasing them, he stepped back.

'Go,' he whispered. 'You are Scompiglio's.'

Gerald looked into his wife's swimming eyes. They joined hands.

And now, with their hands clasped firmly around the wrong end of the stick in the manner representative of religious fanatics the world over, Gerald and Margaret Bailey stepped forward again towards the open French windows. As they did so they began to sing.

⊚ ⊚ ⊚ ⊚ ⊚

# 6

'What about poor Corinne?'

0

Samson raised himself and pushed her back onto the coverlet. He rolled onto her and glued his mouth to hers. He trailed his fingers up the inside of her thigh, coming to rest lightly on the plump bulge of her vulva. Through the thin white cotton of her pants he began to gently palpate the soft flesh.

She had closed her eyes and her breath was coming in small gasps and sighs. Her head rolled to one side as she lifted her bottom, offering herself to his deft ministrations. He knelt beside her now, looking down on her body with an expression of concentrated lust. Her hands reached up to draw down his briefs, and his prick sprang out to hover like a fat fishing-rod above her. She opened her eyes and took it between her fingers and thumb, rolled the foreskin slowly back and forth.

Feeling her panties grow damp he eased the gusset aside. A droplet of clear moisture had gathered at the tip of his penis. They both watched it as it tumbled off, dropping, a fine, transparent filament, onto her breast.

He laid a finger along the length of her slippy little crevice. He let it dip, naturally, slowly, between her swollen labia.

Twisting himself a little now Samson was able to achieve an appraising view of himself with his cock between her fingers and his own fingers paddling in the sweetness of her captivating little teenage honeypot.

0

They had stopped alongside Corinne's chair and were looking down upon her with tenderness and compassion.

'She must come with us, poor thing.'

They managed, with some effort, to haul her to her feet. She hung like a sack of beet-pulp between them, her arms laid limply around their shoulders. Her eyes were half-closed, her head lolling on her shoulders. Her face was white and still streaked with mascara. A slovenly smile appeared on her lips.

'Wasshappin?' she said.

'Corinne darling, you're coming with us,' Margaret told her.

'Nnnmph?'

'We're going to Heaven!'

0

And the doorbell said, '*Door-bell, door-bell. Door-bell, door-bell, door-bell, door-bell, door-bell.*'

0

Margaret resumed her singing again. Gerald cocked a look back over his shoulder to where Rogelio stood behind the sofa, watching them, mauling his hair with both hands and shuffling and dancing agitatedly on his feet. He looked around the room.

'What about the others?' he said as they started forward again.

Margaret threw him a look, regretful and resigned. 'Not everyone can be saved,' she admonished him gently. 'You know that.'

0

And this was the moment Julia chose to stand up. She was insensate with rage.

'You bastards!' she screamed. These were the first words she had uttered all evening. 'You fucking, selfish, feeble-minded bastards!'

She was no longer really aware of what she was doing. All this she had intended for Samson, but as it had grown more and more apparent that he was not going to be returning to the room she had become caught up in the intensity of her wrath. A first impulse had been to go and root him out, wherever he was; but that would have separated her from the others, depriving her of an audience and destroying the effect she wished to create. She was forced to modify her plans. She rushed blindly at the Baileys.

0

She was thrashing wildly now, bouncing on the bed and ramming her cunt onto his plunging fingers, crying out in a delirium of pleasure. She had released his prick and was groping at his muscly thigh, gripping it tightly as she approached her climax.

He worked two fingers in and out of her, probing and exploring

269

her wet flesh, expertly manipulating her clitoris, sensing her moment.

She gave a yell, her body arched and stiffened and her eyes went wide as she orgasmed. Bucking her hips, her fingernails digging into the flesh of his thigh.

Then slowly her body went slack. She sank back, spent, onto the crimson coverlet, moaning softly, still rotating her hips in a lazy movement, reluctant to part company with the fingers inside her.

Half-opening her eyes she peered up at him dreamily.

'Ohh-oooh,' she said.

0

She stopped short, suddenly paralysed with rage again, suddenly without a word to say. She glowered at Gerald, who was closest to her, her lips writhing futilely.

Gerald, recovering from his initial shock at the suddenness of her outburst, smiled apologetically then tentatively resumed his forward motion, his wife doing likewise.

She pushed in front of them and shot out onto the balcony. Her fists closed like twin vices around the narrow iron railing and she glared at the night. Gerald and Margaret, weighed down by their burden, stumbled behind her into the cold, damp, dark air.

Needing to regain her breath Margaret let go of Corinne for a moment and leaned on the railing. Gerald kept hold of her, supporting her unsteadily with his arms around her waist.

0

Now he bent and hooked one arm behind her knees and lifted her – just enough to enable him to slip her little panties over her hips and bottom and down onto the floor. Her white anklets he left as they were.

Leaving the bed he quickly removed the remainder of his own clothes, then returned, kneeling between her parted thighs, swollen with hubris and lust. He gently pushed her thighs upwards and opened them over her chest, exposing her glistening treasure even more fully to his acquisitive gaze. He bent his body and trailed his lips and tongue slowly up the inside of one thigh.

● ● ● ● ●

270

# 7

And Richard Pike looked up and everyone was leaving him.

Everyone.

All the persons he had ever come into contact with in his life had their backs to him, were walking, *pouring*, away from him out of the door.

There was his mother and father. And his sister, Deirdre, laden down with useless presents. There were his old friends and associates from school, and there were the hollow people he had worked with in the carpet shop. He recognized Ralph; he had his pack on his back and his thumb in the air. And Leon and the guys from the band. And there too were all the people he had met earlier this evening: Corinne, with her friends, a small tabby kitten perched clinging to her shoulder. They were all moving away, going somewhere, leaving him behind.

He wondered what was happening.

Richard had ceased thinking in terms of the other Richard Pike now. Sick with fear, mindless with psilocybin and tetrahydrocannabinol, he was making little sense of what was happening around him. His wide, startled eyes were wider and more startled than usual. Skittering through his head was a blur of discrete imagery.

But as he witnessed the exodus before him he was poignantly aware that someone was missing. Jill. Where was she?

0

For some moments now Richard had been caught up again with the idea that Jill might be fucking around with Slider the roadie. He could see her in the back of Slider's blue Bedford van. She was virtually naked. Her legs were clasped around Slider's waist. She was moaning and thrashing ecstatically as Slider slobbered over her, as he stuffed his great hairy prick into her time and time again.

Richard was insane with jealousy and despair. He had all but fully persuaded himself as to the veracity of this suspicion. Jill was not amongst the others, she was not with him, ergo she must have slipped out to keep some secret rendezvous with Slider. Where else could she be?

He hugged himself tightly. A voice was ringing loudly and persistently in his ear. He could not make out what it was saying. He could not tell whether it emanated from inside him or out. He began to rock back and forth on the sofa's edge.

'Jill,' he called softly. 'Jill. Jill. Jill.'

0

She gasped as his tongue arrived at the swollen outer lips of her vagina. He paused there a moment, his face hovering an inch above the precious flesh as he cherished her rising, feminine, sexual heat. It was a sensation he adored. The honey-blonde fluff of her pubes tickled his nose and cheek. He gave a sigh as he felt her fingers slide down to cup and fondle his balls.

He kissed his way with tiny probing kisses around her puffy labia, nibbling and sucking the folds of yielding flesh. Now he lowered his head further and let his tongue run the length of her furrow from bottom to top, wriggling it inside her, like he was scooping out the inside of a singularly appetizing oyster.

Now he rolled his eyes upwards and to the side, manoeuvring her body so that she twisted around a little on the bed. In this position, by inclining his head sideways just a shade more he was able to catch another tantalizing view of himself in the mirror. With his fingers stretching wide the lips of this darling, blonde, nineteen-year-old pussy and his tongue riffling around the tiny pink pearl of her clitoris he was the happiest man in the world.

0

One other thing was bothering Richard.

It stemmed from a magazine article he had glanced at recently. The article, written by an American university professor of environmental studies, enquired into the problem of world pollution. Quoting an abundance of facts and statistics it explained how mankind was progressively crippling the planet Earth.

'No need for nuclear warheads,' the professor had acidly declared, 'for if we continue to pour our unwanted chemicals into the sea, to indiscriminately dump or bury our nuclear waste products, to pump carbon monoxide and other toxic gases into the atmosphere, to spray our crops with poisonous insecticides and otherwise abuse the ecosphere, we can only expect to find ourselves in an environment that is inimical to, and incapable of supporting, life.'

According to the professor not a corner of the planet has remained free of the hallmarks of man's ascendancy. Traces of DDT and oil-slicks and various other sorts of crap that we have no idea what to do with have been found sullying the pristine continent of Antarctica. Penguins there are dying after consuming waste products that men have dumped into the oceans thousands of miles away. Even the regions of space beyond our own atmosphere are daily becoming more and more littered with our unwanted debris.

The professor posed the question, Why is man so intent upon exterminating himself? *What is this perverse bent, this irrational drive we seem to possess which compels us to strive so diligently for our own extinction and the extinction of every living thing with which we come into contact?*

After all, he pointed out, it isn't as if we even get any real fun out of doing it.

He had a particular bone to pick with his fellow countrymen. Americans, he claimed, are among the most polluted individuals in the world. Scientific investigation has shown that a typical American citizen eats, drinks, breathes or otherwise ingests such a vast and varied amount of lethal toxins that he or she cannot be considered a safe form of sustenance for another human being.

And this was the bit that had Richard so confounded. One extract from the entire article had lodged itself somewhere firmly in the back of his brain. The remainder of the article was gone; he had no memory of ever having seen it. But, apropos of nothing, it seemed, a single sentence had lunged forward suddenly to usurp a position of dominance in his mind:

'The average American is unfit for human consumption.'

Taken out of context in such a way it was at the very least disconcerting and bizarre. But viewed through the paranoiac nightmare that Richard was undergoing its implications were horrifying, not to say nauseating, in the extreme.

What did it mean? What was happening in the world? What kind of person would eat an American anyway?

Richard found himself shivering. That solitary voice kept grating, echoing in his head. He let out a moan. Little beads of sweat had appeared on his forehead, had soaked the spiky ends of his dyed blond hair.

He became aware suddenly of Rogelio, who was behind the sofa opposite. He was leaping up and down and clutching his hair, screaming hysterically.

'Aaaaaaaaaarrrrrgggggghhhh!' he screamed. 'Aaaaaa-AAAA AAAAARRRRRRRGGGGGGHHHHHHH!'

As Richard gawked his screams stopped abruptly. He leapt into the air one last time then dropped out of sight.

Richard raked his face with his nails. 'Jill,' he sobbed. 'Jill. Jill. Jill. Jill. Jill.'

0

'*Door-bell*,' the voice said. '*Door-bell, door-bell, door-bell, door-bell, door-bell.*'

0

'My turn,' Jill said. She slipped away from him, and wriggled around, settling herself so that she was seated in front of him, her legs straddling his as he knelt erect. She steadied his pulsing prick with fingers and thumb, smiled as she looked up at him, then brought her head forward. Now it was his turn to moan as her shiny, flickering tongue came into contact with his member.

0

The space beside him, where Jill had been, had grown cold. Icy fingers crept on his skin on his right side where it was touching him. The room felt cold and hostile. He felt that he was being observed by unseen eyes, that he had been singled out for some frightful experiment or trial of some kind.

He turned back to the French windows through which they had all just flowed. He gripped his skinny biceps and bit down hard on his lower lip, trembling uncontrollably.

0

He urged her on with breathless words of encouragement, shifting his weight a little into a more comfortable position. Her tongue chased him like a devoted hummingbird. It raced up and down the length of his shaft, teased around the collar of his glans, probing wetly and lasciviously.

Now she parted her lips and took in the swollen bulb of his glans. He pushed forward involuntarily, eliciting a muffled squeal from her as she was obliged to pull her head back. She swirled her tongue around him, her cheeks hollow as she sucked, her hands tenderly massaging the base.

Samson glanced in the mirror again now to assess himself with his cock in a marvellous blonde teenage mouth. He thought it rather suited him. Her hair had fallen forward, obscuring his view, so he lifted it back. The stout hairy base of his scape stood out at about a forty-five-degree angle from his belly. Approximately half his total length was visible, the remainder disappearing between her sliding red lips.

She withdrew her head slowly and the rest of his penis came into view, glistening with her saliva and his semen. She flickered around the tip again with her tongue. As she did so she too glanced in the mirror. Their eyes met and she smiled at him like a first-class whore.

Stretching her lips wide again she drew him back into the warm cavern of her mouth. Her eyes stayed on the mirror. She gave a little mewl of delight. Samson nodded appreciatively. He thought she looked pretty damn good too.

0

And Gerald and Margaret Bailey were propping Corinne Tallis up against the railing, singing songs of praise and jubilation into the night. And beside them, Julia, growing angrier by the second and not knowing what to do with it all.

● ● ● ● ●

# 8

And Richard looked down and some gigantic hairy insect-creature was coming scuttling towards him across the carpet.

0

'Do you want me to make you come?' she enquired, releasing him for a moment and smiling engagingly up at him, still plying lightly with her fingers.

He thought on this, wondering whether she would take it in her mouth. It seemed likely that she would. She was astonishingly good for a nineteen-year-old; he congratulated himself on his discernment.

'Not yet,' he whispered. He swivelled around and positioned himself over her, between her legs. Her hand snaked down to guide him into her. As the tip of his penis entered her her eyes widened and her lips quivered slightly. She let out a long breath of a sigh. 'Aaaah,' she said.

He held there for a moment then slid his entire length into her. She gasped and closed her eyes. She hooked her feet around his thighs.

He pulled briefly on one nipple with his lips, eased back and glided forward again, establishing a leisurely rhythm.

His backside was to the mirror now but he no longer cared. It did not cramp his style at all.

0

With a sharp, sudden cry his body whipsnapped. It catapulted him upwards and backwards onto the sofa where he crouched, quaking with terror.

The creature shimmied across the floor towards him. As it passed beneath him, where his feet had just been, it suddenly halted, backed away a few inches and rolled over. Then, with a peculiar pushing, rowing motion it continued frantically on its way.

And Richard let out another cry. In his suspended, hallucinatory state he believed he had recognized the creature. He believed it was Rogelio.

0

And it was.

Seized with panic, believing himself doomed, the wretched little beatnik had found himself screaming, leaping up and down in a helpless frenzy.

He knew that it was not for him to go the way of his good friends, and yet the horror that had invaded his mind, that he saw taking over the room, the world!, was preventing him from escaping via the door into the hall. It was seething angrily, it was bulging out towards him, it was growing more potent by the second.

And it had a voice now. It was calling to him.

And then he had spied a chink, a possible route of escape. There was space, he saw. True space. Actually beneath it. Along the floor. A contracting zone of emptiness through which, fortuitously, a small human being might just squeeze.

Immediately he had dropped onto his belly, slithered out from behind the sofa and shot across the carpet.

He covered several feet before he found his passage was narrowing. The belly of the Great Pervader was bearing down upon him, crushing his body, constricting his lungs and throat.

He inched backwards and struggled over onto his back. Whimpering with terror he pushed upwards with the palms of his hands, utilizing all his strength in an attempt to widen his way.

Now he propelled himself forward again with elbows and heels. He continued in this manner until his head came into contact with the wall, directly beneath the one means of escape that was still available to him – the serving-hatch.

0

And the doorbell went on and on.
'*Door-bell*,' it went. '*Door-bell, door-bell, door-bell* . . .'

0

She coaxed him deeper into her with her hands and thighs. She sobbed and writhed underneath him as the rhythm of his thrusts increased. There was a smile on her face as she rode the smooth

277

straights on the gathering crest of her second orgasm. Her eyes were half-open, far away.

Her body tensed and her eyes rolled. Her jaw went slack, though somehow still retaining the smile. Her nails dug deeply into his buttocks. Fireworks exploded outside.

'Oh!' she cried. 'Oh! Oh!'

As her inner muscles contracted spasmodically around him he felt his own climax beginning to build. It came as a great wave, swelling and washing over him, and he let out a loud moan. He began to throb and spatter inside her as he emptied himself in a series of mind-shattering spurts.

0

Trembling with exhaustion and pouring with sweat he pressed himself to the wall beneath the aperture through which he was to make his exit. He closed his eyes and inhaled deeply. He leapt upwards and hurled himself through the narrow opening.

And Richard, seeing this, climbed off the end of the sofa. He tottered towards the French windows after the others, his hands on his ears, bleating like a lamb.

0

He tumbled onto the top of the sideboard in the relative safety of the kitchen. As he did so one hand came to land in something cold and slushy and wet. It sank in half way up his arm and he gave a scream and jerked it away.

The sudden motion sent him toppling over the edge of the sideboard, dislodging at the same time whatever it was he had touched. He hit the floor heavily. Beside him there was a dull crash. He sat up, dazed, kneading a damaged shoulder. His skin and clothes were liberally bespattered with a pinkish, yellowish, visceral mess.

He gave a cry of alarm. He scrambled to his feet, lost his footing on the slippery stuff and fell to the floor again. On hands and knees, then, he scuttered across the linoleum tiles to the nearest cupboard.

Sliding open the door and brushing aside the various bottles and brushes and cloths and the tub of Plumber's Mate that were its contents, he squeezed inside. He pulled the door shut behind him and darkness engulfed him. He closed his eyes up tight. His arms were wrapped around his shins and his head was sandwiched uncomfortably sideways on his knees. In this manner he began to jabber a stream of frantic prayers to his deliverer.

0

'Ooh, I came gallons,' Samson enthused, collapsing over her. 'Did you feel it?'

She tightened her arms and legs around him, holding him more tightly to her.

'Mmm-mmmhh,' she sighed.

● ● ● ● ●

# 9

The Baileys had succeeded in bundling Corinne over the railing now. Somehow they did it. I don't know how.

She was teetering on her heels, on the very edge, on less than two inches of concrete nine floors above the street. Her toes were sticking out into empty space.

The Baileys were hanging on to her when Richard emerged, and she was giggling to herself. Her head had flopped forward and she was dribbling like a cretin down the front of her grey gown. It was drizzling slightly and a stiff, cold breeze was being playful with everybody's hair. As Richard darted to and fro behind them all like a demented glove puppet Margaret, still singing heartily, began to climb over.

And that was when Julia let go of the railing. She wheeled with a yell of fury and lashed out savagely at Gerald, who was nearest to her. The blow caught him on the side of the face, dislodging his spectacles. She raked her nails down his face, leaving four red lacerations on his cheek.

'You bastard!', she screamed. 'You cunt! You fucker!'

She hit him again, closed-handed this time, a staggering blow that all but knocked him to the floor.

Half-blinded and reeling with shock and pain Gerald could do nothing but stoop and grope around his feet for the spectacles. He found them and replaced them, then rose to attempt to defend himself against his assailant.

But she was no longer there.

Gerald, panting, leaned against the railing. He peered over, down to the street below. Julia was lying on the pavement in a crumpled heap.

And before he could fully assimilate what had occurred he was distracted by something else. Someone was tugging at his sleeve. He turned.

'Where's Jill?' Richard pleaded. 'Where is she? What's happening?'

0

'Gerald, come along. Help me!' Margaret called. She had witnessed nothing of what had just taken place. In her ecstasy she was oblivious to all but the imminence of her own salvation. 'Take Corinne's hand! We must go together! Come along, you're not even singing!'

But Gerald, as he swung his legs over the rail, was for the first time beginning to experience grave misgivings as to the wisdom of the action they were engaged in. He blinked several times and shook his head and almost woke up. He glanced down again to where Julia's smashed body lay. Already several people had rushed to her. They were turning their heads upwards to look at him.

'Margaret . . .' he began, but it was too late. Margaret was keen to be on her way. With a song in her heart and on her lips she had stepped over the edge.

'*Scompiglio reigns!*' she sang. '*Scompiglio reigns for all mankind!*'

And she was holding Corinne's hand.

And Corinne's other hand was clutching tightly, reflexively, at Gerald's shirt.

Still dazed, still off-balance, the combined weight and momentum of the two women forbade him any option but to follow.

Down he went.

Down went Corinne.

And down went Margaret, baby and all.

0

Any passers-by observing Margaret's face at that moment – through a pair of binoculars, say – might have noted a sudden change in her expression as she fell. A look not far removed from surprise. As if she had been expecting something quite different.

But, then again, they might not.

0

And Richard hovered at the balcony's edge.

'Come back!' he cried pathetically. He could make out little. He could not see where the others had gone.

He turned and tottered back in through the French windows. And the room told him, '*Door-bell, door-bell, door-bell, door-bell, door-bell, door-bell, door-bell, door-bell, door-bell, door-bell, door-bell, door-bell.*'

Weeping, he tottered back out again.

'Please,' he said. 'Please.'

He was seized with a sudden spasm, a dread of being left behind, all alone.

'Come back!'

He lifted his legs over the railing.

'Jill!' he called. 'Jill!'

He let go. He stepped out into the void.

0

At the last second it came to him that she might be somewhere still inside. She might be looking for him. His hands flew out. They managed to grasp the lower rail, and he was left dangling nine floors above the street.

•　•　•　•　•

# 10

And seconds before he died Richard Pike saw God.

He had never believed in God but he saw Him all the same.

And God's face was ancient and wise. His hair was snowy white.

He was a little way above Richard and a little to his right. He was gazing down at him with an impenetrable visage. And as Richard stared he saw that in God's hand there was a staff and that He had it raised and was pointing it at him. And God's lips moved and a great roaring, rushing wind arose and drowned out the sound of His words.

And Richard knew with sudden certitude that he was going to die and that he did not want to. It came to him that life was not so unbearable after all. All those years of cowering and hiding, terrified of every second of the day, they were suddenly not so bad. They were suddenly infinitely preferable to the Great Unknown that faced him now.

And he realized too that despite all his previous convictions, despite all his earlier protestations to the contrary, he no longer believed he had been deposited on the wrong planet. He no longer believed there was another Richard Pike. He thought parallel universes were a stupid idea. The world was okay the way it was. He never wanted to change a thing.

He began to bawl.

Desperation directed him to make a last attempt. With one hand he released his grip on the iron baluster and reached out for the end of God's staff. But it was in vain; the staff fell well over a yard short of his outstretched fingers.

And God, still floating there above him, continued to aim His staff at him. And His words were still lost in the great wind He had created. But through the wind Richard received God's message. He was telling him he had to go. He was telling him it was Time.

Now he kicked out frantically. He struggled. He failed repeatedly to haul himself back onto the balcony.

'Jill!' he screamed. 'Jill!'

Above him and beneath him and all around him, though he could not see it, was a sea of faces, watching him.

'Jiiiillll!' His strength was failing.

'Jiiiillll! I LOVE YOU!'

With a last drawn-out shriek of horror his fingers parted company with the iron baluster he had been clinging to and he dropped, flailing . . .

0

As mysteriously as it had begun the doorbell now fell silent.

'*Doorbell*,' it said '         .'

0

'Oh God!' Jill had a blissful smile on her face. She gave a great sigh of contentment. 'Oh God, that was fabulous. Oh God, *do it again*!'

● ● ● ● ●

# Epilogue . . .

It's a funny old world . . . but life muddles on somehow.

But that about wraps it up, really, as far as this book, *The Great Pervader*, is concerned. Of course, it doesn't actually end there. Not at all. Its ramifications were, are, and always will be far-ranging and diverse.

One or two of these ramifications have been explored in outline at the beginning of this tale, but there are many, many more. I mean, there are people alive in the world today who would never have been born had not Richard Pike and the others leapt off the balcony of the Tallis's home. And that's the truth. Let me explain.

Remember Cyril Bellows, the tired policeman who found himself in charge of investigations of this bizarre affair? Remember the wry calculation rendered by him as he stood musing on the balcony, gazing down to where the five bodies had so recently lain?

'*No doubt some came and fell in love.*'

That's what he said.

Now there are those who would hold that Inspector Bellows was nothing more than a cynic, and that may well be so. And I for one do not for a moment believe that he was prescient or psychic or any-thing – I just think he had been around for some time – but here's the interesting thing: Two people *did* come and they *did* fall in love.

Their names were Sunanda and Pete.

And here, in a nutshell, is their story.

Pete was a twenty-year-old butcher's assistant from Camberwell. He was up in central London that evening drinking with some mates. Later on they had it in mind to go to somebody's birthday party.

It was as they were heading for their third pub of the evening that Pete, lagging a little behind the others, got held up when the lights changed and the traffic flow prevented him from crossing the road. Waiting for the lights to change back he had happened to glance down a nearby sidestreet and spot a crowd gathering. Intrigued, he had gone to investigate.

When Pete's mind and body subsequently became an essential

element of the corpus that was being born outside Kimberley Mansions, Richard Pike was still hovering and had yet to jump. Pete had no idea at that time that four persons were already lying dead on the pavement up front.

Sunanda, whom Pete had never met, had also made herself a part of this aggregation. She was eighteen years old and of Bengali descent. She was petite and very pretty. She was also very sad, having only ten days earlier reached the endpoint in a relationship that had lasted more than two years. She was out that evening alone, walking her puppy.

The name of Sunanda's pup, by the way, was *Kali-yuga*.

Despite the fact that Sunanda was standing directly in front of Pete he was not actually aware of her presence. This was because his head was turned upwards to the ninth-floor balcony.

A mild disturbance of some sort erupted near the front of the crowd, however, causing a ripple of motion to radiate outwards towards its edges. The ripple grew to be a wave and the wave, when it reached the place where Sunanda was standing, lifted her and pushed her backwards into Pete.

And her heel came down to land quite sharply on his right instep.

Sunanda turned, distressed and full of apologies. And Pete, seeing what a jewel she was, made the most of a God-given opportunity. He pretended she had half-crippled him.

Clutching his instep he hopped on one foot and pulled faces. He hobbled around in a tiny, confined circle and mentioned an operation he had had there. Sunanda wrung her hands and looked doubly distressed.

Then Pete broke into a sunny smile. He told her it was okay, he was just stringing her along. He asked her if she knew what was going on and she said, no, not really.

After Richard Pike had hit the pavement Pete and Sunanda were pressed forward with the rest trying to see what he looked like now. It soon became obvious, however, that they were not going to make it to the front. And Sunanda expressed the opinion that she really had no desire to anyway.

The police and fire brigade were doing their utmost to make folks feel unwelcome, so Pete asked Sunanda if she fancied having a drink with him. She said okay and he took her to a nearby pub – not the one that his mates were in. Later they dumped *Kali-yuga* at

Sunanda's parents' home two streets away and Pete took Sunanda to the birthday party.

And thus was begun something long-standing and beautiful.

Within a year Sunanda and Pete were married. Within two they had their first child, a daughter, whom they named Emily. Soon after that they had a son called Marc.

Incidentally, at the age of twenty-eight Pete was almost going to become famous. He had long taken a keen and active interest in amateur dramatics, and under Sunanda's persuasion and encouragement he would audition for the part of a GPO official in a long-running television soap opera.

The man who was going to beat him to the post, so to speak, would become for a brief period a household name. Then he would fade abruptly after leaving the series and striking out as an actor in his own right. He would become an alcoholic and later would eke out a tolerable living doing voice-overs on commercials for independent television and radio.

And Pete, meanwhile, was to be made manager of the butcher's shop in Camberwell at the age of twenty-nine. He would work there until his retirement.

And Sunanda would stay at home and look after the kids. Over the years she would have two fleeting liaisons with men of no consequence. On the whole though she would prove herself a patient and dependable wife to her husband and a devoted mother to her children.

0

Pete and Sunanda's marriage was to last a lifetime – a pretty remarkable feat in this day and age. Through the trials and sorrows of life they would pull together as a team. Through the good times they would laugh and make love a lot. And although it would be untrue to say that anything particularly exciting or important ever happened to them, and although they never had a big house or a car or very much money to spare, and although they never got to know what the countryside was like, except on a couple of brief vacations, they did in fact manage to live happily ever after.

0

More or less.

• • • • •

# Post Scriptum

Remember the words of Iddio E. Scompiglio:

> 'There is no Love,
> There can be no Life.'

He also says: 'Do not misconstrue my words. To come to a true and full understanding of my works they should be read at least three times.'

**THE END**

(*The Great Pervader* forms the first volume of a three-part work entitled The University Of Life. Part two will be available shortly).